Our Lady of Greenwich Village

A Novel

Dermot McEvoy

Skyhorse Publishing

Skyhorse Publishing books may be purchased in bulk at special discounts for
sales promotion, corporate gifts, fund-raising, or educational purposes. Special
editions can also be created to specifications. For details, contact the Special Sales
Department, Skyhorse Publishing, 555 Eighth Avenue, Suite 903, New York, NY
10018 or info@skyhorsepublishing.com.

www.skyhorsepublishing.com

10 9 8 7 6 5 4 3 2 1

McEvoy, Dermot.
Our lady of Greenwich Village / by Dermot McEvoy.
p. cm.
ISBN 978-1-60239-351-6 (alk. paper)
1. Legislators—United States—Fiction. 2. Political campaigns—Fiction. 3. Pro-
life movement—Fiction. 4. Journalists—Fiction. 5. Irish Americans—Fiction. 6.
Catholics—Fiction. 7. Greenwich Village (New York, N.Y.)—Fiction. 8. Political
fiction. I. Title.
PS3613.C43O97 2008
813'.6--dc22
2008020271

Printed in the United States of America

This book is dedicated to my mother, Mary Kavanagh,

and the grandmother I never knew until recently, Rosanna Conway.

"A politician is an arse upon
which everyone has sat except a man"
—e.e. cummings

"God is a politician; so is the devil."
—Carrie Nation

"We are a nation of believers. We produce anti-clerics, but atheists,
never."
—William Butler Yeats

"If you ever injected truth into politics you have no politics."
—Will Rogers

"We are, to be sure, a strange lot."
—Theobald Wolfe Tone
Eighteenth-century Irish revolutionary

NOW

1.

It was to be a quick trip. Wolfe Tone O'Rourke had flown in from Dublin to stay with his friends Liv and Willie Blumer in their Central Park West apartment. At noon, he took the number 1 train downtown to Christopher Street. He emerged from the subway in front of Village Cigars, which had been there since he was a kid. Instinctively, he looked for the World Trade Center. It should have been just to the right of the slanted slate roof of Greenwich House on Barrow Street, but it wasn't. The twin towers had been immortalized by the politicians and the pundits. The truth, O'Rourke knew, was that they had never really been taken into the hearts of New Yorkers before they died. They had been tolerated, but not cherished like the Empire State or the Woolworth and Chrysler Buildings. Stunningly sterile in their simplicity, most referred to them as cereal boxes. The only time O'Rourke was ever really glad to see them was when they punctuated the flatness of the Jersey Turnpike like paired lighthouses, their beacons reassuring him that he was close to home. O'Rourke could see them from his walk-up tenement on Charles Street. He had watched the towers fall from his living room. When the second plane hit, in fear, he made a Perfect Act of Contrition for himself. Then, feeling ashamed of his solipsism, he said another for the innocents who had been tricked into another dimension. And on September 12, 2001, he had smelled them. As the air from Ground Zero drifted north to the Village it had brought its own pungent scent. At first O'Rourke couldn't place it, but then it came back to him, in a replay from his horror days in Vietnam. It was the smell of incinerated flesh. The aroma made when extreme heat vaporizes human beings. In Vietnam napalm did the trick; here in New York it took Boeing jets. And as O'Rourke stood in Sheridan Square on this clear day and gazed, there was only a ghostly slot where the Twin Towers had once stood.

He had come downtown to say goodbye to Hogan's Moat, the great saloon at 59 Christopher Street. Standing in front of Village Cigars, waiting to cross Seventh Avenue, he could not escape the grip this little square, bordered by Seventh Avenue, Christopher, West Fourth, and Grove Streets, had had on his life. He had crossed it at least once a day for nearly fifty years. His parents had crossed it and his friends had crossed it. They were all gone now, all dead, but if they were to come back they probably wouldn't recognize it.

Sheridan Square had been made possible by the city's growth. During World War I, the city had plowed right down the middle of the Village to make way for the new IRT subway line and the new street that sat on top of it, Seventh Avenue South. Instead of making the street fit the buildings, the city just sawed them off, sometimes right in the middle, to make them fit precisely to the sides of the new thoroughfare.

Still waiting for the light to change, O'Rourke thought back forty years to how the Square used to be. The Starbucks on Grove Street used to be Jack Delaney's, a saloon housed in a wonderful nineteenth-century brownstone. Delaney's was an old speakeasy, and its most distinctive oddity was the sulky cart hanging from the ceiling in the main dining room. The great character actor, the late Jack Warden, had lived in an apartment above. Everybody knew Jack's face, but no one knew his name. He was the trusty enlisted man who protected sub captain Clark Gable in *Run Silent, Run Deep*, and Paul Newman's mentor in *The Verdict*. Most famously, he was Juror Number Seven in *Twelve Angry Men*, the guy who wants to get out of there but fast because he has tickets to the Yankees game. Jack, too, used to drink at the Moat.

As O'Rourke looked at the banal green trademarked veneer of Starbucks he remembered how animated Delaney's façade used to be with its red, green, blue, and white neon sign of jumping steeplechase horses. As a small boy, after shopping at the A&P on Christopher Street with his mother, he would stand absolutely delighted, mouth agape, as the horses hopped incessantly, always clearing the hedges, never falling or hurting themselves.

Next to Starbucks was the Chase Bank. Originally, it had been the Corn Exchange Bank and if you looked closely, you could still see "Corn Exchange" bleeding through the stone, stubbornly refusing to be washed away by time and progress. On the other side of Starbucks had stood the notorious Duchess dyke bar. The doorman was his friend Harry Whiting, who resembled a refrigerator in a pork-pie hat. When men saw women going in they would try to follow, but they would not get past Harry. "This is a ladies' bar, pal," Harry would explain. O'Rourke looked at the sign over the door and began to laugh out loud. Jamba Juice, it said. Yeah, thought O'Rourke, there used to be a lot of Jamba juice going down at the old Duchess.

O'Rourke shook his head. He still didn't like change. They tell you change is good, but the ones who tell you that are always making a buck out of it. "You know," O'Rourke's wife liked to chide him, "for a so-called reformer, you're pretty conservative." She was right, of course. Still, change was mostly good for nothing, life had shown Wolfe Tone O'Rourke.

He crossed Seventh Avenue to the uptown subway island in Sheridan Square that had always had a newsstand. In the movie *Serpico*, Al Pacino had triumphantly bought the *New York Times* here and read about the Knapp Commission. O'Rourke picked up a *Daily News* and turned towards the Moat. He looked up Seventh Avenue and saw his old building on the corner of Charles Street. He heard they had sold his rent-controlled apartment to some hot-shot young actor with a ring going through his nose for $2.5 million. The real estate industry calls it gentrification. What they ought to call it is murder. At first you hardly notice it when the corner deli becomes an antique shop, but then the Chinese laundry becomes a bistro and the corner shoemaker becomes a Marc Jacobs. Soon a movie house like the old Loew's Sheridan is torn down and replaced by a gym for anorexic yuppies. When he was a kid it was always the "Low-ees" where the neighborhood kids went on a Saturday morning—a quarter to get in and fifteen cents for a soda and a bag of popcorn.

Instead of walking straight to the Moat, O'Rourke went into Christopher Park. Everybody thought it was Sheridan Square Park, but it wasn't. Sheridan Square was actually a triangle wedged between Washington Place, West Fourth, Barrow, and Grove Streets, just to the south of Christopher Park, a mystery in plain sight. In Christopher Park he watched tourists taking photos of the oddly-whitewashed statues, two standing male gays and two sitting lesbians, monuments to the Stonewall riots which happened just across the street in 1969. The Stonewall was still there, "the gay GPO" O'Rourke called it. Sometimes the tourists mugged with the statues, or sat in their laps.

O'Rourke thought these pale WASPy figures were the oddest tribute ever paid to a besieged minority.

"Isn't she beautiful?" a middle-aged woman enthusiastically asked O'Rourke. He turned to see that a statue of the Blessed Virgin Mary had been installed where the old drinking fountain used to be, just a few feet from the gay icons. She was a serene presence in the bustle of the Square and her sky blue robe stood out in stark contrast to the gay albinos across from her. It was almost like she was trying to upstage her queer colleagues. O'Rourke smiled at the contrast. He then looked beyond the Virgin Mary to the stern stare that Civil War general Phillip Sheridan, glorious in his patina, was directing at his fellow statues. O'Rourke thought it was ironic that the notoriously politically incorrect Sheridan—the man famous for saying "the only good Indian is a dead Indian"—should be put in charge of this group of motley castings. "They call her Our Lady of Greenwich Village," said the Virgin's guardian, as she offered O'Rourke a brochure. "Do you know her story?"

O'Rourke smiled at the woman and said, "Intimately." He turned before she could proselytize and exited the park on Christopher Street, just across from the Moat. To the left of the Moat was the Duplex, now home to Joan Rivers and other talents. The site had once housed the offices of the *Village Voice*, where many of O'Rourke's friends had found employment. There was longshoreman-turned-writer Joe Flaherty; the poet laureate of the New York Mets, Joel Oppenheimer; the chronicler of New York's soul, Pete Hamill; and the mad gay writer Arthur Bell, who probably would have pissed on the gay monument and pronounced it golden. They turned in their pieces, got their checks, and went next door to spend them at Hogan's Moat. The next-door presence of the *Village Voice* had actually made the Moat successful. That was in the 1960s and '70s, a long time ago. Now Hamill was the only one of the four left with a pulse.

O'Rourke walked across Christopher Street and down the steps into Hogan's Moat Saloon. "Tone O'Rourke," said Saul Shipman, the long-time bartender, as he put the *New York Times* crossword puzzle away. Shipman, heavily bearded with lugubrious but penetrating eyes, was a former sea captain and served as the Moat's own irascible version of Ahab.

"I flew in for the last day," said O'Rourke. "How are you, Saul?" They embraced across the bar, drinking buddies of thirty years.

"Fine," said Shipman, "except for this tragedy."

"What happened?"

"Times change," said Shipman pensively. "The yuppies don't drink. They don't smoke. It's a wonder they fuck. And if they do drink," he continued, passion suddenly in his voice, "they want concoctions called 'Orgasms,' 'Blow-jobs' and 'Slippery Nipples.' Who do I look like? The fucking Mayflower Madam?" Somehow, O'Rourke couldn't see anyone in their right mind ordering a Slippery Nipple from Saul Shipman. He was from the old school where drinking was a religious experience. Now in his mid-sixties, he could still drink men half his age under the bar. "You can't make money," he continued, "on a generation that thinks a swizzle-stick is a coffee stirrer. Then Hogan died and the joint went down the tubes." Saul paused, then brightened as he surveyed O'Rourke. "You look like a gentleman farmer." O'Rourke was dressed in tweed from head to toe. "How's the family?"

"Fine."

"Cognac?" asked Shipman.

"No, coffee will suffice."

"Ah," said Shipman, this time with feigned anger. "Another fucking yup."

O'Rourke knew Shipman's act by heart and smiled. He didn't want to get drunk yet. It could turn out to be a long day and O'Rourke knew from experience that wakes take a lot of stamina. Shipman brought the coffee and O'Rourke went for a stroll around the bar. He looked at all the book jackets, now neatly framed, on the author's wall. They ran the gamut from Fred Exley to Frank McCourt and, in a way, told the history of the bar. And although the bar was empty except for the two men, O'Rourke thought he could hear the laughter of another time. He drank in this bar, sniffed cocaine in its bathroom, fallen in love numerous times, but the thing he always remembered was the laughter. You can't manufacture laughter like this. You can't buy it. You can't even steal it. Laughter, like love, is a kind of chemistry. He could almost hear the boisterous voice of Flaherty throwing another of his insane analogies—this time comparing the poetry of Yeats with the defensive wizardry of Willie Mays—at the ceiling where they rebounded in laughter. He swore he could hear the booming voice of the long-dead Nick Pinto—"Goodness gracious, said Sister Ignatius, I'm shocked that the bishop has piles"—demanding jocularity out of depressed, drunken Irishmen. And he thought he could hear the young O'Rourke, freshly back from Vietnam, cocksure, shooting off his motor-mouth.

"Ghosts," he said to Shipman.

"There've been sightings," came the serious reply.

"Genuine?"

"Yes," said Shipman quietly. "Flaherty was here."

Flaherty was always here and always in O'Rourke's mind. Just after Flaherty died, O'Rourke had an exceptional dream. In the dream he was sitting down at the end of the bar when he saw Flaherty walk in. "I thought you were dead," he said to Flaherty.

"Nah," said Joe, "I was only fuckin' with ya." And with that the dream ended.

"Our Joseph," said O'Rourke, "God bless him."

"Yes," said Shipman, thinking of his old friend, "God bless him." Saul cleared his throat and changed the topic. "What are you doing in Ireland?"

"I'm a family man now," said O'Rourke, not revealing much.

"Who would believe it?" replied Shipman and O'Rourke joined him in laughter as they both thought of the young, feral O'Rourke. "But what do you do over there in County Wexford?" Shipman persisted.

"I think," said O'Rourke. "And I thank God I got out of this country with my life." He went into the rear looking for Flaherty's ghost, but everything was quiet. The back room was as handsome as the front of the bar. It was all brick and dark wood. Three rows of dining tables ran from the twin front windows to the back, their shellacked surfaces gleaming as the sun struck them at sharp angles.

The room was indeed filled with ghosts. As he looked at the big, empty round table in the back he thought he could faintly hear the Clancy Brothers and Tommy Makem belting out "Brennan on the Moor."

Then it materialized to him, clear as the day. All the regulars were gathered around Liam Clancy and his guitar like a bunch of boozy Dutch Masters:

'Tis of a brave young highwayman
This story I will tell
His name was Willie Brennan
And in Ireland he did dwell
It was on the Kilwood Mountains
He commenced his wild career
And many a wealthy nobleman
Before him shook with fear

There was Pinto and Flaherty, the hunchback was Hy Harris, the one with the loudest voice was ace journalist Dennis Duggan, the quiet one Frank McCourt, and the most earnest, off-key ones were actor Val Avery and barman Al Koblin. Was that young Bobby Zimmerman, Liam's acolyte, in the corner? Harris and Koblin, the two Jews in the bunch, actually knew the words. O'Rourke laughed. It always seemed that the non-Irish, especially the Jews, knew all the words to Irish rebel songs best. Then he could hear Koblin's tough Boston accent emanating from under that thick, droopy, Vonnegutian mustache: "The Moat," he said with a crane of the neck, "is the only bar in New York where the Irish think like Jews and the Jews drink like Irish." Once, thought O'Rourke, it was true.

The memories of those happy winter nights faded as he thought of Bobby Kennedy. O'Rourke had been the youngest Moat regular when he rang the bar and told them that Senator Kennedy was on the way down. The kitchen help immediately descended en masse on the men's room wall, scrubbing the salacious graffiti away, as if to protect the emotionally wounded senator. When O'Rourke heard the story days later he could only muse what a middle-class Irish respectable gesture it was. "Didn't have time to procure some lace curtains?" he inquired.

His mood darkened further as he looked to table number one, up front by the window. That's where the filthy deed was consummated. For it was there one early March night in 1968, that as a punk kid, he had sat at a table with Kennedy and pleaded with him to run for president.

"The hottest places in hell," O'Rourke told Kennedy, as he threw one of the senator's favorite quotes in his face, "are reserved for those who in times of great moral crisis, maintain their neutrality."

O'Rourke's words—spoken with the rotten arrogance of the pure-of-heart—had clearly hurt the senator.

"You're right," Kennedy said. "I'll have to run." There was no joy in his voice, only dread at what he knew was coming.

O'Rourke should have just kept his fucking trap shut. But back then, he thought he had saved the world. Little did he know he had set in motion the first major hemorrhage of his soul. There were ghosts here, all right, but they were not talking to O'Rourke right now. They were letting him stew.

"Too bad about Hogan," he said, coming back to the bar.

"The lung cancer," said Shipman, lighting up another unfiltered Camel in defiance of the city's anti-smoking law, "actually metastasized into his testicles."

"Jesus," said O'Rourke.

"They had to snip them off."

"What happened to Barney?"

"You won't believe this," said Shipman. "The dog got cancer of the balls, too."

"Sounds like sympathy balls."

Shipman looked at O'Rourke for a second, then began to laugh. "You still have that vicious sense of humor, I see."

"Did they snip Barney?"

"No," said Shipman, "they put him to sleep. But they buried them together in Green-Wood Cemetery in Brooklyn, within a stone's throw of mobster Albert Anastasia. The mayor himself cut through the red tape to get the dog in."

"You're shitting me."

"It's the truth," said Shipman, pointing to the framed Cyclops Reilly article on the wall. O'Rourke got up to take a closer look at Reilly's "Eye on New York" *Daily News* column: DRUG BUSTING DUO REUNITED IN DEATH. There was a photo of a big coffin and a little coffin about to be lowered into the ground. A priest stood to the side, sprinkling the boxes with holy water. Reilly's piece started out, "I don't care if it rains or freezes, Hogan and Barney will be safe in the arms of Jesus." O'Rourke started to laugh. "Cyclops doing okay?"

"He's the best," said Shipman. "You made him a star. He won that Pulitzer covering your campaign, and now he's on TV all the time.

Yeah," he said, laughing at the thought, "you made him a pundit."

O'Rourke laughed, too. "Who would have thought it?" he said. "The pervasive and invasive power of television. The instrument that turns American minds to dust."

They both looked up at the TV, which was muted. Stock prices ran on a grid on the bottom; above it a generic blond news jockey was yakking away.

"Where do they find them?" said O'Rourke, gesturing toward the TV anchorman. "If he was any blonder, he'd be transparent."

"They miss you," said Shipman. O'Rourke shook his head. "The cable networks."

O'Rourke laughed, thinking about the summer of his infamy eight years ago. It wasn't that long ago, but it seemed a century or more to O'Rourke. "You know, the cable networks still call me in Wexford."

"What do you do?" asked Shipman.

"I hang up."

There was silence broken only by the ship's clock striking the hour. Finally, Shipman asked the hard question. "Was it worth it?"

O'Rourke reflected back to the late winter of 2000 and thought about what he had gotten out of it. "Yes, Saul," he said slowly, "I think it was."

THEN

Greenwich Village
Winter, 2000

2.

At 1:15 a.m. the telephone rang at the City Desk of the *New York Daily News*. "Henry Fogarty?" the voice asked.

"Yeah," said Fogarty, "this is he."

"Fogarty, this is Officer Tessa of the Sixth Precinct. I'm in St. Vincent's Hospital in the Village."

Fogarty began scribbling the information. "Yeah?"

"I was told by Cyclops Reilly that if I ever got a hot tip, I should call you."

"Cyclops told you that?"

"Yeah."

"So?"

There was silence on the wire. Tessa was getting impatient. He didn't realize that Fogarty was already negotiating. "You want to listen to me, or do I call the *Post*?" asked Tessa. More silence.

"What you got?"

"I just got bribed three hundred dollars by Georgie Drumgoole, Congressman Swift's press secretary, and—"

Fogarty interrupted: "You don't have to tell me that. You are protected by the Fifth Amendment."

"Don't be such a smart ass, Fogarty. I might have a bit of a scoop for you," retorted Tessa.

"You mentioned Jackie Swift, I believe."

"Yes, he's here," said Tessa.

"Why?"

"Heart attack."

"What the big deal? Lots of folks, including congressmen, have heart attacks."

"Apparently he had it while ballin' his chief of staff. There's a cover-up going on here. Could be another Bill and Monica."

Cover-up, thought Fogarty. Since Watergate, everything was a fucking cover-up. It had gotten to the point that the media was making up stories so some dumb politician could try to cover them up.

The gotcha mentality, Fogarty called it.

"Bill and Monica are ancient history as far as I'm concerned," said Fogarty. "Anyway, thanks."

"Whatdaya mean, thanks? Cyclops told me you would pay."

"Well, Reilly was wrong."

"You want I should go to the *Post*?" Tessa asked. "Remember HEADLESS BODY IN TOPLESS BAR?" Fogarty winced at the memory of the headline. "This story is right up Rupert Murdoch's alley," continued Tessa. "Fucking *Post* will have a photographer up here in three minutes. Ya wanna let that rag scoop you?"

Fogarty's problem was his personality—or, more specifically, the lack of one. No one, it seems, ever called him Hank. He was not one to joke or have a beer with the boys after the paper went to bed. He had worked for the *News* since Eisenhower was president, yet no one had ever remembered seeing him in the late, lamented Costello's Bar on East 44th Street.

Though he was an emotional cold fish, Fogarty was also a talented and insightful reporter. His personality, talent, and a drunken city editor by the name of Shitty Collins had conspired in 1957 to give him his sobriquet, Peccadillo. Shitty Collins cared about two things: newspapers and drink—and not necessarily in that order. Collins knew talent, and Fogarty had it. Collins also knew how to hang onto his job. In a strange way, the two had taken to each other. Collins gave Fogarty the choicest assignments, and Fogarty's work made Collins look good in the eyes of his superiors. Fogarty was becoming a star, with his byline frequently—too frequently, the gang at Costello's thought—appearing on page three. When one of the rewrite men got into a fight with Collins and mentioned the alleged favoritism between Collins and Fogarty, Collins had condemned the reporter and praised Fogarty in a gin-soaked voice loud enough for the whole city room to hear: "Your sins are mortal compared to Fogarty's peccadilloes." Unfortunately, a just reprimand and a statement in support of Fogarty's skill had created a nickname that at first had been reduced to Pecker and then Peck. Fogarty had suffered silently, if not saturninely—which was his natural state—and had just about survived all his contemporaries, including Collins, who was killed one evening soon after when he had emerged from the old News Building on East 42nd Street under the influence and fell into an open subway grate. A loner in his personal life also—he was another one of those eternal Irish bachelors—Fogarty, his legs shot, had pulled his green eyeshade over his forehead, and retired to the City Desk and the telephone. Even with all the newspaper strikes and labor strifes, the *News* could not get rid of him. "Never met a buyout he liked," they said about Peccadillo Fogarty. He was known to be judicious, circumspect, and cheap. Nothing got by Fogarty. He wasn't about to let a congressman whom he didn't particularly like get by him either.

"No, I'm not going to let that rag scoop me, Tessa. How much?"

"If Swift'll offer three hundred to shut me up, another three hundred from you sounds fair."

"One hundred sounds fairer," replied Fogarty.

"Two," shot back Tessa.

"One-fifty. Take it or leave," snapped Fogarty. He loved it. If there was one thing he hated more than shady congressmen, it was crooked cops.

"One-fifty. You're all heart, Fogarty," said Tessa.

"That's me," replied Fogarty. There was silence on the line.

"I'll take it," Tessa finally replied.

"I thought you would," said Fogarty. Tessa didn't know it, but Fogarty always gave his tipsters $150. It was in his petty-cash budget. "Just don't go away. I'll find Cyclops and send him over. I got forty minutes before the four-star final closes. I'll try to find him."

Fogarty knew exactly where Reilly was. He dialed Hogan's Moat.

"Cyclops Reilly. Telephone!" Zeus, the ursine Moat barman, called out over the crowded Friday night bar. Reilly was in great shape. He was sure that he was about to get laid and he didn't particularly want to be disturbed. "Yeah?"

"Cyclops, it's Fogarty. You got to help me."

"What you want?"

"Jackie Swift was just brought into St. Vincent's with a heart attack."

"Big deal," said Reilly, who looked like a pissed-off Richard Widmark. As he cradled the phone on his shoulder, he pushed his slicked-back blond hair into place and played with one of his out-of-style Elvis sideburns.

"He was fucking his chief of staff when it happened."

"The chief of staff a boy?"

"No. Of course not," said Fogarty, although the thought hadn't crossed his mind. Reilly was good—if you could keep him away from the booze and the broads. "Cyclops," said Fogarty in desperation, "we live in the Age of Clintonian Fellatio. This could be big."

"The Age of Clintonian Fellatio," said Reilly, laughing. "You're beginning to sound like Eric Fucking Sevareid. I like that, but I bet Clinton's getting more pussy than JFK ever got."

"You think?" said the skeptical Fogarty.

"What's the big deal?" stammered Reilly. "Is there a story here?"

"There is," said Fogarty, "if New York City's most reactionary Republican congressman is having sex with someone other than his wife or his hand."

"Good point," conceded Reilly.

"Look, we got the scoop on this one. They bribed your cop friend Tessa three hundred dollars, and he called and filled me in. Get up there, please, Cyclops, and get me a statement from Drumgoole for our last orgasm, which closes in thirty-five minutes."

"Well . . ." said Reilly who almost smiled at the term "orgasm," which only an old-timer like Fogarty would use instead of "edition" to show his love of the newspaper business.

"I wouldn't like to be scooped on this one by the *Times*," said Fogarty, who knew how to push Reilly's buttons.

"The *New York Cocksucking Times*!" yelled Reilly into the phone. Reilly hated the *Times*—or the *Cocksucking Times*, as he always referred to them. He had worked for them for six months and he considered them to be not only trite, but anti-labor and anti-New Yorker. "The only strike they ever supported," Reilly would tell one-and-all, "was in fucking *Poland*!" By now Reilly was shouting into the phone. "I will not be preempted by the *New York Cocksucking Times*," he told Peccadillo Fogarty as bar patrons backed away from him in fear.

"I'll owe you one," said Fogarty.

"Okay. I'll get back to you."

With that he went back to the bar to see the lady whom he was seriously chatting-up when Fogarty had called. She was a blonde from Akron, Ohio, and her name was Paige. She had a wholesome

Midwestern face, which radiated innocence as she listened to Cyclops. Reilly knew that she was a "professional virgin," the type that would coo "no, no, no"—then after four drinks demanded that you fuck her to exhaustion. Reilly had met her about an hour before and they had hit it off immediately. He kept buying her drinks and dazzling her with his newspaper exploits which lately, because of his great affinity with Declan Cardinal Sweeney and the management at the *News*—he had been one of the union point men during the strike—had been reduced to reporting which restaurants in Manhattan and Brooklyn had rat shit in their kitchens. She could play the expert innocent, but Reilly had noticed that she had certain callipygian talents. In fact, she had an ass on her like a wombat. Reilly relished a good sexual challenge.

When he returned from the telephone Reilly explained to her how important he was to the *News* and how he had to run out on this hot tip. Would she wait for him another hour? "Sure," said Paige as she pulled him close and shot her tongue into his ear. "Why do they call you Cyclops?"

Reilly laughed. In one motion he popped his glass eye out and covered the open white eye-pit with a black patch. He deftly dropped the glass eye into his vodka on the rocks. "Keep an eye on my drink, will ya?" he called over his shoulder as he left the bar. He exited onto Christopher Street and started on the quick walk to St. Vincent's. Five minutes later he was conferring with Officer Tessa.

"What's the scoop, Gino?"

"I'm here with a hit-and-run victim, and I see Swift. Drumgoole—who seems to have half a bag on—sees me, turns white, and sticks three big ones in my pocket, saying, 'You ain't seen a thing, Officer.' Ambulance attendant tells me Swift's had a heart attack while balling his cute little chief of staff."

"Boy or girl?"

"Girl, of course. Ambulance guy," Tessa continued, "says they were having a hell of a party."

Reilly's ears shot up like a trained hunting dog's. "Party? What kind of party?"

"Don't know. Just a party," returned Tessa.

"Where is he?" Reilly asked.

"Off duty. Gone for the night," said Tessa. "What do you think?"

Reilly didn't know what to think. "Ah," he said, "our Family Values candidate succumbs. Hypocrite. I'll say this for Peck Fogarty, the old fart's got a nose for news. How much you get from him?"

"Son of a bitch Jewed me down to one-fifty. He drives a hard bargain."

"Four-fifty—still not a bad night, Gino. Where the fuck is Drumgoole?"

"In the emergency ward."

As Reilly walked down the long hall he knew there must be something to this story, especially if that cheapskate Fogarty had promised some cop $150 over the phone. He was stopped by a hospital security guard, flashed his press card, and forged ahead. He was beginning to feel that Joseph Pulitzer had nothing on him.

Reilly headed straight for the ER, which he knew from when he was shot up in a bank heist in Chelsea in 1986. The robbers had tried to break out by having a running gunfight with the NYPD Tactical Force and had ended up winging Reilly in the shoulder. He was lucky he didn't bleed to death right there on 23rd Street and Eighth Avenue. Reilly hated hospitals, from the one in Saigon where they had removed what was left of his eye to the VA hospitals in New York where he had been an out-patient. But if he ever had to be in a hospital, he hoped it would be St. Vincent's. He would never admit it, ever, but that crucifix on the wall still meant something to him, and he got a kick when one of the old Sisters of Charity had come to visit the famous newspaper man who had ended up on page one of the *Daily News*.

Reilly looked in the ER and there was no sign of Swift. There was only a man on a gurney in the middle of a seizure flopping up and down like a flounder out of water. All of a sudden Reilly didn't feel so good and cursed Peccadillo and his fucking story. Out of the ER and into the back. Where the fuck was Swift? St. Vincent's at night gave Reilly the willies. Dark and cavernous, it was like a haunted castle. All the lights were at a minimum, but it was still a working hospital as gurneys and wheelchairs silently moved about on their way to deliver patients for CAT scans, X-rays and MRIs. Hospitals brought back nothing but bad memories to Cyclops Reilly.

He turned the corner and literally ran into Drumgoole. "What's the scoop, Georgie?" he asked with a big smile. When Drumgoole saw

Reilly he almost had a heart attack himself.

"What are you doing here?" he asked incredulously.

"Hear the congressman ain't feeling too good."

"Yes, he's had a very severe heart attack."

"Playing racquetball?"

The booze had lobotomized Drumgoole's brain. He had trouble remembering conversations he had only minutes ago. He concentrated hard, closing his eyes and pinching the bridge of his nose, as he tried to recall what Peggy Brogan, Swift's chief of staff, had said happened to Swift. His brain retrieved bits and pieces of the phone conversation he had with her. Then he remembered Brogan's reference to *The Song of Bernadette*.

"The congressman had a heart attack when the Blessed Virgin Mary appeared to him, urging him to strike against the abortionists."

"What?" Reilly asked, clearly stunned.

"Yes," said Drumgoole boozily, not comprehending what he had just done. "The Virgin appeared to the congressman and told him to fight *Roe v. Wade*." With that, Drumgoole turned, zombie-like, and marched away from Reilly.

Reilly's jaw dropped, and he shook his head. He looked at his watch and saw it was 1:45 a.m. Fifteen minutes to the paper's deadline. He had to find out how Swift was doing. Just then a doctor came through the swinging emergency room doors. "Hey, Doc, you working on Congressman Swift?"

"Yes. Why?"

"I'm Reilly of the *Daily News*. What's his condition?"

"He's holding his own," the doctor replied.

I bet he is, thought Reilly. "He gonna make it, or what?"

"I don't know. The cardiologist is with him now."

"Thanks, Doc. That should be enough." Reilly reached into his pocket for a quarter and came up with a lone crinkled five dollar bill. He had left the remainder of his money on the bar with his drink and his lady sitting in front of it. A smile of anticipation crossed his face. "Hey, Tessa, lend me a quarter, willya?"

"Why don't you use your cell phone?"

"The *News* repossessed it," said Reilly. Tessa shook his head and handed over the two bits. Reilly dialed.

"Yeah?" said Fogarty.

"Peck, Cyclops here. Got the word. Severe heart attack for Swift. Docs don't know if he's going to make it. My guess is that there's a broad and coke involved. Something about a 'party,' the EMS guy told Tessa."

"Doesn't sound like much," replied Fogarty.

"Grab a hold of your balls, Peck."

"Why?"

"Drumgoole's official explanation is that Swift had a heart attack when the Blessed Virgin Mary appeared to him to tell him to, quote 'fight *Roe v. Wade,*' unquote."

Peccadillo Fogarty actually dropped the phone. Picking it up, he said, "You're fucking kidding me."

"That's a direct quote."

"Hold on," Fogarty told Reilly. He picked up another phone and said something he had wanted to say his entire newspaper career: "Stop the presses!" Reilly heard and laughed out loud. "New headline," said Fogarty to the pressman, remembering he owed the Cardinal one. "MIRACOLO!: BLESSED VIRGIN APPEARS TO SWIFT."

"Shit," said Reilly.

"*Holy* shit," corrected Fogarty.

"You owe me," Reilly said and hung up the payphone. "Have a nice night, Gino," he said, as he ran out onto frozen 11th Street and hailed a cab: "Christopher Street and Sheridan Square."

Two minutes later he was back in Hogan's Moat. There wasn't a sign of the lady—or his bar money. "Where's Paige?" he asked Big Zeus.

"Some guy," said Zeus diplomatically as he handed Reilly his drink containing his glass eye, "comes up after you leave, buys her one drink, they swap spit, and they leave."

"Yeah. With my fucking money, too."

"At least they left your eye."

"Yeah," said Reilly. "Zeus, can I run a tab?"

"Sure, Cyclops," Zeus said as he poured an eyeless vodka on the rocks for Reilly. "That's on me."

"Thanks, Zeus," Reilly said as he pocketed his glass eye, gulped the drink and thought bad thoughts about Peccadillo Fogarty. Then he thought about his Virgin scoop and thought good things about Fogarty. It was time to celebrate. He looked to his left. There was a girl with an ass so big and round and firm and perfect that it could stop traffic. The girl was alone. Their eyes met and she smiled at him. Cyclops Reilly was in love.

Again.

"Hi," he said, "can I buy you a drink?"

3.

"**Y**ou. Hey, you. Yeah, you. I'm talking to *you!*"

Wolfe Tone O'Rourke thought someone was in his bedroom yelling at him. He opened his myopic eyes, grabbed his glasses, and saw the disheveled figure on the television screen. He obviously had left the TV on the night before when he had returned from the bar at closing time. "Are you a drunk? A drug addict? Or *both?*" the voice asked in a near-shriek. "Well, you must be if you're lying there in bed, stoned, looking at *me!*"

"Jesus," O'Rourke sighed.

"I'm Bob Stark of the Stark Institute for Addiction, and you can't fool me because I *used* to be a junkie just like you! *You* need HELP!" Bob Stark shouted at O'Rourke. "Call 1-800-ADDICTS. Remember," Stark continued, "*I* can't call *you.* Get off your sorry, addicted butt and help yourself. Call me NOW! We take Medicare, Medicaid, and most HMO and union-sponsored plans. You supply the addict. We'll supply the tough love."

"Fuck you," said O'Rourke as he grabbed his remote control and flung it at the TV, hitting the cable box and turning Bob Stark's red whiskey face to black. O'Rourke couldn't believe it was already Saturday morning.

Saturday mornings always brought supreme hangovers and this one wasn't any different. It was the cotton mouth that killed him. The dry-caked taste of last night's beer and whiskey was too much. O'Rourke pushed the sheets away, put his chin to his chest, and surveyed the wreck he'd become. He was swollen with fat, an off-shade of battleship gray, and quite ugly. O'Rourke was honest enough with himself to acknowledge that it was another sign that his skirt-chasing days were over.

Naked to the kitchen for his relief—a Coke gargle. It was the only thing that exorcised that taste of yesterday's frustration from his body and brain. The fridge door opened to a lone slice of two-week-old green pizza and not one old-fashioned eight-ounce glass Coke bottle. There was something magical about those thick greenish bottles that made Coca-Cola taste the way it tasted when you were a kid. To O'Rourke, everything was beginning to taste the same. It wasn't often that he could recapture a small part of the innocence of his youth. O'Rourke closed the refrigerator door, decided he would not vomit, fetched his clothes, and knew he had to seek the cure.

Wolfe Tone O'Rourke was an anachronism. In an age of physical and mental narcissism—when it seemed that everything and everyone had been molded into snobbish and pretentious three letter sequences, be it GAP or BMW or MBA—he didn't give a fuck. His personal appearance was a clue to his splendid indifference. Now the head "mover and shaker" (according to *Newsweek* magazine) at one of the most prestigious political consulting firms in the country, Northern Dispensary Associates, he dressed in what one of his colleagues had once ruefully described as "early stevedore." This took courage because the firm was populated mostly by young eager-beaver Generation-X-types, who thought culture had begun in the United States with the invention of rollerblades and the cell phone. They were hip, but they didn't know shit. O'Rourke's shabby blue jeans and corduroy jackets tended to stand out. He would not go with the flow. Also the look of his plump appearance, his full beard set against long black, graying hair, and taut eyes guarded by thick bifocals, tended to distract and dismay the staff and clientele whenever O'Rourke escaped his corner office and poked his head around a bend.

Just after eight o'clock, Tone O'Rourke bought a *Daily News* at the newsstand in Sheridan Square and looked at the morning headline: MIRACOLO! He stopped dead in his tracks and followed the story to page three. BLESSED VIRGIN APPEARS TO SWIFT, the headline said. REP. CRITICAL AFTER HEART ATTACK, read the deck. O'Rourke forgot all about his hangover as he read the byline: Benedict Reilly. "GOP Congressman Jackie Swift is resting in critical condition this morning at St. Vincent's Hospital in Greenwich Village after suffering a heart attack at his West 10th Street apartment. According to Swift's press secretary, George Drumgoole, the congressman was stricken after the Blessed Virgin Mary appeared to him and urged him to 'fight *Roe v. Wade.*' Neither his wife, fellow U.S. Representative Madonna-Sue Fopiano Swift, nor his father-in-law, former Staten Island congressman Vito Fopiano, could be reached for comment." The item concluded by saying that additional reporting was supplied by Henry Fogarty.

O'Rourke turned the corner onto Christopher Street and dropped the three steps into Hogan's Moat. And a typical Saturday morning it was at the Moat, as the bar jumped from end to end with the same febrile crowd. O'Rourke needed a taste desperately and he swung into the corner of the bar by the window.

"Oh, don't we look like hell this morning, Doc," said Cyclops Reilly, his one eye dancing. Reilly stood out in any room because of his mismatched eyes. The right one was like a brilliant blue gemstone while the left eye looked like a cheap replacement, which, in a way, it was.

"Fuck you," said O'Rourke. He turned to the barman. "A Remy and coffee, please." Reilly was unshaven and looked a mess. "What's with the eye patch?"

"I can't get used to that fucking glass eye," said Reilly.

"The new one?"

"The new one, the old ones," said Reilly. "It's like sand in there. I'd rather wear the fucking patch." Then Reilly brightened, relishing O'Rourke's sorry condition. "Jesus, Doc, you look great. Your fucking eyes look like maraschino cherries floating in sour cream!" Reilly roared with delight.

"Cyclops," said O'Rourke, "as Betty Ford would put it, I think I 'over-medicated' myself last night—again." O'Rourke looked up as a cup of black coffee and a snifter of Remy Martin were placed in front of him. "Congratulations," O'Rourke said as he held up the *Daily News* headline. Reilly grinned feverishly. "The fucking *Virgin*?"

"Well," said Reilly, "that's Swift's version of the story."

"Drumgoole didn't actually say that, did he?"

"Yes, he did," said Cyclops.

"The shit will be hitting the fan this morning,"warned O'Rourke. "I think Madonna-Sue and Big Daddy Vito will be personally removing Swift's balls, one at a time. What really happened?"

"My educated guess," said Reilly as haughtily as he possibly could, "is that he was balling his chief of staff, Peggy Brogan. Apparently there was also some 'magic' involved."

"Magic?"

"Coke that wasn't cola."

O'Rourke shook his head. He wondered how politicians got themselves into such jams. "How was the *craic* last night?" he asked.

"The *craic*," said Reilly, referring to the Irish word for fun, "was grand. But there was no other kind of crack to be had," meaning crack, as in the crack of a woman's backside, or the kind that was either sniffed or smoked.

"You need more crack," said O'Rourke, "like Custer needed another Injun." O'Rourke, looking for an immediate caffeine boost, dropped the Remy into the coffee, took a taste, and shook his head violently. "Jesus, how do we keep drinking this shit?"

Cyclops pointed to the money on the bar and said, "That's with me."

"God bless you," said O'Rourke as he again tasted his coffee. As O'Rourke looked down the cacophonous bar of morning he knew that those who had opposed Franklin D. Roosevelt and the repeal of the 18th Amendment to the United States Constitution had been right.

The Moat, as the regulars called it, was narcotic. They cashed your checks. They extended credit. They took telephone messages. They mothered their drunks. It was, thought O'Rourke, the only bar that had actually been left a suicide note by one of its writer patrons. ("Best fucking thing he ever wrote," was the consensus of the regulars.) But the Moat in all its wood, brick, and darkness was only a room. To outsiders—"tourist" was the pejorative term with the Moat regulars—it was a "literary bar." Dust jackets haphazardly clung to every available wall space, stuck there with yellowing scotch tape.

Most of the professional writers in the Moat were either too drunk to write or ended up getting their work published between beaver shots in "gentlemen's magazines." Once, a little old lady from Des Moines asked, "Is this the place where writers with drinking problems come?" To which one of the regulars replied in truth, "No, this is where drinkers with writing problems come."

But to O'Rourke it was the people who came there regularly—who actually lived there—that gave the Moat its personality. O'Rourke loved rogues and he found plenty of them in the rhythmic, decadent cadence that defined Village drinkers. Most of those at the bar had closed the Moat at four o'clock that morning, gone to one of the illegal after-hour places that were known as "blind pigs," and as the sun approached, had swayed back to the Moat before it opened at eight. The porter usually had to sweep around the customers, they flooded in so fast, the bar filling with ladies and gentlemen left over from the night before embracing each other in some sort of sexual glide that would never be realized—at least not this morning. Men, alone, slumped over the bar, cognac in front of them untouched, fighting and defying the sleep that had already slugged them. What were they looking for? Why had they reduced their lives to the companionship of a bar and neutering alcohol? Why had they allowed life to reduce their will power so that comatose alcoholism was preferable to the dread of reality—reality being failure and loneliness? One only had to look to figure out that the regulars were the legion of men who habitually woke to empty beds and rolled naked by themselves, pushing the piss hard-on against cool sheets with the wish that the one girl that they had once loved, that one girl with the pretty face and the ass chiseled by the Almighty Himself, were there. But of course she never would be. There would be no morning rolls, just laments for a lonely hard-on. Relief was just a drink and a laugh away at Hogan's Moat. And O'Rourke, no matter how many times he would try to deny it to himself, knew it. He couldn't escape and he knew that the Moat, in a benevolent way, was slowly killing him.

O'Rourke heard the door opening and in walked Aloysius Hogan, proprietor of the Moat, and Barney, his trusty German shepherd. Barney looked at the customers and growled. Then his eyes met O'Rourke's and a whine came out of Barney as he backed away and tried to slide under the cigarette machine.

"Fucking pussy," said Hogan to his dog.

Hogan was in his early sixties and although now slightly stooped, you could see that he had once been an athlete. He had played Class D ball in the Milwaukee Braves organization in the early '60s, but his inability to hit the curve ball had sent him back to New York. Not lacking in ego, he saw himself as Humphrey Bogart in *Casablanca* with the Moat being his Café Américain. Essentially a shy man, conversation did not come easy to him. Often he threw out curious asides such as "An unemployed jester is nobody's fool" and "Did you know that Cy Young never won a Cy Young Award?" to the bafflement of his customers. When silence followed, he would head for his office in the basement.

Barney was a retired DEA cocaine detection dog who had been given to Hogan as a birthday gift by his old handler. Hogan, an ex-cop himself, had kept friendly with the law, which was a good thing to do if you were sniffing three grams of coke a day. Hogan's coke habit had put the Moat in financial jeopardy as the profits went up his nose rather than to the IRS.

First day on the job, Barney came through. Hogan moseyed up to a regular at the bar and whispered, "Got any blow?"

"Not today, Hogan," the regular lied. Immediately Barney jumped on the man's back and pinned him to the bar. "On second thought, I remember I do have some." Barney had saved the Moat from the IRS. Hogan still did three grams a day, but he wasn't paying for it anymore.

O'Rourke had already seen Barney in action before Hogan approached him one night and squeezed in beside him to ask, "Holding?" Out of the corner of his eye O'Rourke saw Barney approaching and as he began to pounce, O'Rourke spun and cold-cocked the dog between the eyes, sending him flying across the bar where he landed in a heap, whimpering. "Well," said Aloysius Hogan, "I guess you don't have any."

Barney never forgot O'Rourke, and neither did Hogan. "How's it going?" asked O'Rourke as Hogan passed him, grunted, got his ever-present cup of coffee, and headed for his basement office, which was often referred to as "Little Peru."

"Hey, Hogan," said Reilly.

"What?" said Hogan as both he and Barney turned around.

"You should do something about that dog's balls," said Reilly.

"What's wrong with them?"

"For Christsakes, Hogan, they almost hit the floor," said Reilly.

"Yeah, Hogan," said O'Rourke, "willya put a jockstrap on him for decency's sake?"

Hogan peered down at Barney's swaying genitalia, then looked up to find both O'Rourke and Reilly with wide grins on their faces.

"Fuck you guys," said Hogan as he and Barney again headed for Little Peru.

"What a personality," O'Rourke said, laughing.

"Yeah," said Reilly, "he could be the advance man for a famine."

O'Rourke looked down the bar and saw Nuncio Baroody. Nuncio was a diminutive Irishman who spoke with the Liberties nasal twang of his native South-side Dublin. Nuncio was becoming seedier by the year. His hair was always cut as if a bowl had been placed on top of his head and the remaining hair cut away. He now shaved but twice a week and his nose and face were mapped by roads of thin blood vessels that, thought O'Rourke, must run with Jameson. If Nuncio was to be played in the movies it would be by the late Irish actor Jack MacGowran. In fact, it had been rumored that Jack MacGowran, dead these many years, probably looked better than Nuncio Baroody.

Nuncio—no one remembered his real first name—had come by his sobriquet (if you could believe the mendacious Nuncio) through scandal. He had once been a priest, and he served as the secretary to the Papal Nuncio in Paris. His downfall had been the whiskey and Pernod and the occasion when the real Nuncio caught him in the confessional in a pederastic act with an 11-year-old boy. The Church had suspended him *a divinis*, banning him from celebrating mass and other sacraments. They had also "read him out" in *L'Osservatore Romano*, letting the world know that he had been formally *laicized*, a form of ecclesiastical castration. It was believed that he now taught Latin in some Catholic high school, where it was assumed that Nuncio's proclivity toward pederasty was being fulfilled nicely.

"Hard night, Nunce?" asked O'Rourke.

"Not a-tall," twanged Nuncio as he staggered up to O'Rourke and put his arm around him. "Sure I met a lovely young lad just in from Dublin and we had a grand fook. Sure I'm just back from the Plaza Hotel meself."

"Nunce, you're a fucking degenerate," said O'Rourke as he physically removed Baroody's arm from around his neck.

"Well," said Nuncio with conviction, "I'd rather be a pedophile than an Anglophile."

O'Rourke looked at Baroody with appreciation. "I can't argue with that," he said. "Buy the little prick a drink—on the condition that he drinks it at the other end of the bar."

"Ah, sure ya toooo dacent," said Nuncio as he scooped up his Pernod and waddled back down to his end of the bar.

"Jesus, Cyclops," said O'Rourke, "it seems to get worse by the year. A hell of a way to spend your life."

"Fucking A," said Reilly as he waved the barman for two more drinks. O'Rourke dropped a twenty and gazed out the window, as if searching for the meaning that his life now lacked.

For as long as anybody could remember, Tone O'Rourke, with his creative profanity, Village street smarts, and outrageous wit, had been sitting in the corner of Hogan's Moat every Saturday morning with his friend, Cyclops Reilly. The two of them told everyone that they were cousins—which they were not—and that their family came from the same small town in Ireland—Ballyslime.

The two of them had met in Vietnam in 1970 when Reilly was a Marine PFC, or, as he liked to say, "Young. Dumb. Full of cum," and O'Rourke was a Navy Corpsman—a medic—assigned to their platoon.

Reilly had actually joined the USMC to escape some trouble with the Westies in his native Hell's Kitchen and a pregnant girlfriend. Eighteen and mean, he went to Vietnam *looking* to kill Communists.

O'Rourke was a far different case. He thought he had beaten the system. He had just finished a master's degree in political science, and he thought that no army would want anything to do with his 20-500 vision. He was half right. The army didn't want him, but the navy sure did.

Even after being drafted, O'Rourke, always the impossible romantic, thought of himself on the flight deck of the U.S.S. *Enterprise* directing jet launchings and landings. Those dreams dissipated when he found his ass at the Great Lakes Naval Station training to become a corpsman. Upon graduation O'Rourke went right past the *Enterprise* and directly to Saigon. Within a week he was dropped out of helicopter in a rice paddy—how ironic, thought O'Rourke, a Paddy in a paddy—in Qua Dong in northern South Vietnam into the waiting arms of the 3rd Marine Division, whose previous corpsman had stepped on a landmine and had come up two legs and two balls short—or, as the doctors liked to write in their reports, "avulsion of testicles."

In a platoon populated with "Gomers and Homers," as Reilly put it, the two New Yorkers had taken to each other. Reilly was born in Hell's Kitchen and had gone to parochial school and Power Memorial High School. O'Rourke, although born in Dublin, had grown up in Greenwich Village and had the same background as Reilly. Soon, the "Two Harps," as the good ol' boys referred to them, were inseparable buddies.

One day, Reilly took one look at O'Rourke and declared to the whole platoon, "How does he do it?" There was O'Rourke, all five-foot-seven, 135 pounds of him, packed from head-to-toe with equipment. Helmet flopping down on the bridge of his nose, flak-jacket open, heavy medical bags on his left side, M-16 on his right side.

"Fuck you, Reilly," said O'Rourke that fateful day when their lives would change forever. "If I don't do it, you certainly won't."

"Up yours," replied Reilly as they went out looking for the "dinks" that had been ripping the marines to shreds in recent weeks.

"We got to do something," declared Second Lieutenant Howland Meager of Falls Church, Virginia.

"Hey, Howland," said the ever-irreverent Reilly, "what'd they teach you about this in OCS in Quantico?"

"They didn't," said Meager.

"Well, you better hurry up," said Reilly, "your time is almost up." Meager knew what Reilly meant—the average life span of a marine second lieutenant in Vietnam was six weeks.

"The cocksuckers got to sleep," said O'Rourke. "They're killing us by night with their mortars. Why don't we kill them by day?"

And that's just what they did. They went looking for the dinks in the daytime—when the VC were sleeping. They came across them in a wooded area and they were up in the trees, in rolling hammocks. Most of the VC never knew what hit them as the M-16 rounds torn into them, twirling their hammocks around, turning them into human sausages, dripping blood onto the Marines below them. The VC lookout had tossed a grenade before being hit in the head by Marine fire. The grenade exploded and managed to miss all the Marines except O'Rourke, who took a chunk in the fleshy part of his right arm and Reilly, who was hit with a tiny sliver of shrapnel, right in his left eye. He left out a scream that would frighten a banshee. "Tone, Tone, Tone!" Reilly cried and O'Rourke, bleeding heavily himself, was at his side in a second.

"Cocksucking VC!" O'Rourke yelled. He pulled his belt off and looped his own arm, pulling it tight in one motion. "Fuck," was all O'Rourke could muster as the makeshift tourniquet slowed the bleeding to a trickle.

Blood was gushing out of Reilly's eye. "I can't see," he screamed. Then, in a voice suddenly quiet with resignation, "Doc, I can't see."

He couldn't see because his eye was mush. O'Rourke was afraid he would bleed to death. He quickly put a field dressing over Reilly's ruined eye and plunged a syrett of morphine through his fatigues. He stuck the spent syrett in one of Reilly's buttonholes to alert the MASH surgeons that morphine had already been given. "I don't wanna die, Tone," Reilly said slowly as the morphine began to take effect.

"You'll be okay, kiddo," O'Rourke said, but he wasn't so sure. The morphine had put Reilly on queer street, and he was beginning to drift off. O'Rourke didn't want to take any chances. He put his mouth to Reilly's bloody ear and began to recite a Perfect Act of Contrition in Irish.

Reilly awoke and heard the Gaelic. "What Tone? What are you saying?"

"*Cad a dhéanfaidh mach an chait ac luch do mharú?*" replied O'Rourke, again in Irish.

"What?"

"What will the cat's son do but kill a mouse?"

"Oh, of course," said Reilly completely baffled as he fell into a morphine-induced coma.

Soon Reilly was on a copter and out of Vietnam forever. O'Rourke, though wounded, stayed. He didn't want to leave his men without a corpsman. But the trauma had left O'Rourke with a stone-empty feeling in both his gut and his heart. Since that day O'Rourke could not stand the sight of blood—his or anyone else's. And as a corpsman, he was done.

O'Rourke couldn't believe it, but that had been 30 years ago. Back in New York after a prolonged AWOL hiatus in Dublin, O'Rourke had done his time in the brig in the Brooklyn Navy Yard and the Navy had finally discharged him. The two of them had again met up at the Moat and their friendship, based on insults and a battlefield bond, had continued.

The front door opened again and the procession of mourners paraded in, led by Napoleon Quirkle, an itinerant carpenter—"Just like Jesus," he liked to remind—who always referred to himself as a "published poet" based on the one poem he had published in the *Village Voice* in 1974. The bar was now two-deep as the mourners tried to drown their sorrows.

"How did the funeral mass go?" asked O'Rourke of Quirkle.

"It was a moving experience," replied Quirkle haughtily as he sipped a glass of Chablis while he prepared his Holmesian Calabash pipe for a smoke.

It was the burial day of vainglorious Michael O'Dote, the legendary Moat bartender who had finally succumbed to terminal laziness after all these years.

Quirkle cleared his throat and the Moat went silent. "To Mikey O'Dote," he said, "a legend in his own time."

"Here, heres" were heard around the room.

Cyclops turned to O'Rourke, "A legend in his own fucking mind," Reilly said and Quirkle turned to him sharply.

"What's that?"

"Ah, Cyclops was saying," said O'Rourke, "that that was a lovely sentiment of yours they quoted yesterday in the obit in the *News* about Mikey. What was it you said, exactly?"

"I said," said Quirkle posturing in his sensitive poet's mode as he tugged on his beard, "that Michael O'Dote was 'a true renaissance man.'"

"Yeah," spat Cyclops, "the only problem was that he couldn't spell fucking *renaissance!*"

Quirkle was thinking of a comeback for Reilly's "renaissance" crack when Fergus T. Caife entered. The sea of mourners and drunks parted as the famous Donegal poet made his way to the center of the bar.

"Irish whiskey, Lady Mountbatten back. Any of my fags back there?" asked Fergus T. looking for his Capri cigarettes behind the bar and Nuncio Baroody snapped to attention and began to rise from his seat.

Fergus would have none of it. He flipped his hands up as if to say: *Stop!* "Don't touch the poet!" Caife intoned in Nuncio's direction.

The threat abated, Fergus slipped in next to his old friend Tone O'Rourke, whom he had known since Dublin in 1971 when O'Rourke was getting IRA men out of the country with phony American passports and Fergus was establishing himself as a poet and lecturer. They had spent hours drinking together in the Bailey on Duke Street and the Palace Bar on Fleet Street, just across from Trinity College.

"How's it going, Fergus?" asked O'Rourke.

"Awful."

"How so?"

"Do you know what I had for dinner last night?" he asked. "The wife ordered in *sushi*. I washed it down with a *Moussey*. It all tasted like *pussy!*" O'Rourke and Reilly roared.

Fergus T. Caife looked like a bewildered Edgar Allan Poe. He was now the Distinguished Professor of Celtic Poetry at NYU, but at the Moat he was always referred to as the "Pussy-Whipped Poet." His American wife, the former Maggie Yeats—a distant, distant cousin of the great Irish poet—had met Fergus in McDaid's Pub on Harry Street in Dublin. She was looking for the ghost of Brendan Behan when she came upon Fergus, who had been reciting verse for his drinks. He looked her sincerely in the eye and declared:

"Stroked:
A wife stroked me in my dream
I turned, laid a hand on a breast—a scream
She turned away, her own Aran Isle
Leaving me barren, astir, in my Celtic bile."

A torrid romance had followed filled with drugs, wine and passionate and creative love-making. Marriage soon followed and a move back to New York. With the arrival of their first child all his vices were declared null and void by his wife. Thus he was referred to as "pussy-whipped" because his wife wouldn't allow him to drink or smoke in his own apartment. "I married a smoke detector," he was honest enough to admit. So he got his drink and smoke surreptitiously on the run at the Moat as he ran out for groceries or the paper.

"Caife," said Cyclops. "You got to put your foot down. Remember," he continued in his best Ralph Kramden imitation, "you're the King of the Castle."

"And every castle," returned Fergus, "has a vassal!" Sometimes there was no arguing with Fergus T. Caife.

Fergus sipped on his whiskey and cleared his throat. "Ha'penny," he said. There was absolute silence in the bar.

"She had red hair and I was on the hunt
She turned away as if to shunt
I knew she was a right cunt
So I asked her how much in *punts*
She turned around and said, 'But I'm just a nanny!'
So I offered her a ha'penny"

"Good Jesus," said Reilly.

"Get the fuck out of here, Fergus," added O'Rourke, "you fucking fraud!"

Fergus finished his whiskey, washed it down with his non-alcoholic Lady Mountbatten, then turned and started to exit the bar.

"Fergus T.," said Napoleon Quirkle. "Do you have a poem in memory of Mikey O'Dote?"

Fergus stood in the middle of the floor, his feet wide apart, his thumbs tucked inside his vest and cleared his voice: "For Mikey O'Dote:

Mikey O'Dote in now in the grave
For in matters of pussy he was always brave
A man only talked to because he was as handsome as a Cheshire cat

It won't do him any good now that he is as dead as a fucking bat
Still stiff, now, a necrophiliac's delight
The big donkey is dead and gone is his bite."

The bar was hushed in memory of O'Dote. Fergus turned, winked at Reilly and O'Rourke, and ran out the door. "How moving," said Quirkle. In silence O'Rourke and Reilly looked at each other, smiled, and clicked their glasses together.

With the after-hours drinkers, the mourners, and the other Saturday morning regulars, the Moat was soon so loud that you could hardly hear yourself think. The door opened once more and in came Dr. Moe Luigi, fresh from his morning rounds at St. Vincent's Hospital, and J. Howard Byrne, professional grief counselor.

Luigi and Byrne were the original Mutt & Jeff tandem. Luigi, diminutive, intense, minutely-groomed was just the opposite of Byrne who was nicknamed "The Commandant" because he looked like an IRA commandant, circa 1920, sent by central casting. It was said that you could tell the changing of the seasons by observing Byrne, because he was either wearing his winter tweeds or his summer tweeds.

"What's going on here?" asked Byrne as he looked at the mourners.

"Mikey O'Dote's funeral," said O'Rourke. "Do your stuff, Commandant."

Byrne had a Ph.D. and a sharp bite. In the touchy-feely '90s, he had put a hard Irish gaze on life, the antidote to the saccharine voices on TV and in public life who took delight in grief and mourning, like President Bill Clinton. ("He gives good eulogy," Byrne liked to say of the president.) From the bombing in Oklahoma City to the latest teenage nuts with AK-47s shooting up their high school, Byrne gave the same advice on national television as he would to Mikey O'Dote's mourners: "They're dead. Get over it. Move on."

"You show great sensitivity," said Quirkle with an edge as he pulled on his pipe.

"Fuck you," said Byrne. He ordered his morning soda. "Never trust a pipe smoker," he added as he went to read the papers.

"Good morning, Tone, Cyclops," said Luigi, surveying the bar. "I see they've rounded up the usual suspects."

Dr. Moe Luigi, according to a fawning profile in the *New Yorker*, was the famous "Proctologist to the Stars." He was referred to simply in the Moat as "the asshole doctor." And as Luigi himself often proclaimed, "What's all this veneration for me? A doctor's a doctor and an asshole's an asshole."

"How's it going, Moe?"

"The same, Tone. I look at assholes from nine to five. I stick my fingers in them. I peer up them. I shove proctoscopes up them. I wink at them, and they wink back at me. If I never see another asshole again, it'll be too soon!"

"Moe, you're in the wrong saloon." O'Rourke smiled.

"Touché," said Luigi, as he raised his glass of anisette in salute.

The story of Moe Luigi was the stuff that the American Dream was made of. The son of an immigrant Italian shoemaker, Giacomo Luigi was his father's first American-born son when he made his belated appearance in a railroad flat—the "dumb-bell" apartments of New York lore—on Mulberry Street in 1930. A graduate of Brooklyn College just before the Korean War, he too, like O'Rourke, had started out as a navy corpsman. After the war he entered the Cornell University Medical School on the GI Bill and finished first in his class in 1957. Declining offers from such places as the Mayo Clinic, he worked at St. Vincent's Hospital on the causes and cures for colorectal cancer. Over his long career he had peered up the rectums of such varied celebrities as Marilyn Monroe ("Nice," he said), Francis Cardinal Spellman ("He liked it too much"), Roy Cohn ("Clean as a whistle"), and President Ronald Reagan ("There was nothing at my end either"). But the thing that endeared him to the other regulars at the Moat was his plain speaking. The man had absolutely no pretensions. He was also a man of humor and kindness who had taken care of many of his impoverished drinking pals and their families free of charge.

"How's it with you, Tone?" asked Luigi. "How's the glamorous world of political consulting?" O'Rourke did not answer. He just looked at Luigi and gave the old jerk-off sign with his hand. "My boy," Luigi responded, "you have a lot to learn. Life was meant to be a giant circle jerk. You just can't beat the bastards. It's their game. They made the rules."

"But Moe," O'Rourke said, "look at you. You've done it. They always want you for some committee or panel or commission. They respect you."

"My boy, you're wrong. They don't respect me. They need me." Luigi pulled out a pack of Chesterfields from his jacket pocket and stuffed one into a long cigarette holder. He stuck it in his mouth, lit it, and slanted it upward like a grand erection. FDR couldn't have done it better. "I'm the best there is," he continued, blowing smoke through his nose. "I've forgotten more about assholes than those bastards could learn in a lifetime. I'm a pro's pro. So when some WASP President is worried why there's blood in his stool, and he doesn't know if he has cancer or just some temperamental hemorrhoids, he calls Luigi. He doesn't give a fuck about me. All he knows is that I'm a greasy little Wop who knows more about his dreaded malady than anybody else in the goddamn world. Always remember that. People want you for what you can do for them. Always stay on top of the bastards and fight them toe-to-toe and you'll win because most of these assholes have nothing but air between their ears. Just keep fighting."

"Moe, I'm tired of fighting. I just want to snooze for a while."

"My boy, you'll be snoozing for all eternity. Have fun now. What did the great Red Smith say about the eternal snooze? 'Dying is no big deal. The least of us manage that. Living is the trick.' See you dumb mick, living is the trick!"

"Moe," said O'Rourke, turning dead serious, "I'm having second thoughts."

"About what?"

"This business I'm in. It stinks. It's a filthy business full of filthy people."

"What does that make you?" said Luigi, blowing smoke in O'Rourke's face by way of punctuation. It was not the answer O'Rourke wanted to hear. "You think," continued Luigi quietly, "they give you all that money for doing good?"

"And that," said O'Rourke, "is part of the problem."

"Problem?"

"I should be ashamed of myself for consorting with these bums, these politicians," said O'Rourke. "What a bunch of scumbags." O'Rourke was becoming animated. "I'm not even talking about the right wingers," said O'Rourke. "I'm talking about the fucking phony liberals I get elected. They don't believe in a fucking thing, and the only thing that qualifies them for office is their mommy's money. Trust fund patriots. Jack Kennedy said, 'I'm an idealist with no illusions.' Well, I've become an illusionist without ideals."

Luigi saw O'Rourke was in genuine distress. He knew O'Rourke liked to avoid confrontation if he could, and now it was obvious that O'Rourke couldn't look him in the eye. He was slowly turning his body away from Luigi as they talked. "It's alright, Tone," Luigi said quietly, feeling for his friend, "it's just the *dybbuk*."

"The what?"

"The *dybbuk*," repeated Luigi. "You got the *dybbuk*." For a minute O'Rourke thought it was a disease. "You've been possessed by a demon." O'Rourke looked skeptical. "It's from Jewish folklore," Luigi added.

"A *dybbuk*?" said O'Rourke.

"A *dybbuk*," repeated Luigi, then added, "you always try to do good, Tone, but there's a terrible side to your business, politics. It is a business of the bought and sold. No matter what good you do, your means of doing it—deception fueled with money and lies—has its evil side. You want to do good like your heroes—Roosevelt, the Kennedy brothers— but they sold part of their souls to do good. You are no exception. First and foremost, you are a politician, and that puts your soul in jeopardy. Most of them don't care; they check their conscience at the door. You, Tone, I'm glad to say, are different."

"Moe," said O'Rourke, "I think you're more priest than doctor." Luigi smiled. "I must be the perfect politician," O'Rourke went on sadly, "because I am delighted by idiots and thrilled by stupidity." *Dybbuks*, thought O'Rourke, fucking *dybbucks*.

He still possessed the conscience of his mother and the nuns. There was right and there was wrong and O'Rourke knew the difference. It had been taught to him first by his mother and the indoctrination had continued with the Sisters of Charity at St. Bernard's Parochial School on 13th Street in the West Village. He still remembered the time he had stolen a peapod at an Italian fruiters on the corner of West 4th and 12th Streets in 1950. He had been apprehended by his mother who made him apologize and surrender the kidnapped pod to the proprietor. He had never forgotten that. Later, the good nuns had continued his mother's work with the help of the *Baltimore Catechism*.

The Red Chinese and all their devilish brain-washing schemes had nothing on the Sisters of Charity and the *Baltimore Catechism*. He still remembered what Sister Perpetua had said to her first grade class: "What you are in the first grade, you'll be for the rest of your life." Years later he sometimes thought about what Sister Perpetua had said, but discarded it as the philosophy of a narrow, sheltered woman. But lately he had begun to rethink Sister Perpetua's logic and realized she was probably right. Nearly half a century later he thanked both his mother and Sister Perpetua for the strong hand they had applied to his moral till.

Suddenly he brightened. "Did you see this?" He picked up the *Daily News* headline about Jackie Swift. "Do you believe we have morons like this representing us?"

Luigi read and started laughing. "The Virgin Mary," he said, "has Swift flipped his lid? What's the story, Cyclops?"

"Swift," said Reilly, "had nothing to do with the story. The Virgin shit, it's pure fiction, I guarantee it. That drunken press secretary of his, Drumgoole, must have fucked up the real story from his chief of staff, Brogan. I bet the story behind the story is a doozy. What I do know is that they were screwin' and snortin', and Swift's heart attacked him."

"Is that really true?" asked Luigi.

"Sure it is," said Reilly. "Word on the street is that Smilin' Jack loves the white powder."

"I've heard rumors," said O'Rourke.

"Well," said Reilly, "Jackie Swift has been in and out of Betty Ford more times than Jerry. He's disappeared about three times in the last three years. Supposed to be on some fucking fact-finding tour of Southeast Asia. Vito and Madonna-Sue packed him off to Betty Ford to clean up his act. He can't get straight. Loves the shit too much."

From the other end of the bar Nuncio erupted: "Moses, Moses, King of the Jews. Wiped his arse in the *Daily News!*" Baroody hit the deck as Cyclops's shot glass shattered against the wall where his face had just been.

"Fuck you, and fuck James Joyce," Reilly yelled in Baroody's direction. He clearly was in no mood to have his scoop belittled by the likes of Nuncio Baroody.

"How do you prove the Virgin story is bogus?" asked Luigi as if the histrionics in front of him never happened. "You know there are true believers."

"I'll have to pump my source," said Reilly.

"You have a source?"

"I have a mole."

"Where?"

"Deep inside the GOP."

O'Rourke threw out the first name that popped into his head. "Vito Fopiano?" he surmised.

"Close," said Reilly, putting his index finger to his lips to keep his secret, "but no cigar." Both Luigi and O'Rourke looked at him with renewed admiration. Cyclops was on a roll, and he knew it. "Moe, would you do me a favor?" he asked.

"Oh, no, you don't," said Luigi. "Whatever you're thinking, the answer is no."

Reilly's query had roused the politician in O'Rourke. "Are you thinking what I'm thinking?" O'Rourke asked his buddy.

"Fucking A," replied Cyclops.

"Moe," O'Rourke said, "do they do toxicity tests when a patient comes in? You know, for drugs and stuff."

"That would be part of the blood work-up," said Luigi.

"Would you take a little peek for me?" asked Reilly, sweetly.

"You two are something," said Luigi. He knew they were both rogues, and he couldn't resist them.

"Well?" said O'Rourke.

"I'll see," said Luigi as he took the cigarette out of its holder and snuffed it out in an ashtray, then threw a five-dollar tip on the bar. "I'll see." With that Luigi got up and exited the bar.

"What do you think?" asked Reilly.

"I'll guess we'll see, like Moe said," returned O'Rourke. Two more drinks were placed in front of them.

J. Howard Byrne ambled over. "Nice job, Cyclops," he said gesturing toward his copy of the *Daily News*. "This Swift guy is something. I was on a TV show with him after some kid shot his calculus teacher in Rathole, Montana, last year, and he said we should get rid of all the gun control laws. He even said, God help me, 'Guns don't kill people. People kill people.'"

Both O'Rourke and Reilly laughed. "Well," said Reilly, "he's right. If he dies it will be: 'Pussy doesn't kill people. Cocaine doesn't kill people. But the combination of both will give you a hell of a send-off.'"

"What do you think this 'visitation' means to Swift's career?" asked O'Rourke.

"It's a fucking mess," said Reilly. "How's he going to undo the Virgin Mary? Every religious nut in the country will be coming out of woodwork to embrace him. Just watch."

"Maybe it will go away," said O'Rourke.

"My job is to make sure it *doesn't* go away," said Reilly. "How's the Family Values congressman going to explain away the girlfriend?" Reilly got a twisted look on his face. "I'm going to *stick it* to him."

"What will your cousin Johnny Pie think of that?" said O'Rourke, referring to Monsignor Seán Pius Burke, Reilly's first cousin and the Cardinal's right-hand man.

"He knows," said Reilly. "You expect him to tell his boss, the Cardinal?"

"Declan Cardinal Sweeney might be very interested," said O'Rourke.

"Monsignor Johnny Pie ain't gonna tell the Cardinal squat about Jackie Swift. Swift is the Cardinal's favorite congressman. Right-to-Life and true-blue to Holy Mother Church. I can read my cousin like a book. I'm older than he is, but remember, we grew up in the same tenement together. No fucking way. Johnny Pie will keep quiet, won't rock the boat, and be a fucking bishop before he knows it. Shit, he's no help. He's a fucking politician just like Swift—and the Cardinal, too, for that matter too. There's got to be a better way."

"Another two here," said O'Rourke.

"You know, Tone," Reilly said changing the subject, "I saw *her* the other day."

"Who?"

"Deirdre." Something flip-flopped in O'Rourke's stomach. Deirdre was his last lover and he didn't want to think about her. He didn't say a word. "She still has the face of the Irish Madonna." All of a sudden, O'Rourke wanted to smash Reilly's fucking mug. It had been a year, and it still hurt. "Tone, she's so fucking beautiful."

"I don't want to talk about her. Forget it. Leave me alone." But

Reilly had the arrogance of the drunk and would not be silenced.

"What a face. What a body!" he said.

What does he know of her body, thought O'Rourke. He's never seen it. Or has he? Probably tried to make her like the rest of this fucking bar. O'Rourke would be at her place when the phone would ring. He would pick it up and as soon as they heard his voice he would hear the click of a hang-up.

"You expecting a call?" he would ask the lovely and mendacious Deirdre.

"No," she would say, looking innocent.

But she was expecting a call and she would lie and deceive and O'Rourke had had enough. He was going to make sure that Deirdre was the last woman who would ever hurt him. He hadn't slept with anyone since. He just drank.

"That's your problem, Tone," slobbered Cyclops, "for you to get laid you have to love them."

And Reilly was right. O'Rourke remembered them on leave in Saigon. While Reilly would be down at the local whorehouse, O'Rourke would sit in a bar alone, drinking until he could hardly see. O'Rourke looked at Reilly. It was thirty years since Saigon. The anger, the hurt, of a moment ago was gone. Reilly was now just another drunk.

"Cyclops," said O'Rourke, "you don't tell me about my romantic inclinations, and I won't tell you when you've had enough to drink. Okay?"

Just then the Moat's phone rang. "Cyclops, telephone," yelled the barman.

"Moe Luigi here," said the voice on the phone. "Your source is right. Cocaine was found in Congressman Swift's system."

"Christ!" said Reilly.

"I've got another surprise for you, too," said Luigi. "His Eminence, the Cardinal, will be making a private visit within the hour."

"I love you, Moe Luigi, even if you do drive a Lambor-guinea."

"You're incorrigible," said Luigi, breaking into a smile on his end of the phone. "Just do me a favor, Cyclops: Forget where you learned this. Forget my name."

Reilly heard the click as the phone line went dead. He returned to the bar, threw back his drink, and said, "I got to get to St. Vincent's."

"Why?" asked O'Rourke, still morose over Deirdre.

"Big shit happening. See you later."

O'Rourke shrugged and went to the head. At the urinal O'Rourke stared straight ahead at the smudged graffiti, looked down at his limp member—as it always seem to be now—and watched as steam rose up off his piss as it contacted the stone cold urinal. He then thought of Deirdre Gonegal and wished he was dead.

4.

"**M**y cock is killing me," said Jackie Swift. He was closer to the truth than he knew. Swift slowly opened his eyes. Even in his anesthetized state, he was in agony. "Pain," he mumbled. "Get me something for the pain."

"The worst is over," said Peggy Brogan reassuringly. "The doctor says the Demerol should be enough."

Swift wanted to say "fuck the doctor," but he didn't feel he had the strength. Swift was in the cardiac ICU at St. Vincent's and had an oxygen tube up his nose, an IV in his left arm, and wires running out of his chest, which were hooked up to a monitor that displayed his heartbeat in a red-line that jumped up into a miniature Gibraltar every time his heart pumped. His chest was sore, but his penis was pounding. He motioned Brogan closer to him. She put her ear close to his mouth. "My cock," whispered Swift.

"What?"

"It's awful sore."

Brogan lifted his smock and surveyed his genitals. "It's the Foley catheter," she said.

"Foley," said Swift, alarmed. "Get that cocksucker away from me!"

It took Brogan a second, but she realized that Swift was talking about fellow Republican congressman Mark Foley of Florida, who had a penchant for chorus boys and congressional pages. Foley hated the closet, but so far the GOP leadership had managed to bar the door.

"No," said Brogan. "Your pee tube, it's called a Foley catheter."

"Oh, okay," said Swift, relieved. "My balls feel like they're swollen."

Brogan looked again. They had run a tube up through Swift's groin to do the angioplasty and he was all black and blue down there. "They look okay," she said to him. If everything was normal, Brogan knew, Swift would have asked her to rub them for luck. No matter how sick Swift was, Brogan knew she had to bring him up to speed. It was her job as his chief of staff, and she would do it. "Honey," said Brogan, "I have good news and bad news."

Swift couldn't believe he was hearing such drivel. "Do I have a choice?" he said in a hoarse voice. Brogan shrugged her shoulders. "Bad first," he finally said. Brogan held up the *Daily News* headline: MIRACOLO!: BLESSED VIRGIN APPEARS TO GOPer. Swift read the headline and turned red. "What the hell is this?" he said trying to use the elbow of his free arm to push himself up in the bed. "What Virgin? What the fuck are they talking about?"

Brogan was in a fix. She could see that Swift was getting more agitated by the second. The last thing he needed was another heart attack. She would have to break the news to him gently. "Honey, remember *The Song of Bernadette* last night on the TV?" Swift shook his head no. Brogan was taken aback. "Don't you remember," she said lowering her voice, "when we made love?"

"Of course."

"And your attack?" Swift nodded. "Well, remember *The Song of Bernadette*?"

Oh my God, thought Swift. *The Song of* Fucking *Bernadette*. He closed his eyes as his head landed hard on the pillow and everything became frightening vivid.

*   *   *   *   *

The mirror rested on the bed between the two naked bodies.

Swift shook the vial of cocaine in his fist as if it were dice. He unscrewed the cap and tapped it onto the mirror. The razor scratched the mirror as Swift laid six lines. Neat in reflection. Glassy gutters to give them dimension. A thing of beauty.

He took the straw to his nose and snorted once left and then right. Four sat. "For you, Brogan. You can handle it. You're younger." He smiled at her.

"Yeah," said Brogan. "I can handle it." Left, then right like a shot. She took her index finger and wiped line five onto her upper gum, front, then left. Then six.

She reached between his legs and took his balls in hand. "Ah," said Swift. "Jesus," followed as his dick shook and things started to look up. Brogan's head went for it with a gigantic lick. Swift fell back on the pillow, almost in orgasm already. Hard now, Brogan in control, Swift's cock rode the coke wake between Brogan's lips and tongue. In and out as it grew. Harder still, she pumped, until he was purple, hard, and anaesthetized. Ready for action.

Brogan went to turn out the light. "Ah, don't do that," said Swift. "You know I like to fuck to light."

"It's too bright," said Brogan, who had fought this losing battle before. "Here," she said, reaching for the remote as compromise, "let's use the TV for light."

That was fine with Swift. "Let's go," he said. "Get on top."

"You always make me do all the work," said Brogan, telling the truth about their relationship. "If you want it, take me from behind." She got on her knees and stuck her rump into the air. "Oh," she said, laughing as she reached into the drawer of the night table, "I forgot something."

A buzzing filled the room as she revved up the vibrator.

"Oh," said Swift, "not that fucking thing again. Ain't I man enough for you?"

"Yes," Brogan said, a touch of unctuousness in her voice, "you're man enough, but men do need help sometimes, you know."

"Great."

"Did you know that some woman in Texas was arrested last week for using one of these?" asked Brogan. "You should ask your pal DeLay about that." It was a gentle jab at Swift because Brogan knew that when Tom DeLay—the Texan Republican enforcer in congress known as The Hammer—said "jump" Swift replied "how high?" "I wonder if Mrs. DeLay has one?" opined Brogan.

"I wouldn't bet on it," said Swift, and they both laughed.

"It's better than a hammer," said Brogan coyly, "*that* I can assure

Mrs. DeLay. If DeLay ever finds out how great these things are for women, he'll be introducing bills banning them on moral grounds. Sometimes makes you wonder if you even need a man."

Swift laughed and held his hands in front of him like he was holding a gun on a suspect. "Drop that vibrator or I'll legislate!"

"What if DeLay did propose legislation?"

"I'd vote for it," replied Swift honestly.

Brogan laughed. "Someday," she said, "we'll wonder how an imbecile like DeLay got so powerful. In the meantime," said Brogan airily as she positioned her rump on the side of the bed, "you can do to me what DeLay has been doing to the country."

"If you say so." Swift got out of the bed and stood behind her. Before he could help himself, he smacked her generous ass cheek.

"Oh, doctor," she said, giggling.

"Shut up," he said lightly as he whacked the other butt cheek. Brogan did as she was told and Swift slid himself into her and they became one. This was Brogan's favorite position and she knew all the nuances of it. She also knew that men were longer and harder when standing. Plus, the sight of her great, ample upturned ass guaranteed granite-like hardness. She was a pro at lovemaking. Basically, she used Swift as a prop. He stood there and she did all the moving. In and out and back and forth. For variation she would arch her back and find a different angle. With power, she would slam her ass back into Swift as she touched herself with the vibrator, triggering a set of multiple orgasms. It was her show and she knew it.

Swift loved fucking Brogan. Until he met her, he thought it was just about time for the Viagra. Unlike his wife, Madonna-Sue Fopiano, Brogan loved sex. Sex to Madonna-Sue was a chore. She rationed it out like it was gasoline during World War II. Once every six or seven weeks was enough—and no speeding. When they were courting, the sex was rampant. They couldn't strip fast enough. But when she became pregnant, and they had gotten married, everything changed. Now she was always covering her nakedness and making excuses of why she couldn't do "it." When they conceived their last child in a wine-induced quickie, Madonna-Sue had managed to somehow preserve her modesty during the act. Sex and modesty, Swift knew, don't mix. He became depressed just looking at those ankle-length flannel nightgowns she had taken to wearing. Madonna-Sue was the kind of woman who closed the door on her spouse to pee. Brogan had no such qualms.

The first time Swift saw Brogan, he fell in lust. She had been sent over by Vito, his father-in-law, to interview for chief of staff. "My God," Swift had said to himself, "what a beautiful woman." She was deeply tanned and wore her brilliant platinum blonde hair pulled straight back, revealing her extraordinary facial features, which included high cheek bones and a prominent Celtic forehead. It was a sign of sheer beauty, Swift knew, when a woman could pull her hair back to reveal her features, naked to the world. She bore a remarkable resemblance to the Maureen Dean of 1974, stoically sitting behind her husband John as he testified before the Watergate committee.

Madonna-Sue had not been happy when Swift hired Brogan. Although Madonna-Sue was cute and came across well on TV, she knew she was not in Brogan's league in looks, and maybe brains. "Nice call," she had said coldly when Swift introduced his new chief of staff. That night as they prepared for bed, she asked, "Why her?"

"Vito sent her over," said Swift.

"I said 'why her?'"

"She's qualified," said Swift defensively.

"I bet she is," said Madonna-Sue, precisely dissecting the way both her husband and her father thought: competence counts—especially if a big round ass is attached to it.

"Look," said Swift in the middle of the fuck, "it's Charles Bickford!"

Brogan, in heat, gave a look that Swift couldn't see. She should have gotten on top after all, she thought. At least then he wouldn't have had a straight line of vision at the TV. Swift loved old movies. He knew every old character actor who ever lived. "John Ridgely," he would declare as if anyone cared, pointing out Bogie's foe in *The Big Sleep*, "died in 1968 of a heart attack."

While watching *The Quiet Man*—he was a ferocious John Ford fan—he would always point out the Irish actor Arthur Shields. "Who does he look like?" he would demand of Brogan.

"Helen Hayes," she would say.

"Not at all," would reply Swift without humor. "Barry Fitzgerald. Do you know why?"

"Because they're brothers."

"How do you know?"

"Because this is the seventh time you've told me."

Now, watching *The Song of Bernadette*, he was utterly distracted by the cast. "Look, there's a young Lee J. Cobb. And there's William Eythe. Remember him?" Brogan couldn't believe this conversation was going on. "He's the American double-agent in *The House on 92nd Street*. Didn't have much of a career. Drank himself to death."

The movie had distracted Swift. He wasn't as hard and he just kept missing her "spot." She was all business and she would get Swift back up to speed. The vibrator buzzed as Brogan rubbed herself, then grabbed a handful of balls with her fingers, causing Swift to step up and relentlessly pound her. It was all in the balls, Brogan knew, as she pulled Swift up into her.

"Jesus," said Swift. "My God, that feels good" as he curiously thought of Captain Queeg and the ball bearings.

"Mother of God," said Brogan in orgasm. "Mother of fucking God." Swift had climbed up on the bed and was now standing over Brogan pumping away, hands on his knees like an infielder waiting for the pitch. It was supreme sex. They had ceased being human and had turned animal. "Fuck me, you bastard," said Brogan as the vibrator flew out of her hand and she ejaculated heavily on the bed, pushing Swift out of her.

"Oh my God," he said as he stood up and straddled her, holding his arms out like wings, fists clenched. He tried not to come, but she had been too much for him and, involuntarily, he shot thick streams of semen on Brogan's freckled shoulders and back. They collapsed on the bed, each one's body fluids smeared on the other as they laughed the sex laugh, the laugh of relief and total satisfaction.

"Thanks be to God," intoned a solemn voice from the television.

"What's that?" Brogan said as she turned the vibrator off.

"It's *The Song of Bernadette*," said Swift. "That's what I was trying to tell you. Every great character actor in Hollywood is in it. Jerome Cowan. You remember him, don't you? He was Bogie's partner in *The Maltese Falcon* and the district attorney in *Miracle on 34th Street*. Vincent Price from *Laura*. Even Sig Ruman, the Nazi sergeant from *Stalag 17*."

"My God," said Brogan, "it's Jennifer Jones."

"You know," said Swift as if revealing something, "she was married to David O. Selznick."

Brogan had to laugh at the irony. They couldn't escape it, the knowledge that the Church, all important in their political lives, was still somehow looking over them, even in bed. Swift, exhausted, rested his perspiring forehead in the valley of Brogan's robust breasts, looked up into her eyes, and smiled again.

"Jackie," said Brogan in her state of relieved passion, "I love you so much." She looked at Swift, who smiled sweetly back at her with that boy-Irish look that he had never lost and that the sisters at St. John the Evangelist's had always loved. A good Irish-Catholic lad he would always be.

"Me too," replied Swift as he went back to playing with the cocaine on the mirror. Brogan saw how ravenous Swift was for the powder. No matter how good in bed she was, she always seemed to be playing second fiddle to the "magic," as he sometimes called it. What a waste, she thought. He was scraping the residue together for one more line. The razor scratching across the glass made a sound that forced Brogan to grimace. Swift shot half the line up his left nostril and the other half up the right.

"Honey," said Brogan out of the blue, "did you ever think of having a baby with me?"

Swift laughed. "Brogan," he said, "remember? I'm already married. My wife's pregnant. I'm the 'Family Values' Congressman from the Sodom and Gomorrah called New York City."

"You're also for mandatory sentences for drug abusers," Brogan said as she gestured towards the mirror with the cocaine on it.

"What's that supposed to mean?" asked Swift, annoyed. Brogan had noticed that after Swift used cocaine his personality had a tendency to change. He was developing an edge. "Don't start with me now," said Swift. "I feel bad enough about having another kid with Madonna-Sue."

"How could you do that to me?"

"Do what?"

"Get her pregnant."

"I didn't plan it," said Swift. "It just happened. I told you. We went to get our coats after Thanksgiving dinner at Vito's house and the next thing I know we're screwing on the bed. Drink was taken."

"The Irish excuse for *everything*."

Swift gave her a look and there was no smile attached. "Don't start now," he repeated as he stood up to go to the bathroom, but he immediately sat back down on the bed. "I don't feel so good," he said. "My God!" he said grimacing. He flung both hands across his chest as he fell across the bed. "Jesus," he said as he gasped for air. "Mother of God, help me!" he uttered as the pain exploded in his chest and rushed down his arms and disintegrated his elbows. He felt nothing as a blackness engulfed him and then he thought he saw the light, so far away, but getting closer by the second.

*   *   *   *   *

The memory of the whole sorry episode had totally deflated Swift. "How," he said, "in God's name did the *Daily News* get the idea that the Virgin Mary appeared to me?"

"Georgie Drumgoole," said Brogan.

"Oh, no," repeated Swift knowing he was doomed, "not Drumgoole."

"Drumgoole got it wrong," said Brogan. "I called him as soon as they took you to the hospital and told him we were watching *The Song of Bernadette* when you had your attack. Somehow he misconstrued that into an appearance by the Blessed Virgin."

"Was he drunk again?" asked Swift.

"What do you think?"

Swift was beside himself. "How," said Swift with growing agitation, "could he think—if that's the word—such a stupid thing? It's the most asinine thing I've ever heard of." He plopped back onto his pillow, near exhaustion.

For a solid minute, there was nothing but silence. "You want the good news?" Brogan finally asked.

"Good news?" shouted Swift, seemingly overwhelmed by events. "What good news? That my wife and father-in-law are going to kill me? That my political career is over? What good news could you possibly have?"

Brogan went over to Swift and put her hand on his arm. "It's okay, Jack," she said, "everything will be all right." She kissed him on his unshaven cheek. She took his hand in hers and stroked his manicured fingers. She could see him become calmer. "In fact," she said, "I have two pieces of good news for you." For the first time, she could see a trace of hope in Swift's eyes. "First, your cardiologist says you're out of danger."

"Thank God," said Swift sincerely. "And?"

"The Cardinal will be visiting you shortly."

"Not the Cardinal," said Swift, visibly slumping again. "Not the fucking Cardinal." Swift looked like a beaten man, resignation clearly on his face.

With that the door opened and in stepped Declan Cardinal Sweeney, sprinkling Holy Water. "The Lord is my light and salvation," said the Cardinal. "Though I walk in the shadow of death, I will fear no evil, for you are with me." Swift knew instinctively that it was the last of the seven sacraments: The Sacrament of Anointing the Sick. An uneasy smile crossed Swift's face, for he knew it was an ecclesiastical euphemism. It used to be called Extreme Unction, the sacrament of the dying. Swift was Catholic enough to know that the Cardinal thought he was on the way out. The Cardinal stood over him and nearly drenched him with more Holy Water. "The Lord is my shepherd," he said, "I shall not want. In verdant pastures he gives me repose." Oddly enough, the very presence of the Cardinal seemed to comfort Swift. Swift laid back in the bed, watched the Cardinal's theatre, and felt at peace. He almost felt like going to confession because it was the first time he had been honest enough to admit to himself that it was his cock and his coke that was always getting him into trouble. They had gotten him into this holy mess and now he would have to face the music, which was being orchestrated in front of him by a Prince of Holy Mother Church.

5.

Vito Fopiano had been Jackie Swift's Dr. Frankenstein. For without Vito, there would have been no Congressman Swift.

It had all started in 1979, when Vito Fopiano, the New York City Council minority leader from Staten Island—who also happened to be the lone Republican on the council—had watched a made-for-TV movie about old Joseph P. Kennedy, the chieftain of the Kennedy clan. "If a mick prick like Kennedy can do that, why can't I?" he asked his empty living room. Unfortunately, Fopiano had no Jack, or Bobby, or even a Teddy to work with. All he had was his daughter, Madonna-Sue. Since his wife's death, he had been both mother and father to Madonna-Sue. And she had thrived, especially as a high school and college athlete. An All-American in both tennis and lacrosse, Madonna-Sue more than made up for the son that Vito never had.

New York, city and state, was solidly Democratic in 1979. Mayor Koch, Governor Carey, and Senator Moynihan were all Democrats. And the other senator—"Javits the Jew," as Fopiano referred to him—might as well have been a Democrat. He was one of the last Rockefeller Republicans—a cross of Lincoln, Teddy Roosevelt, and Nelson's money. He was about as conservative Republican as Vito was liberal Democrat.

It was about this time that Fopiano stumbled across Alfonse D'Amato, who strangely enough, would one day become the King of the Jews. Jewish voters, that is. At that time, D'Amato was the obscure Presiding Supervisor of the Town of Hempstead, out on Long Island.

"How'd you like to be a United States Senator?" asked Vito Fopiano of D'Amato over a delightfully sautéed veal scaloppini.

"How'd I do that?" D'Amato asked, his mouth full.

"What do you get if you divide one Italian by two Jews?" asked Fopiano, as a delicate mushroom sauce inched down D'Amato's chin. There was no response from D'Amato. "A United States Senator," said Vito Fopiano.

D'Amato's dull eyes didn't move for a second, then he nodded, swiped his chin with the sleeve of his jacket, and pumped his arm in the air. "Yes!" D'Amato said, his beady eyes ricocheting wildly in their sockets, sounding like Marv Albert.

A year later, two Jews—Jacob Javits and Elizabeth Holtzman— divided by one Italian would equal one Senator Alfonse D'Amato. It was becoming obvious that Fopiano could plot politics like a member of the Curia in a papal conclave. There were other worlds to conquer, thought Vito Fopiano. No office was too insignificant; he would start with the New York City Council.

The first thing he did was get his chief of staff, Smilin' Jackie Swift, to run as a Republican for the city council on the East Side of Manhattan. The East Side from 14th Street to 96th Street was a mixed bag. Upper-, lower-, and middle-class. Lots of rich, but most stuck solidly in the middle. Some browns, mostly white. Still a lot of ethnic Irish left over from before the war. It was the district of Roy "The Conscience of the New York State Senate" Goodman, famous for displaying his conscience on every bus in New York City every four years at election time. It became a running joke—the very notion that either Roy Goodman or the New York State Senate had a conscience, that is. And Vito Fopiano instinctively knew that this was a district where he could get Jackie Swift elected councilman.

Jackie Swift was perfect for this district. As an Irish Republican—GOPer, that is—Jackie was a total fraud. In fact, he wasn't even a Republican—he was still registered as a Democrat. But no one could wear a two-thousand-dollar suit like Jackie Swift, not even John Gotti. He was immaculate. He loved to shake hands, and he had the smoothest hands of any politician in New York. They were as pink as a baby's bottom and had done considerably less work. He had hands softer than an archbishop's, with beautiful sculptured cuticles and fingernails that gleamed from their careful biweekly shellacking. Not a Thursday or a Monday went by without Jackie Swift getting a manicure. And he was a master of the two-handed handshake. The right for the shake, and the left for the top of the other man's hand. Jackie, as he liked to say, could "cup-it with the best of them." He had learned it by watching John Ford's *The Last Hurrah*. He loved the scene where Spencer Tracy worked the wake, "cupping" hands left and right.

But Jackie Swift had many flaws, all of which were exacerbated by his laziness. Swift's idea of a hard day was going to City Hall at 10:30 a.m., returning a few phone calls, then heading over to Harry's at the Woolworth Building for a three-hour lunch. After such a lunch Jackie often felt, well, tired. He found that a little white "Peruvian marching power"—as he called it—could get him through the rest of the day's boring meetings and another little pick-me-up could propel him onto the cocktail circuit looking wide awake. Soon Jackie began using a little cocaine in the morning, "just to get the heart started," as he liked to say.

And he had something that Vito Fopiano envied: he was well-liked. Jackie could work a bar from one end to the other like an old Tammany politician. Soft handshake here, tap on the back there, a condolence whispered in an ear. Everyone knew he was lazy, but they all liked him. And Vito Fopiano's firebrand Republicanism (basically: let's scorch the niggers and the poor) left many feeling threatened. Jackie, like Ronald Reagan, was the antidote for the firebrand—he put a happy face on misery.

Of course, the Democrats cooperated in the election of Jackie Swift to the city council. They ran two candidates, the regular Democrat and a Democrat on the Liberal line. Vito Fopiano had taken care of that. Everyone knew that the Liberal Party was the ultimate political oxymoron—it wasn't a party, and it wasn't liberal. Fopiano had made a deal, and two divided by one still meant a win for the Republicans. Smilin' Jackie Swift was to become the second Republican on the city council.

Not that Jackie was without enemies. His career had started in 1968 as a young deputy press secretary for Paul O'Dwyer's U.S. Senate try. Over the years many had observed that Jackie Swift had come a long way—from working for a great man like Paul O'Dwyer to getting into bed with sleaze-bag like Vito Fopiano. In fact, many Democrats and lefties had never forgiven Swift for what they considered the ultimate betrayal. Even O'Dwyer himself refused to talk to Jackie. Swift had finally cornered O'Dwyer at City Hall one day and asked why the cold shoulder.

"Jackie," said O'Dwyer in his soft County Mayo accent, "you don't understand." O'Dwyer put his hand on Jackie's shoulder, "If me own brother had joined the Black and Tans I wouldn't talk to him either." Jackie Swift felt as though he had been slapped across the face.

But now it was now time for Vito Fopiano to fry bigger fish. He was going to run for Congress and his beloved daughter, Madonna-Sue Fopiano, was about to take his seat in the city council. Madonna-Sue was cute. She was photogenic. And she learned quickly. The first time she saw herself on TV she was accompanying her father to the Al Smith Dinner at the Waldorf-Astoria. She was appalled at the way she looked on the small screen—dark Italian hair, shades of a mustache and a wide, frumpy butt. She went back to running, cut out the pasta, experimented with electrolysis, and bleached her hair blonde. And she was good. She came across as the girl next door. And although her opinions were carbon copies of her father's, she didn't frighten people the way Vito did. She always put a happy, perky face on things.

Perky.

That was the adjective most used to describe Madonna-Sue Fopiano. She had a perky nose. A perky personality. A perky sense of humor. And, as Jackie Swift would soon realize, she had perky tits.

But it was all an act. Madonna-Sue Fopiano couldn't give a fuck about the national debt, drugs, abortion, or the regulations on rent control. She was only doing what her father wanted her to do. Vito Fopiano thought, some said, with Alfonse D'Amato getting on in years, that maybe, just maybe, she would some day make a United States senator.

Vito was no fool. Before he left the City Council to move on to Congress he got Madonna-Sue a job in the office of his friend, Councilman Menachem Mandelstam of Brooklyn. Mandelstam was a nominal Democrat—he would later change to the Republican Party at Vito's urging—and his job was to teach Madonna-Sue the ropes, out of the presence and spotlight that Vito Fopiano inevitably had focused on him. Mandelstam was a politician made out of the same mold as Vito Fopiano—divide and conquer. He was a master at using the race card. He could play it better than Fopiano and Johnnie Cochran combined. If things got tough in Crown Heights, he would hiss one word—*schwartze*—and his problems were over. He told Fopiano and Rudy Giuliani to use it against African-American David Dinkins in the 1989 mayor contest, but Giuliani wouldn't. By 1993 he had no such qualms. "It'll look like the second parting of the Red Sea," said Mandelstam to Fopiano and Giuliani, "with all the Jews rushing to the polls to vote against the *schwartze*." It took Giuliani two tries to get it right, but in the end Mandelstam's theory stood up. Madonna-Sue couldn't be in better hands. She kept her mouth shut, learned the routine, and was ready when her father did his Mr.-Smith-Goes-to-Washington routine.

So when Vito went to Washington as a congressman, Madonna-

Sue went to the City Council, representing the whole of Staten Island and parts of Brooklyn. She sat on the Finance, the Environmental, and Zoning committees, just as her father had. And the money, most of it meant for Vito, flowed in. It flowed in in briefcases from landlords and developers disguised as campaign contributions. Wall Street contributed in the form of lucrative preempted stock market IPOs and insider information that had once allowed Vito to make $27,000 in the market in one day. But, of course, Madonna-Sue Fopiano was for campaign finance reform. Vito would write the bills and she would introduce them and more money would flow to the elected representatives of the people of the City of New York, slowly strangling the political process into an absolute plutocracy.

And while she sat on these committees, her father managed to get three more Republican members elected to the city council. By 1990, forty-four-year-old Smilin' Jackie Swift was the minority leader and Madonna-Sue was his whip. She would often end the day in Jackie's office, and they would go out for a drink near City Hall. Then they would work their way to one of the small, discreet restaurants around the Village, where Jackie would regale her with stories of the Irish rogues he grew up with on the East Side. He was so smooth. Soon Madonna-Sue was using Jackie's cocaine. Then the whip ended up getting spanked.

Then she missed her period.

What was she to do? Jackie was terrified. "Maybe an abortion?" Jackie, the anti-abortion candidate, meekly offered.

"Marriage sounds better," said Madonna-Sue curtly.

Marriage it was and Vito pulled the strings—St. Patrick's Cathedral and Declan Cardinal Sweeney himself presiding. The Cardinal owed Vito big-time for his opposition to abortion and this was a good way to show that the Cardinal would always back his friends to the limit.

"Lord, bless this marriage," said Declan Cardinal Sweeney, "like you would sanctify the hands of a great surgeon—or a Hispanic shortstop." People looked around St. Patrick's Cathedral at one another and it was the first clue that the Cardinal was beginning to lose his marbles.

Seven months later a baby girl, Vitoessa, was born at St. Vincent's Hospital in Greenwich Village. George Drumgoole, Swift's press secretary, called an impromptu press conference in the lobby of St.

Vincent's to announce the birth. Abe Stein of the *New York Post* began counting on his fingers. "That's seven months, Georgie." Drumgoole looked baffled. The reason Drumgoole looked baffled was that he was drunk. In fact, he was drunk so frequently that he was known as George the Fifth, for the fifth of bourbon he nurtured throughout the day until he could do some real drinking, come cocktail hour. Then he was terrified. Seven months! He could see the foggy *Post* headline now: GOP BABY WAS IN OVEN! "Seven months," Abe Stein repeated, a small smile appearing on his face. This was better than covering Al Sharpton, Stein was thinking as he watched Drumgoole in an alcoholic daze try to figure out what to do.

"The baby's birth was normal," Drumgoole muttered, "and Councilman Swift is doing fine."

"How's the *mother*?" Roche of the *News* asked pointedly.

"It would be," began Drumgoole onerously, "premature of me to comment on Madonna-Sue Fopiano Swift's condition at this time."

Abe Stein was beginning to feel sorry for Georgie Drumgoole. "Did you say the baby was premature, Georgie?"

The light went on. "Yes, that's it," said Drumgoole. "The little bastard was premature!"

"You owe me one," said Abe Stein.

"This is just what the GOP needs!" said Vito Fopiano as he bounced little Vitoessa on his knee for the TV cameras. "We are the party of family values!"

George H.W. Bush heard the soundbite on CNN and called Vito. "Like that 'Family Values' stuff," the president told him. "Keep it up agin the heathen." (Even Vito Fopiano wondered why the president of the United States spoke the way he did.)

But it would pay off big. At the 1992 Republican Convention there were Vito, Jackie, and Madonna-Sue before the crowd waving the kid around—the placard for family values. Abe Stein looked up at the TV in Hogan's Moat and said, "I bet Madonna-Sue Fopiano can lactate on cue."

By 1994, Vito Fopiano and Newt Gingrich were making big plans for New York and their "Contract for America." They had decided that it was time for Vito to retire from Congress and take his anointed place on the Republican National Committee. (Mayor

Rudolph Giuliani, grateful for Vito's benediction, had even named the newest Staten Island ferry after him—the *Congressman Vito Fopiano*. Jimmy Breslin in his column commented that after a bottle of chianti christened the boat, his eyes were strangely drawn to the bridge where he "expected to see Captain Smith on the lookout for the first New York City harbor iceberg.") Madonna-Sue, naturally, would take his place in Congress. And Vito Fopiano's eyes immediately went to New York's 7th Congressional District where Fat Max Weissberg—Vito referred to him as "The Jowly Jew"—was ill and obviously not up to a strenuous defense of his seat. When Vito told Gingrich about his plan to have *both* his daughter *and* his son-in-law elected to Congress out of the same congressional delegation, Gingrich started babbling about his own august destiny as Speaker of the House: "I am an arouser of those who form civilization," Gingrich actually said. Vito didn't know what Gingrich was yapping about; he only knew he had lots of work to do.

Smilin' Jackie Swift was a superb candidate. "Just don't talk about abortion, prayer in schools, or rent control, and you're in," cautioned Vito Fopiano. The 7th C.D., which covered the Upper West Side down to the Battery and part of the East Side, had been in the hands of the Democrats since the days of FDR. In this decidedly left-of-center district, there was only one way for Jackie Swift to win: divide by two.

Fat Max Weissberg was old and sick. People knew he was sick because he was down to only four double chins. The mounting questions about his health had some saying he should retire. One of these "voices of concern" belonged to Thom Lamè, the gay city councilman whose ambition was legend. "Think of your health, Max," Lamè said in his patterned lisp.

"Fuck that professional homo," said Weissberg, and Vito Fopiano licked his chops. The Democrats were committing suicide again and he was going to help them by making sure that Thom Lamè ended up with the Liberal Party endorsement.

Divide by two.

Swift won easily.

Newt Gingrich's Republican Revolution had reached into New York and sent to Washington a married congressional couple. It could happen only in America.

And they were off and running until Madonna-Sue found Jackie Swift's diary.

Jackie, like Garry Moore, had a secret. But only Jackie Swift was stupid enough to write his down in a diary. Only he didn't exactly "write" it down. He had used a code. Jackie Swift loved movies and mysteries. His fascination with codes had started back in 1958 when he was a kid. Every Sunday, right after mass, Jackie would rush home to watch old Sherlock Holmes movies on Channel 11. These were the old flicks from the 1930s and '40s starring Basil Rathbone as Holmes and Nigel Bruce as Dr. Watson. One of his favorites was *Sherlock Holmes in Washington*, where Holmes has to figure out the significance of the "Dancing Men," little figures on a matchbook cover. Each one stood for something important. Jackie Swift had been mesmerized by the movie, and the Dancing Men had stuck in his mind even into adulthood.

Then he made a mistake. He invented his own Dancing Men, his own private code. The code stood for sex. No one, Jackie thought, not even Madonna-Sue, if she ever came across it, would know what it meant.

But Swift had underestimated his wife. Madonna-Sue, like the British in Bletchley Park reading a German enigma machine, knew immediately what it meant. She kept a diary, too. It was full of her most intimate thoughts—and the mating habits of Mr. and Mrs. Jackie Swift. Like good Catholics they both over-estimated the sex act. They were fascinated about doing "it." Madonna-Sue's diary even recorded the positions used. It also reported the data on her menstrual cycle. Madonna-Sue suffered from PMS, which made her crampy and cranky. The last thing Madonna-Sue wanted to do when she was suffering from PMS or having her period was to have sex. Any sex. She had informed Jackie Swift in no uncertain terms that during her period her least favorite word was "fuck." Her second least favorite word was "suck." Jackie Swift duly noted the situation and went looking for a remedy for one week of every month. It was to be his undoing.

Madonna-Sue had found the diary, had figured out what the little man that looked like the symbol for Leslie Charteris' "The Saint" stood for. It meant that Jackie Swift was cheating. Jackie Swift was dead meat. But Madonna-Sue kept her counsel. If there was one thing she had learned from her father it was never to show your cards. She would wait—but she would also cut Jackie off, and soon they would begin to drift apart.

Jackie Swift had met Peggy Brogan when she worked on Vito Fopiano's staff at the National Republican Committee. Working for the inventor of the GOP's "Family Values" campaign could be trying. Vito was a widower, he was lonely, and he was sixty-six. But he still woke up in the morning with a hard-on. Soon, Brogan found herself in hard escape from the roving hand of Vito Fopiano. He was so quick you could hardly feel or see them. The glancing tip of the buttock was a favorite of Vito's. He also liked to feel for "the good part" of the breast. That's when he would stand on Brogan's right and paternally put his hand around her back and get a piece of the "good part" of the left breast, the area where the breast descended from the armpit. To Vito Fopiano it was a test of means; if the "good part" was good, the rest of the tit was tremendous. Showering one morning, Brogan discovered that her ass and tits were black and blue from the reconnoitering of Vito Fopiano's hands. She wanted out. And Jackie Swift would be her ticket.

With the Republican Party's takeover of Congress for the first time in forty-two years, young staffers were scrambling for the best jobs on Capitol Hill. Swift's chief of staff had left to work on Bob Dole's presidential campaign, and he needed a replacement. He called Vito, and Fopiano, reluctantly, recommended Peggy Brogan. She was smart. She had kept her mouth shut, hadn't ranted and raved about sexual harassment, and had upped her salary to ninety grand a year. It was incestuous, working for Vito's son-in-law, but she didn't care. She was in for the long run, and she knew she was just as tough as Vito Fopiano and his "*capos*," as she referred to the people who were loyal to Vito.

She was immediately surprised by Jackie Swift. He was not a hood like the rest of them. He was a gentleman. He was funny and as he liked to describe himself, he was, indeed, "as affable as an Irish cop." As chief of staff she was around him constantly. Preparing him for congressional hearings; basically making sure he didn't make a fool of himself. Brogan soon learned that Jackie was as lazy as he was affable, but he was also lucky.

Soon she was traveling with him back to New York for his "working weekends." Working weekends soon meant walking through a neighborhood street fair, pressing the flesh, then retreating to Swift's West 10th Street ground-floor garden apartment where Swift would press Brogan's flesh. After the discoveries of the infamous Swift Diaries by Madonna-Sue, the Swifts had surreptitiously separated—they didn't want to damage either of their political careers—and Peggy Brogan had quietly moved in with Jackie. Peggy ran the man, but was still jealous of Madonna-Sue. Jackie and Madonna Sue still appeared together on the Sunday morning network talk shows, eagerly blasting Bill Clinton's morals, hugging each other for the cameras. Jackie had *savoir faire* and Madonna-Sue was perky. Brogan had felt betrayed when Madonna-Sue had become pregnant again at Thanksgiving, 1999. The Swifts, still separated, would be having another baby just in time for the 2000 Republican National Convention.

Brogan had worked for Swift for five years and had been his lover for nearly four. Without her Swift's career would be in ashes. She knew it, Vito knew it, and Madonna-Sue especially knew it. Vito and Madonna-Sue had given the two of them space. At this point in their congressional careers, it was paramount to keep this political marriage alive. It wouldn't look good to have two of Clinton's biggest moral critics involved in their own little sordid matrimonial mess. This was the hand Brogan had been dealt. She didn't like it, but that's how it was. But still, Madonna-Sue's pregnancy haunted her, tormented her in a way that made her jealous and vengeful at the same time. She could be a dangerous woman and the Fopianos, father and daughter, knew it.

6.

For over twenty years the professional lives of Wolfe Tone O'Rourke and Winthrop Pepoon had been intimately intertwined. It was almost impossible to find two men with such diverse backgrounds and personalities. Where O'Rourke was the Village drinker, the censorious Dublin-born, Greenwich Village–bred Irish Catholic, Pepoon was the eternal preppy, the Ivy Leaguer WASP with a lifestyle and family right out of *The Great Gatsby*. Pepoon's playground was the Hamptons, O'Rourke's the Moat. Where Pepoon wore seventy-five dollar silk ties, O'Rourke—when he remembered to wear one—got his for five bucks at Tie City. O'Rourke was a Democrat, Pepoon a Republican. O'Rourke was abrupt with Pepoon, who was his boss. Pepoon was terrified of O'Rourke, whom he considered *the* brightest mind in the political consulting business. They should have hated each other, but there was a strange bond and respect between the two of them. They had their corporate ups-and-downs, yet when Pepoon took his accounts elsewhere, Wolfe Tone O'Rourke was sure to follow. They were known best throughout the industry for their great American Express fiasco/success.

If there was anything O'Rourke liked better than drinking and talking at the Moat, it was hanging out at the original Palm Restaurant on Second Avenue. The Palm was one of those places without pretenses. What you see is what you get. It was the ultimate cholesterol palace featuring succulent food, drinks strong enough to fell a horse, and efficient, no-nonsense service that tended to be brusque.

It was to the Palm that O'Rourke had gone on his day of infamy. His lunch-mate that day was the CEO of the Ambrosia Winery of Rome. Ambrosia was trying to break into the U.S. market, and O'Rourke was trying to get the account. Their meal went well with lots of spirits and wines flowing around the lobster. At three o'clock, O'Rourke strolled back into the plush Third Avenue offices of his firm and was immediately reminded by his terminally enthusiastic secretary, Bonnie, that there was the big American Express account meeting in thirty minutes. Usually, Winthrop Pepoon made all the presentations, but he had been called away to London on business. It wasn't that Pepoon didn't trust O'Rourke to give presentations which, by the way, were O'Rourke's creations, it was just that Pepoon felt he had a more even temperament than the abrupt O'Rourke and there was less chance of somebody being called an "asshole" around the conference table. But this time fate had intervened and there was no choice. The London business had been an unforeseen emergency and American Express would be put off no longer. They wanted to see how the campaign was progressing and the ball was now in O'Rourke's court. There was only one problem: O'Rourke was totally unprepared. He immediately drank five cups of coffee and decided to fake it. But O'Rourke's whiskey lunch and the absence of Pepoon's smooth tongue would betray him this time.

"Well, Mr. O'Rourke," said Cyril Hawkesworth, the head of the agency, in his usual pompous manner, "we are anxiously awaiting your suggestions for the new ad campaign." Hawkesworth and O'Rourke were like oil and water. Hawkesworth bore a remarkable resemblance to John Houseman as he portrayed Professor Kingsfield in *The Paper Chase*. He loved wearing double-breasted suits and droopy dickie bows and often walked around the office with a book clutched to his chest. He was also quick to remind everyone of his family's wealth. Once O'Rourke had stood behind him in a crowded elevator and imitated in the perfect Houseman pitch for the Smith-Barney commercial he had created: "We make money the old-fashioned way—we *inherit* it!" Hawkesworth was not amused.

Now what to do? Thoughts of Ambrosia and Rome were rattling around in O'Rourke's brain-cell challenged mind. All of a sudden there came a vision. Divine inspiration had struck.

"Well," said O'Rourke, "I've put a lot of thought into this and I think that American Express needs to spruce up their image a little bit. People are sick and tired of Karl Malden, his hat and nose, and his dire warnings of muggers and thieves. American Express has to think positively. It needs a little glitter." O'Rourke paused for effect. Looking around the table everybody was nodding soberly. O'Rourke had them in the palm—he loved the pun—of his hand.

"Yes, gentlemen," O'Rourke continued, "glitter. Some big names. And a format. Well, the first one will be terrific. We'll get ah, ah...." His tongue was now out of control. He couldn't stop himself.

"Gentlemen, we take the pope—you know, Paul VI—and we put him in the Sistine Chapel. The pope is dressed up in his white cassock, satin red cape, and papal stole, white zucchetto"—he knew he must be impressing these five WASPs and one Jew with his Catholic terminology and he was sure glad he had been an altar boy—"and as the camera zooms in on him he says, 'Do you know me? Here in the Sistine Chapel everybody knows who I am. But when I leave Vatican City sometimes it isn't always that way.'

"Now," continued O'Rourke, "we have the viewer fascinated." The gentlemen were beginning to shift uncomfortably in their chairs, but O'Rourke couldn't stop. "So we go into the whole spiel about where the American Express Card is accepted by everybody all over the universe and then we shift back to Pope Paul and the Sistine Chapel. This time he has a blank card in his hand and at this point we print his name, in Latin—*PAULUS PP VI*—on the card with a real zap, zap, zap kind of special effect. Then the Pope ends it with the tag-line: 'The American Express Card. Don't leave *Rome* without it!'"

Hawkesworth coughed, and Coolville, the chairman of the board of American Express, cleared his throat. The rest of the gentlemen just stared straight ahead with their mouths open. But O'Rourke wouldn't let up.

"And the great thing about this format is that you can get different celebrities to do it. It'll be terrific."

"Thank you, Mr. O'Rourke," said Hawkesworth, "that will be all for now."

Later that afternoon O'Rourke was made—as Hawkesworth succinctly put it—"redundant."

When Pepoon returned from London the following day, there was hell to pay. When he was told that O'Rourke had been canned, Pepoon—totally out of character—had burst into Hawkesworth's thickly carpeted office with its panoramic view of the East River and shouted at him: "You asshole. Nobody, but nobody, not even the chairman of this goddamn firm, fires one of my people. You can take this job and shove it. I quit." Pepoon turned on his heel, ignored pleas for calm and reason from Hawkesworth, and headed back to Sag Harbor. He was damned if he was going to take this kind of abuse from some guy who knew nothing about the ad business except that he was supposed to reassure clients by looking grandfatherly.

O'Rourke handled his unemployment in another way—he went out and got shit-faced for two weeks. After that he calmed down and collected his unemployment checks and drank afternoons and evenings at the Moat. One evening about three months later as he was preparing to go out to the Moat for his second drinking shift of the day, he turned the television set on and, as he sat reading his mail, he heard the voice of Benny Goodman utter the familiar words, "Do you know me?" O'Rourke couldn't believe it. By the time Goodman had uttered, "don't leave *home* without it," his phone was ringing. It was Pepoon.

"Tone, old chum," he said, "I think we have them now." With not too subtle threats from Pepoon's lawyers, O'Rourke found himself within the week holding a check for $75,000 for "consultation fees." Right then, O'Rourke knew that he would never again have trouble finding and holding a job, no matter what a classic fuck-up he was.

Neither Pepoon nor O'Rourke would be unemployed for long. Soon Pepoon bought the long vacant Northern Dispensary building at the corner of Waverly & Waverly in the Village and set up Northern Dispensary Associates, which specialized in ad campaigns, and many of his old accounts came over. Then luck took over in the form of Harris Landsdown, Pepoon's classmate from Harvard, who was running for the Republican nomination for Senator in California.

Landsdown was in trouble. He was terrible on the stump and all he had was money. But Cranston, the Democrat incumbent, was thought unbeatable, so there were few who wanted the Republican nomination. In any election, Landsdown thought, there was always that chance of winning. And he wanted that chance. There was only one thing between Landsdown and the nomination—Charlton Heston, who was also looking for the Republican endorsement.

Landsdown turned to Winthrop Pepoon for some media advice. Pepoon wasn't quite sure what should be done. He called in O'Rourke. After being introduced and told the situation O'Rourke was blunt. "I don't work for Republicans," he said. "Sorry."

"For Christsakes, Tone," said Pepoon, "Harris here isn't a bad guy. Look at Heston. He's a lackey for the goddamn NRA."

"Okay," conceded O'Rourke. "I'll help you this time, but only against Heston. I'm for Cranston in the general election."

"That's fine," said Landsdown. "I can live with that."

"But you have to do what I say," said O'Rourke. "Okay?"

"I'm in," said Harris Landsdown. Winthrop Pepoon began to feel uncomfortable.

O'Rourke sent a researcher to find pictures of Charlton Heston in *Planet of the Apes*. When the researcher returned, O'Rourke flipped through them, selected one, and went to the typewriter. He typed less than thirty seconds before pulling the paper out of the machine and showing it to Landsdown. In it was Charlton Heston in a G-string, his back to the camera. He handed the paper to Landsdown. It read: "Isn't it time we put Charlton Heston *behind* us? Vote Landsdown on primary day."

Landsdown started laughing. "What do you want me to do with this?"

"I want you to put this up on a billboard on Sunset Boulevard, as big as possible. You won't have to worry about Chuck Heston any more," assured O'Rourke.

"I can't do that," said Landsdown.

"You can't beat this guy one-on-one. He's got the recognition factor, he's smooth, a professional actor, for Christsakes. He'll kill you. You have to shame these guys. You can't believe the egos on them. This will work."

"What do you think, Winthrop?" asked Landsdown.

"Let's face it, Harris. It's worth a try. You'll be spending your money for nothing if this guy builds up momentum."

Harris Landsdown did as he was told and Charlton Heston decided that he had to go to Australia for the summer to make a made-for-TV movie. O'Rourke had literally laughed him out of the country. Harris Landsdown won the nomination for the U.S. Senate and was beaten by Alan Cranston in the general election. And Northern Dispensary Associates got a reputation.

"I killed Moses," bragged O'Rourke.

As the word spread about O'Rourke's campaign, other politicians came looking to O'Rourke for salvation. Pepoon, always the astute businessman, split the business in two: half ad agency and half political consulting, which was under O'Rourke's wing. O'Rourke only did Democrats and referred Republicans back to Pepoon. They began to make money hand over fist.

The reputation of the firm continued to grow when they saved the Dannemora Brewing Company from bankruptcy. Charles Hodding's family had owned Dannemora Brewing for nearly 100 years. Pepoon had been their account executive going back to the 1960s. He had come up with the immortal tagline that was heard on radios all over upstate New York:"Things Go Better with Dannemora," sung to the tune "How Are Things in Glockamora?" from *Finian's Rainbow.* When O'Rourke heard it for the first time he told Pepoon, "You should be ashamed of yourself."

"I thought it was rather good," said Pepoon.

"You would," replied O'Rourke.

Now the Brewery was in sad shape. It was being squeezed by Anheuser-Busch and also by several Canadian breweries to the north. Their market was dwindling. Fifteen hundred jobs were at stake.

"I don't want to sell out," Hodding told Pepoon. "If I sell out to Budweiser, they'll shut the brewery down. I'm the biggest employer in Dannemora, along with the prison. I have to do something." Pepoon called O'Rourke in.

"What's the problem?" said O'Rourke.

"I have a shrinking market," said Hodding.

"Find a new market," said O'Rourke.

"Not so easy," said Hodding and Pepoon almost together.

Then the light bulb went on. "Queer Beer," O'Rourke said.

"What?"

"The faggots," said O'Rourke.

"What are you talking about?"

"Who has more money to piss away on themselves than anyone? Fags, of course. I see them in those bars on Christopher Street drinking Bud from the can until they're absolutely polluted. Who's vainer than fags? Nobody! They'd love to have their own brew."

Hodding was that desperate. Within six weeks, the first Queer Beers rolled out of the Dannemora Brewing Company. O'Rourke pulled Juanita, the Puerto Rican transsexual from Pepoon's mailroom, to be the first Queer Beer sales-whatever in New York. Within weeks, every homosexual on Christopher was standing outside their favorite joint with a Queer Beer in his fist. O'Rourke packed Juanita off to San Francisco where the response was also overwhelming. Hodding couldn't brew Queer Beer fast enough. Within a year Hodding had beaten off Budweiser. To rub salt in Anheuser-Busch's wounds O'Rourke was now referring to Queer Beer as "The Queen of Beers" in his ads. Hodding had even acquired one of the Canadian breweries that had been trying to acquire him. He couldn't thank Pepoon and O'Rourke enough.

"Where can I go from here?" he asked.

"Dyke Lite," replied Wolfe Tone O'Rourke.

7.

Tone O'Rourke, being the creature of habit he was, always arrived at Northern Dispensary Associates at precisely 6:30 a.m. For the next hour he read the four New York newspapers, the *Washington Post*, the previous day's *Irish Times*, and immersed himself in the politics of the day.

"How'd it go this weekend?" asked Winthrop Pepoon, another early riser, as he stuck his head into O'Rourke's pocket office.

"Lovely. Hardly remember it at all. How'd you like that stuff with the Virgin Mary and Congressman Swift?"

"Virgin Mary?" said Pepoon. "What are you talking about?"

"Don't you get the papers?"

"Nothing about it in the *Times*."

"Figures. Big news in the tabloids. Cyclops Reilly broke the story."

"I didn't think Cyclops was ever sober long enough to break a story," said Pepoon haughtily.

"Don't give me any of your Chablis morality," said O'Rourke and Pepoon backed off.

It was time for Pepoon to change the subject. "When are you going to hire your new chief of staff? We have a busy primary season ahead of us."

"You know, Winnie, I don't like anybody sticking their nose in my business."

"Jesus, Tone, who the hell is sticking their nose in your business?

I just wish you'd hire someone. What is it now, for God's sake, three months?"

It was more. O'Rourke was procrastinating. He hated hiring people. "Well," said O'Rourke, "I'll think about it."

"Fine. I'll have Human Resources call you later this morning."

"Okay."

At 10:00 a.m. the phone rang and it was Human Resources. Human Resources, thought O'Rourke, another euphemism for the solipsistic times. What ever happened to Personnel?

"I hear you're *still* looking for a C of S, Tone," said Mrs. Dooge, the HR Director. "Have you decided exactly what you're looking for?" Mrs. Dooge was trying to pin O'Rourke down.

Resisting the cheap, smart answer, O'Rourke said he was looking for someone who was bright and had a passing notion of how the American political system works. O'Rourke was lousy with people who worked for him. He couldn't motivate them and if they were duds, he almost had to beg them to do their jobs.

"In that case, Tone," said Mrs. Dooge, "you may be in luck. I have someone here who just graduated from Columbia with an M.A. in political science. Also worked for Senator Schumer. When would it be convenient for me to send Sam McGuire up?"

"How about now?" said O'Rourke.

"Fine. We'll be right there."

Minutes later, when Mrs. Dooge and Sam McGuire approached O'Rourke's third floor corner office that looked out onto Christopher Street, they were stopped in their tracks by a flying cell phone. "And keep your fuckin' beepin' cell phone out of my fuckin' office. You couldn't sell whiskey to drunken fuckin' Injuns," O'Rourke said as the hapless account executive scampered to safety.

"Is this a good time, Mr. O'Rourke?" asked Mrs. Dooge.

"As good as ever," replied O'Rourke calmly.

"This is Sam McGuire."

O'Rourke had a look of surprise on his face. For Sam McGuire was female, black, and beautiful. "Won't you come in?" asked O'Rourke smoothly as he closed the door on Mrs. Dooge.

She certainly was different from the female Teutons—all Protestant Amazons, six-foot-two with flowing blonde hair and brilliant white teeth as big as tombstones—whom he had been forced to interview before. To say Sam McGuire was different was an understatement. She was immaculately dressed in a dark blue pinstriped skirt and a burgundy sweater that showed off her collarbone. Black boots rose to just below her knees. She looked a little like Leslie Uggams, her skin a radiant caramel. O'Rourke guessed she was in her mid-thirties. He examined her hands, which were bereft of jewelry, and her bosom, which looked ample. She squirmed her bottom in the chair, getting comfortable, before she crossed her legs, revealing shapely thighs.

"What the hell was that all about?" she asked with the most stunning smile O'Rourke had ever seen. He also liked her bluntness.

"Oh, he's one of those Gen-X types I can't stand. He's not much of an account executive, but he has all the toys in the world. I hate fucking cell phones, and he's always playing with his fucking laptop. Toys for the dopey generation," said O'Rourke gesturing toward his corner window, which gave him a panoramic view of Christopher Park and the entrance to Hogan's Moat. "I see him coming out of fucking Starbucks on Sheridan Square with a cup of shit corporate coffee. Then I see the dunce coming up Grove Street on a fucking scooter. Twenty-nine-fucking-years-old and he's riding a fucking scooter to work! He also has braces. What's with adults wearing fucking braces on their teeth? He's even studying for an MBA, for Christsakes. The most useless fucking degree ever invented. Bunch of lazy fucks with fucking spreadsheets who think they know something about nothing. Christ, what a dopey, money-grubbing, dunce-ridden generation."

"Are you through venting?" asked Sam.

"You're a cheeky one," said O'Rourke, laughing. "I guess I'm full of piss-'n-vinegar this morning."

McGuire looked around O'Rourke's office and noticed what was probably the last rotary telephone in the city of New York. She also spied O'Rourke's trusty electric typewriter, circa 1974. There wasn't a computer in sight. "Early Luddite," she said to O'Rourke.

"You know what a Luddite is?" asked O'Rourke.

"I sure do," she said. "There are a lot of positive things to be said about Luddites."

"Can't argue with that."

"No computer? How do you send emails?"

"I don't," said O'Rourke, "that's *your* job."

"I'll change that."

"You think?"

"Sure," said McGuire, cocksure. "I hear you're one of the great copywriters, right?"

"I guess."

"Well, every writer loves computers. They make it easier to write." O'Rourke looked dubious. "And you'll *love* email."

"Another distraction," O'Rourke scoffed.

"Boy," said McGuire, laughing, "you're a *confirmed* Luddite."

"Not completely," protested O'Rourke, holding up his caller ID box. "I like this one. Allows me to speak to as few assholes as possible."

McGuire looked at O'Rourke's wall, which showed the story of his life. On it were photos of O'Rourke with many of the politicians he had dealt with over the years. There he was with Bobby Kennedy, taken just two months before the senator was assassinated. Another showed him wedged between Teddy Kennedy and Tip O'Neill. "Not bad company," said McGuire, "I see you get around," as she looked at O'Rourke with President Bill Clinton. "You were pretty cute in that picture with Bobby Kennedy," she added.

"*Were?*" O'Rourke deadpanned.

"Oops," said McGuire covering her mouth. Then she began to laugh.

"What's so funny?"

"That picture of Rockefeller," said McGuire.

Stuck in the middle of his wall was the famous picture of Nelson Rockefeller, vice president of the United States of America, giving the finger to some student demonstrators in 1976. "That's the picture that best describes politics in America in the last quarter of the twentieth century," said O'Rourke. "Fuckyouism."

"You knew Rockefeller?"

"Only over the phone," said O'Rourke. "He called me up once when he was trying to get Roy Goodman elected mayor. Goodman was the Ex-Lax heir," said O'Rourke, laughing at the thought, "one of those ersatz Republican liberals. 'Hiya fella,' Rocky said to me. 'Wouldya like to help Goodman?' I told the governor in no uncertain terms that I wouldn't piss on Goodman if he was on fire."

"Oh," said McGuire, laughing, "you didn't!"

"I did," continued O'Rourke, "and Rocky said to me, 'Okay, fella, I can't stand the little shit either!' Nelson was a mixed bag. Great state university system; terrible, stupid drug laws. 'Every law not based on wisdom—'"

"—Is a menace to the State," finished McGuire.

"Who said that?"

"I don't know," replied McGuire. "I found it on the New York State Appellate Courthouse on East 25th and Madison."

"Me too," said O'Rourke. He was piqued that they both, apparently, thought alike.

She looked at a photo of O'Rourke and a woman standing by a bus in the Connemara countryside. "How's President Robinson?"

"You know the former president of Ireland?" he said, truly astonished.

"Sure," said McGuire, "I do have an M.A. in political science from Columbia, you know."

"Sam," said O'Rourke, "I've had people in here with Ph.D.s who didn't know who the fucking president of the United States was."

McGuire laughed. "So how did you meet President Robinson?"

"We're old friends going back to the early 1970s. When she decided to run for president on the Labour Party ticket in 1990, I asked if I could help."

"Well," asked McGuire, "did you?"

"See that sound truck?" O'Rourke asked, pointing to the van in the photo. "It played nothing but 'Mrs. Robinson' by Simon and Garfunkel. When she started, out nobody knew who she was. By the time that truck waded its way from Connemara to the Ring of Kerry and up to Dublin, everyone knew who Mary Robinson was. A great candidate, and a great woman."

"Why were you in Dublin in the '70s?" asked McGuire.

"Had to flee this country," said O'Rourke.

"Flee?"

"Yeah," said O'Rourke, "went AWOL for six months and the U.S. Navy was not amused."

McGuire looked at O'Rourke's wall again and saw a photograph of O'Rourke's Marine platoon. Underneath it were three framed medals.

"Deserters don't usually win Purple Hearts."

"Yeah," said O'Rourke, "I'm the hero deserter. Purple Heart, Navy Cross, and Bronze Star with Combat Ribbon. All that got me was a one way ticket to Dublin in 1971 and that's how I met Mary Robinson."

"Why Dublin?"

"They were about to pack my ass back to Vietnam for another tour, and I had had enough. I was supposed to be finished. Then they pulled the 'stop-loss' shit on me."

"Stop-loss?"

"Yeah," said O'Rourke, "stop-loss. That's what the military calls it today. It allows them to keep you in. They were almost out of corpsmen, so they extended me by six months. I was steaming. I was at Kennedy Airport, waiting to head back to 'Nam and I said 'fuck this.' I'm an Irish citizen, born there. So I went from American Airlines to Aer Lingus and found my ass in Dublin for six months. Happiest six months of my life."

"Wow," was all Sam McGuire could say.

O'Rourke didn't go into it, but there was more to his sojourn. He had arrived back in Dublin just as internment without trial was introduced in Northern Ireland and with his radical, Irish Republican contacts it wasn't long before he was running fugitives from the North into New York using phony American passports that friends from the States had conveniently "lost" while they were on holiday in Ireland. It was a time of healing for O'Rourke as his soul slowly recovered from his Vietnam ordeal. He had met the likes of Mary Robinson and Fergus T. Caife and had gotten his life together. One day he was on the top of double-decker bus when it went by the American Embassy in Ballsbridge and he saw his old buddy from Vietnam, Kevin Griffin, one tough Bronx Marine, doing embassy duty. He got off the bus and walked up to Griff. "Hey, Kevin," he said to the stunned Griffin, "how does an old corpsman get home?" The Navy and the Marines knew their men. O'Rourke returned to New York under his own authority, was arrested, and thrown into the brig at the Brooklyn Navy Yard. They could have court-martialed him and sent him to Leavenworth, but they were not vindictive. Three months later he was released with an honorable discharge.

"Why didn't you just go to Canada?" asked McGuire.

"Because I didn't want to freeze my ass off," said O'Rourke, who then paused before continuing. "But that really isn't it."

"So?"

"I had to go, morally wise."

"Morally?"

"Yeah," said O'Rourke, "I couldn't allow someone else to go, some other hapless soul from Brooklyn taking my place. I had an obligation to that fellow, whoever he was."

"So, your obligation wasn't necessarily to your country?"

McGuire had caught him. "Not necessarily," he replied softly.

"You're a moralist?" she asked, laughing. "Last thing I thought I'd ever find in this business."

With a thunderous knock, the office door opened and Tommy Boyle burst in. He took one look at McGuire, said "Sorry," turned and slammed the door behind him.

"Tommy!" O'Rourke called out.

Tommy, in response, burst back into the office. "Sorry," he yelled again, just high enough for Sam to realize that Tommy Boyle was not normal.

"What is it, lad?"

"The papers," said Tommy.

"What papers?" asked O'Rourke.

"The Irish papers," said Tommy as he again began to turn and retreat.

"Tommy," said O'Rourke, "come here."

"*Irish Times*," said Tommy in a voice that could be heard in the basement.

"Just a minute," said O'Rourke as he rummaged in the pile of newspapers behind his desk. He came up with a week's worth of *Irish Times* and gave them to Tommy.

"Thank you," said Tommy as he rushed to leave.

"Tommy!"

"Yes."

"Say hello to Sam McGuire."

"Hello, Sam McGuire," Tommy said, his fair skin turning a sunburnt red in embarrassment.

"What's wrong, Tommy?" asked O'Rourke.

"Sam," he replied, "that's a boy's name."

"You're right," said McGuire, standing and taking Tommy's reluctant hand to shake. "My real name is Simone McGuire, but my little brother had trouble pronouncing Simone so he turned it into Sam."

"Okay!" said Tommy. "Doc, I gotta go."

"Doc?" said McGuire.

"They call him 'Doc,'" said Tommy, "because he was a hero in Vietnam."

"They call me 'Doc,'" said O'Rourke, "because I was a navy corpsman."

"That's like a medic," said Tommy to McGuire.

"I see," said Sam.

"I gotta go," repeated Tommy and he disappeared like a spirit in the night.

"That was Tommy Boyle," said O'Rourke. "He's shy around girls."

"I see," said McGuire. "Is he special?"

"Yeah," said O'Rourke, smiling because McGuire had used the very same Dublin term his mother often did, "he is. He's a good lad. We're in this program with the archdiocese that supplies jobs to the mentally handicapped. He's been with us since we opened this joint. He's our janitor, handyman, painter, whatever. Likes to look at the *Irish Times* because his parents are from Leitrim and they go back in the summers for holidays."

"He your idea?"

"Yep," said O'Rourke quietly, "I have several cousins back in Dublin who have Down's Syndrome. Geraldine and Ross. I just wish God would pay more attention sometimes. I think it's His way of pricking human hubris. Trying to make us pay attention to the least among us. It breaks my heart the way they're treated sometimes. You know, I once went with Bobby Kennedy to visit his retarded sister. . . ." O'Rourke's voice trailed off and he went quiet.

"You okay?"

"No, I'm not," said O'Rourke as he got up and turned his back on McGuire. He went to the window and watched the traffic going west down Christopher Street.

McGuire could hardly believe that this was the same man who had thrown the cell phone at the account executive just minutes before. She got up and went to him, putting her hand on his arm.

"Did you just feel that God was in this room?" said O'Rourke in a whisper.

McGuire, stunned by O'Rourke's statement, looked at O'Rourke, a tear running down his cheek. "Yes," she said, her breath almost taken away by O'Rourke's outburst, "yes, I think maybe you're right."

"Who will speak for them?" O'Rourke asked rhetorically. "No one cares anymore. No one gives a shit about people anymore. It's all about sound bites and how important *I am*." O'Rourke returned to his desk and McGuire to her chair. "I'm sorry," he said.

"For what?"

"My display of middle-age crisis."

If O'Rourke was a moralist, right now he was a very angry moralist. He had always believed in the system, that the system was the way to change things. Just as his hero, Bobby Kennedy, had always maintained. Now, in his fifty-third year, he had begun to realize that everything he believed in was a sham. And as someone who helped elect frauds to Congress, he was part of that sham. In a way, the greatest thing that had ever happened to O'Rourke was getting drafted. It had defined his life. He had done his duty for his country, and he was proud of it. It had also made him wary of politicians who wanted to send other people's sons to fight in America's wars while their sons hid out with a deferment. He referred to it as the "Dick Cheney Factor." While others were getting their asses shot off in Vietnam, Little Dick Cheney was hiding out in the Yale Divinity School. He was another of those right-wingers like Pat Buchanan and George Will who, when they had a chance to kill Communists—which they urged every American to do—took a safe pass. O'Rourke despised them, and now he despised himself for being part of the same corrupt system.

"God forgive me," said O'Rourke. "I should be ashamed of myself for representing these bums, nothing but spoiled, selfish little shits looking for attention and someplace to spend their trust funds."

"They pay well."

"Yeah," said O'Rourke, "that may be the problem. Money. I can't believe some of the guys I represent. Miserable human beings. The only thing they have in common is that they're Democrats, and they're millionaires. It would be nice to have a truck driver in Congress. He might have a clue about what's going on in the country."

The conversation was interrupted by a knock on the door. "Come in," said O'Rourke.

"Oh, excuse me," said Winthrop Pepoon, "I didn't know you were busy."

"I'm only doing what you ordered me to do," said the now composed O'Rourke.

"What?"

"You told me to hire an assistant. This is Sam McGuire. We're talking about the job."

"Oh."

"Well, what's the problem?" asked O'Rourke.

"It's the 'I Can't Believe It's Not Butter' campaign," said Pepoon.

"What's wrong with it?"

"It's not coming along. Could you sit in at the meeting?"

"Oh, stop," said O'Rourke. "You and your fucking meetings."

"I'm only asking," protested Pepoon. "I'm sorry."

"I got it!" said O'Rourke.

"Got what?"

"Your campaign," said O'Rourke and Pepoon had a sinking feeling in his heart.

"What?"

"*Last Tango in Paris.*"

"*Last Tango in Paris*? What in God's name are you talking about?"

"Remember that old Brando movie in the early '70s with that big-titted slut, what's her name?"

"Maria Schneider," interrupted Sam McGuire.

"Yeah," said O'Rourke with appreciation, "Maria Schneider."

"What about it?"

"Remember the butter scene?"

"Butter scene?" said Pepoon. "What butter scene?"

"I do," said McGuire, covering a giggle with her hand.

"Well," said O'Rourke, "how can I put this judiciously? They need lubrication for a certain sexual act."

"What does this have to do with the 'I Can't Believe It's Not Butter' campaign?" asked a clearly exasperated Pepoon.

"Well," said O'Rourke, "we get a clip of the film, and when he takes out the butter to lube Maria's ass, we can dub and have Schneider say: 'I can't believe it's not butter!'"

McGuire laughed harder, but Pepoon looked perplexed.

"It's genius!" said O'Rourke.

"Thank you," said Pepoon, exiting. "Nice meeting you Miss McGuire." With that he closed the door.

"You're insane," said McGuire.

"I'm the best!" replied O'Rourke and McGuire didn't doubt it for a moment. "Where were we?"

"You were telling me how much you hate the business of politics."

"Yes," said O'Rourke, "it's lost its magic."

"Well," said McGuire cutting him no slack, "why did you get into politics, if it's such a hideous business?"

"Because politics used to be fun," replied O'Rourke. "Not only were you changing the world for the better—you hoped—but you were having fun doing it."

"Such as?"

"Well," recalled O'Rourke with a smile, "you ever hear of Dick Tuck?"

"No."

"What do they teach you up at Columbia?" O'Rourke asked as he punched the air in defiance. "Dick Tuck used to work for Jack Kennedy. Bobby, too. Dick taught me a lot. He hated Nixon and used to drive him crazy."

"How?"

"Well, there's the famous stunt he pulled in 1962. Nixon was running for governor of California, and JFK sent Tuck out there to make sure Nixon didn't get a head of steam for 1964. Nixon's giving a speech from the back of a train, and who shows up but Tuck, dressed like a railroad worker." O'Rourke stopped to laugh and savor the moment before continuing. "Anyway, Tuck waits until Nixon starts his speech, then starts waving his railroad lantern. The train pulls out right in the middle of Nixon's speech," said O'Rourke, laughing out loud.

"You're kidding!"

"He was something," continued O'Rourke. "At the 1968 Republican Convention, he hired pregnant black women to parade in front of the convention center with NIXON'S THE ONE signs." McGuire howled. "He ran for state senate in California once on the slogan, 'The job needs Tuck, and Tuck needs the job.' He got *killed*. So on election night, he comes out to give his concession speech and says: 'The people have spoken—the bastards!' It was another time."

"It's brutal today," McGuire said.

"Brutal is not the word," agreed O'Rourke. He turned around to his wall and pointed out a photo. "Look at that. Nineteen-sixty-nine. Norman Mailer, Jimmy Breslin, Joe Flaherty, and me."

"The 51st State."

"Right you are, McGuire," said O'Rourke brightening. "Now, *that* campaign was fun. It was just before I went in the navy, and, boy, did we cause havoc that spring. We knew we weren't going to win, but we had ideas, and we drove the establishment crazy. Flaherty ran a great campaign. Mailer was bombed most of the time, but he was great. Someone asked him how he'd remove the snow from Queens and he said—"

"I'd piss on it," interrupted McGuire.

"You know!" said O'Rourke, "God, I wish politicians talked like that today."

"Well, why don't you make them?"

"That's not my job," said O'Rourke.

"Maybe you should make it your job," returned McGuire, nudging O'Rourke's conscience.

"How do you know about the 51st State?"

"I read Flaherty's book *Managing Mailer*," said McGuire, further impressing O'Rourke. "It's a textbook to a very important time in the history of the city of New York."

"You know," said O'Rourke quietly, "Joe was a very close friend of mine."

"I didn't."

"Yeah," said O'Rourke, "I loved the guy. Everybody loved him. Funniest man who ever lived and also a superb writer. I cherish his memory every day." O'Rourke was silent for a second. "Back then we had all these dreary old farts like Mayor Wagner," continued O'Rourke, "a liver-spotted Dalmatian of a politician. Then there was Mario Procaccino, the eventual Democratic nominee for mayor."

"He was preposterous," replied McGuire, echoing Flaherty's opinion.

"Well, Mario was something," said O'Rourke laughing. "He once introduced somebody by saying, 'He grows on you—like cancer!'"

McGuire could see that O'Rourke was warming to the memories of his youth. "Then there was Herman Badillo, the great Puerto Rico liberal. Flaherty called him 'a Puerto Rican Robert Goulet.' Nothing more devastating than that has ever been said about a politician. I think it was Doug Ireland who said that Badillo campaign literature was bilingual—English and Yiddish!

"That phony," continued O'Rourke, rising out of his chair, "used to have a sound truck working the Bronx. In the Spanish neighborhood, it was 'Vote for Ba-dilllllo.' In the Italian neighborhood, it was 'Vote for Ba-dil-ooo.' In the Jewish neighborhood, it was 'Vote for *Herman!*'" McGuire laughed. "And that old starched pseudo-PR prick is still drawing a city paycheck from Giuliani. They are good at one thing— cashing checks. Not helping the people. Fuck the bunch of them." McGuire could see that O'Rourke's mood was turning black again.

"Your midlife crisis coming back?" asked McGuire.

"Oh," said O'Rourke, "that's just self-indulgent horseshit on my part, too. Every time I want to give up, pack it up, get away from those frauds, and move back to Ireland, I come up against this," he said, pointing to the Monday morning edition of the *New York Daily News*. The Virgin's appearance was the talk of the town, a topic almost as hot as Cyclops Reilly's prose. BOGUS, proclaimed the *News* headline. Rupert Murdoch's *Post* was just as strident: MOTHER OF GOD! "I can't take it," said O'Rourke laughing.

"So you don't believe the Virgin appeared to Congressman Swift," said McGuire. "What kind of a Catholic are you, anyway?"

"What the hell do you know about being a Catholic?"

"Twelve years with the nuns," said McGuire with passion. "I attended *The* Mary Louis Academy in Queens."

"Oh," said O'Rourke, "not any old Mary Louis Academy, but *The* Mary Louis Academy."

"Yes," said McGuire, laughing. "We had the best of pretensions and sophistication and Catholicism."

"Hard time?" said O'Rourke, also laughing. "Not that many black Catholics around."

"I'm not black."

"What?"

"Well," she continued, "not all of me. My father is a Harp, just like you."

"Bullshit," was all O'Rourke could muster.

"Honest Injun," she said, holding up her right hand.

"That's some mix," said O'Rourke.

"Yeah," McGuire said, "tell me about it. I've got an Irish liver and a black booty."

"That," said O'Rourke, shaking his head, "is an awesome combination. Let's see your resume."

He looked it over and said, "That's good, no picture."

"Picture?"

"Yeah," he said, "I refuse to hire anyone who has their picture on a resume or uses the words *synergy, proactive,* or *execute* in the resume."

"*Execute?*"

"Yeah," continued O'Rourke, "you know, will 'execute' this or 'execute' that. The only executing around here is done by me!"

"I get your point," said McGuire.

"I see you worked every losing Democratic campaign in the last ten years."

"Hey," said McGuire, "I also worked Schumer's."

"What do you think of him?"

"He'd talk to a fire hydrant," she said. "God, I hated those Sunday morning news conferences he loves so much. That was my job— weekend flack."

"Yeah," said O'Rourke. "Old Chuck should take a valium or something." He went back to looking at the resume. "I see you worked for Bobby Abrams against D'Amato and Ruth Messinger against Giuliani the last time out."

"Abrams, to put it mildly, was not John F. Kennedy on the stump."

"And Messinger?"

"She didn't have a chance," said McGuire, starting to laugh again.

"What's so funny?"

"She has the biggest ass on any white woman I've ever seen!" McGuire responded bluntly.

O'Rourke savored her laughter, then said, "I'm glad *you* said that, because if I had even thought it, the National Organization for Women would be demanding that this misogynist pig be fired. You learn anything up there at Columbia?"

"Yes," said McGuire. "Drink in the West End Bar as often as possible."

"What did you write your master's thesis on?"

"Bobby Kennedy's three-month campaign for president."

O'Rourke was quiet for a second. "What did you think of it?" he finally asked.

"It," said McGuire with authority, "was flawed." O'Rourke nodded, beginning to feel uncomfortable. "Did you know the senator well?"

"No," said O'Rourke with a small smile, "not that well." McGuire knew he was lying. O'Rourke got up and walked to the window again. He wanted to change the subject again. "You really want to work for me?" he asked. "You know I'm crazy."

"I'll take my chances."

"What I need help with is the culture."

"Culture?"

"Yeah," said O'Rourke, "I am completely oblivious to popular culture. Until a few months ago, I actually thought it was Gladys Knight and the *Pimps*."

"Oh," said McGuire, "you didn't!"

"Yes, I did," said O'Rourke. "I'm at that stage in my life where the cover of *Playboy* magazine says 'So-and-so Naked!' One, I don't know who she is, and two, I don't care. I need help. I think I started blocking out popular American culture about 1985."

"I'll cover your ass."

O'Rourke smiled. "Okay, let me test your political acumen."

"Try me."

"Name me," said O'Rourke, "every one of FDR's vice-presidents."

"John Nance Garner of Texas," said McGuire, "twice. Henry Wallace of Iowa, once. And Harry Truman of Missouri for a couple of months."

"Pretty good," said O'Rourke.

"Pretty good?" said McGuire. "That was *very* good."

She was right. O'Rourke knew that she was perfect for him. He had to admit it. "Fuck, you're good."

"Yes," said Sam McGuire with another beautiful smile, "I know."

8.

The five o'clock alarm rang, and Monsignor Seán Pius Burke awoke with a start. For a moment, he lay in bed and listened to the occasional passing car on Madison Avenue. It was still dark, but he knew his boss, Declan Cardinal Sweeney, was already saying his five o'clock mass in the chapel of his private apartment, located just across the hall. Burke swung his legs out of the bed and stiffly stood up. At forty-one he was one of the youngest monsignors in the New York Archdiocese. "A man going places," everybody—including the Cardinal—said. Burke slid into the hot shower, and the stiffness left his athletic body. As he scraped his face with his razor, he turned on the radio to WINS to find out what was going to befall him this day.

He knew the news would be bad. The Cardinal had once again attacked everybody in his Sunday sermon at St. Patrick's Cathedral. He said he had been inspired by the Virgin's appearance to Jackie Swift. He started with the homosexuals, went on to the abortionists, and then attacked every politician who supported abortion. The phones had not stopped ringing all Sunday afternoon as the governor, the mayor, and then congressman after congressman had called to ask, basically, if the Cardinal had flipped his lid.

Burke didn't know what to tell them. He couldn't tell them that, yes, the Cardinal had torn up the truce between the Catholic politicians and himself—a truce that Burke had worked so hard to declare. Burke had a doctorate and a law degree, but when it came to reasoning with the Cardinal, it often was an impossible task. Burke couldn't control the man. He looked in the bathroom mirror and smiled. What was he going to do? The Cardinal, he thought, was the Church's answer to George Steinbrenner. The poor man couldn't help himself: He was a media contortionist. He loved mugging and posing. Give him a baseball cap to wear for the camera and he was as happy as a child. Let him see a TV camera, and he went berserk. He was good copy, always talking off the top of his head, throwing out names and issues. One week the evils of rock music, the next the problems with condoms, the next, the insidious filth of Channel 35 on Manhattan Cable Television. ("Eminence, who brought this filth to your attention?" Billy "Eminence" Owens, the obsequiously pious religion editor of the *Daily News,* had innocently asked at a press conference one Sunday to the howls of the press—and the cold stare of Declan Cardinal Sweeney.) His Sunday sermons, which were carefully monitored by the New York press corps because they often turned out to be great copy, had become circuses, and the press conferences afterward were just as wild. In the immortal words of Abe Stein from the *Post,* "You just can't make this stuff up."

Cardinal Sweeney's Sunday morning sermons had been intensely covered by the media since his infamous Palm Sunday sermon. It had all started rather innocently as the Cardinal had ascended the pulpit to talk about Jesus's triumphant entrance into Jerusalem and the events that would lead up to his crucifixion by Friday of the same week.

"Jesus," began the Cardinal, "rode into Jerusalem on his ass." He paused for effect, then almost shouted, "His *bountiful* ass." There was total silence among the congregation. "Yes," the Cardinal added, lowering his voice for effect, "his bountiful ass." This time the silence was interrupted by a snicker, then a cough. The Cardinal arched an eyebrow. "I see that, even in this holy house, the simple, innocent-sounding word *ass* can be misinterpreted." By now there was shuffling in the seats as the Cardinal, clearly distracted, had turned beet red.

"We are reduced to this," he said deliberately, sadly shaking his head. "Our liturgy has been reduced to this, a mere television sitcom." He remained silent for what seemed a minute. You could hear a pin drop in the cathedral. "Yes," he thundered, "we have been reduced. And reduced to what?"

By this time the Cardinal even had the attention of Cyclops Reilly, who had a feeling that his Eminence was about to blow a circuit.

"We are reduced, like a television sitcom, to tits and ass!"

There was a collective gasp from the congregation.

"Tits-and-ass!" screeched the Cardinal as he reached his hands toward the heavens, beseeching the Almighty. Reilly got up and headed for the back of the cathedral so he could beat the others to the telephone.

"And where," asked Declan Cardinal Sweeney, "does tits-and-ass lead us?" He paused for effect. "It leads us to *masturbation!*" shouted Sweeney. "Oh my God, silly, sinful masturbation!"

Reilly stopped in his tracks. He could see the Cardinal was clearly out of control and he waited anxiously to see what was coming next.

"Masturbation," the Cardinal continued, "is not merely the spilling of God's precious seed. Masturbation is murder! First-degree murder!"

Cyclops Reilly nearly broke an ankle as he tore from the church. He decided to forego the telephone and hailed a cab and headed for the *Daily News* on West 33rd Street. He burst into the near-empty city room and headed straight for his computer. At the city desk, Peccadillo Fogarty raised his head as Reilly passed by in a blur. He picked up his phone and dialed Cyclops at the other end of the city room.

"What's up?" Fogarty asked.

"The Cardinal has lost it," Reilly said and relayed the Cardinal's performance to Fogarty.

"Write it," said Fogarty.

"Let me do an in-person sidebar," said Reilly.

"Go to it, Cyclops." And Cyclops did. After writing a straight factual story, he began his sidebar with the memorable sentence: "If masturbation is murder, then there's a holocaust going on in my bedroom every night." He then called several lawyers and got differing opinions on whether masturbation was first-degree murder.

"Yes," said Carney of the DA's office, "there is definitely premeditation to an act of masturbation."

"Manslaughter is more like it," said Sapperstein of the Legal Defense Association.

"Are you nuts?" screamed Horowitz of the ACLU.

The headline of Monday's *New York Daily News* shouted: MASTURBATION MURDER! The *New York Post* declared: NO HAND JOB! The *New York Times* thoughtfully scribed: IS *IT* MURDER? Wednesday's *Village Voice* finally got it right: JERK-OFF!

Reilly's sidebar column was titled: "The Secret Holocaust?" Reilly had had his fun. Now the Cardinal would demand retribution. Reilly found himself writing about rat shit in restaurant kitchens and Fogarty found himself working the lobster shift. But what goes around, comes around. And with the appearance of the Blessed Virgin, the Cardinal found himself battling his two adversaries again.

"How are ya, Johnny Pie?" the reporters would tease the monsignor. He was one of them. They knew him and his cousin, Cyclops Reilly, well. "What's the Red Hat going to say today, Johnny Pie?" "I need some good stuff, Johnny Pie. Any idea what's up?"

The newspapermen were good guys. Some were from the old neighborhood and he had gone to school with some of them. They were only doing their job. You couldn't blame them. Sweeney was great copy. And they sure knew how to get him into a lather.

Yesterday's debacle had started innocently enough. The theme of the Cardinal's sermon the Sunday before St. Patrick's Day was to be, in fact, the patron saint of both Ireland and the Archdiocese of New York, St. Patrick himself.

At his regular ten o'clock mass, the Cardinal took the pulpit. "The best day of the year," began the Cardinal, "to many of us Irish New Yorkers happens this week, when we celebrate the feast of St. Patrick."

From the sides of the cathedral a chant began: "GAY-LICK!, GAY-LICK!, GAY-LICK!, GAY-LICK!." Irish tri-colors and banners proclaiming "Cardinal Unfair to Irish Gays" were unfurled as the NYPD, always on guard when the Cardinal spoke, raced down the aisles to intercept the demonstrators before they reached the pulpit.

GAYLICK was a militant organization that supported the right of Irish homosexuals and lesbians to march in the St. Patrick's Day Parade. They had been reviled by Francis X. McNamara of the Ancient Order of Hibernians as a "bunch of faggotry queers." It was noted by several columnists in the tabloids that Francis X. McNamara was a master of hyperbole, not to mention redundancy. McNamara had retorted with a straight face that he was "a master of Hibernians."

Monsignor Burke had only sighed. "Let them march," he had urged the Cardinal. "The more you point them out and fight them, the more you legitimize their cause."

"Not after what they said about my priests," replied the Cardinal.

The monsignor just shook his head. After the Cardinal had declared on TV that there would be "no homosexuals" marching in the parade, Bull O'Shea, the lesbian leader of GAYLICK, had responded in her thick Derry accent, "Sure, what's he talking about no homosexuals in the parade? What about all his priests!" As the Cardinal watched Bull O'Shea on TV, the color of his face began to match his red vestments.

It was obvious there was going to be no solution this year. Monsignor Burke had met with GAYLICK secretly, but they were as adamant as the Cardinal. Burke always thought that if they just didn't take themselves so seriously, if they had called their group the Casement/Pearse Brigade—in honor of Roger Casement and Patrick Pearse, two of the 1916 rebels who were executed and who were also probably homosexual—they might have shamed the AOH into granting a marching permit. But to Burke it seemed that everybody wanted more to make a statement than to find a solution.

As they drew closer to the Cardinal in the pulpit, GAYLICK changed its chant to "SHAME! SHAME! SHAME!" The cops caught up to them well before they could get to the Cardinal and dragged them by the necks out the side doors into 50th and 51st Streets. The congregation hummed in horror.

"Please, please," said the Cardinal. "Please be seated. It's over." He could still hear the chant from the street outside, "GAY-LICK! GAY-LICK! GAY-LICK!" The Cardinal had had enough.

As the congregation reseated itself, he began. "Shame," he said. "Did you hear them, lecturing me about shame? What is shame? Do they know shame? Does this feckless generation of MTV and abortion rights know shame? Do their parents know shame? Do their politicians know shame? Do the governor and the mayor know shame?" He was silent. You could hear the rustlings in the cathedral and people nervously clearing their throats.

"*Shame*," he shouted into the microphone, "unfortunately, is not in the vocabulary of this country! Seemingly, we have no shame. Who are the good people? Who are the enlightened few? As I look at the trash that just used this holy house as their personal hate toilet, I feel shame. They have shamed me—my own Irish—in the presence of the Lord. Yet, I am reminded of some of the good people. The people, like yourselves, who have not forsaken Holy Mother Church. I think of Representative Jackie Swift, the congressman who represents the district where this holy house sits. I think of Congressman Swift, in

St. Vincent's Hospital, fighting for his life—and our way of life. Jackie Swift is a man of principal who goes against the grain. You don't see Congressman Swift voting to extend abortion rights to every feckless woman in this country—as our governor and mayor would like to do. You don't see Congressman Swift voting to legalize pornography so little children can be photographed naked by perverts." He stopped momentarily. "NAKED!" he shouted for emphasis. There was absolute silence in the cathedral. It reminded many of the journalists of nine o'clock mass when they were kids. After some forty years, many of them were terrified again.

"And don't you doubt for a second," said the Cardinal, "that the Blessed Virgin Mary appeared to Congressman Swift. You'll hear them snickering in the media about how this appearance is 'bogus.' But what do they know? We know the Virgin appeared to Jackie to tell us—her children—of her abhorrence of filthy abortion."

The Cardinal was caught up in his own voice now. His mind was racing. He remembered the subway ad that someone had pulled from a number 1 train and mailed to him. The ad was for the "Doggie Gynecologist," a veterinary clinic that promoted veterinary medicine with a modern twist. Not only would the vet, Helen McManus, DVM, do the regular spaying, but she was also an expert on championship dog breeding, doing DNA testing to make sure that championship parentage was indeed confirmed. She also did canine abortions if the bitch's mate wasn't up to snuff, so to speak. The "Doggie Gynecologist" was sent by a devout Catholic who found any kind of abortion abhorrent. Now, all the Cardinal could think of, as he began to froth at the mouth, was the "Doggie Gynecologist." Unfortunately, it didn't come out that way.

"Brethren," he began again, "we have gone too far. We have no shame. None whatsoever!" More silence. "Last week, one of my flock sent me a subway ad. Maybe some of you have seen it. Do you know what it was for? It was for the 'Bitch Abortionist!'"

A gasp went up from the congregation. "The Bitch Abortionist," the Cardinal cried. "Will they stop at nothing? Pulling little puppies from the bellies of poor bitches and throwing them in the garbage! Feckless garbage!" The Cardinal sought to regain control of himself. He was wild-eyed now. "Let us pray for this feckless Bitch Abortionist!"

He spun and left the pulpit and flung himself prostrate in front of the main altar. People could hear him praying through his portable microphone. Every journalist in the place raced out to use their cell phones. They were fighting for a scoop. "Where's Johnny Pie?" they all shouted at Father Parnell Dowd, the public information officer of the Archdiocese. The monsignor was quietly reading the Sunday papers in his bedroom and was preparing for the Cardinal's post-mass comments to the press, if he had any. When Father Dowd knocked on his door and explained the situation, the monsignor put on his clerical stock with its stiff white Roman collar over his T-shirt, grabbed his jacket, and headed for the cathedral steps where the Cardinal liked to be interviewed after mass.

Outside, it was like the first day of spring, with the sun brightly shining on Fifth Avenue. "Cardinal," said Abe Stein of the *New York Post*, "who's this 'Abortion Bitch?'"

"Bitch Abortionist, Abe," said the Cardinal with great seriousness. "I don't know her personally, but an abortionist is an abortionist. They're all the same. Human. Animal. There's no difference between them. In God's eyes, every life is sacred. To God, they're all murderers!"

"Eminence," said Billy Eminence, "should good Catholics take steps against this bitch abortionist?" The other reporters looked at Billy like he was nuts.

"Catholics now know who this feckless woman is," said the Cardinal as Father Dowd handed out photocopies of the subway ad, "and they should take appropriate action."

"What about the governor and mayor?" a voice from the back of the crowd yelled.

"What about them?" replied the Cardinal.

"What should they do about the Bitch Abortionist?"

"They should close her down. Revoke her license. Prosecute her for murder! Do anything they can. But they won't. They don't care about human life, why should they care about a poor puppy's life?"

"Cardinal Sweeney," said Abe Stein, exasperated, "she's only a veterinarian."

The Cardinal shot a look at Stein that made him glad he had been born a Jew. Now he knew why all the Irish guys on the paper drank.

"Only a veterinarian," the Cardinal continued. "She is a doctor with the gift of healing."

"Don't you think you've gone a little far on this, Cardinal?" asked Stein, hoping to give the Cardinal a way out.

"Oh, some Catholic bashers will think I've gone too far, but I don't think so. Every time I defend the doctrine of Holy Mother Church, they say I've gone too far. The bashers will always come after me, calling me names. But I know I'm right. God tells me I'm right."

"Eminence," said Billy Eminence, "does God speak directly to you?"

At that Burke had had enough and grabbed the Cardinal by the elbow and said to the press and the electronic media, "The press conference is over. His Eminence will be leaving for Rome right after the parade on Friday and he has to prepare for his meetings with the pope." With that he took the astonished Cardinal and handed him over to Father Dowd, who hustled him back to the living quarters. The monsignor went looking for Abe Stein.

"What do you think, Abe?" said Monsignor Burke.

"Johnny Pie, I don't call him '*Oy vey* Sweeney' for nothing," said Stein as he hit himself on the side of the head.

"That bad, Abe?"

"That bad."

"*Oy vey*," said Burke.

"*Oy vey*," returned Abe Stein. "Johnny Pie," continued Stein, "what's for lunch today? Bashers and mash?"

Bashers and mash. Burke smiled. "I think I'll try a little humble pie today, Abe." Some feckless humble pie, thought Monsignor Seán Pius Burke to himself.

*   *   *   *   *

"You give us twenty-two minutes, we'll give you the news," said the announcer on WINS. And the news was worse than Monsignor Burke thought it would be. On Monday morning the television and radio media had run with the Bitch Abortionist story as their lead, actually pushing the Blessed Virgin off page one. "The Cardinal has sparked another media debate about abortions and Catholics with his comments about the Bitch Abortionist. After being heckled in St. Patrick's Cathedral by protesters from GAYLICK, the militant

Irish homosexual organization, the Cardinal attacked many in the pro-choice movement, including the governor and the mayor, both Catholics. After praising Congressman Jackie Swift, to whom the Blessed Virgin Mary purportedly appeared days ago ..."Burke couldn't take anymore. He switched off the radio and began to dress.

After saying mass, Burke entered the dining room and looked at the morning papers while he ate his breakfast: "BITCH ABORTIONIST," screamed the *Post*. "CARDINAL K-9," said the *News*. "PUPPY LOVE," cried *Newsday*. Burke didn't know if he wanted to laugh or cry. Only the *New York Times* could dull up this story, which they did by hiding it in the Metro section with a headline that said: "CARDINAL GOES FURTHER ON ABORTION." The lads at the papers were having a field day.

Father Dowd interrupted Burke's breakfast. "Seán," he said, "I think you should come to the TV."

On Channel 5's *Good Day New York* program, veteran reporter Ollie Dunkirk stood in front of the Doggie Gynecologist Veterinary Clinic in Soho as protesters from Operation Free Fetus (OFF) picketed in front, carrying signs that read BITCH ABORTIONIST and SAVE THE PUPPY FETUSES.

"Oh my God," said Monsignor Burke to no one in particular.

"With us this morning," said Dunkirk, "we have the Reverend Chester Cockburn of Operation Free Fetus. Reverend Cockburn, why are you picketing the Doggie Gynecologist?"

"We're here, Ollie," he said earnestly in a high-pitched voice, "to save lives."

Burke looked at the Reverend Chester Cockburn in his purple stock and collar, his moony eyes, his flat blond hair pasted against translucent skin, and said to Father Dowd, "that's the guy my mother told me to stay away from when I was a kid." Dowd laughed.

"We are here," continued Reverend Cockburn, "to stop the senseless killing of innocent puppies."

"Reverend Cockburn," said Oliver, "some people would say they're only dogs."

"Only dogs," shot back Cockburn, "only animals. Did not St. Francis of Assisi love animals? What would St. Francis say to this? This is criminal. This is murder!"

"Ah, thank you, Reverend Cockburn," said Dunkirk. "I've just been informed that we have to go back to the studio for an interview with Dr. Helen McManus, the vet who's at the center of this controversy."

"The Abortion Bitch!" cried Cockburn.

"The Bitch Abortionist," said Ollie Dunkirk.

"Whatever," said Jim Ryan back at the studio, as he smiled into the camera. Ryan had been in the news business forever. He had forgotten more about New York City politics than most would ever learn. With a great shock of Paul O'Dwyer-esque white hair and a puckish manner, Ryan loved covering the eccentricities of his city, and it showed. "We have with us Dr. Helen McManus, the veterinarian at the center of this storm. What do you have to say when the Cardinal calls you the Bitch Abortionist?" asked Ryan.

"I don't know what to say, Jim," she said nervously as she stared into the camera. McManus was thirty-eight, attractive, and totally bewildered as to how she had become the focal point in the Cardinal's war on abortion. "I was only trying to be cute drumming up business by calling myself the 'Doggie Gynecologist.' I'm only a vet. I do some advanced work in breeding pedigrees, but I also give shots and set broken legs. In fact, my associates and I haven't done an abortion this year. I'm dealing with dogs, not human beings. I'm a Catholic, too, and I think the Cardinal has gone out on the limb a bit."

"Ah, Dr. McManus," interrupted Ryan, "we have to cut back to Ollie. It seems that a counter-demonstration group is showing up."

"Yes, Jim," said Dunkirk, "animal lovers are showing up to show their support for Dr. McManus. Many are holding signs that say, 'We Support Our Doggie Gynecologist.'"

"Fuck-OFF, Fuck-OFF, Fuck-OFF," they chanted.

Reverend Cockburn tried to stop a woman from bringing her dog into the clinic. "Stop now, before you regret this," cried Cockburn into the TV camera.

"What's wrong with you?" yelled the woman. "I'm only bringing Angus in for his shots!" Cockburn grabbed the woman by the arm and Angus, an ambitious cairn terrier, took umbrage, and lodged his teeth into the Reverend Chester's ankle.

"Ah, ah, ah," cried Cockburn, "I'm being attacked."

"Leave my dog alone, you pervert," said the woman as she clocked

Cockburn with her pocketbook.

"Jim," said Ollie Dunkirk with a straight face as the enraged Angus dug his teeth deeper and Cockburn howled louder, "the battle for abortion continues in the most unlikely places. Back to you." Ryan smiled into the camera and broke for a commercial.

"What do you think?" asked Father Dowd.

"I think," said Monsignor Seán Pius Burke, "I'm going to have a little chat with his Eminence."

9.

Jackie Swift looked up from his hospital bed to see he was surrounded. Everybody was standing around his bed, but no one was paying any attention to him. Their eyes were either riveted on the television, waiting for the nightly news to begin, or on Peggy Brogan. Brogan was on his left, flanked by Georgie Drumgoole. On his right his wife, Madonna-Sue, concentrated on the TV. After his emergency triple angioplasty, his heartbeat was steady; it was his familial support that worried him. There was tension in the air—both political and sexual. Vito couldn't take his eyes off Brogan and Madonna-Sue knew exactly what her father was thinking. She looked at Brogan and felt a deep hostility and jealousy for the woman who ran her husband's life. How had this woman managed to come into the Fopiano household and, like a magnet, demand the attention of her husband and her father?

Swift didn't know if he could take the stress and pressure that was sure to come. Until the Fopiano entourage had arrived, St. Vincent's had been an oasis of calm for him in his most eventful weekend. He was just the latest in a long line of colorful events that had taken place at the hospital over the years. The survivors of the *Titanic* were taken there when they arrived on the R.M.S. *Carpathia* at the foot of 14th Street in April 1912. It seemed the bizarre was the commonplace at St. Vincent's. Actor Jack Nicholson, Swift had read, was born here to his mother, whom he thought was his sister, and was raised by his grandmother, whom he thought was his mother. By the Nicholson criteria, Swift was living an uneventful life. The hospital was also been the checkout point for Dylan Thomas. Everybody thought that Thomas had drunk his twenty-two whiskeys, or whatever it was supposed to be, at the White Horse Tavern on Hudson Street, just four short blocks from St. Vincent's, and dropped dead on the floor. But in truth he had been taken back to the Chelsea Hotel on West 23rd Street and from there to St. Vincent's to finish the verse of his life. The hospital had survived the *Titanic*, the confused Easy Rider, and the bloated Dylan. Swift just hoped that his name would not be etched next to theirs in hospital infamy.

Swift was well aware that Drumgoole's news about the Blessed Virgin had thrown the press into a feeding frenzy. He just knew he was the next O.J. Simpson for the networks and cable channels after the Cardinal visited him on Saturday. Although nearly out of it, he was shocked to see His Eminence in such an obsequious state towards him, thanking him for the Virgin's appearance while blessing him and sprinkling him with Holy Water. As he took his leave, the Cardinal had bowed over and kissed him on the forehead. His nostrils now ventilated, Swift thought the Cardinal smelled of warm milk and cereal. Later, on New York One cable TV, Swift had seen the Cardinal talking to the press outside of St. Vincent's. "Congressman Swift is our Joan of Arc," said His Eminence. Swift immediately buzzed the nurse for another Demerol.

They were all waiting for the 6:30 p.m. broadcast of the *CBS News with Dan Rather*. They had been tipped off that Rather was going to lead his telecast with the Virgin story. The whole family was laying low, refusing to be interviewed. The hospital wanted to release Swift, but Vito decided he would stay put until the storm blew over. It had hit the newswires on Saturday and by Sunday it had spread to all the talk shows on Fox, CNN and MSNBC. Everybody had an opinion and they were all cocksure of it. All the fundamentalist Protestants—who incidentally didn't believe in the sanctity of the Blessed Virgin—thought it was historic that a deity they considered false had taken their side in the abortion battle.

"God has shown us He's on our side by sending His most Holy

Mother, Mary, to take up the anti-abortion banner," declared Jerry Falwell, his well-jellied jowls flapping in conviction. "His will be done."

"We are fools for Christ's sake," the Reverend Pat Robertson had declared on *The 700 Club*, his little head bobbing like Howdy Doody's. "We must pray for the courage to endure the scorn of the sophisticated world." Robertson gave that loony look of his that in the past he had used to direct hurricanes away from his headquarters in Virginia and north toward the Godless hedonists of New York City. "Remember," he added for good measure, "we are awash in the blood of Christ, Our Lord."

"I quake with humility in the shadow of the Lord," said Declan Cardinal Sweeney as he began his Sunday sermon, "and I am thrilled by the appearance of His most Holy Mother to Congressman Swift. God Almighty be praised!" Then he was forced to take a breather for ten minutes to have a good cry in front of a packed St. Patrick's Cathedral. The appearance by the Virgin Mary had sapped him of his energy. "Mother of God," he finally continued, "thank you from the generations of the unborn."

"Anyone have a cigarette?" asked Madonna-Sue. Drumgoole eagerly reached into his jacket pocket and offered her his pack of Chesterfield's, a Bic lighter lodged in the cellophane. He was happy that he had finally done something right. Madonna-Sue put a cigarette in her mouth and frantically began trying to light it with the recalcitrant Bic. It was a sure sign of nerves on her part. Very seldom did Madonna-Sue ever light up any more. Not even after sex.

Jackie Swift began waving his arm, pointing to the clear tube he wore. "Oxygen," he said. "Oxygen!"

Madonna-Sue took one look at him, then went over to the wall and turned the oxygen gauge to the "off" position. "Shut up," was all she said. On the seventh attempt, the Bic worked, and she lit her cigarette. The room was soon choked in a Chesterfield fog.

Rather's theme music began blaring and there was a picture of Congressman Jackie Swift with a portrait of the Blessed Virgin in the background. "Miracle or Hoax?" said Rather's voice-over. Vito and Madonna-Sue looked at each other and thought about killing Georgie Drumgoole right then and there.

Rather was getting on in years. He now had taken to wearing his hair like an eleven-year-old rural schoolboy, right down to the little ski-slope in front and the cowlick in back, bringing to mind the old slogan, "Brillcream, a little dab will do ya." Rather had come a long way from his outstanding work on the JFK assassination, reporting from the jungles of Vietnam, and confronting Richard Nixon over Watergate. Once known as the "ironcock" around CBS, he acted like someone who might take a nip now and then before he went on the air. One wondered why CBS had decided that a cogent Walter Cronkite must retire at sixty-five, yet Rather, with his jumpy eyebrows ("Courage," he had once said bizarrely when signing off) and darting eyes ("Kenneth, what is the frequency?") had been allowed to stay on.

Rather looked straight into the camera and started to speak. "Not since Fatima in 1917 has there been a reporting of this magnitude of an appearance by the Blessed Virgin Mary," he said. The picture then went live to Swift's apartment building on West 10th Street where a candlelight vigil was being held. People were holding pictures of Our Lady of Greenwich Village—as she had been dubbed by the tabloids—as others placed flowers or knelt to pray. Some were trying to catch rain water—Holy Water—as it came cascading out of a drain-pipe at the side of the building's entrance. Others were spooning out the dirt between cracks in the sidewalk to save as relics. A lineup was reciting the rosary and with every Hail Mary their voices would raise in unison as they shouted "thy womb Jesus." As they pronounced Jesus's name, they gave an exaggerated bow of their heads. It looked like an Olympic event in the making—synchronized praying.

"I don't believe this," said Madonna-Sue Fopiano.

"Un-fucking-believable," said her father.

"My God," said Brogan.

Drumgoole was smart enough not to open his mouth.

"Ah," said Jackie Swift, trying to make up and play up, "I see where I'm famous now."

"Just shut the fuck up," said his wife, and the smile immediately disappeared from Jackie's face.

Rather continued: "The Vatican, so far, has not made a comment on the visitation. President Clinton, as he boarded his helicopter at the White House this afternoon, said he was noncommittal on the appearance because, after all, 'he was just a country Baptist.' Many

Republicans were reluctant to comment. Because of the explosive repercussions of this purported sighting of Our Lady of Greenwich Village, some believe the Republicans are being more cautious than two herds of nervous cattle in a small pasture full of cactus. Fraught with political dangers. . . ."

"Oh, shut up," said Fopiano as he hit the power button on the remote and Dan Rather disappeared. "I can't stand it when he does that Texas shit-kicking bullshit," said Vito. "Where do we stand?"

"How the hell did this all happen?" asked Madonna-Sue. There was no answer out of Brogan or Drumgoole. "Well?" she said with agitation, taking another Chesterfield drag.

"We were working on the omnibus pornography bill," began Brogan, who was interrupted by Madonna-Sue's shrill laughter.

* * * * *

"The fucking pornography bill," thought Madonna-Sue Fopiano. "Couldn't they come up with anything better than that for an excuse?"

Here she was, pregnant, stressed out, and puffing away. She wondered what the hell she was doing in politics in the first place. Every man in the room had his eyes on Brogan. As much as Madonna-Sue disliked her, as a woman she had to admire her. She was picture perfect. She wore a dark blue suit that highlighted her cleavage, her impossibly round ass, and her stunning legs. Madonna-Sue felt like Aunt Bee from Mayberry standing next to Sophia Loren.

It was Brogan's sex appeal that bothered Madonna-Sue the most, the way she was always flaunting her physical attributes. She had the tan and every piece of blonde hair was meticulously combed into place. No wonder their marriage had cooled. Madonna-Sue knew she could not compete with Peggy Brogan. At least not sexually. Madonna-Sue looked at her father and saw a sexual stalking by eye. For Christsakes, even Drumgoole looked interested.

She wished that she could just fire Brogan, but it wasn't that easy. Who would run the man? Who could control, manipulate, and basically frightened the indolent Jackie into doing his job? Madonna-Sue didn't even want to think about that. She couldn't do it; she had her own office to run. They had no choice. She needed Brogan and she hated herself for it.

* * * * *

Madonna-Sue had an aura about her that could not be explained. She had worked the cute-little-Staten-Island-girl act of hers to the hilt. They loved her on the Sunday morning talks shows, alone or holding hands with Jackie so the whole country could see their devotion to each other. So photogenic with such well-rehearsed replies that Tim Russert or David Brinkley or Sam Donaldson were reduced to smiles no matter how outrageous her opinions had been.

The real Madonna-Sue was just like her father—as tough as nails. The current pregnancy was a slap in the face to Brogan. She could just see the two of them fucking on the Thanksgiving coats, Jackie pinning Madonna-Sue's ankles behind her ears as he gave it to her, but good. Brogan looked across the room at Madonna-Sue and shook her head. There was the congressional icon, four months pregnant and puffing away on her Chesterfield with a desperation that was shocking, even to Brogan. Five months from now Madonna-Sue and Jackie would be waving the newborn for the cameras at the Republican National Convention in San Diego. Family Values, thought Brogan. Dysfunctional family values.

Brogan looked at Vito Fopiano, the proud grandfather with the aphrodisiac hands, and wondered what she had gotten herself into. The Fopianos knew she was fucking Jackie, but nothing had ever been said. This was politics, the dirty politics of 2000. Everybody was looking into Bill Clinton's bedroom to see who he was doing and so they had to be careful that the media didn't start looking into their own bedrooms. But Brogan would somehow survive. She was a tough girl from Queens, and she could handle herself. As she looked at Madonna-Sue, Brogan realized that she might have to extract the ultimate revenge on the congresswoman. "Tread softly, Madonna-Sue," she thought, "tread softly."

* * * * *

"The omnibus pornography bill," repeated Madonna-Sue Fopiano with a laugh.

"Yes, we had the television on," continued a distracted Brogan, "and *The Song of Bernadette* was on Turner Classic Movies. I told Georgie on the phone what had happened and, apparently, *The Song of Bernadette* became an appearance by the Virgin Mary when that little cockeyed shit Benedict Reilly of the *Daily News* got a hold of Georgie at the emergency ward." Everybody looked at Drumgoole and knew they didn't call him George-the-Fifth for nothing.

"So it never happened?" said Vito.

"Of course it never happened," shot back Brogan.

"You should be fucking fired," said Madonna-Sue to Drumgoole.

"Madonna-Sue, Vito," pleaded Drumgoole.

"Oh," said Madonna-Sue, "fuck off."

They were squared off against each other. Brogan and Drumgoole on one side, the Fopianos on the other, with Swift, trying to look innocent, lying between them.

"Nobody is going to get fired," said Vito.

"He deserves it," replied his daughter.

"That's not the way *I* do things," said Vito sternly to his daughter. "Anyway," he continued, "I'd rather have Georgie inside the tent pissing out, than outside pissing in—especially under these circumstances." Drumgoole was so happy he was staying that he'd piss wherever they told him to.

"What are we going to do?" asked Brogan. "How are we going to handle it?"

"We don't have a choice," said Vito. "The Cardinal's already praised Jackie. Remember, he's the new Joan of Arc of the GOP. Calls are running 9 to 1 in favor of the Virgin at both your offices. We're stuck. Our Lady of Greenwich Village *did* appear to Jackie."

Everyone was silent, all the energy drained out of them by the weekend's events. Finally, Vito wearily turned to his son-in-law, "What do you think, Jack?"

From the movie encyclopedia in his head Swift retrieved the answer. "Mother of Mercy," said Jackie in a dead-on impersonation of Edward G. Robinson's death scene in *Little Caesar*, "is this the end of Jackie?"

No one smiled, but Vito was thinking that maybe Jackie was right. It might be the end of Jackie—and maybe the Fopianos too.

10.

St. Patrick's Day.
It was all a sham. It was a date reserved for acne-faced teenagers from the suburbs who celebrated by throwing up on each other. An excuse to get drunk and talk about the "Troubles" and the "Risin' of '98," "good ould Dev," and what a marvelous literary tradition *we* had.

When O'Rourke walked into the Moat at the end of the day the only familiar face he saw among the loud green throng was Clarence Black. "What the fuck are you doing here?" asked O'Rourke.

"I don't know, Tone," said Black. "I keep telling these harps that I'm black Irish."

"Black Irish," said O'Rourke.

"Black Irish," laughed Black, who was, in fact, black.

Clarence Black was a retired New York City firefighter. In his twentieth year on the job as a river fireman, a burning pier had fallen on him, and after a long convalescence he had hung them up. Clarence had been around a long time. When he had started in the FDNY, the notorious "black bed" was still in fashion in the firehouse. The black bed was reserved for black firefighters and only black firefighters. It was a way of reminding the few blacks that managed to make the cut that that this was still a department run by the Irish. Black, a very sociable and sensitive man, had been hurt. After enough abuse, he took his hurt to the river, where he put in most of his career. It had been an exciting time, the last epoch of the ocean liner, big beauties like the *United States*, the *France*, and the two Queens, *Mary* and *Elizabeth*. But it all ended that day in 1973 when that old, abandoned, rotting pier had come down on him. Several homeless men, trying to make a fire for warmth in winter, had almost killed him. After retirement he went to work for an insurance company as an arson investigator. Taking the next step, he ended up working as a PI. Now, he lived on his pension and operated his own one-man private investigation agency. When asked what he did for a living he would smile a piano smile of white teeth that lit up that unlined black face, making it years younger, and say, "Me? I'm a private dick."

"You out to keep an eye on my fellow countrymen today, Clarence?" asked O'Rourke.

"Shit, Tone, you keep your own eye on your own. I had to deal with these fucking harps for years in the department. I don't need to do it now."

"Absolutely right, Clarence. I know exactly what you mean, but after what I did to you years ago on this day I thought you still might be gun-shy."

Black laughed, "Shit, Tone, I ain't afraid of much, but you're right, I must be nuts to come out on St. Patrick's Day."

"Buy that man a drink," said O'Rourke and two Remys were placed in front of them.

"*Sláinte*," said O'Rourke.

"*L'chaim*," returned Black.

Five years ago to the day. O'Rourke, after a bitch of a day at the office, had come in for his evening "pop." The Moat was raucous with people drinking beer and wearing pointed green leprechaun hats. O'Rourke swung into the corner bar at the Moat where Clarence Black was standing. "How's it going, Tone?"

"Fucking amateurs, Clarence."

"I know what you mean, Tone."

"Clarence, do you know what's long and green and has assholes on both ends?"

"Nope."

"The St. Patrick's Day Parade." Black laughed. O'Rourke did not.

The drink was poured and the two men stood there in silence as the noise level seemed to grow and grow, as it reached for some impossible apogee. As he looked around the crowded bar O'Rourke could feel himself growing depressed as he saw in his people everything he hated so much about them and himself. They were fools, parodying themselves, with a distinct meanness and ungraciousness that brilliantly pierced through the thin veneer of the camaraderie of the slurred words. He wished that St. Patrick's Day would just disappear. Forever. He was growing more depressed as he looked down toward the beer pumps and saw a cute little college girl with red hair and freckles on her nose raise her mug of green beer in toast.

"God Bless the Irish!" she said in a voice that told O'Rourke she would have her next beer on July 4th.

O'Rourke was no longer depressed. He was mad. "Fuck the Irish," O'Rourke said.

The bar suddenly grew silent. It was as if O'Rourke only wanted to think it, but the words jumped out of his brain and dashed out his mouth before he could stop them. O'Rourke then realized that Clarence Black was standing beside him, the only black face in a joint full of bombed harps.

Black Irish.

A blurry figure pushed in front of the cute red-haired girl. O'Rourke and Black took one look at the guy and had him cut and quartered immediately. Long Island Irish. The kind that had a defiant strut—so similar to that of a black ghetto kid's, yet so different—instead of a walk. The kind of a guy who had a chip on his shoulder. The kind of guy who liked his beer with the boys at The Holy Ground Pub, watched the Yankees at the Stadium regularly, and jerked off more than he ever got laid. The kind of guy whose idea of a date was going to an Irish writer's bar in Greenwich Village on St. Patrick's Day to drink green beer. The petulant kind of Irish kid whose every third word was "fuck," but who, if you said "fuck" in front of his cute little red-haired date, would react like a priest who had been just told that Sister Ignatius was blowing the whole Fordham basketball team.

"Hey," said the big Irish kid from halfway down the bar, "what's your name, boy?"

It didn't register with O'Rourke. It did with Black, who reached inside his jacket to instinctively feel his revolver. It also registered with Big Zeus, the bartender, who snapped up the bridge of the bar and prepared for a preemptive strike. Then O'Rourke realized what "boy" he was talking to. Clarence Black just stared.

O'Rourke broke the silence. "Wolfe Tone O'Rourke. What's yours, fuck face?" There was more silence. Fordham Joe had just realized he had broken a very important bar law—don't cause trouble on foreign turf. There was a prolonged silence. The two Irishmen stared at each other.

"Wolfe Tone O'Rourke," the cute, little red-haired girl said as she finally broke the deafening pause. "I guess we can't top that. God bless you, Wolfe Tone O'Rourke."

O'Rourke nodded. "Zeus, buy those nice people a drink." The crowd began to hum again. "Sorry, Clarence, I forgot you were here."

"That's all right, Tone. I would have whipped that fat sucker senseless." He meant it. He leaned over and whispered in Tone O'Rourke's ear, "Fuck the Irish."

O'Rourke smiled. "I owe you one, Clarence."

* * * * *

So it's come down to this, thought O'Rourke.

It was after ten o'clock and leaning against the side-bar, Remy still in hand, he surveyed the ever-increasing madness.

His people.

He was too drunk to laugh at the idea. His glazed-over eyes only smiled at the absurdity. He couldn't escape them. What had that mad chronicler of Irish ghosts and their random hauntings, Eugene O'Neill, said? "One thing that explains more than anything about me is the fact that I'm Irish."

"May God help us," thought O'Rourke.

O'Rourke now saw the procession to the men's room. Lots of people going in and lots of people coming out rubbing their noses. O'Rourke was beginning to get the itch. He hadn't used the shit in a long time—as his weight would confirm.

"Anything shaking, Zeus?" O'Rourke said to the barman, elegant at three hundred pounds and mightily bald.

"Not a thing, son," said Zeus. "The Fish hasn't shown up tonight. Must be afraid of our people. Maybe it's time to invoke the intercession of St. Leroy."

"St. Leroy?"

"St. Leroy," said Zeus. "The patron saint of drug abusers."

"Yeah," said O'Rourke, "better say a prayer."

"The Fish" was Fischbein, the house Pablo Escobar. Thirty years ago they used to give rent parties for the Fish so he wouldn't be thrown out of his $126 rent-controlled apartment. Thanks to the cokeified '80s and '90s, Fischbein now had a house in the Hamptons, investments on Wall Street, *and* his $126 rent-controlled apartment. Fischbein wasn't the best dope dealer in the world, but he was the only one in the Moat. It was said that beer drinkers had their six-packs, but the Moat's coke-heads had their "Fish-packs." In fact, Fischbein's stuff was so diluted with baby laxative that the saying around the Moat when John Belushi checked out was that he'd still be alive if he was using the Fish's shit.

Fischbein recently had a habit of talking to himself. "Met the Fish on the street yesterday," Zeus once told O'Rourke, "and the three of us had a nice conversation." Fischbein had deluded himself into thinking he was providing a middle-class service, not breaking the law.

Aloysius Hogan and Barney walked into the Moat, and the bathroom immediately cleared out. "Anyone see the Fish tonight?" asked Hogan.

"Not a sign," said Big Zeus.

"Yeah," said Hogan, a man who liked to brag about his coke-induced deviated septum, "dope dealers are getting to be like cops—can't find one when you need one."

Hogan poured himself a cup of coffee and set it down in the waitress station. The section was defined by a brass pole that ran from ceiling to floor. Everyone in the place, for some reason, called it Hogan's Pole. A pretty young woman sat down on the other side of the pole. She had a sweet smile, but Hogan's eyes—on instinct—roamed lower. Hogan noticed her superb breasts. Hogan had a thing for breasts. The bigger, the better. She began jotting things down in a notebook. Hogan's grip on his pole became taut.

"You a writer?" asked Hogan as he began the chat-up. The answer was in the affirmative. "I must introduce you to Mailer the next time he drops by."

"That would be swell," she replied with genuine enthusiasm. Soon Hogan learned that she was working on her first novel.

"Yes," said Hogan as he took a swig of coffee, "I may go back to Paris this summer and finish *my* novel."

"What are ya *reading*?" said Zeus to the laughter of the bar.

With that, Fischbein walked in the front door. Big Zeus's eyes implored the heavens as he quietly intoned, "Thank you, St. Leroy." Barney howled at the ceiling, and the Fish went to work. Hogan moved so swiftly toward the Fish, he looked like a wolf in search of a pork chop in Fischbein's coat pocket. Fischbein surrendered an offering to Hogan, who immediately went with Barney to Little Peru.

"I'm a bold Irish navvy, I work on the line . . . " sang the Clancy Brothers on the jukebox. To O'Rourke it sounded like ". . . I work on the lines." O'Rourke gave Fischbein the high sign and headed for the bathroom.

"I thought you gave this stuff up."

"I did," said O'Rourke. "Just for tonight."

"Well," said Fischbein, "you sure you want this?"

It was like trying to buy dope from your mother, thought O'Rourke. "For Christsakes, yes," said O'Rourke. "Give it to me before you talk me out of it." Fischbein slid him the package and O'Rourke passed him two Jacksons. O'Rourke went in the toilet stall and tried to open the aluminum foil. That son of a bitch, thought O'Rourke. He's still too cheap to buy proper wrapping paper. Still using the foil. Must have stock in Reynolds Wrap. He shot a couple of lines and rubbed some of the shit on his gums. Things were looking up.

Back to the bar for another cognac. That was the trouble with coke users, thought O'Rourke. They had no self-control. The only reason anyone continued to use coke, O'Rourke believed, was that they were trying to rediscover that first coke high, which can be almost spiritual. The hope of that return-high was based on wishfulness. It would never be felt again. And that's why, O'Rourke surmised, coke made people crazy. O'Rourke was drinking with a friend one afternoon who went on and on about conspiracy theories when he was using the shit.

"You're paranoid," an exasperated O'Rourke finally said.

"No," said the friend in dead earnest, "I'm not paranoid. I'm *real* annoyed."

It wasn't working. Hardly surprised—having suckered himself— O'Rourke went back to the bathroom for more. This time the whole contents of the aluminum foil went up O'Rourke's desperate nose. That was better.

Coked up, O'Rourke stood, just looking at people. Wondering what it all meant. It was beginning to catch up with him. All the work, the drink, the loneliness—they were all too much. He couldn't think straight. He felt depressed. Or was it repressed? Was there a difference? His lack of functioning, his lack of life, his lack of women. He lacked everything except drink, and that, there was too much of. O'Rourke knew that his alcoholism was nothing more than a manifestation of his fear. Alcohol fueled his inability to change, to do something about his stagnant life.

Then he thought of Sam McGuire and smiled. She was now an integral part of his team. She was smart, funny, and on the ball. She liked the give-and-take that O'Rourke was always supplying. She loved his double entendres and even shot back a couple of her own. But it was her eyes that enchanted O'Rourke the most. McGuire had the bluest gray eyes he had ever seen. Or were they the grayest blue eyes he had ever seen? They were extraordinary, especially for a black woman. He just wished he was twenty years younger. Maybe then she would have gone for him. But that was all supposition now. What would a woman like Sam McGuire want with a broken-down old drunk like O'Rourke? O'Rourke knew there was no chance, not a single chance, that this exquisite human being would fall for him. He had forsaken relationships for booze. And this night, cocaine. What a fucking dunce he was.

Sometimes he could not remember things. Sometimes he didn't want to remember things. With the drink, the night before sometimes became a mystery. He simply could not remember. Then there was the fright of awakening in the middle of the night with a dry mouth and those curious little pains that probably meant nothing, but one just didn't know. He felt sluggish, slow moving. It was hard to pinpoint. He didn't feel like himself. And at this point, he didn't like himself. This was what bothered him the most. He didn't know if he was sick or crazy. Probably a little bit of both. He sipped his Remy and thought of Sam McGuire's eyes.

Something was wrong. As he stood there his lips went dry. Probably the coke. His knees weakened. Something was happening. O'Rourke was scared. Then he wasn't. Three thoughts shot across his mind.

He didn't want to die in a saloon.

He wanted to die in a state of grace and say a Perfect Act of Contrition—but he couldn't remember the words.

And he wanted to die in Ireland.

Then something exploded on the right side of his head like a Bob Gibson fastball, and Hogan's Moat, with all its raucousness, neatly faded away.

11.

"I've put off my trip to Rome for a few days," said Declan Cardinal Sweeney to Monsignor Seán Pius Burke.

Burke just knew it was coming. The St. Patrick's Day Parade the previous day had turned out to be a fiasco. GAYLICK had somehow infiltrated the parade disguised as the County Louth Association. They had marched up Fifth Avenue as far as the cathedral. There, they had stopped and with fists pumping in the air began to shout, "GAY-LICK, GAY-LICK, GAY-LICK," in front of the enraged Cardinal. As the police moved in to arrest them, they had turned their backs to him, dropped their jeans, and exposed their naked buttocks directly at the Cardinal. They had brought along a boom box on which blared the music of the day, albeit with a queer twist:

" . . . By the Rising of the Moons, By the Rising of the Moons, and Arise All Queers for Freedom, By the Rising of the Moons!"

"Did you see this?" the Cardinal asked Burke. It was the front page of the *New York Post*, whose headline proclaimed: MOON OVER ST. PAT'S. "Apparently," the Cardinal said evenly, "we've helped sell a lot of newspapers in town this week."

Burke could see the other side of the Cardinal now. He was composed, in control. Burke knew he was plotting. At seventy-seven, the Cardinal could still be awesome when he put his mind to it. Now, the Cardinal had something on his mind and Burke was afraid what it might be.

"I talked with His Holiness this morning," said the Cardinal. Burke was silent. "We discussed the events of the last few days. The disturbances with these queer Irish hooligans. The Blessed Virgin's appearance and the abortion question. His Holiness agrees with me that this is a very special time for Holy Mother Church, and it's time to make a stand."

"What do you have in mind, Eminence?" said Burke.

"I think we're going to endorse an anti-abortion candidate this year," said the Cardinal.

Burke didn't like it. It was getting into sticky territory. Church and State. He didn't like it at all. "Are you sure this is the right tack to take?" he asked.

The Cardinal shot him a look. "His Holiness agrees with me," said the Cardinal tersely.

"I see," said Burke. "Do you have anyone in mind?"

"You know whom I have in mind."

"Congressman Swift."

"Congressman Swift," repeated the Cardinal. "I want to show our support and appreciation for the congressman. And I want to focus the media on the Blessed Virgin's appearance and its significance."

"Significance?" asked Burke tentatively.

"Its significance as a sign to all of us in the anti-abortion movement."

"You really believe the Virgin appeared to Swift?"

The Cardinal shot him a glance meant to make him cower, but Burke stood his ground. "You are close to blasphemy, Monsignor," the Cardinal finally said.

"I am not a blasphemer," replied Burke. "But I am not a fool either."

There was silence before the Cardinal replied. "You'll do as I say."

Burke bowed his head in submission, "Yes, of course, Eminence."

"I also want to get other religious leaders in on this," continued the Cardinal. "We have stood together alone on this anti-abortion front too long. There are others who think the same way we do and I think we should all get together and pose a united front in the sacred and holy fight against abortion. Dr. Costello agrees with me."

*   *   *   *   *

Breakfast at the chancery—the Cardinal's house at the Madison Avenue end of St. Patrick's Cathedral—was often an occasion of surprise. On any given day you might find the Cardinal dining with the papal nuncio, a visiting bishop, or even the vice president of the United States.

Perhaps the thing Burke hated most about living in the chancery was the dress code. The Cardinal insisted that all his priests be properly dressed in a black suit and a hard white Roman collar, which was forever chafing Burke's fair Irish skin. There was no privacy in the house. Dignitaries and politicians were showing up at all times of the day and night for meetings. There was no room to sit around with the guys, chew the fat, and watch the Mets game. To Monsignor Burke, it was a dignified prison.

"I'm Seán Burke," he had said to the stranger seated at the breakfast table.

"Dr. John Costello," the priest said, standing and reaching out his hand to Burke.

"Nice to meet you," Burke paused, "Doctor." Burke had a doctorate too, but he didn't go flaunting it. So did Dowd and the Cardinal. Burke loved hubris—he loved bruising it.

With his left hand Costello tightly grasped a gold and silver crucifix that hung around his neck. The cross and chain were silver; the body of Jesus gold. Burke noticed that Costello's fist had engulfed the cross as if it were a talisman that could protect him. Burke was forced to do a double take as he shook hands because Costello looked like he had stepped out of another time. He was wearing an old-fashioned soutane, a cassock more common to European priests of fifty years ago then to the modern clergy. It had to be specially tailored, thought Burke. His curiosity had been piqued. Even the Cardinal bought his suits and cassocks off the rack. With his cross, Costello almost looked like a bishop. Burke himself, although a monsignor, rarely wore a cassock with his red stripe of rank. But this guy really went for the clerical sartorial of the anointed. Why did he think he was so special?

"Do I detect an accent?" asked Burke as he sat down to have his breakfast. Then he cocked his head. Something definitely was wrong.

"You have a good ear, Monsignor," said Costello. "I grew up in Dublin." Costello was about sixty-five and pink the way elderly Celts are. The Irish come into this world with pink bottoms and leave it with pink faces. It is the stamp on their passport of life.

"Do you still live there?" Burke asked.

"No, no," said Costello, "when I left Maynooth, I left Ireland too. I've been up in Canada for the longest time. Niagara Falls."

Something was bothering Burke. "Cos-TELL-o," he said. "What a great name! Lou Costello."

"Abbott and Costello," said the priest, smiling perfunctorily, fingering his cross.

"Frank Costello," said Burke.

"A mobster sent from central casting," said Costello, this time without the feigned amusement.

"John Costello," repeated Burke. "Yes, you share the name with the former *Taoiseach*."

"John Costello?" asked Dr. Costello, shaking his head.

"Yes," said Burke, "he was prime minister of Ireland twice."

"Must be before my time. Anyway, I'm not that political."

Irish-Catholics had many ways of identifying their own. They knew, as they always had known, that language was their greatest weapon. You could tell by the way they spelled their names. You could always tell the Green from the Orange by the spelling. James Connolly, the 1916 patriot, was green. John Connally, the Texas governor shot in Dallas with JFK, was orange. Eugene O'Neill was green, but Shaquille O'Neal was not. Clare and Denis were Irish spellings; Claire and Dennis were not. If you knew how to play the letters, it wasn't that hard. There was also the way the Irish pronounced their names on either side of the Atlantic. Mahon in the United States was pronounced "Mann." In Ireland, it was "MA-han." Mahoney in New York was "Ma-hone-ey"; in Dublin it was "Matt-han-ee." Shaughnessy morphed from the American "Sean-a-see" to the Gaelic "Shock-nessy."

Costello in America had always been "Cos-TELL-o," as in Lou and Frank. In Ireland it was "COS-ta-low." Dr. Costello had failed the mean's test and Burke knew there was something wrong.

"Have you been back recently?" asked Burke.

"Back where?"

"Dublin."

"No, not since Maynooth."

"I studied in Dublin," said Burke, buttering his toast.

"Great town," said Costello noncommittally.

"I have people there, you know," continued Burke, "on both sides of the city." There was nothing Dubliners—and Burke had lived there for three years—loved more than chatting with fellow Dubliners, finding common ground in pubs, restaurants, or bookshops they both knew. Burke noticed that Costello didn't share his enthusiasm. "My mother's people are on the South Side," Burke continued, "off Cork Street between Dolphin's Barn and the Guinness Brewery. And my father's people are in Phibsborough on the North Side." Burke paused. "Where are you from?"

"I grew up in Donnybrook," said Costello.

"On the North Side," said Burke.

"Yes, that's it."

There was silence. Liffey geography, thought Burke. Costello had gotten it wrong.

"Are you staying with us long?" asked Burke.

"I won't know until I meet with the Cardinal," replied Costello.

"Well," said Burke, "I hope you enjoy your stay."

With that, a burst of energy entered the room. "Monsignor, Monsignor," said the excited boy, "can I go now?"

"Where's your brother, Felipe?" asked Burke.

"He's out in the sitting room," said the boy impatiently, pounding his baseball mitt. "Can I go now?"

"You rang the bell too long during the transubstantiation," said Burke, suppressing a smile.

The smile left Felipe's face, and he stared at the floor. "I know," he said.

"So it'll be a shorter ring tomorrow?"

"Yes, Monsignor," said Felipe. "Short and sweet!"

Burke laughed. "Felipe, say hello to Dr. Costello. He's visiting with us."

Costello pushed his chair away from the table and tapped his lap. "Come here, son," he said, and the boy followed his order. Costello picked him up and placed him on his knee. "Short and sweet. I'd say that that's a pretty good description of you!" The boy smiled perfunctorily. "Transubstantiation. That's a pretty big word. Do you know what it means?"

"Yep," said Felipe, "that's the consecration of the mass."

"When the bread and wine are turned into the body of Our Lord, Jesus Christ."

"Yep."

"Look at Jesus, Felipe," said Costello, pointing to the gold figure on his cross. "Would you like to feel my cross? Would you like to feel Jesus on the cross?"

It was getting creepy. Burke had been down this road too many times before. He wanted to say, "That's enough," but he didn't want to frighten the child. "Come on, Felipe," he said taking the child by the hand and pulling him off of Costello's lap, "your brother's waiting. Time for baseball practice."

"Yes!" said the boy as he ran toward the door. In the doorway he turned around and gave the two priests a little wave goodbye.

"He's precious," said Costello. "Sometimes you only see God in the eyes of a boy."

Burke looked at Costello and knew. "Yes," said Burke evenly, "sometimes you only see God in the eyes of all his children." Costello knew he had been caught, but he didn't seem to care.

"Well," said Costello with a chuckle, "that's what I meant."

"I'm sure you did."

Within minutes Costello had wiped his lips with his napkin and risen. In his left hand he held a briefcase, the kind you didn't see much any more, the kind where the front and the back came together on a V-frame and a flap dropped down the front and snapped into the lock.

On the flap were the letters, embossed vertically in gold:

I.

H.

S.

Burke at first wanted to smile, but then he grew concerned. When he was a kid he was told that I.H.S. stood for "I have suffered," supposedly Christ's lament on the cross. In reality I.H.S. was a Greek truncation of the first three letters of Jesus' name. "It's kind of like Christ's monogram," Burke used to joke as he explained it to laymen. Unless Costello's real name was Isaac Henry Sullivan, there was something very wrong here.

Burke looked up to see Costello, carefully holding his cross in his other hand, bow in an old-fashioned way, then back away from the table before turning and leaving the room.

The Westie in Burke had been piqued, for he knew Costello was not what he purported to be. He picked up the phone and called an old friend from Dublin, Monsignor Vincent Bartley, now the parish priest of St. Paul's on Staten Island.

"Vince," Burke said, "I gotta be quick."

"Sure," said Bartley in his soft North Side Dublin accent.

"Did you ever run into a priest back in Dublin by the name of John Costello?" Burke pronounced it the American way.

"Costello?" said Bartley, pronouncing it the Irish way.

"Costello," said Burke, agreeing with Bartley's pronunciation.

"You mean *The Reverend Doctor* Costello," laughed Bartley into the phone.

"The Reverend Doctor?"

"Indeed," said Bartley. "I know your man, but not from Dublin. I knew him when I was studying in Spain."

"What do you think?"

"I have only two words for the Reverend Dr. John Costello," said Bartley dryly.

Burke knew of Bartley's Fenian connections and became concerned. He knew it was going to be bad news. "And those two words are?"

"*Opus Dei.*"

*   *   *   *   *

More trouble, Monsignor Burke thought to himself. "Who are you thinking of, Eminence, the Christian Fundamentalists?"

"The Christian Fundamentalists, exactly," said Cardinal Sweeney. "Let's hit these abortionists hard, and let's do it now. I want you to get in touch with Reverend Cockburn."

"Eminence," said Burke defensively, "do you mean that hysteric who picketed the veterinary clinic?"

"That man who was cruelly assaulted right in front of that feckless clinic," added the Cardinal.

"By a cairn terrier, I believe," countered Burke.

The Cardinal shot him another one of his looks, made to intimidate. "I don't want to argue on this, Monsignor. This has to be done. What I'd like to do is get together with Swift and Cockburn and hold a press conference. If the Congressman is up to it, we could even have it at St. Vincent's, where no abortions are performed. Let's set it up as soon as you can do it."

"Yes, Eminence," said Burke quietly as he stood up to leave. The more he thought about the press conference, the more it disturbed him. Back at his office he put in a call into his cousin.

"Cyclops Reilly here," said the voice over the phone.

"Benedict," said Burke, "it's Johnny Pie."

Reilly cringed. He hated being called Benedict. "Well, well, well, Monsignor," he said, "what have I done to rate a call from a dignitary of the Church like you?"

*   *   *   *   *

It was hard to believe, but Benedict Reilly and Seán Pius Burke were first cousins. They grew up in the same tenement on West 49th Street across from the old Madison Square Garden. They shared the same grandmother, old Masie Scully, late of the Falls Road, Belfast.

Masie was a piece of work. The special branch of the Royal Irish Constabulary had made her a widow in 1920, and by 1924 she was in New York living with her two young daughters in Hell's Kitchen. During World War II the daughters had married a couple of Irish tough guys from the neighborhood. The two men, Tom Reilly and Dominick Burke, took odd jobs at the Garden, working the floor, changing the arena from boxing to hockey to rodeo to basketball. On the side, they were "boyos," doing jobs for the mob. Everybody knew them as auxiliaries in the Westies, the Irish gangsters of Hell's Kitchen.

It always amazed Cyclops that the Mafia would hire the Westies to do their dirty work. For all the intermarriage between the two nationalities, there remained a deep schism. The Italians, by personality, were solitary figures, more comfortable at home with family, while the Irish were gregarious gladhanders. The Italians aspired to be Westchester Republicans, while the Irish knew there was a little bit of John F. Kennedy in each of them. It was an odd business arrangement.

Masie Scully didn't even have her own apartment. In each daughter's railroad flat she had a room, and she ruled the two households as if she were Pope Masie I. She went to mass twice a day. She ignored whatever Westie work her sons-in-law were involved in, and generally dictated the lives of her two families. She had even named the two children. Benedict was named after Pope Benedict XV, who had been Pope during the Troubles. Young Benedict hated the name, especially when the neighborhood kids called him "Benny" and implied that he was the only Irish Jew in the neighborhood. In fact, his nickname as a kid had been "Briscoe," after Robert Briscoe, the first Jewish Lord Mayor of Dublin. Benedict had actually been glad when the boys down at the *Daily News* had given him the obvious nickname "Cyclops" because he hated his childhood moniker so much. Later he would explain Benedict away by saying that he was named after the Pope by his grandmother because "he gave good encyclical or something."

Seán Pius had been named after Masie's murdered husband and Pope Pius XII, the Teuton-loving Pontiff of World War II infamy. But Seán Pius, younger than Benedict, had gotten off much easier with the neighbor kids. To them he was the popular "Johnny Pie," the handsomest and smartest kid in the class.

They were complete opposites. Cyclops was a character right out of *Angels with Dirty Faces*, while his cousin would be more comfortable singing in a Bing Crosby–led choir. Cyclops would go to Vietnam and return to a job as a copyboy at the *Daily News*. Johnny Pie would go off to college, then to seminary and graduate school. Cyclops was street smart; Johnny Pie knew which fork to eat his salad with. It was extraordinary that they could come from such a close gene pool. But there were two things they shared: a Hell's Kitchen toughness and an extraordinary Irish willingness to resist.

* * * * *

"I been reading your stuff on Jackie Swift," said the monsignor. "Very interesting."

"Yeah," said Cyclops Reilly, "I'm keeping a close eye on the creep. What's it to you? Or are you calling on behalf of the Cardinal? He didn't fall for Swift's Virgin shit, did he?"

"Hook, line, and sinker," said the monsignor. "We're having a press conference at St. Vincent's tomorrow. The Cardinal is going to endorse Jackie Swift for Congress. . . ." He paused to let it sink in, ". . . because of his Right-to-Life stance." Reilly whistled at the end of the phone. "I know Billy Eminence will be there because it's his beat, but I thought you should know about this because of your interest in Swift. Just in case your name slipped through the cracks and you didn't get an invite."

Cyclops Reilly's mind was racing now. "Yeah, thanks, Johnny Pie. I really appreciate this."

The monsignor continued, "The Cardinal is also going to bring along the Reverend Chester Cockburn, who'll also endorse Swift."

"That nut from OFF who picketed the vet's clinic?" asked Cyclops.

"Yes, that's him," said the monsignor. "His Eminence wants to present a united front on abortion."

"Aren't you supposed to talk him out of shit like this, Johnny?" asked Cyclops.

"Not this time," continued the monsignor. "This comes from higher up."

"Higher up?" said Reilly. "You don't mean The Dour Slav?"

"I don't mean anything, Benedict," said the Monsignor, suppressing a smile at his cousin's unique sobriquet for Pope John Paul II. "You can take that any way you want. But if I were you I'd look into the background of Reverend Cockburn. You may want to ask him a few questions at the press conference."

"Does this have anything to do with your special work for the Cardinal?" asked Reilly.

"Yes, it does, Benedict," replied Burke. "See you there?"

"Yeah," said Cyclops Reilly. "I'll be there."

*   *   *   *   *

"Does this have anything to do with your special work for the Cardinal?" The sentence had curiously bounced back into Monsignor Burke's mind after he had hung up the phone on his cousin.

The "special work" was routing out pedophiles for the Cardinal and it had earned him his red stripe. Being a lawyer, he had been assigned to negotiate with the families of the abused. Negotiate was a euphemism. Badger, intimidate, twist, coerce was more like it. If they didn't take the money and run, he often ended up cross-examining them in court. Make the victims the predators so the archdiocese could save a little of its dirty money. It had made him sick to his stomach. Once, while talking to his cousin about a family matter on the phone, he had let it drop how much he hated his job, being the Church's persecutor of innocent victims, all children.

"Fuck you," said Cyclops Reilly, "it's your own fucking fault."

"Benedict," Burke had said icily, "how is it my fault?"

"It's your fault," replied Reilly with vitriol, "because if you don't like doing it you should tell your superiors the truth."

"And what is that truth, Benedict?"

Reilly had had enough. "Look, you smart prick, the truth, if you really want to know, is that the Church should just get rid of these guys, not rotate them. If you didn't have these cocksucking scumbags as priests you wouldn't have a fucking problem."

It was as clear as that and the tirade had changed Seán Pius Burke's life. He went into the office of the monsignor who ran personnel in the New York Archdiocese and told him straight: "Your problem is not these children and their parents. Your problem is your priests. Why don't you eliminate your problem?"

The monsignor had hemmed and hawed, but Burke had put it in writing and sent it to the Cardinal. The monsignor was furious when the Cardinal told him about the letter. He was furious until the Cardinal told him what a great idea Father Burke had. The monsignor went back and told him he had the blessing of the Cardinal. "What are you going to do?" asked the monsignor.

"I'm going to round up the usual suspects," Burke had replied without humor.

He pulled the personnel files of every priest in the archdiocese and red-dotted those who had had problems with sex and children. Then he had the Cardinal send a letter inviting all of them to lunch at St. Joseph's Seminary in Dunwoodie. The Cardinal told them how wonderful it was to see them and that he hoped they enjoyed their lunch. Then he got up and walked out the door.

Seán Pius Burke stood up and looked at their mostly Irish faces and their soft, well-padded bellies, and he went at them. He was no longer the smooth priest with the law degree and the answer for everything. He was now the kid out of Hell's Kitchen who knew how the game was played. "Listen up, you cocksuckers." A hush fell over the crowd. Burke picked up the foot-thick personnel files from the table and slammed them down with a thud. He could see Adam's apples bouncing up and down behind Roman collars. "The party is fucking over. Do you understand? Over. I am going to get rid of as many of you bums as I can. And the ones I can't get rid of, I'm going to hound night and day. I am your worst fucking nightmare. Is that understood?" There wasn't a sound in the room. "Good day, gentlemen. Enjoy your lamb chops."

Soon after he had told his cousin Cyclops about the meeting. "You going to get rid of all of them, Johnny Pie?"

"Impossible," replied Burke. "They're too embedded. I'll get rid of as many of them as possible and put the fear of Jesus into the rest of them."

"Do the best you can."

"Thank you, Benedict."

"For what?"

"For showing me the light." For once, Cyclops Reilly was mute.

Burke went to work at a job that no one wanted him to do and soon learned what an impossible task it was. It was impossible because he was sabotaged at almost every juncture. There was a massive conspiracy of the cloth underway. Everyone was in denial. It seemed that every pedophile priest had a rabbi. And that rabbi had a rabbi in Rome. He soon noticed a disproportional number of priests had been sent down to New York from Boston. They were in as bad a way for clergy as New York was, so why were all these guys suddenly showing up in New York? It didn't take Burke long to figure out that it was Bernard Cardinal Law up in Boston and his two pimps, Bishops Thomas Murphy and William Daly, who were doing the dirty work. Burke had enough problems with his New York pedophiles, and now Boston was sending him theirs.

He went to the Cardinal and explained what Law was doing. The Cardinal listened without saying a word. In those days the two

Cardinals were known as "Law & Order," Sweeney being the order part. They were partners in orthodoxy, but Law was closer to the Pope. "I'll see what I can do," the Cardinal told Burke after he had finished with his presentation.

Days later the phone rang. "Father Burke?" It was the Cardinal. "Cardinal Law denies he's using New York as a dumping ground."

"He's lying," said Burke, the words jumping out of his mouth.

"He is a Prince of the Church," said Sweeney.

"He's still a liar," responded Burke, sure that his career had taken a sinister turn.

Three months later, Father Brendan Quiver—late of West Roxbury, Massachusetts, but now parish priest at St. Charles Borromeo in Harlem—was caught with his underpants around his ankles and his penis in the anus of a nine-year-old boy who was a student at the St. Charles parochial school. Burke was put on the case. He called the Cardinal.

"Was he one of Law's?"

"Yes, Eminence."

"How much?"

"One point four million."

"Pay it."

"Yes, Eminence."

"And get rid of Quiver. No counseling this time. Get him out of here."

"Yes, Eminence."

"And forgive me."

"Why, Eminence?"

"Because you were right and this will never happen again. You taught me a valuable lesson."

Burke wondered if he was changing anything. It was depressing work. Several months later Burke got a call from the Cardinal, who needed a personal secretary. Would Father Burke take the job?

"Yes, Eminence," said Seán Pius Burke, taking the job and the red stripe that went with it.

* * * * *

After Googling both the Reverend Chester Cockburn and OFF, Reilly still didn't know much. He learned that OFF was created after the *Roe v. Wade* Supreme Court decision in 1973. They were active in picketing abortion clinics, and the home office was in Buffalo, New York.

Buffalo, New York. Reilly picked up the phone and called his friend Joe Barry, reporter for the *Buffalo News*. "What say you from the mistake by the lake?" inquired Reilly of Barry.

"Fuck you, Reilly," said Barry to his old friend.

Reilly got right to the point. "You know a guy called the Reverend Chester Cockburn? He's with this anti-abortion organization, OFF."

"You mean Chester the Molester?" said Barry.

"What?" said Reilly, suddenly very attentive.

"You heard me right," said Barry. "He's one of those born-again Christian types that hates everyone," said Barry.

"Like who?"

"Like the blacks, the Catholics, the Jews . . ." said Barry.

"Sounds like he belongs to the KKK," said Reilly.

"Well, he's pretty good at baiting. He's cooled his act recently. Tries to play the man of God. He's had his own problems in the past."

"Problems?"

"That's where he got his nickname," said Barry. "Let's just say that if he has one more child molestation charge, he gets his own parish!"

"What are you talking about?"

"You never heard of the GodScou✝s?"

"GodScou✝s?" said Reilly. "What the hell are the GodScou✝s?"

"That's his front organization," said Barry. "They're like fundamentalist boy scouts for God. They sit around the campfire and sing hymns."

Cyclops Reilly started laughing. "Are you thinking what I am?"

"Yes, I am," said Joe Barry. They were both a couple of cynical Harps.

"I can just see it now," said Reilly, "hymns, marshmallows, and sodomy—all by the light of the silvery moon."

"I like the way you think."

"I can't help it," said Cyclops. "I'll never forget what my old man said: 'Any guy who works forty hours a week and wants to spend his weekend sitting in some swamp with a bunch of eleven-year-old boys is not right.'"

"You should inspect his closet," said Barry.

"For what?"

"GodScou✝s's underwear, methinks."

"Jesus," said Reilly. "But is that all you have on him? The fucking GodScou✝s?"

"He's got a rap sheet," said Barry. "He got booted as associate pastor about ten years ago over a child molestation allegation."

"What happened?" Reilly asked.

"Some kid in the parish said they used to pray together, then later they would seal the prayer with a blow job," said Barry.

"Explosive stuff," said Reilly.

"Yeah," said Barry, "but the kid wouldn't testify in court. His father had the corporation he worked for transfer him to Indiana, and he let everything drop. So they let Chester the Molester slide."

"But the church fired him?" asked Reilly.

"Yeah, the Presbyterians kicked him out," said Barry. "Landed running. He was made director of OFF soon after."

"Wasn't OFF worried about the allegations about the boy?"

"Cockburn got everybody to think the boy made the whole thing up," said Barry.

"How about his other troubles?"

"OFF wasn't too disturbed over that either," said Barry.

"What did he do, exactly?"

"Oh, some do-gooder Catholics were helping some blacks fix up their houses. You know that shit that Jimmy Carter does?"

"Habitat for Humanity?"

"Yeah, that's it," said Barry. "Well, he makes it out that it's a Papist plot to get all the blacks—who are all Baptists—to convert to the Catholic Church."

"You have to be kidding," said Reilly.

"Wish I were," said Barry. "The bishop up here, Malloy, denounced him as a Catholic basher."

"When was this?"

"Around 1988," said Barry.

Reilly—the epitome of the lapsed Catholic—was pissed off. "Joe," he said, "can you email me some clippings on this guy, pronto?"

"Yeah, Cyclops," said Barry. "I'll email it right down. What's up?"

"Read the *Daily News* on Friday," said Reilly as he hung up the phone.

After Reilly read Barry's emails, the first person he thought of was Abe Stein of the *New York Post*. Abe had been the *Post*'s chief court reporter for over thirty-five years, covering the most notorious murders and mobsters the city had to offer. Over the past several years he had covered the Cardinal's Sunday sermons and news conferences. Abe knew how to frame a story and he had become the *Post*'s de facto Religion Editor. Since Stein was Jewish, the Cardinal didn't try to intimidate him like he did the Catholic reporters. Stein had an ingenious way of framing his questions in a way that always made the Cardinal stick his foot in it. Reilly was in a quandary. He didn't want to share his story with Stein—he might be able to run with the front page with this one—but he didn't want to be accused, God forbid, of "Catholic Bashing." Abe Stein could help him out on this. He decided to show Abe only the story concerning the Reverend Chester Cockburn's encounter with Bishop Malloy. The rest—the Chester the Molester allegations—he would keep for his own ammunition.

12.

A specter for a guilty conscience. There she was in front of him, floating, high up. Speaking, but O'Rourke could not hear what she was saying. Her arms were outstretched to him, but O'Rourke did not reach out to her, to touch her hands. He didn't know if he was afraid or not. He tried to see her face, but it was obscured by fog or clouds or smoke; he couldn't be sure. He thought it was Mary, the Blessed Virgin. Why was she appearing to him? It must be important, but he was flummoxed by her.

Why was she here beckoning O'Rourke? Didn't she belong to

Swift? That was the political thinking. The papers made it sound like Swift and the Virgin were a gossip item. Were they dating or going steady? It was really blasphemous, but the Swift camp encouraged it. Even the Cardinal knew that the Virgin was in Swift's corner, like she was a registered Republican.

She must want something, O'Rourke thought in his dream state. She swirled around again and O'Rourke remembered the Virgin of his childhood. She was the Virgin-in-the-Box. Every kid in the classroom got to take the Virgin-in-the-Box home so the whole family could kneel and say the rosary in front of her. The box was her home and her mode of transportation. Every kid in the first grade got the Virgin-in-a-Box for a night. O'Rourke remembered kneeling with his mother and father in their living room at 349 West Fourth Street. Today that behavior would be considered to be very serious Catholicism, but back in the early 1950s every Catholic family in the parish was extremely devout. Life revolved around the school and the church. Even his father, still in his work clothes, was on his knees and saying the Hail Marys which came out like whispers on steroids; more of a buzz than words. After the rosary was done the Virgin returned to her box and the next day was passed on to the next family.

In O'Rourke's youth, the Virgin was like a member of the family. The nuns at St. Bernard's Parochial School talked about the Blessed Virgin incessantly and how much she was loved by her son, Jesus. The nuns also said that May was named after Mary, and was the Virgin's month. Every May the whole student body went up on the roof of St. Bernard's and sang songs to a statue of the Virgin. "Bring flowers of the rarest, bring flowers of the fairest . . . Oh, Mary we crown thee with blossoms today . . . Queen of the angels, Queen of the May." And all the children wrote notes to the Virgin—little prayers the nuns called ejaculations—and O'Rourke remembered how they were offered up in a fire, the smoke rising to the heavens where the Virgin now resided. O'Rourke's prayer was that Willie Mays would not be killed in the Korean War and safely returned to the Polo Grounds. O'Rourke could remember the brightness of the day and the heat of the early summer as it made tar bubbles on St. Bernard's roof. Then there was the smell of the still busy river, only blocks away, and the aroma of the bloody meat market around the corner. Today developers kill for the warehouses in the Meatpacking District; then it was an Irish-Catholic neighborhood full of stevedores.

Mary was also his mother's name. Mary Kavanagh. Named by his grandmother, Rosanna. O'Rourke never knew his Grandma Rosanna, for she had died so, so long ago. All he had was an old sepia photograph of her, sitting at a table with his grandfather. Henry Street, Dublin, was stamped on the back of it. His grandmother was a Conway and from the photograph he could tell she had a big bust and a serene face. And she was devoted to the Virgin Mary, naming her only daughter, O'Rourke's mother, after her. That's all he had of his grandmother: an old picture, a statue of the Blessed Virgin Mary that was hers, and a tombstone in Glasnevin Cemetery in Dublin with her name on it. His grandmother had a kind face, a young face. How old was she when she died? O'Rourke didn't know. His mother had few memories of her own mother because she was just seven when God had called Rosanna to heaven. "The good die young," his mother had told him. His mother ended up in an orphanage in Sandymount. The Black and Tans used to visit, looking for rebels in the basement. But that photo of his Grandmother Rosanna stuck with O'Rourke. A mystery woman, like this mystery woman—the Virgin Mary?—in his dreams.

And now the hot roof of St. Bernard's was out of O'Rourke's dream and the mystical figure was back, dancing in front of him. Was this Virgin coming to tell him something important? The fog was lifting from the Virgin's face. He could see her white scarf and her blue wrap, which she used like a burka, and there was a lone eye and it was familiar and, my God, could it be—

"You fucking asshole," said Dr. Moe Luigi.

"Mother of God," replied O'Rourke, waking up.

"Dr. Luigi!" said the woman in white.

"Oh," said Luigi embarrassed, "excuse my language."

"Where are my fucking glasses?" said O'Rourke to the white figure. O'Rourke was out of it. He didn't know where he was. He was woozy and still high and everything seemed out of sync. Plus he couldn't see a goddamned thing.

"Here you are, Mr. O'Rourke," said the woman.

O'Rourke put his glasses on and saw the aged nun in the white Sisters of Charity habit. She must be eighty. She looked just like Sister Perpetua from the first grade. "Oh, Sister," he said, "where am I?"

"You're in St. Vincent's," the nun said.

"What in God's name were you doing?" demanded Luigi.

O'Rourke was embarrassed. "I was fucking around." He looked at the nun and felt remorse.

"With what?" asked Luigi.

"Cognac and blow." The nun wondered what this blow was.

"Fool!" said Luigi. "You almost blew a gasket. Your blood pressure went through the roof, and you fainted. Lucky you didn't have a stroke. Better clean up your act!"

"Moe," said O'Rourke, "I'm sorry."

"You'll be sorry if you continue like this." Now Luigi felt remorse because of the way he had read down O'Rourke. "I'll never get any rest with friends like you," he said by way of apology. "Why does stuff like this always happen in the middle of the night?" Luigi covered his friend with a sheet and brushed O'Rourke's hair off his forehead. "Sister says you have a visitor. Do you want to see him?"

"Who?"

"Sam McGuire. Want to see him?"

O'Rourke smiled at Luigi's misdirection. "Sure."

"You'll feel better in the morning," said Luigi. "The blood pressure's coming down. Then we'll do some tests. I'll send your friend in." He put his hand on O'Rourke's wrist and squeezed. "I'll see you then."

"Moe," said O'Rourke sincerely, "thanks."

Both Luigi and the nun left, leaving O'Rourke alone in the room. His eyes grew heavy and the truncated dream came back and he cocked his head at the ceiling, as if a slant would make the apparition reappear. He almost knew who it was when he was awoken by Luigi. Just a few seconds more and he would have solved the mystery.

"You okay?" asked Sam McGuire.

"Thanks for coming."

"That's my job."

"How'd you know?"

"Mr. Pepoon called me," she said. "I came right over."

"Sorry I'm such a sorry pain in the ass."

"You're not," said McGuire as she slowly bent down and kissed him on the forehead. She hesitated. "You're my hero."

"I'm nobody's hero."

"Well," replied McGuire, "you're mine."

"Why?"

"Let's see," said McGuire, beginning to count on her fingers. "You're kind. You're passionate. You care. And even more important—you make me laugh."

"All I am," said O'Rourke, "is one drunken, fat Irish fuck."

"Hey," returned McGuire, "we'll knock thirty pounds off you, and you'll be a new man."

O'Rourke shook his head. "I'm an asshole."

"Yes, maybe," she said, "but you're *my* asshole." Now McGuire showed her edge. "You're too hard on yourself. You put yourself down too much. Everybody loves you. Don't you know?"

O'Rourke was actually embarrassed. "Thanks, honey," he muttered under his breath, afraid that the "honey" would insult her. O'Rourke knew he didn't deserve to be treated this kindly.

"Get some sleep. I'll see you in the morning."

O'Rourke cocked his head. "Do you hear it?" he asked McGuire.

"Hear what?" McGuire thought he was hallucinating; maybe he was still high.

"The keening."

"I don't hear anything," said McGuire, "and I think it's time for you to go to sleep." She took O'Rourke's hand in hers and O'Rourke wanted to hold her all night, but she slid from his grasp and left with a wave and that dazzling smile.

Why him? What did the Virgin want? It was haunting O'Rourke. He had never had a dream like that before. Who was it? He almost knew. He almost saw the Virgin's eyes. He was full of *pishogue*, as they say in the Irish. Full of ghosts, full of superstition, full of the unknown. He remembered that his mother fervently believed in the "Three Knocks at the Door" as a harbinger of death. She swore it had happened to her in the late 1920s as she was caring for a dying boy in Dublin. All alone in the house with the child, she went to answer the door. No one was there. When she went back to the lad, he was dead. O'Rourke wondered about all the ghost stories his parents had regaled him with when he was a child. He smiled at the memory of his wonderful childhood, his wonderful parents, and wondered about the wail of the banshee that he was sure he just heard, out there, on West 12th Street.

13.

Coming from three different directions, Cyclops Reilly, Abe Stein, and Seán Pius Burke found themselves alone in the same elevator. The diminutive Abe looked up at the two tall Irishmen on either side of him and smiled. "I feel like a pastrami on Irish soda bread," he said. Both Irishmen smiled back at him.

"You get my email?" asked Reilly.

"Sure did," said Stein. "What are you up to?"

"Me?" said Reilly innocently. "What would I be up to?"

"Johnny Pie," said Stein, "you know anything about this?"

"No," said the monsignor, "and I don't want to know anything about anything."

The news conference took place in the small auditorium that was adjacent to the St. Vincent's Hospital press office. The congressman was not crazy about the idea, but there was little he could do; in fact, coming back to the hospital made him feel like he was revisiting the scene of the crime. Madonna-Sue and her father had spoken with the Cardinal and had, reluctantly, agreed to attend. It was all for show and they had no choice. Peggy Brogan was there also, separated from the clique, a political wallflower who knew where all the bodies were buried.

When all the television lights and radio microphones were set up, the Cardinal stepped to the podium. On one side of him was Congressman Jackie Swift and on the other was the Reverend Chester Cockburn. "We are here," the Cardinal began, "to put a moral imprimatur on this year's elections."

There was a hum from the group of reporters and the only thought on their minds was "Church and State."

"For years now, Catholic politicians have run for office," began the Cardinal, "freely disregarding the moral teachings of Holy Mother Church. The Church will not stand for this amoral conduct any longer." He paused for effect. "Therefore, breaking tradition, I am endorsing Congressman Jackie Swift in his reelection bid. I am supporting the congressman specifically because of his stand against abortion and his efforts for Right-to-Life legislation." The Cardinal turned to Swift, shook his hand and said, "Thank you, Congressman Swift." Expecting applause, the Cardinal was taken aback by the silence in the room. He returned to the microphone. "It is not often that a crusade like the anti-abortion movement is given a signal from above," the Cardinal said as he raised his eyes toward the heavens. "And God chose to send his most Holy Mother to Congressman Swift to deliver his message on high—abortions must stop!

"Also, I want to take this a step further," said the Cardinal. "From now on, in the Archdiocese of New York, any Catholic politician who defies the teachings of Holy Mother Church on abortion will be denied Holy Communion. No one has an absolute right to the Eucharist." There was a palpable tension in the room, for the press knew the "Wafer Watch" was underway. The Cardinal cleared his throat. "The Reverend Chester Cockburn of Operation Free Fetus also has a statement to make."

Cockburn, ever so proud as he shook the Cardinal's hand, knowing the Cardinal's endorsement helped legitimize his organization, stepped to the podium. "Never again in this country," the reverend began, "will little fetuses be left defenseless. We will fight these Godless heathens in the Congress, in the streets, in the abortion clinics. We will do whatever it takes to stop the maiming of the innocent!" His eyes were raised to the ceiling as he spread his arms apart in imitation of Christ on the cross, looking instead like a loony bird about to take flight.

Swift was next. He looked sharp and healthy in his three-piece suit. "I just want to thank His Eminence, the Cardinal, and the Reverend Cockburn for their endorsement. I would also like to thank," he added with a straight face, "Our Lady of Greenwich Village for her inspiration." There were snickers from the media. "Now, we can begin the fight, and the fight will be right!" Swift was beginning to sound like Ian Paisley. With Cockburn on one side and the Cardinal on the other, Swift took their arms and raised them in triumph, like he had just won a heavyweight championship. The Cardinal surveyed the reporters. "Any questions?"

Abe Stein looked at Cyclops Reilly and knew the floor was his. "Ah, Reverend Cockburn," began Stein, "as you may know, the Cardinal is very wary of so-called Catholic bashers. I have a report here that after you accused the Buffalo Archdiocese of building low-income housing for poor blacks solely for the purpose of converting blacks to Catholicism, Buffalo's Bishop Malloy accused you of Catholic bashing. What do you have to say about that?"

"It's a canard," said Cockburn. "I have nothing but the utmost respect for the Catholic Church."

"So you're saying Bishop Malloy is a liar, then?" continued Stein.

"Yes, wherever you got that information from, it's a lie."

Cyclops Reilly was ready. "Reverend *Cock*-burn," he began.

"Ah," said the Reverend, "that's Co-burn. It's pronounced Co-burn."

"Nevertheless," said Reilly, "you're accusing the bishop—a member of the hierarchy of the Catholic Church—of lying? The Cardinal is always talking about Catholic bashing. Eminence, is this man a Catholic basher?"

"Who are you?" demanded the Cardinal, unaware of the connection between Reilly and Monsignor Burke.

"Cyclops Reilly, *New York Daily News*."

"I know your stuff, Reilly," said the Cardinal sharply. "Very biased reporting."

It didn't faze Reilly one bit. "Nevertheless, Eminence, is this man a Catholic basher?"

"Eminence," interrupted Billy Eminence, "could you define 'Catholic bashing'?"

"Catholic bashing," said the Cardinal, "is the abuse of Catholics by Catholics and non-Catholics alike."

"So Catholics can be Catholic bashers, too?" said Billy Eminence.

"Yes, Billy, Catholics can be accused of self-abuse," continued the Cardinal. With that answer howls went up around the room as the reporters started laughing. Monsignor Burke turned his head to the wall so the Cardinal couldn't see him.

"Friends," said Cockburn, "let's not fight over our differences. I happen to be a Protestant. But we all have lots in common. Like the Cardinal, I'm anti-abortion. I quake in the shadow of the Lord, for I am a man of God."

"But are you a Catholic basher?" demanded Reilly. Cockburn was stonewalling him.

"You said before, Reverend Cockburn," continued Abe Stein, "that you would 'do whatever it takes to stop the maiming of the innocent.' Are you advocating violence against doctors and women who use abortion clinics?"

"I said that we will take action to stop this holocaust of the fetus."

"How?" asked Stein. "What are your means?"

"We will do what it takes!" A look came over Cockburn. "My heart leaps for joy every time one of them gets popped." His face crunched into a scowl. "You won't find me weeping over the grave of an abortionist. It's time to scream bloody murder!" The Cardinal took a step back, disbelief on his face. Swift looked like he wanted to disappear.

"Reverend," said Reilly as he went in for the kill, "you seem to be more interested in fetuses than in living human beings."

"Fetuses," said Cockburn, "are living human beings."

"As alive as teenagers?" asked Reilly.

"Certainly."

"I hope you don't treat your fetuses like you treated that teenage boy up in Buffalo that you sodomized," said Reilly.

"I never touched that boy," protested Cockburn. "I have a wife and three boys myself."

"Does your wife let you near them?" yelled Reilly.

"This is an outrage!" Cockburn screamed at Reilly.

"You're more interested in fetuses," yelled Reilly, "than the living who you are accused of sodomizing! Are you a sodomite?"

"I'm not. I'm not a sodomite," shouted Cockburn into the microphone as the Cardinal came forward to try and calm him.

"How about you and your GodScou✝s?" continued Cyclops. "There've been allegations."

"I demand the right to face my *alligators!*" said Cockburn desperately, unconsciously stepping into a Joycean word maze from which there would be no escape.

"These allegations are outrageous," the Cardinal said into the microphone. "The Church would never associate with a man accused of doing such terrible things."

"How about your association with Father Bruce Ritter, Eminence?" said Reilly, referring to the notorious celebrity pedophile founder of Covenant House, who was feted by everyone from Sweeney to President Ronald Reagan as a hero savior of defenseless children.

With that Father Parnell Dowd, the archdiocese's information director, stepped to the podium and took the Cardinal by the elbow and led him out of the room.

Congressman Swift, wondering how he ended up in the middle of this circus, searched the crowd for his wife and Vito Fopiano, but they had already left. He decided to do the same. He caught Brogan's eye and they both headed for the exit. "I didn't touch that boy," the Reverend Chester proclaimed, over and over again. "I didn't touch him." The podium was now empty except for the Reverend Chester Cockburn, protesting his innocence.

Cyclops Reilly went to the pay phone and called Peccadillo Fogarty. "I got your headline for tomorrow, Peck."

"Yeah?" said Fogarty.

"I AM NOT A SODOMITE!"

14.

Sam McGuire came into O'Rourke's room at St. Vincent's with a shopping bag filled with his clothes. After two days of blood tests, probes, and scans, it was finally check-out day. He would live, Moe Luigi had told him. Only with no booze, no drugs, a new diet, and lots of exercise. With those admonitions weighing on him, O'Rourke would be going home.

O'Rourke was asleep when she came in, his hairless chest quietly going up and down. There was no hospital attire in evidence. O'Rourke hated pajamas. He always slept nude. Peacefully asleep, O'Rourke showed none of the inner turmoil that daily tortured his very being.

* * * * *

McGuire remembered vividly the first time she had seen O'Rourke. She was a junior press secretary in Chuck Schumer's campaign in February 1998 when panic had started to set in. Schumer was sitting at 17 percent in the polls, and everyone thought Geraldine Ferraro—the woman who had helped Walter Mondale lose forty-nine states to Reagan in 1984—was going to be the nominee against Senator D'Amato.

Schumer called in Northern Dispensary Associates for a consultation. McGuire was shocked the first time she saw O'Rourke, all beard, hair, and glasses, with an attitude that said, "I don't give a fuck." He was just the opposite of the slick operators who had been kissing Schumer's ass all winter, telling him what he wanted to hear. Schumer was tentative in his approach. O'Rourke had cut him off. "Geraldine Ferraro is a professional loser," he said, as mouths dropped open. "She's a lousy candidate, and her husband is mobbed up. And you're worried about *her*?

"Go out," O'Rourke had told Schumer straight to his face, "and punch them in the fucking mouth and see if they like it. The problem with the Democratic Party is that Clinton and the rest of those pussies at the Democratic Leadership Council"—McGuire knew immediately that O'Rourke was referring to the likes of Joe Lieberman and Lanny Davis—"have turned the party into GOP Lite."

The "GOP Lite" line had stuck with McGuire and was the reason that when she needed a job she came first to Northern Dispensary Associates. She also came because of O'Rourke the man. This was a real man. She was tired of boys disguised as men, with their toys and their solipsism. Hard dicks with soft heads, she thought of them. And although she had worked for him for just short of a month she knew O'Rourke was special. The way he took care of Tommy Boyle, the enthusiasm he showed when talking about issues, showed character. Even the things he didn't want to talk about—Vietnam and Bobby Kennedy—showed what kind of a man he was. What O'Rourke had was decency, something that had seemingly gone out of fashion. And, really, he wasn't that bad looking a man. In fact, in a saloon society kind of way, he was cute, even ruggedly handsome.

She knew O'Rourke was interested in her—a woman always knows. But he would never make a direct approach because, even at his age, he was still shy with women. It would be up to her to get the romance going. Seduction, she knew, could be fun. She smiled at her opportunity.

*　*　*　*　*

A sheet came up to O'Rourke's waist. He continued his quiet snooze. McGuire surveyed him and she couldn't resist. Gently, she lifted up the sheet and looked at his genitals. She held the sheet just a few seconds, but it seemed like a long time.

"What da ya think?" said O'Rourke out the side of his mouth.

Stunned, she dropped the sheet. Her black face blushed and she took on a purplish hue. "They're," she stuttered in embarrassment, "they're humongous!"

"Yeah," laughed O'Rourke at the sound of such a ridiculous word, "I've heard that before—mostly from my political opponents."

"But they're nice," said Sam, giggling. "Like ripe avocados."

"I like them massaged," replied O'Rourke, figuring he had nothing to lose.

Without saying another word, McGuire put her hand under the sheet and cupped his balls, slowly rotating them.

"Deeper," said O'Rourke.

McGuire dug her fingers deeper into his groin, and O'Rourke shut his eyes. His head dropped back on his pillow. McGuire's middle finger teased his anus, and O'Rourke found himself with his first erection of the year. Neither spoke.

Then the door opened. It was old Sister Perpetua. McGuire withdrew her hand.

"Ready to go home this morning, Mr. O'Rourke?" she pleasantly asked as she looked around the door.

"Yes I am, Sister," said O'Rourke. "Miss McGuire here is, ah, giving me a hand."

"Wonderful," said Sister Perpetua. "I'll see you downstairs at the check-out."

Sister Perpetua closed the door and O'Rourke, with McGuire holding his arm for support, helped him stand up out of the bed. He was naked with a full-blown erection.

"I'm all right," he said to McGuire with no self-consciousness. He was amazed at the weight of his hard-on. McGuire stared at it then looked up at O'Rourke, who was looking as frisky as a happy unicorn. "I wasn't sure it still worked," he said. They smiled at each other, now not sure if they were embarrassed or not. O'Rourke thought that an erection was the closest thing to a truth that was to be found in the world today. It was, after all, the most honest of reactions. "Get my clothes, honey." McGuire offered socks, which O'Rourke put on sitting on a chair, then underwear. "No underwear today," he said, "I want to let this thing breathe."

"Yeah," she said as she laughed out loud, "we're *really* going to let it breathe today."

* * * * *

They walked the two short blocks from the hospital back to O'Rourke's walk-up tenement apartment on Charles Street. O'Rourke knew he was not up to snuff because it took him ten minutes to walk up the six flights of stairs. They went to his bedroom where O'Rourke immediately sat down on the bed. McGuire stood facing him and began to unbutton her blouse. She reached for her bra and stopped, looking down at O'Rourke.

"Turn around," he said. "Keep me in suspense."

She did as she was told and the bra hit the floor. She undid the buttons of her skirt and let it slide down her legs. She was now standing right in front of O'Rourke's face and she slowly slid the panties down, exposing her crack. They also hit the floor and she moved backwards slowly, towards O'Rourke.

O'Rourke loved backsides and Sam's was round and firm, with a one-foot crack which made her buttocks look deliciously inflated. As she moved back into him, he noticed the splendid marbling on the side of her ass, dark to light to lighter then back to dark. O'Rourke's grabbed her hips and pulled her ass to his face and he kissed it, then licked it, moving toward the middle where he slid his tongue down her long crack and he could smell her true scent for the first time. He slid his middle finger between her legs and she was moist. "Tone," was all she said as she turned around and O'Rourke pressed his lips to hers.

"My God," said O'Rourke in awe, "surprise, surprise."

McGuire laughed. "You like my hot Brazilian wax job?"

"I *love* your hot Brazilian wax job," he said and then licked her bare pubis and slid his tongue down farther. She put her left leg on the bed, and O'Rourke's tongue pushed deeper until her clitoris began to surface, as big and hard as a hooded filbert.

"Stop, stop," she said, pulling her leg down and steadying herself. "God, you know how to travel below the Mason-Dixon Line!"

"I really was whistling Dixie, wasn't I?" All McGuire could do was hold her stomach and laugh nervously. For the first time O'Rourke saw the silver navel ring decorated the middle of her soft belly. O'Rourke looked up and realized McGuire didn't have a hair south of her eyelashes. Her breasts were bigger than O'Rourke thought they would be and their weight made them sway away from each other. Her nipples were like bolts, blacker than herself, with aureoles a good three inches in diameter, dotted with those magic bumps that made them look like chocolate chip cookies. Then he caught a shine from her left nipple. "What's that?" he said standing up and undoing his pants, his erection just as hard as it was back at the hospital.

"I'm pierced."

"Only one breast?"

"Just for a little attention."

"You got it," he said. "How do you get through the metal detector at the airport?"

"I have my ways."

"You're full of surprises," he said as he pushed his erection against her. He hadn't had an erection like this, he thought, since he was fifteen.

"I have *lots* of surprises for you, Wolfe Tone O'Rourke," and with that they fell into each other and onto the bed.

"I don't know if I'm up to this," said O'Rourke.

"Oh," smiled McGuire, "you're *up* to it, all right."

"I don't mean that."

"I know what you mean."

McGuire got on top of him and placed O'Rourke inside her. She moved back and forth in a rhythm. She smiled at him and he had his hands on her ass, as if holding on for dear life. They went on for minutes before she spoke. "Back at *The* Mary Louis Academy," she said as she stopped to laugh, "we called this 'The Proud Mary.'"

"The Proud Mary!"

"The Proud Mary."

"She will be proud," said O'Rourke as he found the perfect rhythm for McGuire, driving himself in at the perfect angle, finding her groove again and again. He could almost hear Tina Turner sing "Rollin', rollin' on the river." "Oh, my God," said O'Rourke quietly, "oops!" He shot. "Don't move," said O'Rourke with urgency.

"Wasn't that a little premature?" said McGuire with a look of disappointment on her face.

"Premature for *whom*?" answered O'Rourke. Then, retrieving a sexual trick from his youth, he started slowly moving again like a piston engine.

"What?" she said.

"I'm still hard. Let's keep going."

"Yeah, let's."

For forty-five minutes they rode. That was the amazing thing about good sex. The time flew. For the first time in years, O'Rourke felt like a real man. It was a gift to have someone like Sam McGuire for a lover. He had been a lucky man throughout his life with his lovers. But there were always two he thought of, even thirty-odd years after he had lost track of them—Rebekah Hoffman and Grace Phelan. They came back to him now and he began to drift in attention until McGuire suddenly stood up.

"You still with me?" she asked.

"Forever, sweetheart."

She turned around and O'Rourke—a man who loved shapely women—admired her abundant chocolate rump. He looked down at his wet cock and he thought he saw it grow even more in front of his very eyes. Then McGuire lowered herself down on him and pulled herself forward, grabbing his ankles, and started pumping her bottom. In and out, up and down. O'Rourke's panoramic view made him so hard he was afraid his dick would explode.

"At *The* Mary Louis Academy," she said as she laughed again, "the girls called this 'The Reverse Proud Mary,'" she said, throwing the words over her shoulder.

"What the fuck kind of Catholic school is *The* Mary Louis Academy?" O'Rourke said, joining her laughter.

Soon both O'Rourke's hands were on the top of McGuire's wonderful bottom. She was still pumping with the robust energy of a very sexual and horny thirty-five-year-old. He moved his hand across her chiseled backside and his pinky found her other hole.

"You dirty bastard," she said, but she really didn't seem to mind.

In and out, in alternate rhythms, they perfectly played. Then she stopped but O'Rourke continued to play her solo.

"My God," she said.

"*Whence did all that fury come?*" he said.

"What?"

"*Whence did all that fury come? / From empty tomb or Virgin womb?*" McGuire craned her head over her shoulder to look at O'Rourke, his head comfortably on his pillow. "*Saint Joseph thought the world would melt / But liked the way his finger smelt.*"

"You filthy, blasphemous bastard!" she said as she leapt off him, and O'Rourke began to laugh uncontrollably.

"Who wrote that?" she demanded.

"I shan't tell."

"Sounds like the work of that drunken poet friend of yours, Fergus T. Caife."

"Fergus," said O'Rourke, "would love the compliment."

"You," said McGuire accusingly, "didn't write that, did you?"

"Nope."

"Well?"

"William Butler Yeats," said O'Rourke with triumph. "It's called 'A Stick of Incense.'"

"You're kidding!" said McGuire laughing, then slapping him playfully on his Vietnam scarred arm. O'Rourke winced. The smile left McGuire's face. "I didn't see that before," she said quietly. "I was looking at your *thing* too much."

"That's all right, Sam."

"I'll never hurt you again," she said kissing him and they embraced, not saying a word for the longest time.

* * * * *

Soon after, McGuire fell into sleep. Although O'Rourke came twice, he was still rock hard. McGuire turned her back to him and O'Rourke, looking to dock, slid his erection into the pier between McGuire's ass cheeks. Her hand in sleep reached back and pulled his hip closer to her. "Yes, honey," McGuire said in sleep, "yes, that's it."

O'Rourke's hand patted McGuire's soft belly and he began to drift back in time once again. Again it was the two loves of his life, Rebekah Hoffman and Grace Phelan. They had one thing in common: Rebekah was the only woman O'Rourke had ever asked to marry him and Grace was the only woman who had ever asked marriage of O'Rourke. Rebekah wisely had said no and O'Rourke, although it broke his heart, had given Grace a negative reply. He was 0-for-2. O'Rourke had slept with enough women, but these two kept bouncing into his mind. Thirty years and they would not go away. He didn't even know where they were anymore and wondered if they had grown gray and fat like he had.

Naked with Sam, O'Rourke felt very comfortable. There was no inhibition and that reinforced his ease. It was the same with the other two. You would never find three women as different as Rebekah, Grace, and Sam, but O'Rourke loved them all. With Rebekah and Grace he had been too young and immature. O'Rourke, in his fifty-third year, had learned that he should enjoy women, do exactly what they told him, and everything would be fine. His decreasing testosterone, O'Rourke was happy to concede, had been replaced by common sense. He leaned forward and kissed McGuire on the shoulder. In response, she squeezed the hand that rested on her belly.

O'Rourke thought that he had never had as much fun in bed as he had with Rebekah. They were at once complete opposites and still strangely alike. Over the years O'Rourke had to smile at the thought of him and Rebekah. She was a Mennonite and he was an Irish-Catholic. There just *had* to be a law. O'Rourke once, trying to be a smart ass, had introduced her as "Rebekah, the Amish."

"How would you like me to introduce you as 'Tone, the Orangeman?'" she said, clearly annoyed.

O'Rourke had gotten the message. Rebekah reminded him how the Mennonites had suffered martyrdom at the hands of both the Catholics and the Protestants during the Reformation. "They refused military service and would not baptize their children," she lectured him. "They were considered subversives." Rebekah knew of O'Rourke's Dublin passport shop and how he liked to disrupt.

"Subversive?" said O'Rourke, delighted, as he gently kissed her lips.

"Subversive," replied Rebekah as she teased his tongue with hers.

Rebekah felt guilty about everything and O'Rourke felt guilty about almost everything—except sex. Sexually, Rebekah was a walking dichotomy. To her sex outside of marriage was wrong, but, God, she loved it and she was expert.

O'Rourke had met her at the Moat and had taken to her immediately. To this day, he didn't know why. There was just something about Rebekah, a genuineness and goodness that, frankly, reminded him of his mother, Mary Kavanagh. She was a good conversationalist, liked a drink, and loved to laugh. She was a handsome woman, not a great beauty, but whatever it was, for O'Rourke, she had it.

It had taken O'Rourke two months to bed her, but it was worth the wait. She hesitated to take her clothes off, but when she finally did it was as if she was totally liberated. She was a true exhibitionist. She loved to walk around naked, posing her pouting bush and making sure O'Rourke saw enough of her curvaceous ass. After a mutual shower, she would put her hair up in a towel and hold her hands around the towel so her full breasts would stick out tautly. Tastefully, she was a great tease. She had a great body and she knew it. O'Rourke was thirty, she was 22. Just out of college, she was trying to fit into the New York publishing scene. There was no denying their animal attraction to each other. The only sex apparatus they needed was a towel to dry Rebekah, she was so excitable. Missionary, cowgirl, doggie, they would pump for hour after hour. They would fuck in bed. They would fuck in her rocking chair. They would fuck on the floor in front of a mirror so they could check themselves out in action. She would pose naked for Polaroids, staring into the camera defiantly or flipping her rump out provocatively. "I want to be," she would say in an imitation of Greta Garbo, "your Priestess of Love.'" And the thing that made sex so much fun with Rebekah was that she felt so guilty about it.

"Oh, we shouldn't be doing this," she would say in the middle of coitus.

"Shut the fuck up," would reply O'Rourke with the sensitivity of the horny.

Never was fucking so good, and never was fucking so bold.

O'Rourke loved her, and for the first and last time, he had asked a woman to marry him. She sadly shook her head and told him that it just wouldn't work. He would get drunk and show up at her apartment and pull his limp cock out, and she would be patient and he would fall asleep, his head on her shoulder. He just couldn't understand why she just didn't love him when he loved her so much, so much that he had exposed himself to her in every way. And her rejection had deadened part of his heart forever.

Grace was something else. She was probably the most beautiful women he had ever seen. She had the face of the Irish Madonna, resplendent with fine Celtic features including a broad forehead and high cheek bones. She looked like a young Gene Tierney, only more beautiful. He had met her, too, at the Moat. The first time he saw her, he desperately wanted her. O'Rourke wasn't often like that, but the look of her drove him insane. Grace loved a drink and pretty soon she had found her way down to the end of the bar where O'Rourke and his cronies sat, night after night. At first, he was very shy in front of her, as her beauty intimidated him. He didn't know what to say after he was introduced, so he offered to buy her a drink. She accepted. O'Rourke soon learned that Grace Phelan loved booze so much she would accept a drink from even Adolf Hitler. One night, drunk, O'Rourke had asked if she would like to have dinner with him. When he didn't call, Grace went right up to him and said, "You owe me a dinner." O'Rourke didn't think the dinner had gone that well. He was a good conversationalist, but there were lots of awkward silences during the meal. The next day she called. "That was the best first date I ever had," she said. "Want to come over to my place for dinner tonight?"

O'Rourke showed up with a bottle of champagne at her door on Grove Street and Grace answered the door in her birthday suit. "Grace, I don't think . . ."

She took the bottle of champagne and put her index finger to his mouth, quieting his lips. Then she started undressing him. Apparently, he was on Grace's menu that night. He couldn't believe this absolutely beautiful woman wanted him. He looked at her, mouth open. She was the most exquisite woman he had ever seen. She had dark hair parted in the middle that fell to her hips. Wonderful active eyes, a narrow nose, and soft, soft lips. She wasn't as voluptuous as Rebekah, but her breasts were superb with lovely pink nipples. Her bush, like every bush he had seen before Sam McGuire's, was full and her bottom was small and tart.

They drank and they made love every night of the week, month in, month out. Grace's mouth was expert. She had an oral fixation, be it booze or cock. She would work O'Rourke for hours with her mouth, especially during her periods. "Where'd you learn to do this?" he demanded of the twenty-three-year-old.

"I read it in a book," she had innocently said and it was true. She said she heard when she was seventeen in Catholic high school that boys liked getting head and had bought *The Joy of Sex*. O'Rourke couldn't believe how lucky he was. She was the most desirable woman at the Moat and somehow O'Rourke, the ultimate fuck-up, had won her.

Then she began dropping hints.

Grace was from Staten Island. She dreamed of the house in the suburbs, kids, and a backyard swimming pool. She tried to domesticate O'Rourke by taking him to see her parents and to her sister down at the Jersey Shore. Her sister had taken him aside. "She's not for you," she said bluntly. "She's a drunk."

It was true; they were both drunks. But O'Rourke was functional and would work all day, while Grace, who couldn't hold a job, sat home all day drinking gin and listening to Billie Holiday records. She would be plastered by the time O'Rourke got home.

"I'm so depressed," she said to him.

"No wonder," he would say viciously. "What do you expect, drinking all day and listening to fucking Billie Holiday?" He had hurt her and regretted his brutal honesty. O'Rourke had finally convinced her to visit a psychiatrist. By the second session the doctor had told her to stop drinking. Grace immediately found a new psychiatrist. O'Rourke would try to break up with her, but she would drop to her knees as if to pray and pull his zipper down. Like Neil Sedaka, he would find that breaking up was hard to do—especially when your cock was in Grace Phelan's proficient mouth.

Their relationship was turning into a fucking disaster. "Marry me," she said, clutching at O'Rourke's sweater. "Please, marry me." But O'Rourke could not. He loved her more than anything in this world, but he could not marry her. She was a really good, gentle, but confused person. And all he could see was some shitty house in the suburbs and coming home to an empty bottle of gin on the dining room table night after night, for the rest of his life.

That was more than twenty years ago, and he still felt the hurt. He had loved both Rebekah and Grace, but the energy and impetuousness of youth had destroyed both relationships. He pledged to himself that it would not happen with Sam McGuire.

*   *   *   *   *

"What are you thinking about?" asked McGuire, yawning as she came out of her nap.

"That fucking *dybbuk*," O'Rourke responded.

"The what?"

"The *dybbuk*—my own personal demon." McGuire didn't say a word. "I've got to change my life, Sam. Will you help me?"

"I'll do anything so long as it makes you happy," said McGuire. "Just name it."

"You ever run a congressional campaign?"

"No," said McGuire with concern. "What are you thinking?"

"I'm thinking that for once, Sam, I have to do something good in my life, something truthful."

"I love you," said McGuire as she kissed him. O'Rourke wanted to say the same thing, but he thought of Rebekah and Grace and the words just wouldn't come.

What was wrong with him?

Love was the most misused word in the language. Everybody used it, but few knew what it meant. Its twin was *truth*. Everybody demanded truth, but truth, like love, was always in the eye of the beholder. Love and truth. Truth and love. No two words were fraught with more potential and no two words could destroy so quickly. Sam moved to the edge of the bed and lit her cigarette, taking heavy drags and pushing the smoke out through her nose, and O'Rourke began to doze.

Then he thought he saw *her* again, out there in the shadows of his subconscious, telling him to do something. Her head was still covered, but it looked like she was speaking to him. She motioned him towards her and he tried and tried, but he could not reach her. He thought he could hear her voice, but then he wasn't sure. And in a flash she was upon him and he wanted to back away, but he couldn't. She had the eyes of his Grandmother Rosanna. Those eyes from the old sepia photograph. They were the same eyes as his mother, Mary Kavanagh. And they were his eyes also. That was the nicest thing Rebekah—or anyone else, for that matter—had ever said to him: "Tone, you have kind eyes." The same eyes as his mother, his grandmother, and the specter. He thought he could now hear her. He tried hard. "In the cause of truth and mercy," the specter said, "and for the sake of justice: may your right hand show your wondrous deeds." A coldness and fear ran through O'Rourke.

As she stood and snuffed out her cigarette in a tea cup, McGuire caught the terrified look on O'Rourke's face as he began to awake. "What's wrong?" she asked.

"Oh, Sam," said O'Rourke as he took McGuire's hand and pulled her into the bed and his arms, holding her tight in case she might try to escape. McGuire kissed his cheek, but O'Rourke's gaze shot right past her.

Then he remembered what he had recited to Sam before, during their love-making: "*Whence did all that fury come? / From empty tomb or Virgin womb?*" And only then did he realize who the specter was. He was pretty sure it was her, Our Lady of Greenwich Village.

15.

"**I** am not a sodomite!" shouted Chester Cockburn on New York One, the local New York City cable news channel.

Thom Lamè smiled, almost feeling empathy. Lamè was anxious. In the past twenty-four hours, New York One had run the clip over and over of Cockburn melting down like the Wicked Witch of the West. And every time Lamè had seen it he had grown more anguished. He knew this was the time to make his move. He thought, one-on-one, he could beat Jackie Swift. He knew he could corral the nomination for the Liberal Party— they owed him one from the last time he had run against Swift. That time he had split the vote between himself and the Democratic incumbent, Fat Max Weissberg, which allowed Jackie Swift to go to Congress with only 37 percent of the vote. Fat Max loathed Lamè, and he had let the world know that the only reason Swift had been elected was because of Lamè's naked ambition. Lamè had indeed sucked up to the powers in the Liberal Party, who were helping out their patronage pals in the GOP. That debt had been paid off. This time Lamè wouldn't have to worry about Fat Max Weissberg—he had died shortly after the election. Still, Lamè agonized about getting the Democratic nomination. People had long memories. Even inside the gay community, he was not well liked for what he had done to his city council primary opponent, Lizzie Townsend. If he could only get Tone O'Rourke to work for him.

It had been a disastrous courtship. Lamè had tried to woo O'Rourke several times in the past, without success. The last time was when he had made his successful run for city councilman. Lamè had found O'Rourke standoffish. He had not returned his phone calls, and when Lamè had finally gotten him on the line, O'Rourke had been dismissive.

"You can't afford me, Mr. *Lame*," O'Rourke said, testing the size of Lamè's political ego, eschewing the accent and intoning the synonym for "crippled."

"It's *La-may*," Lamè replied, clearly annoyed, "Lamè. Accent grave over the E."

O'Rourke smiled. "You still can't afford me."

"Yes, I can," said Lamè stridently.

"Not this year," O'Rourke had said and hung up the phone.

Let him wait, thought O'Rourke. He had been keeping an eye on Lamè. In the political consulting world the creed read that "Politics was show business for ugly people," and that description fit Lamè perfectly. O'Rourke knew that every politician he had ever met was an opportunist, but Lamè seemed to go out of his way to highlight his opportunism. The campaign against Max Weissberg and the Democratic Party had been bad enough, but after watching the way Lamè had run his campaign for city council, O'Rourke realized that no gutter was too dirty for Lamè.

If it had anything to do with gays, he was out there, as though he had been given the tablets by the Gay Moses at the Stonewall that June day in 1969. Lamè was for mom, apple pie, and the repeal of the sodomy laws. He demanded that the cops crack down on gay bashers. He sought free "condoms on demand" for school children, even at the elementary school level. His work would be done, he told cheering throngs on Gay Pride Day, when same sex marriage was made legal. "I may not see the Promised Land," he said, mimicking Dr. Martin Luther King, Jr., "but I know *you'll* eventually get there." Thom Lamè had absolutely no shame.

O'Rourke had been amused by gay politicians for years. He had told his friend Congressman Barney Frank, "Thirty years from now you'll be a Republican." Frank had laughed, but he knew what O'Rourke meant. The thing that O'Rourke admired so much about gays was that they had political power, and they knew how to use it. They wielded a devastating disproportionate political clout that the city's other minorities had never achieved. And because they voted en masse, it gave them political power that the blacks and Latinos could only dream about. Not for one second did O'Rourke think that any politician, be it Bill Clinton or Rudy Giuliani, gave a fuck about the gay agenda. What they did understand was that gays voted in a solid block and used that power like a political blunderbuss. The gays, like the Irish before them, knew how to work the vote. And like the Irish they were slowly beginning to evolve. O'Rourke was amused to note that gays, once proud of being outcasts and pariahs, now wanted to be part of the homogenized mainstream. In an age where Americans had basically repudiated the sanctity of marriage by their spiraling divorce rate, gays had embraced the institution that the masses now found less than sacred.

What particularly disturbed O'Rourke was Lamè's campaign that had gotten him elected to the city council in the first place. It was a tough battle between him and Lizzie Townsend. In the beginning, the campaign had been fought completely on the issues, but as primary day approached the gay cajoling had become acute. First Lamè had adopted a gay lisp. O'Rourke noticed that at no time when he talked with Lamè on the phone had he lisped. Subtlety, O'Rourke presumed, was not one of Lamè's strong points. O'Rourke, being the student of American politics he was, thought it great theatre.

The lisp was a harbinger of things to come. Although a champion of gay rights, Lamè had never officially revealed his sexual orientation. The time, as they say in politics, was ripe. "I'm gay, I'm queer, I'm out of the closet!" Lamè had told a candlelight rally in Christopher Park, right across the street from Hogan's Moat. There had been tears and hugs and everyone had told him how brave he was. Even better, he had made all the newscasts that night. The ball was now in poor Lizzie Townsend's court.

Three days later Lizzie came out. "I'm a lesbian. Have always been a lesbian. Will always be a lesbian."

"After seven innings of play," O'Rourke had told his staff, "Cocksucker 1, Muff Diver 1." He could hardly wait to see what knuckleball of a pitch Lamè had hidden in his arsenal to close out the game.

The Sunday before the primary, Lamè made his move. "Not only am I gay," he said to a packed house at the Stonewall, "but I'm also HIV-positive!"

"Game, set, match. Lamè," O'Rourke declared.

"I'd love to see Lizzie beat this guy," said Pepoon.

"Don't hold your breath," cautioned O'Rourke. "She can't beat him. The logical conclusion to this little pissing match would be for Townsend to declare that she had AIDS and would soon be fucking dead!"

Lamè had polarized the gay vote, much in the same manner that Vito Fopiano liked to play one ethnic group against the other. Gay men—numerically superior in the district—had embraced Lamè, while lesbians had backed Lizzie Townsend. O'Rourke was impressed with Lamè. He didn't approve, but he admired his superb manipulative techniques. Lamè, O'Rourke knew, was thoroughly ruthless.

At the top of the hour Chester Cockburn was again shouting on New York One that he wasn't a sodomite. "I'm going to run," said Thom Lamè to himself, "and I'm going to get Wolfe Tone O'Rourke to manage my campaign."

Congressman Thom Lamè.

He liked the sound of that. But Thom Lamè had secrets, dirty little secrets, and Wolfe Tone O'Rourke had a pretty good idea what they were.

16.

Sam McGuire proved a tough taskmaster. There was never any talk of her moving in with O'Rourke—she never left after that first day. She would get up with O'Rourke every morning at five o'clock, and make a simple breakfast of fresh-squeezed orange juice and an English muffin while he showered. He stubbornly refused to join a gym, so she would send him off before the dawn broke. But not to the office; O'Rourke would take the number 1 train to Columbus Circle and begin the long walk down Seventh Avenue to the Village and his office on Christopher Street. As she pushed him out his own door, McGuire would kiss him gently on the lips and sweetly say, "I'm going back to bed for awhile. I'll see you at the office later."

And O'Rourke, finally wise after all these years, would nod and say the smartest thing a man could be trained to utter, "Yes, dear."

O'Rourke was already beginning to look better. She had brought him to his barber and said, "Cut it off. Give him a Steve McQueen haircut." His long locks hit the floor and pretty soon you could see the O'Rourke of his youth emerging. His beard was now trimmed tight, and new, smaller glasses gave him a cut, smart look. At lunch time they would walk south for an hour, down into SoHo.

At night, he did all the cooking simply because he was better at it and McGuire had absolutely no interest in it herself. While O'Rourke was puttering around with the spaghetti and sausage or chicken in a mushroom sauce or the steak au poivre she would sit in her underwear and paint her toenails. O'Rourke thought it was great. He didn't miss the drink at all because he was happy. He soon realized that the booze was an empty friend. It never spoke to you or hugged you or kissed you, did nothing for you but dulled you and begrudgingly got you through another day. Within weeks the McGuire Regimen had begun to turn O'Rourke into a new man. With just sensible diet, exercise, and no booze, O'Rourke was losing pounds by the day.

But not all was sunshine. O'Rourke still awoke in the small hours of the morning, his demons pursuing him. Sam would be lying in his arms, but there would often still be terror in his heart. O'Rourke had become obsessed with Fat Max Weissberg's old congressional seat. Should he run or not? O'Rourke would decide to go for it, then change his mind the next day. He would lie awake in the middle of the night with nothing but the sound of traffic going down Seventh Avenue and the small bursts of air coming out of Sam's nose as she slept with her head on his shoulder and chest.

Then O'Rourke would begin to drift off, and the dream would come again. Our Lady of Greenwich Village. O'Rourke wondered if they were now sharing the Virgin, he and Jackie. O'Rourke didn't know what the Virgin wanted of him, but he knew she was *of* him.

The Blessed Virgin was deliberately tempting O'Rourke, like a chaste seductress. She was cute, elusive—as if she wanted O'Rourke to pursue her. He didn't know if he should chase or not, because sometimes, frankly, she frightened him. He had spoken with Sam that night and told her he was going to run for Fat Max's old seat. He wanted her to be his campaign manager. "What do you think?" he asked Sam.

"I think you should run," she replied.

"What if I fail?"

"We'll pack up and move to Ireland," was her perfect reply. O'Rourke knew he had nothing to lose.

They had made love, but O'Rourke could not fall asleep afterward. His mind was too active with plans that he would announce to his staff in the morning. Slowly he had drifted off with only the sound of Sam's little snores that he had grown used to. That is when Our Lady of Greenwich Village had come back to him. She was again swimming in nothingness, darting to and fro, like a celestial stripper. What did she want?

"Tone," she said in a whisper. "Tone."

O'Rourke, in sleep, could see himself trying to pull his head away, but his body was too heavy and he was trapped, a captive audience to this apparition. She would not show her face. The veil hung loosely over her eyes and he tried different angles to see who it was. It was no use. But he knew he knew her.

Out of frustration he said, "Should I run?"

There was no response.

"Should I?" he repeated.

The Virgin said, loud and distinct: "Grace is poured out upon your lips: thus God has blessed you forever." O'Rourke shook his head, totally befuddled. "I think I will leave you now, Tone," said Our Lady of Greenwich Village and she began to back away, sliding as if on tracks.

Strangely, O'Rourke felt betrayed.

"No," he snapped, his fear of her dissipating. "Don't leave me now. I need you to guide me." He wanted to reach out to her, to jump into the dream, but he couldn't.

For some reason he thought of his mother. And the day she died. He was with her that morning, but had to meet an important client. "Now don't work too hard," was the last thing she said to him. She was the only person who had ever said that to him. A strange thing to say, but also a sweet thing. She had always worked hard in the kitchens of the Anglo-Irish in Dublin, and of the Jews and Protestants in New York. "Now don't work too hard," was maybe her way of saying, "because look where it's gotten me."

She had said she wasn't feeling well, but O'Rourke was not concerned. His mother would never die on him. He must go to this important meeting. When he returned later that day she was dead and stiff and cold, and O'Rourke had never forgiven himself. They say death is one of the three things that every person must do alone. "Be born.

Die. Testify," Mayor Jimmy Walker had once joked. But it was not true. You are not born alone, and you should not have to die alone. When he was born in Hollis Street Hospital in Dublin his mother had been there, and when she died he had cruelly left her alone. Perhaps Our Lady knew of his mother. Perhaps Our Lady could take a message to Mary Kavanagh. "I need you," he heard himself say. "Please help me."

With that plea he could see Our Lady returning to him. He knew she was smiling behind her veil. Why? He only wished he could see her full face. "Sing to the Lord a new song," she said, "for He has done wondrous deeds."

All he could see was that one damn eye. An eye that he knew. And then the most extraordinary thing happened. Our Lady of Greenwich Village winked at him. And his dream ended.

* * * * *

"Is everyone here?" asked Tone O'Rourke of the throng that had overrun his office and was hanging out the door and into the hall. Pepoon and McGuire were standing behind him at his desk. Fergus T. Caife and Moe Luigi were huddled in a corner. Tommy Boyle was standing next to Clarence Black. Cyclops Reilly was alone by himself sitting in the windowsill, ogling the young female assistants. Nuncio Baroody was on the other side of the office, ogling the young male assistants.

"Tone has an announcement to make," said Winthrop Pepoon, and the hum dissipated.

"Ladies and gentlemen," O'Rourke began, "I have decided to run in the Democratic Primary in June as a candidate for the 7th Congressional District." He was met with a round of applause and whistles. He put up his hand for quiet. "It's April now. We don't have much time to file our petitions and get on the ballot. Sam McGuire will be my campaign manager and everyone will report to her. We have much work to do, starting immediately. We will need buttons, posters, T-shirts. I will need a personalized 800-number. Clarence Black," O'Rourke said as he pointed him out, "will be in charge of security. Nuncio Baroody—give a wave Nuncio—will be our liaison with the gay community. And the indispensable Tommy Boyle will be the keeper of the petitions. I will make the official announcement within days. Any questions?"

"What will the buttons say?"

"NO MORE BULLSHIT," said O'Rourke with glee. "I'm stealing this directly from the Mailer-Breslin campaign of 1969. They were right then, and I'm right now."

"How about the 800 number?"

"I'm still working on that," said O'Rourke, "but it will have to be catchy, because this is how we're going to raise funds. Same with the T-shirt. Right now VOTE FOR TONE will suffice, but there'll be more. Let's see how the opening weeks of the campaign go."

"What exactly," asked Nuncio Baroody, "am I supposed to do with my fellow cocksuckers?"

There was embarrassed laughter, then silence. "Get used to it folks," said O'Rourke. "This is not going to be the kind of boring campaign that has forced the voters of this country into a coma. We are going to be audacious, and we are going to be tough. We are not taking shit from anyone. To answer your question, Nuncio, you're going to be my floor manager at the caucus of the VQD, the Village Queer Democrats. I want their endorsement. Got it?"

"Got it," said Nuncio. "When do I get paid?"

"Don't worry, Nuncio," said O'Rourke amid the laughter, "you'll get yours. Anything else now? Okay, if you have any questions, direct them to Sam. Let's get moving!"

The room cleared, and O'Rourke was left with his friends.

"You are out of your fucking mind," said Pepoon.

"No hope," said the poet Caife.

Black, Baroody, and Luigi nodded their heads in agreement. McGuire slid her arm inside of O'Rourke's for support, and pulled on his wrist to bring him closer to her. The statements had stung O'Rourke. Even with Sam's armlock, he felt alone. Strangely, he again thought of Mary Kavanagh on the morning of her death. Sam could feel the chemistry of his body language change. He was in doubt again. Maybe he had made the wrong decision.

"I don't think so," said Cyclops Reilly. "I think Tone can win." Reilly stood in the middle of the room alone, all eyes on him. He looked like a tired soldier-of-fortune with his eye patch and his hands dug into the pockets of his tweed jacket. "I remember being very frightened one time in Vietnam when I got hit by shrapnel," he softly said. "I couldn't see. I was in shock. And I thought I was going to die." Still facing the small group he started to walk backwards, then stopped. "There was this little prick of a navy corpsman who stopped me from bleeding to death and got me into a helicopter. As they were putting me on board, I noticed he was bleeding on me from a huge hole in his arm. But he stayed with me. And then he shouted over the din of the copter blades: 'Cad a dhéanfaidh mach an chait ac luch do mharú?' I didn't know what the fuck he was saying to me. Then he gave me the translation: 'What will the cat's son do but kill a mouse?' He told me it was an old Westie saying—from the Gaelic, no less—which I found out later it wasn't. But I held onto that saying like it was a sacred talisman. Like it alone could save me. It stuck in my head as I got out of that rice paddy, out of the hospital, and out of fucking Vietnam forever.

"Now," continued Reilly, "that same corpsman is in this room and he's going to run for Congress. I know this man better than I know any other human being on this earth. He's scared right now because he's always scared. He's tormented now because he's one of the few men I know who really cares. He's looking for some kind of redemption. From what? I don't know. Redemption for Vietnam? For what he did to Bobby Kennedy?" O'Rourke looked at the floor when Reilly mentioned Kennedy, and McGuire's jaw fell open in shock. "Well, Tone," Reilly went on, "there is no salvation, no redemption for any of us in this fucking life. When Tone goes out there he will be vulnerable. They will call him a terrorist because of what he did for those IRA guys back in Dublin in the '70s. They will call him a traitor for going AWOL. He will be an easy target—like I once was—so there's only one thing I can say to him: 'Cad a dhéanfaidh mach an chait ac luch do mharú?'"

Cyclops Reilly tugged at his patch and looked directly at his friend Tone O'Rourke, then turned to walk away, "Yeah," he said as left the office, throwing his voice over his shoulder, "let's go kill some fucking mice."

There was an awkward silence as they listened to Reilly's footsteps echo down the hall. "I'm sorry, Tone," said Pepoon. "I shouldn't have said that. You know we're all with you."

"You can depend on us," added Fergus T.

O'Rourke, clearly moved, nodded. "I know I can," he said. O'Rourke squeezed McGuire's hand and thought of a dead mouse on its back with four little legs standing up straight. But that vision soon became Bobby Kennedy lying on the filthy floor of that kitchen in the Ambassador Hotel in Los Angeles. There he was, a big hole in the back of his head, his eyes wide open, as if astonished by the absurdity of it all.

"What did Cyclops mean about Bobby Kennedy?" asked Sam. O'Rourke's lips were clenched as he shook his head back and forth. Then he recalled what he had dreamt: "Sing to the Lord a new song," Our Lady of Greenwich Village had said, "for He has done wondrous deeds." But O'Rourke could not sing for he had been struck dumb by the vision of the dying Bobby and his pleading eyes.

17.

"Which way?" the voice, calm amid the ruckus, asked. O'Rourke was pushing forward, and he could feel the senator holding onto the tail of his jacket. "Which way?" he said again.

"That fucking Bruno," thought O'Rourke. His boss, Jerry Bruno, was the best advance man in the business, but he had headed back to New York to work on the primary, leaving O'Rourke to advance the senator on the day of the California primary. Truth was, O'Rourke didn't know which way he was going. He caught the gleam of the stainless steel refrigerators. They were like a beacon and he lowered his head and pushed ahead. Get through that kitchen, he thought, and we're home free. He could now feel the senator's fist in the small of his back as he clutched O'Rourke's jacket for dear life. Although he was always in them, the senator hated crowds. He never said why, but O'Rourke knew. With the pop of every flashbulb, the senator would involuntarily wince at his own mortality.

Pop. Pop. Pop.

O'Rourke thought it was another photographer's flash. There was a scream and the fist was gone from his back. On the floor the senator, eyes wide open, looked right up at O'Rourke. The floor, where the senator's head rested, looked like Jackson Pollock had taken a bucket of barn-red paint and just dumped it. O'Rourke was wild-eyed. "Is everybody else all right?" were the last words Kennedy whispered before lapsing into a coma. But to O'Rourke the only words out of Robert Kennedy's mouth as he lay on a blood red floor on the next to last day of his life were, "Which way?"

"Which way?"

"What?" Sam asked.

"Which way?" said O'Rourke, sitting up in the bed, arm jabbing the air. "Which fucking way?"

"Tone, Tone, Tone." She grabbed him under his arm and O'Rourke's eyes flew open, terrified. "It's all right, Tone," Sam said, "you just had a nightmare."

For a second O'Rourke didn't know where he was. Then he recognized Sam and slumped into her arms. "Which way?" he said again and began to cry uncontrollably, the heavy tears running down Sam's bare breasts.

*　　*　　*　　*　　*

"Kennedy once asked me," said O'Rourke, "'Why do I like you?'"

"What did you say?" McGuire asked, lighting a cigarette. It was a cigarette of tension, unlike the smoke after sex, which was pure relief.

"I said 'Senator, you like me because I'm a little Irish prick, just like you.'" McGuire and O'Rourke laughed simultaneously and the horror of a few minutes ago evaporated. O'Rourke put his hand on McGuire's smooth knee, almost petting it roundly like the head of a dog.

"You don't really think you killed Bobby, do you?"

"Of course not," said O'Rourke, "but I'll never get over that fucking night, that fucking moment. There's always guilt in my mind. What if I had turned the other way? What if I hadn't been mesmerized by the shine of those refrigerator doors? That little shit Sirhan would never have gotten near him. Sirhan Sirhan. A double-barrel of mindless hatred. If I had gone the other way, we'd been out of California and into New York and God knows what might have happened."

"As FDR used to say," said McGuire, blowing smoke in O'Rourke's direction, "that is a very 'iffy' question."

"Yes, it is," said O'Rourke absently. "I often wonder what Jerry Bruno would have done? No matter what, the candidate was killed on my watch."

"Just like JFK was killed on Bruno's watch."

"Yeah," said O'Rourke with a little smile, "we're the advance men from hell." McGuire leaned over and kissed O'Rourke and took his penis into one of her soft hands. It remained flaccid. "Not tonight, dear," he laughed.

"That's a change," said McGuire.

"Come on," he said. "Big day tomorrow."

"So Bobby getting shot is your big secret," said McGuire.

"One of them."

"You want to tell me about any of the others?"

"Not now."

"When?"

"In time."

"You loved Kennedy, didn't you?"

"Like I love you."

The answer caught McGuire by surprise and she felt her heart jump and she gave O'Rourke a wonderful smile and a peck on the cheek. "How long did you work for Senator Kennedy?"

"I started in the 1964 senatorial campaign," said O'Rourke. "After the election I worked in his New York office while I went to CCNY. Then I found myself spending time in D.C. and pretty soon I ended up working for Jerry Bruno as an apprentice advance man."

"What was Bobby like?"

"I know it sounds funny," said O'Rourke pensively, "but I still have trouble explaining him. I suppose it was his great gifts, his great touch, which you don't find in people anymore—especially politicians. The best word for him is *empathy*. He could—"

McGuire cut him off. "Yeah, the empathetic millionaire."

"You didn't like Bobby?"

"Nothing personal," said McGuire. "He was really before my time."

"What bothers you?

"McCarthy."

"Gene?" asked O'Rourke.

"No. Joe." O'Rourke gave a big laugh. "What's so funny?" asked McGuire.

"People always hated Bobby because of one of the two Senator McCarthys," answered O'Rourke. "Kennedy found it rather amusing."

"There was nothing amusing about Joe McCarthy," said McGuire adamantly.

"You're right," agreed O'Rourke.

"So?"

"People change," said O'Rourke.

"No, they don't."

O'Rourke looked at Sam and nodded. "You're right. People don't change, but they evolve. Without evolution you don't grow. Would FDR have been the same politician if he hadn't had polio? Bobby evolved. Without the death of his brother, he would have remained the same, just interested in power, not what power could do for the people. He learned to direct the toughness—the Irish malice, you could say—toward the enemies of the people."

"How?"

"He became a champion of the blacks, the Latinos, the middle class, the disenfranchised."

"You think?"

"You think there's any votes in this fucking country being for poor blacks and Latinos?"

"I *know* for a fact there's no votes being for blacks and Latinos!"

The laughter broke the debate. "You know, Bobby could give a speech and bore you to death, but in person he was dynamite. I remember once in '68 for the presidential campaign I got a haircut and shaved my beard and started wearing a suit and tie and he pointed it out to the whole office and it got a big laugh. I was terribly embarrassed. Here I was this twenty-two-year-old kid with a degree from CCNY and all these other guys and girls were from Harvard and Yale. He saw me blush so he came over to me and stood behind me and put his thumb and index fingers around the back of my neck, slowly massaging it and in a few seconds I felt like a million bucks." With that he wrapped his hand around McGuire's neck and rubbed it, just as Kennedy had kneaded his. He then put both arms around her and hugged her with all his might. And as he did he thought he might get hard, but he didn't.

"Maybe one time, for Bobby?" Sam joked.

O'Rourke shook his head. He recalled the saturnine Kennedy quoting Aeschylus to a crowd of blacks in Indianapolis after he had informed them that Martin Luther King had just been assassinated. "'In our sleep,'" began O'Rourke, "'pain which cannot forget falls drop by drop upon the heart until, in our own despair, against our will, comes wisdom through the awful grace of God.'"

McGuire was mesmerized. "Where do you come up with this stuff?" she asked. She stifled an embarrassed laugh with the lift of her hand. It was the wrong reaction, but she couldn't help it.

"Someday I'll tell you," replied O'Rourke.

"How about Marilyn?" she impishly asked, suddenly changing the subject.

"Monroe?"

"Is there any other Marilyn?"

"It was before my time."

"But was the great moralist Bobby *fucking* her?" McGuire used *fucking* like she would say "The Nazis just *invaded* Poland."

"How would I know?"

"You never asked him?"

"Hey," said O'Rourke, clearly on the defensive, "you didn't talk about stuff like that back in 1968."

"Do you *think* Bobby fucked Marilyn?"

O'Rourke was getting exasperated. "Christ, even *I* would fuck Marilyn Monroe," he said.

She let that sit in the air for a moment. "Me too," said McGuire with a smile that in a mild but wonderful way shocked Wolfe Tone O'Rourke.

18.

N ew York John Mellor's stretch limousine pulled up in front of
the Old Town Bar on East 18th Street and O'Rourke emerged,
followed by Nick Pinto, Neil Granger, John Hamill, and Mellor. The
five men were old and trusted friends. Pinto was a legendary Village
bartender, restaurateur, and convicted felon. "Hey, nobody's perfect,"
he offered. He told the best stories about the old Village—before
it became de-gayed, yuppified, and colorless—be they about 86ing
Brendan Behan from Stefan's bar on Christopher Street or baking
bread before dawn with Frank Sinatra at Zito's Bakery on Bleecker
Street. Granger was a Marine buddy from O'Rourke's Vietnam
days. He was a big man physically and looked like Fred Flintstone's
doppelganger. All his friends called him "The Corporal," his finishing
rank in the Marines. Hamill, big and handsome, had that rare gift
of Irish laughter that would leave a condemned man smiling about
his fate. Mellor was a retired banker and man-about-town who split
his time between New York and New Orleans, where he earned the
handle "New York John." He was as comfortable rubbing elbows with
Bobby Short at the Café Carlyle as he was with the local bookie at
Hogan's Moat or mini-skirted devotees on the carpet of his condo off
Bourbon Street. Pinto, Granger, Hamill, and Mellor were rogues, but
O'Rourke knew there were few better men.

A photographer came up and snapped a picture of the five of them.
"If that makes the paper," growled Pinto, looking into the camera but
talking to O'Rourke, "you can kiss your campaign goodbye. Fuck, I'm
going to have to explain to my parole officer why I'm *consorting* with
fucking politicians!"

"It is sometimes better to know the judge," said Hamill slyly, "than
to know the law."

"Now he tells me!" laughed Pinto.

The five men began to climb the stairs leading to the second floor
dining room, where O'Rourke would announce his candidacy for
Congress. The steep twenty-six steps demanded sobriety. At the top,

out of breath, they were greeted by Larry Meagher, the proprietor. "If it isn't the limousine liberal himself," he said to O'Rourke.

O'Rourke knew he was just breaking his balls. "How's my favorite right-wing nut? How ya feeling, Larry?"

"Lost another toe to diabetes," he said, pointing a cane at his bandaged, tender feet. "I'm like an old leper with various digits falling off by the week. Otherwise, I'm fit." Larry was old and tough. He did not complain. "You're looking good, Tone. Sharp suit."

"Thanks," said O'Rourke, knowing Larry was about to hammer him.

"I always say," said Meagher, "if you're going to be *im-PO-tent*, you got to dress *im-PO-tent*!"

"Larry," said O'Rourke, laughing, "do you know John Mellor, Neil Granger, Nick Pinto, and John Hamill?" Meagher nodded. "So, how's the family?"

"Doin' okay," said Meagher. "I got six kids," he said to O'Rourke's group. "Two redheads, two towheads—and two shitheads!" Larry Meagher was a pistol—an old, rusted pistol, but he still had perfect aim. "I hear you're the fags' favorite candidate."

"I hope to be," said O'Rourke. "I can use their votes."

"They've turned Horatio Street," deadpanned Meagher, "into Fellatio Street." Amid laughter, Larry shuffled away.

"He's a piece of work," said Pinto.

"Yeah," said O'Rourke absently as he surveyed the scene, "going to be a good crowd."

"Fuck all of 'em," said Hamill with a Belfast wink, "except the six that will carry your coffin." Wolfe Tone O'Rourke loved Johnny Hamill.

The Old Town was a *real* bar. Almost church-like with beautiful, high tin ceilings, tall, narrow booths like confessionals, lots of wood, marble, tiled floors, and stained glass windows. The urinals—not on the scale of the ones at McSorley's Old Ale House, but pretty damn impressive—were almost four feet tall and were so comforting in their stolid, milky gleam that they made peeing an event. The original gas fixtures were still there, recalling the time when the bar had opened in 1892. On the wall were pictures of Teddy Roosevelt, photos of regulars like Liam Neeson, and book jackets belonging to Frank McCourt and

Billy Collins. A political poster from the 1928 presidential race of Al Smith and his running mate, Joe T. Robinson, declared the candidates "Honest, Able, Fearless." Nothing about being Catholic. Also on the wall were pictures of Larry's uncle, William J. (Willie) Meagher of the "Regular Democratic Organization." Although Larry now bent his elbow to the right, his blood was deep in Brooklyn Democratic politics. One headline from the *Brooklyn Eagle* about the avuncular Willie Meagher declared: "Spurned All Jobs!" "Just like Gerard!" Larry Meagher said, nodding at his son—the saloon dauphin—resplendent in his Hawaiian shirt, with hand to forehead, puzzling over the intricacies of the day's menu, as though he were Einstein doodling with the theory of relativity.

O'Rourke knew how to throw a party. Especially if he wanted to attract the media, those poor put-upon souls of the fourth estate who received little respect and less money. Noon sharp. A buffet consisting of shrimp cocktail, slabs of prime rib, lobster tails. And most important, an open bar. In fact, on the invitation, OPEN BAR stood out in fifty-two-point type. O'Rourke knew his announcement would be well attended.

"You guys get the envelope I left you?" he asked Amy Yax and Christine Reynolds, who were bartending and ministering to the culinary treats. He was talking about the gratuity he had left for them with Larry. Yax and Reynolds—they sounded like a slightly shady law firm—were favorites of O'Rourke. Yax had one of the most devilishly dirty laughs in the city, and shared O'Rourke's political views; she was a dark-haired beauty who ran marathons and wrote wonderful short stories.

Reynolds was Yax's complete opposite—the daughter of a cop, who studied law at Fordham, sweet and upright. O'Rourke had met Reynolds originally on one of his trips to Dublin. He had run into her at the Olivier St. John Gogarty saloon in Temple Bar, where she worked. She had a wonderful disposition and a marvelous sense of humor. One night at the Old Town, a young yuppie sat down next to her at the bar while she was waiting to order drinks. "You come here often?" asked Joe Smooth, shaping his mousse-soaked hair.

"Every night."

"I'm a Sagittarius."

"I'm a waitress," she said without missing a beat.

She now studied law and ravenously read Dostoyevsky. O'Rourke had a sneaking suspicion that she was more interested in the punishment than in the crime.

Sam McGuire entered the room and immediately went up to O'Rourke and gave him a peck on the cheek. "I did good, right?" McGuire had been in charge of the invitations and making sure everyone in the media showed up.

"It's a small room," said O'Rourke.

"So?"

"It's easy to fill a small room." She looked hurt, and O'Rourke felt bad. "Sam, remember, I earned my bones working for Jerry Bruno. He never got out of high school, but he was fucking brilliant. Anyway, I was working for him in Oregon in 1968 on Bobby's last campaign. Oregon was a mess, poorly organized. Bobby wasn't popular out there because he was for gun control laws. He wasn't drawing well and the press was on to it. POOR CROWDS GREET KENNEDY. Kennedy was going insane. So we're having this big rally and Bobby says just three words to Bruno: 'Don't disappoint me.' So—"

"Let me guess," said Sam.

"Go ahead."

"Bruno rented a small hall and people were hanging from the rafters."

"Sam," said O'Rourke, "I knew there was a reason to love you." It was only the second time he had mentioned the most treacherous and dangerous word in the English language to McGuire. It was as if he was defying the ghosts of Rebekah and Grace. Sam glowed and O'Rourke felt embarrassed. "Well," said O'Rourke, trying to cover up his feelings and move on, "the local big-shot Democrat supporting RFK gets up in front of this fire hazard crowd, points her finger right at Bruno, and says, 'You can blame all this overcrowding on that man over there!'"

"What happened?"

"Bob Kennedy looked at Jerry Bruno and gave him the most dazzling thank-you smile you ever saw!"

"Let me guess," said Sam. "Next day the papers said Kennedy spoke to an overflowing crowd."

"You're learning, Sam. You're learning."

McGuire looked O'Rourke squarely in the eye. "You bet I am."

"Let's make the announcement," said O'Rourke and McGuire went to shoo the press away from the bar and the buffet table. O'Rourke, almost unconsciously, touched McGuire slightly on the buttock as she turned away. She turned and smiled and O'Rourke knew exactly how Bruno felt that day when Kennedy had smiled at him.

"I am here today," began O'Rourke, "to announce my candidacy for the 7th Congressional District. I am running for this office for just two reasons: First, to bring this traditionally Democratic district back into the fold; and, secondly—and even more importantly—to tell some truths about the American political system and how it works. I will tell you what I believe to be the truth, whether you agree with me or not, whether it is politically correct or not, whether an election hinges on it or not. The floor is open to questions."

"How do you stand on abortion?" was the first question.

"I'm for it."

"Even partial-birth abortions?"

"What is it," said O'Rourke with a hard stare, "that you don't understand about the three words 'I'm for it?'"

"How about welfare reform?" yelled Wellington Mulvaney of the *New York Post*, his Australian accent conspicuous in the roomful of New Yorkers. Mulvaney hadn't changed much over the years; he still wore those shiny Italian suits that went out of vogue in 1975. It was early in the day and Mulvaney was already on his fourth Bloody Mary. The years since Rupert Murdoch had brought Mulvaney in from Australia to type his column had not been kind to him. Like his ideas and prose, his body had taken on an embalmed look. As the years passed and his drinking increased, the average length of Mulvaney's columns had shrunk to less than 250 words. It had gotten so bad that the *Post* had started printing his columns in 16-point type in order to fill out the page.

"I'm for a fair and just welfare system," O'Rourke continued. "I have no respect for any politician who takes bribes from corporate scumbags—you can fill in the blanks here, Wellington—but wants to act tough with some poor black woman with three kids getting $320 a month from the city. I think that's despicable."

"I think what you're saying is despicable," returned Mulvaney.

"Wellington," said O'Rourke dead-on, "this is my party. If you don't like it, you can go downstairs and buy your own fucking drinks."

"But why," Mulvaney continued, "should the citizens of this fair city have to pay for welfare cheats?"

O'Rourke had had enough. He was getting that look in his eyes and McGuire was getting alarmed. Then Larry Meagher came to the rescue. Larry's raspy voice interrupted the dead silence. "I would *never* trust an Irishman named Wellington," was all he said. Soon there was laughter, followed by applause. Mulvaney blushed. O'Rourke had been saved by his favorite right-wing nut job, very late of the Brooklyn Regular Democratic Machine.

But Mulvaney wouldn't give up. "The president says he never inhaled. How about you? Have you ever used drugs?"

"Yes, I have," said O'Rourke as he prepared to hit the loaded question out of the ballpark. "I have not lived in a cocoon all my life. In fact, I've used drugs with many of the people in this very room. And," O'Rourke added, "I hope you'll ask Jackie Swift the very same question." O'Rourke knew his people. There was no follow-up on the drug question. Mulvaney was done.

"Are you for school teachers being paid on merit?" another reporter asked.

"No," said O'Rourke, "I'm for school teachers getting raises. But I *am* for politicians getting paid on merit. By that standard every single one of them would owe the treasury money."

"Will you take campaign contributions?"

"I will only take *bribes* of twenty-five dollars or lower. And for that twenty-five dollars the contributor will get my everlasting gratitude and a 'Tone for Congress' T-shirt and 'NO MORE BULLSHIT' buttons."

"How do you feel about NAFTA?"

"I'm against it," said O'Rourke. "I'm against anything that takes American jobs out of the country. In my opinion, this is a conspiracy by the Clinton administration and corporate America to screw the American worker. Pretty soon they'll want to pay Americans in *pesos*." There was a slight buzz from the crowd.

"What do you think of Clinton?"

"I think he should get some backbone," said O'Rourke. "He's

been a disaster for the Democratic Party. He's lost the House to the Republicans. In fact, he acts like he's afraid of the Republicans. He's turning the Democratic Party into a bunch of spineless pussies. In fact, he's the best fucking president the Republicans have ever had." O'Rourke looked at McGuire and could see she was not enamored with his use of the word *pussy*, which had escaped his fast-moving lips.

"How about State Senator Thom Lamè?"

"What about *Lame*?" O'Rourke, still needling the councilman.

"The rumor," said the reporter, "is that he'll run in the primary, also."

"That's his right," replied O'Rourke.

"What's your stand on the death penalty?"

"I'm against it," said O'Rourke.

"Why?"

"I'm sick and tired of politicians—most of them without morals themselves—seeking easy solutions to very difficult problems. It's nothing but political grandstanding. Look at Texas. The governor down there—great Christian he is—brags about executing human beings."

"But it's the law in Texas."

"I am not exactly awed by the law either," said O'Rourke. "The law is made by men, some of whom are more corrupt than the people they proudly punish. After the basic laws—those against murder, robbery, rape, whatever—the laws every decent person can agree on, just what are the laws and who is writing them? Take bankruptcy. Who's interested in bankruptcy laws? Banks and credit card companies. Certainly not the schmuck up to his neck in hock. And who's writing those laws? Congressmen who take bribes—excuse me, I misspoke, I mean *campaign contributions*—from those same banks and credit card companies. Yet no one gets outraged over that. This government is bought and sold on a daily basis, and I want to change that."

"How about the Liberal Party endorsement?"

"I won't seek it or accept it."

"Why?"

"Any party," replied O'Rourke with vehemence, "that would endorse Rudy Giuliani over David Dinkins should be airbrushed out of New York City history. One of my objectives in my lifetime is to see the Liberal Party extinct. I know you've heard the refrain before, gentlemen, but one, it ain't liberal, and two, it ain't a party. It's more of a dry cleaners, if you ask me." Laughter went up from the crowd.

"Any other questions?" asked O'Rourke.

"I have one," said Mulvaney, hoping for a comeback. "How do you feel about being denied Holy Communion because of your stand on abortion?"

O'Rourke did not mince his words. "Boots," O'Rourke began, and Mulvaney winced at his hated nickname, "the Cardinal should be ashamed of himself, setting Catholic against Catholic. Requiring a litmus test for faith. In Jack Kennedy's time it was Protestant bigots questioning his religion and his patriotism. Now, unfortunately, it's the bigotry of my own Church. It's no big deal for me personally," added O'Rourke, "because I haven't been in a church except for a marriage or a funeral in over thirty-five years." He paused. "And may I add that I preferred the funerals, because at least I knew the suffering was over." It got a big laugh and Sam McGuire wanted to kick O'Rourke in the shin. "One more thing on the Cardinal. I didn't hear a word out of him on the death penalty. Apparently, it's okay for Catholic politicians to be for the death penalty. If he wants to pontificate on theology, at least the Cardinal should be consistent."

"And gentlemen," added O'Rourke, "don't forget to tip Amy and Christine—the booze and food were on me. Don't be cheapskates." Both Yax and Reynolds burst out in applause.

O'Rourke worked the crowd before ducking into a corner to do quick stand-ups for Channels 2, 4, 5, 7, 11, and New York One. When he was finished, Sam McGuire joined him. "You were great," she said.

"I know," said O'Rourke, tongue firmly in cheek.

"Except for that marriage crack. You're such a fraud," she said, laughing, and as she looked down at his pants, she saw a growing pyramid.

"No, I'm not," said Wolfe Tone O'Rourke.

"You know you're such a *pussy*," said McGuire as she ran her tongue between her lips. They embraced, oblivious to everything and everyone around them.

19.

New York Post, April 20, 2000

THE CHUTZPAH CATHOLIC

By Wellington Mulvaney

Frankly, it was disgusting listening to Wolfe Tone O'Rourke announce that he was going to run for Congress yesterday at the Old Town Bar on East 18th Street.

The only word that comes to mind is "chutzpah."

It's amazing how this man, a man in favor of murdering fetuses, has the gall to defame His Eminence, Declan Cardinal Sweeney.

In front of the free-loading liberal press of this city he had the nerve to bash Cardinal Sweeney, who, as all true Americans know, is one of the great men of this nation.

When questioned by this reporter O'Rourke laughed off being denied Holy Communion because of his Godless beliefs. He made himself out as being some kind of latter-day John F. Kennedy, for defying the tenets of his faith. He even had the nerve to accuse the Cardinal and the Church of being bigoted.

I know it's hard to believe, but he even came out against the death penalty. What right-thinking American is against the death penalty in this day and age?

I have just one question for Mr. Big Shot, Wolfe Tone O'Rourke: How do you sleep at night with the murder of fetuses on your alleged conscience?

20.

O'Rourke took the dusty statue in hand. Everything in his apartment was dusty. McGuire had begun to vacuum, scrub and dust. "The only thing dirtier than this apartment," she had said, adjusting a bandanna on her head, "is your mind."

"Quentin Crisp once said," O'Rourke returned, "that after the first four inches of dust, it doesn't matter." McGuire looked at him with a fair measure of doubt.

O'Rourke began to examine the white statue of the Blessed Virgin, only it wasn't white anymore. It was a weary gray. It had belonged to his grandmother, Rosanna Conway Kavanagh, and somehow it had survived her and made it all the way to New York. He didn't know how, but it had. He thought his uncle, Dick Kavanagh, had somehow brought it with him when he emigrated to New York in the 1930s. Dick was O'Rourke's favorite uncle. Thinking back, he was Jack Paar's doppelganger. He lived in Queens and he was an elevator operator at the Manhattan Hotel on 45th Street and Eighth Avenue. ("It has its ups and downs," he used to tell his young nephew—who finally got the joke.) Next to a civil service job, working at a big hotel was pretty good for a lower-middle class Irish-Catholic back in the 1950s and '60s. Dick was married to his Auntie Rose, the first woman O'Rourke had ever seen with blue hair back in the '50s. They had married in middle-age and O'Rourke's father, always casting a cold eye on matters of the heart, had declared at their wedding: "As He made them, He matched them."

O'Rourke hadn't thought about it until now, but Dick had married a woman with almost the same name as his mother. Dick was also devoted to the Blessed Virgin. He had once been a drunk—being AWOL with the drink, he had missed his ship, saving him from Omaha Beach on D-Day—and to occupy his time he had taken up photography and building altars for the Virgin Mary in his apartment in Jackson Heights. By the time he died, every room in the apartment had an altar, including abbreviated ones in the kitchen and bathroom.

The dissolution of the whole Kavanagh family had begun with O'Rourke's grandmother's death. Mary and Dick in orphanages and young Joe and Frank in the IRA. Up into the Dublin mountains, "on the run," the proverb of the day said. Irishmen hiding in their own country. If the Tans got them, they would be done.

The appendix jutting from the South Circular Road turned into one long thoroughfare with many street names: Camden, Wexford, Aungier and Georges. A crooked street, long and narrow with terrible blind spots. The Auxiliaries and the Tans in their trucks would come down this road and your man, as innocent as could be, would pull the pin and give it a good toss into the lorry. The result would be a Union Jack on a wooden box and a one-way ticket home to England. Soon Camden Street was known as "the Dardanelles." But the British had built their empire on ingenuity and they would not be easily defeated by insurgent hand-grenades. A wire screen was slung over the truck so the grenade became superfluous as it bounced back to the rebel and put him in his own snug box.

"Improvise," Michael Collins would rant to his men. And improvise they would. A fishhook and the grenade stuck to the wire mesh and they began to pile more boxes on the North Wall for their trip home to England.

"Find a solution," commanded the Lord Lieutenant, Field Marshal John French, sartorial and clueless. The solution was found at number 31 Aungier Street, where Joseph Kavanagh had his barber shop and living quarters above.

"Where are ya fucking lads?" they wanted to know. A knee in the kidney did no harm when looking for an answer. "Where are ya fucking IRA sons-of-a-cunt?"

Sons-of-a-cunt.

Out of Rosanna's cunt and into this terrible world, and like Molly Malone no one could save them now.

Sons-of-a-cunt. Was that all Rosanna was to the Black and Tans? Would she know what the word even meant? Her precious privates reduced to fodder to punish her husband and her sons and her country. Did the Tans know that the boys were conceived in love just down the way on Camden Row? Did they care? Poor Rosanna up in Glasnevin. The Tans wanted to know where the Kavanagh cunt was, but this time she was safe. There was nothing they could do to her now. Joseph remembered making love to Rosanna, then closed his eyes as his kidneys absorbed another blow.

They picked Joseph Kavanagh up and in a bum's rush he was sitting up there in the lorry with the wire mesh over it. High up in his own fucking chair, like the King of the Dardanelles. He was a free pass, for when his neighbors saw Joseph Kavanagh up there, high and mighty in a very bad way, there would be no tossed grenades. The Auxiliaries and Tans would be able to wind their way down to Dame Street, make their left, and continue up to Dublin Castle. Home, safe and sound. Then they would beat the consciousness out of Joseph Kavanagh before driving him back to 31 Aungier Street and dumping him like a sack of potatoes on his own doorstep. Then the next day they would do it again.

Joseph Kavanagh would suffer and Michael Collins would cop the revenge. He would end it on a Sunday morning with a squad of boys with Mausers and Lugers and fine aim and the English would leave Dublin City, first in boxes, then marching along the quays with their famous bands playing the Garry Owen.

And the Kavanagh boys would come out of the mountains and they would never be the same. Frank was wild and alcoholic and Joseph was quiet and studious. Then they went against the treaty and Collins's government was after them. Frank skipped the country, going to America to be a merchant seaman, and Joseph ended up in a Free State court for treason. "How do you plead?" asked the judge of the new Irish State in his old English judge's wig.

"Oh my God!" said young Joe Kavanagh. "I am heartily sorry for having offended Thee, and I detest all my sins, because I dread the loss of heaven and the pains of hell."

The Act of Contrition was the wrong response and the Free State would give young Joe a lifelong vacation up in Portrane by the sea, a haven for gentle lunatics. Up there he was harmless and he would study the dictionary, memorizing page after page, just in case someone might need the lend of a word. And he would be a special patient. He would be the patient who went out to fight for his country, went into the mountains like a modern day rapparee and, seemingly, came back into Dublin City as if he had been touched, somehow indefinably, by God.

And it would get worse. Collins would die and Mary Kavanagh would be taken by her father to see him lying in state in Dublin's City Hall, right next to Dublin Castle, recently denuded of English embezzlers. She would look in the coffin at Collins, and she would not believe he was dead because he was so handsome in his general's uniform. But Collins was dead and Ireland was changed forever. Her father, prematurely old from blows of His Majesty's forces, would soon join Rosanna up in Glasnevin. His kidneys were black and blue from the Black and Tans. In less than a decade, disease and revolution in a mad, wet country had taken an ideal, loving family and, with disdain and mindless filth, had destroyed it. The rich don't die for freedom, the aristocrats wouldn't think of it, and the bureaucrats will serve any master. It is the working people who always die for freedom, because they are the ones with impossible dreams and disposable families.

Mary Kavanagh was the only fertile one of the bunch and now O'Rourke was the last Kavanagh. A Kavanagh by the name of O'Rourke. All he had of his mother's family was two photos and a plaster statue of the Blessed Virgin. Except for them, the Kavanaghs might have never even existed. But they must have existed because he was here.

"What are you cooking tonight, honey?" Sam asked. O'Rourke didn't answer and McGuire, scrubbing the kitchen floor on her knees, didn't ask again. She was attacking the floor as O'Rourke searched the statue for clues. She was pretty typical, for a Blessed Virgin. She stood about ten inches tall and he could see where his Uncle Dick had repaired her broken neck and replaced her broken fingers with golden digits. She is stood on the globe with a serpent running under her feet and her arms were outstretched, supine hands open in greeting. The only manufacturer's mark O'Rourke could find is "R & L" on the base of the statue. He took the statue into the bathroom and in the basin places it in lukewarm water, dish detergent and a drop of Clorox. Soon the gray became clear and the statue gleamed white again. He dried it with a bath towel and saw for the first time what a handsome work it was.

"I have to go out for some flowers," he told McGuire.

"For me?"

O'Rourke, still not fully trained or domesticated, almost told her that the flowers were for the Blessed Virgin, but stopped himself in time. "Yes," he said in an epiphany of love, "who else would I buy flowers for?" But as McGuire kissed him and sent him out the door, O'Rourke felt in his heart that there was some kind of womanly competition going on for his very soul and he didn't know why.

21.

"Why me?" asked Nuncio Baroody.

"Because you're perfect for me," replied O'Rourke as he sipped a club soda at his end of the bar at Hogan's Moat.

"How so?"

"You know the gay community," said O'Rourke. "You know how they think. You also know me and know how I think."

"Aren't you afraid I'll embarrass you?"

"No, why?"

"You've heard the rumors, I'm sure," said Baroody, his eyes lowered. O'Rourke hadn't often seen Nuncio sober. He had always been impressed with his sharp wit and utter disregard for protocol. O'Rourke loved people who liked to stir the pot.

"Ah, *roomers*," said O'Rourke, inferring an Irish twist to it.

"Exactly."

"Don't worry about anything," said O'Rourke. "Just do your job and keep your ears and eyes open." As an afterthought O'Rourke added, "And your mouth shut."

"Got it."

"You hire the ringers?"

"They'll be there," Nuncio assured.

"Okay," said O'Rourke. "The campaign begins." The two men left the Moat and walked straight across Seventh Avenue to the headquarters of the Village Queer Democrats. The VQD was created after the gay riots of 1969. They had become a force and every Democratic politician had come to them as supplicant. O'Rourke and Baroody entered the building on Fourth Street, just across from the back of the Riviera Cafe, and walked the lone flight of stairs. They could smell the gym next door before they could hear the grunts and groans of the weightlifters. Inside the drab room there were only a few people. O'Rourke was drawn to their Wall of Fame, where photographs of the famous and the infamous showed the VQD's political clout. The wall also showed the part sex had played in New York City politics over the past thirty years. In the middle was a huge picture of Bill Clinton speaking before the group in 1992, just before the New York primary that had saved his candidacy. There was a photo of Harvey Milk, who was literally blown away, posing with an obviously uncomfortable Senator Pat Moynihan. O'Rourke's eyes were drawn to a picture of Thom Lamè and Malcolm Forbes, the sissy capitalist. "What the hell is this?" he asked Nuncio Baroody.

Nuncio shook his head. "Don't ask."

O'Rourke just smiled and replied, "Don't tell."

There was a wonderful picture of Barney Frank and the late liberal congressman of the district, Fat Max Weissberg. Then O'Rourke started to laugh. He was looking at a photograph of Ed Koch and Bess Myerson, obviously taken in 1977 when Koch won the mayoralty. "The Immaculate Deception," said O'Rourke to Baroody. He was referring to the master chicanery that Koch had pulled off with Myerson. It was the first time the middle-aged Koch had *ever* been seen in the company of a woman, a ploy he used to assuage the fears of the middle-class of Queens and Staten Island. It had been his way of combating the bumper stickers the Cuomo camp had put out leading up to the primary: "Vote for Cuomo, Not the Homo."

"Ed Koch," said Nuncio, "has to be the biggest *a*sexual of all time—but he'd suck you off for your vote."

"Agreed," said O'Rourke. Just then he felt a tap on his shoulder. It was Lizzie Townsend. "Liz, how are you?"

"I don't believe it, Tone," she said as she hugged O'Rourke.

"Don't believe what? That I want the endorsement of the VQD?"

"No," said Townsend, "that you're *actually* running for Congress."

"Why not?" replied O'Rourke. "Life is short."

Lizzie and O'Rourke had met after Thom Lamè had defeated her for City Council. They had run into each other at the Moat and she was distraught. O'Rourke had comforted her and told her that she had done everything right, but that she just didn't have the votes. Lamè had played the numbers—gay males—perfectly.

"Do you have the numbers?" she playfully asked him.

"No," said O'Rourke, "I don't. But I hear there is going to be media here tonight."

"Yeah," said Townsend, "New York One is going to cover the caucus." Right then Lizzie Townsend got suspicious. "What are you up to?"

She caught O'Rourke off guard. "Why would I be up to something, Lizzie?"

"You don't have numbers and you're not upset, that's why," said Townsend.

"In politics," said O'Rourke, "sometimes you have to lose a battle to win the war."

At that moment Sam McGuire and Clarence Black entered the room. McGuire saw O'Rourke chatting up Lizzie Townsend and immediately headed for them.

"Hi honey," said McGuire without warmth.

"Sam," said O'Rourke, "this is Lizzie Townsend. You remember Lizzie, she lost to Thom Lamè for city council a couple of years ago."

A cloud lifted from McGuire as the obvious became clear. "Oh, yes, Lizzie," she said. "Tone told me all about you." Lizzie gave her a smile that said "I'm no threat."

"You still deputy leader of the VQD?" asked O'Rourke, although he already knew the answer.

"Yep."

"You must be excited that Lamè will be here tonight," said O'Rourke with enough sarcasm.

"I am," said Townsend with a big, false smile. "If he wins the congressional seat, maybe I can get his council seat."

O'Rourke laughed, but he was disturbed that he hadn't thought about that. "Who you gonna root for tonight?"

"I am not a political exhibitionist," said Lizzie Townsend lightly as she turned to walk away.

O'Rourke looked at McGuire and gave a tentative look. "You want me to wipe the egg off your chin now," asked McGuire, "or later?"

"Not egg," said O'Rourke. "Grand Clong."

"What?"

"Grand Clong is when you fuck up so bad, you get a rush of shit to the heart." O'Rourke was thinking Congress and Lizzie Townsend was thinking city council. Lamè and Townsend in bed together and things were getting hot.

The crowd began to pile in and O'Rourke saw how conservative they all were. There were a few with earrings and leather pants, but it was nothing like 1975. Back then the members of the VQD looked like The Village People. A mohawk here, a jockstrap, chaps, and a pierced nipple there. With the thought of a pierced nipple he looked at McGuire.

"What?" she said.

"Nothing," replied O'Rourke.

Dominick Carter of New York One arrived with his crew. O'Rourke introduced his people then jabbed the rotund Carter playfully in the belly. "How's it goin' Dom?"

"I'm *really* looking forward to tonight," said Carter with his patterned enthusiasm. "I can't wait to see how you relate to the prestigious VQD," he said laughing.

"When are you going to go live?" he asked Carter, without answering his observation.

"As soon as the caucus endorses," Carter replied. "They won't allow us in here live, but I'll catch the candidates as they come out the door."

"Be glad to accommodate you, Dominick," said O'Rourke.

"I'll look for you later," said Carter.

"What was that all about?" asked McGuire.

"Setting up the stand-up later with Dominick," he said as he turned to McGuire and said seriously, "You must manipulate the media always, and not let them manipulate you. Do you understand?"

McGuire was taken aback by O'Rourke's vehemence. "Yes, I do," she said.

He saw he caught her off guard. "Sorry, honey," he said as he hugged her. "I'm putting on my game face and I want to psych myself up." McGuire saw for the first time how O'Rourke played political hardball.

Thom Lamè entered the room and was mobbed by the VQD members. He saw O'Rourke and his face went hard. He had never dreamed that O'Rourke himself would run. He thought the primary was going to be a cakewalk. Lizzie Townsend walked up to Lamè and a photographer from the *New York Times* snapped a photo of the beaming couple.

"We are," said McGuire, "in deep doo-doo."

"You're a riot, Alice," said O'Rourke, stealing a line from the *Honeymooners*.

"Can we have some silence here?" said Lizzie Townsend into the microphone. "Tonight's a big night for the VQD," she said, "for tonight we are going to endorse a candidate for the 7th Congressional District in the upcoming primary. So far the field contains only Councilman Thom Lamè and longtime Villager and political consultant Wolfe Tone O'Rourke. Mr. O'Rourke has insisted that Councilman Lamè, since this is his home political club, be introduced first."

"Fellow queers," Lamè lisped to the thunderous applause and laughter. He went through his spiel about how long he was a member of the VQD and how he would fight to make sodomy and gay marriage legal. He was passionate, but he was speaking to the choir.

When O'Rourke's turn came he praised Lamè for his courage in supporting repeal of the sodomy laws and the legalization of gay marriage. "I hate to sound like a 'me too Democrat,' but I agree with Councilman Lamè on these important gay demands." O'Rourke was met with polite applause. "But I think there are more immediate matters on the agenda. We are in the grasp of a right-wing hold in this country," began O'Rourke, "that threatens not only gay Americans, but the freedom of every American. Bill Clinton is a Lamè duck." O'Rourke was stopped by the laughter at his Freudian slip. "Sorry about that, Thom," he said laughing himself. He noticed Lamè's hard stare. "As I was saying, Clinton is a *lame* duck. Who will be the next president? This election is about who will be picking Supreme Court justices. We can't go back to back-alley abortions. Now that would be a crime."

"Who cares about abortion?" came a voice from the back. "We're queer. It's not our problem."

"You should care," said O'Rourke with a sudden intensity. "Because if you don't care about what's important to other people, why would you expect others to care about gay rights? To build coalitions you have to compromise, you have to bend. I dare you to stand up to some girl who's been raped and is pregnant and tell her 'It's not our problem.' It *is* your problem. You don't change things by being selfish. You have to empathize."

O'Rourke was surprised by the applause. He stepped from behind the podium. "How many of you are employed?" Most of the hands went up. "How many of you have health insurance?" The show of hands was halved. "What Councilman Lamè spoke about is very important," O'Rourke continued, "but so are other things that are important to both gay and straight Democrats of this district. The need for universal health insurance should be one of the crucial themes of the Democratic Party." O'Rourke had caught their attention and there was silence. "How about adoptive rights? Are there any adoptive gay parents here this evening?" Four hands shot up, a male couple and a female couple. "How easy was it for you to adopt?"

"It wasn't easy at all," said one of the males. "They practically called us perverts."

"Same with us," said one of the females. "You knew they were thinking 'dyke' from the get-go."

"Adoptive rights," said O'Rourke, "are important. That's another area that should be investigated in Washington. And if you adopt, education is important, as is health insurance. It doesn't matter if you're gay, straight, or asexual," he said, thinking of Ed Koch. "We all have so much in common that we must not divide our attention and our efforts. There is only one way to march and that is together and forward as we uphold the great traditions of the Democratic Party in America."

To O'Rourke's complete surprise he got a loud ovation. The two gay couples he had spoken to stood up to applaud and the rest of the audience followed their example. He looked at Nuncio Baroody and smiled, for Nuncio had done his job superbly.

The votes were tallied and Lizzie Townsend came back to the podium. "The vote is as follows. Councilman Lamè 105. Wolfe Tone O'Rourke 25. Thus the VQD endorsement for the 7th Congressional District goes to Councilman Thom Lamè. This meeting is adjourned."

O'Rourke went over to shake Lamè's hand and say congratulations. Lamè ignored him and headed straight towards Dominick Carter of New York One. "How do you feel?" asked Carter.

"Just tremendous," Lamè gushed. "What a tremendous victory. We will go on from here to win the primary in June and the general election come November. God bless America and sodomy on demand!" said Lamè as he and his followers left the building. O'Rourke shook his head in astonishment at Lamè's statement. He knew Lamè had just frightened half the Upper West Side into his camp.

"What's your reaction to your devastating defeat here tonight, Mr. O'Rourke?"

"Geez, Dominick," said O'Rourke, "he didn't say what I thought he said, did he?" Dominick Carter gave a nervous laugh and O'Rourke could see the plea in his eyes. If he was in a barroom he would break Carter's balls, but right now he decided to let him slide. "I didn't think it was that devastating," continued O'Rourke. "After all, I am playing in the other guy's ballpark."

"That may be true," said Carter, "but remember the VQD endorsement packs a lot of electoral wallop."

"You may be right," said O'Rourke, smiling as he remembered a lesson he had learned from LBJ. "At least after tonight, Dominick, I now know the difference between a caucus and a cactus."

"And what might that be?"

"On a cactus, all the pricks are on the outside."

* * * * *

The phone had started ringing the next morning after CNN picked up the feed of New York One.

"They're going crazy," said Sam McGuire to O'Rourke.

"Really."

"You knew all along, didn't you?"

"I figured this might happen," replied O'Rourke.

"How?"

"New York One is affiliated with CNN," said O'Rourke. "I thought there was a good chance of being picked up if I said something to pique their interest. Cable channels can't help themselves. You can bet that CNN wants to beat Fox to *any* kind of political news, no matter how spurious it is."

"CNN wants you," said McGuire.

"Let them wait," replied O'Rourke. "I want something with a little more fire."

"Like?"

"Like Liam Hanrahan of the Fox Network."

"Are you crazy?"

"Like a fox, my dear," and O'Rourke laughed at his simile.

"You are one lucky son of a bitch," said Pepoon as he walked into the office.

"I am never lucky," said O'Rourke with an edge. "I don't believe in luck. I planned this just as I planned those ringers in the audience last night."

"Ringers?" asked McGuire.

"Yeah, those two gay couples with adoptive kids."

"I thought you were lucky they were there," said McGuire.

"They were there because Nuncio did his job and planted them there," said O'Rourke. "And 'all the pricks are on the outside' is ancient history also."

"LBJ," said Pepoon.

"Right you are," said O'Rourke, and McGuire raised an eyebrow in surprise. "Said it right after he was fucked in a caucus. One of the funniest lines in American political history."

"Here it is again," said Pepoon as he took the remote and released the mute button. The three of them looked on in anticipation.

"God bless America and sodomy on demand!" said Lamè once again.

"That should go over big in Middle America," said Pepoon. "He's his own worst enemy."

"He couldn't help himself," said O'Rourke. "Pure hubris. Big win and he's flaunting it—and frightening half the people in the district. He's an amateur."

O'Rourke was now on the TV screen. "At least after tonight, Dominick, I now know the difference between a caucus and a cactus."

"And what might that be?" said Dominick Carter perfectly.

"On a cactus, all the pricks are on the outside!"

"What is our political dialogue coming to?" said a perplexed Wolf Blitzer of CNN into the camera.

"It's Wolf on Wolfe," said Pepoon.

O'Rourke laughed. "Blitzer's the dumbest kraut since Rudolf Hess."

The phone rang again. "It's Liam Hanrahan's people. They want you tonight," said McGuire.

"I thought they would," said Wolfe Tone O'Rourke.

22.

O'Rourke and Clarence Black took a cab up Sixth Avenue to the Fox News Studio on West 48th Street. O'Rourke was silent, which was beginning to drive Black nuts.

"What the fuck you up to?" asked Black, clearly annoyed.

"You packin'?"

"Yeah, I'm packin'," said Black. "That's what you pay me for. What the hell you up to?"

O'Rourke looked at Black and smiled. "It's time for the dry run, Clarence."

"Dry run?"

"Yes," said O'Rourke, "we're going to find out if my plan will work, starting tonight."

O'Rourke was immediately taken to makeup. As he sat there in the chair they powdered his nose and swabbed the sweat pockets from underneath his eyes. He was not nervous. He was focused on Liam Hanrahan—Fox's highly-rated political pundit and bestselling author of *God Made America Just for You!*

Hanrahan was 48. He wore impeccable dark blue suits. Recently he had abandoned his tie and had taken to wearing turtlenecks. Turtlenecks, it appeared, were the leisure suit of the new millennium. One surmised that he thought this fashion statement made him more a man of the people. In reality, it made him look like he had a foreskin crawling up his neck. But the one thing that got everyone's attention immediately was his immaculate razor-cut. His black hair was all shiny. It would not move in a tornado. In fact, his hair made it look like he had a permanent black hockey helmet cemented to the top of his head. He had teeth that glistened like fine china. You could always tell when the Irish in America had made it because their kids had teeth so perfect it looked like Michaelangelo had personally chiseled each and every one. And of course there was that famous, square-cut Hanrahan jaw. Rock solid, with a tiny Cary Grant cleft. Hanrahan was almost perfect.

But almost doesn't count.

He had a flaw and O'Rourke knew what it was—16 years of Catholic education, topped off with a B.A. from Manhattan College in the Bronx. This was something that Hanrahan didn't shout from the mountain. In fact, he was embarrassed by it. Not exactly the kind of pedigree he wanted to flaunt. He wanted to be accepted by all those rich Republicans, those Texas oilmen, those moral crusaders from the prairie with their stark Protestant beliefs and their steady trust funds. They had all gone to places like Princeton and Harvard, not, for God's sake, Manhattan College run by the De LaSalle Brothers. So he didn't like to talk about his pedestrian Catholic education. He also knew his Republican friends really didn't trust Catholics all that much. Papist plotters, that's what they really thought of Catholics. It bothered him, but he had put his lot in with them and there was no going back. He knew they didn't like Catholics, but they absolutely abhorred Jews. They were all for a right-wing Israel, which they would defend with their aircraft carriers and someone else's sons. They just didn't want Jews, or Catholics for that matter, playing golf at their country clubs on the weekend. But that Protestant attitude—we're better than you because we were here first and we have old money—would not stop Hanrahan. He would overcome his background. He would do it by being to the right of the right-wing. He had won their admiration by relentlessly attacking Clinton and he would not stop now. And why should he? Clinton bashing had made him famous—and rich. Without Clinton he had been nothing, just another gasbag talk-show host on an obscure Riverhead, Long Island, radio station. With Clinton he was a star. Bashing Clinton had propelled him to *Celebrity Felony*, the TV tabloid show where he had managed to turn the raised editorial eyebrow into his smug trademark. Deep down, Liam Hanrahan loved Bill Clinton. Then the Fox Network came calling.

Hanrahan was fourth-generation Irish-American. The first Hanrahans had shuffled off the boat at Ellis Island before World War I. They had been working class and Democrats right up through the '60s, when their fear of a socialist state—they apparently didn't need handouts themselves anymore—and New York Mayor John V. Lindsay had chased them into the hands of the Republicans of Nassau County. Hanrahan was typical of the devolution of many of the Irish. He was handsome. He was opinionated. He thought he was tough, but he didn't know the meaning of real toughness—the ability to overcome, to put food on the table for the family while worrying about how to pay this month's late rent. He was like the rest of the bought-Irish, thought O'Rourke—a narrowback without a spine.

O'Rourke was shown into the studio. As he was being seated and miked, Hanrahan perfunctorily nodded at him, then went back to his notes. The red light on the camera went on and Hanrahan looked straight into it and electricity bolted through his body. This is what turned him on.

"You're on *The Hanrahan Debate*," boomed Hanrahan into the camera. "Tonight our guest is Wolfe Tone O'Rourke, Democratic candidate for Congress for Manhattan's 7th Congressional District." He paused for effect. "You might be the only man in the world named after a terrorist," said Hanrahan, his way of baiting O'Rourke, taking him down a notch before a word had even come out of his mouth.

O'Rourke had been dealing with smarmy punks like this for years. He would not be baited. "Well, Liam," O'Rourke began, "I'll have to disagree with you there."

"How so?" Hanrahan said, his voice soaked in a feigned mock.

"You never heard of George Washington Carver? He was named after a terrorist. An American terrorist who also fought the British."

"Ah," said Hanrahan, showing good cheer, "you got me there. But President Washington was a freedom fighter."

"So was Theobald Wolfe Tone," replied O'Rourke. "As was Nelson Mandela. As was David Ben-Gurion."

"Well," said Hanrahan, "let's move on. How does one get named after an Irish Revolutionary?"

"My parents were Fenians, fervid Republicans," replied O'Rourke.

"Yes, Republicans," said Hanrahan, beaming. "Everyone will be one soon!"

"Not your kind, Liam," O'Rourke said evenly. "My parents were Republicans in Dublin. But they were Democrats in New York!"

"Hmmm," smiled Hanrahan into the camera. "Let's move on. Why are you running for Congress?"

"It's about time this district, overwhelmingly Democratic, was returned to the people. It's time this district stops being exploited by Republican sorcery." O'Rourke thought Hanrahan would bite at that statement, but he didn't.

"What do you think about Our Lady of Greenwich Village appearing to Congressman Swift?"

"It's possible," said O'Rourke. "I believe in the Virgin Mary. My mother was named after her. I was born a Catholic, and I'm going to die a Catholic."

"But aren't you a little ticked off that she's on *our* side?" responded Hanrahan.

"Your side?" said O'Rourke. "Which side is your side?"

"Opponents of *Roe v. Wade*."

"Believe me," said O'Rourke evenly, "if Our Lady had a legal message, the last person on earth she'd bring it to would be Jackie Swift."

"That's pretty condescending," said Hanrahan.

"The only thing Jackie Swift knows about *Roe v. Wade*," said O'Rourke, "is that he thinks those were George Washington's options when he was preparing to cross the Delaware."

Behind the scenes, a cameraman started laughing. Hanrahan, distracted by the laughter, squinted into the camera. "Let's move on," he said. "How about your opponent in the primary, Thom Lamè?" Before O'Rourke could respond, Hanrahan said, "Let's run that tape."

There was Lamè on the screen from the VQD caucus: "God bless America and sodomy on demand!"

"Sodomy on demand!" said Hanrahan. "That sums up the agenda of the Democratic Party."

"Why are you so homophobic, Liam?" shot back O'Rourke.

Hanrahan jumped out of his chair and to his own conclusion. "Don't you dare call me a sodomite."

O'Rourke didn't move a muscle, and Hanrahan saw the coldest pair of eyes he had ever seen. Rebekah's "kind eyes" had vanished. Hanrahan retook his seat. "You always hit below the belt, don't you, Hanrahan?"

"Well, O'Rourke," said Hanrahan, "my staff has compiled a dossier on you." He hastily pulled papers from a folder. "Your rap sheet goes all the way back to Bobby Kennedy in 1968. You're a leftist, O'Rourke," said Hanrahan as he stuck his neck out of his turtleneck like a turkey. "Admit it!"

"And you're a right-wing asshole."

The set went dead quiet.

A blush bloomed on Hanrahan's face, which was soon as red as an apple. O'Rourke thought blood was going to gush out Hanrahan's ears any minute. He had him just where he wanted him.

"How dare you!" said Hanrahan, almost in stroke. "How dare you use such filth on cable television."

"Why not?" replied O'Rourke. "The airwaves belong to the American people—not Rupert Murdoch. You propagate filth daily on this channel with your lies and half truths. Fox is to journalism what Adolf Hitler is to the *B'nai Brith*!"

"Fox adheres to the highest journalistic standards."

"You're not journalists," said O'Rourke, "you're keyhole peepers."

Journalists, thought O'Rourke. He no longer believed a thing he read. He knew the *New York Post* made up most of their stories. And he wasn't paralyzed by the sterling reputations of the *New York Times* and *Washington Post* either. American journalism, as O'Rourke saw it, had plummeted from the halcyon days of Edward R. Murrow on radio and TV and David Halberstam reporting in print from the jungles of Vietnam. How could you ever believe someone like the pontificating George Will, infamous for coaching Ronald Reagan for his debate with Jimmy Carter, then hours later declaring as a commentator on ABC News that Reagan had walloped Carter in the debate? O'Rourke knew there was more hard journalism in one of Jimmy Breslin's columns on Marvin the Torch then in all the predictable, flaccid prose of David S. Broder and William Safire combined. But what really ate at O'Rourke were the so-called TV journalists, like Hanrahan. They were good at doing two things—looking pretty and reading a teleprompter. O'Rourke had never forgotten the reader on *Eyewitness News* who had put on a morose face and announced "We have sad news tonight. Isaac Bashevis, the singer, is dead."

"Do you see this?" said Hanrahan pointing to the American flag in the lapel of his blue suit while trying to change the subject and regain control of the debate at the same time.

"Yeah," said O'Rourke, "so what?"

"Men died for that flag!"

"I know," said O'Rourke. "I was with them. Where were you?"

"What?"

"I was in Vietnam. Where were you?"

"I had a deferment."

"Oh, yes," said O'Rourke with a laugh, "you couldn't go because you had an anal cyst, right?" Again, there was laughter from behind the camera, which only encouraged O'Rourke. "You know what an anal cyst is, America? It's a pimple on the ass. This man couldn't fight for his country because he had a pimple on his ass. Imagine that. Meet the patriot from the Fox Network—Anal Cyst Hanrahan!"

Hanrahan was beginning to wonder who had the dossier on whom. "We're getting way off track here," said Hanrahan, still pointing to the flag for all America to see. He was ruffled. He needed a comeback. "You have a warped view of this world and a warped view of this country. Why aren't *you* wearing an American flag!" He thrust his arm at O'Rourke, his index finger pointing accusingly.

"Because I don't have to," said O'Rourke flatly.

"You should be ashamed of yourself, exploiting Vietnam vets," said Hanrahan, his voice dripping with reproach.

"Look in your little dossier," said O'Rourke. Nobody had ever talked to Hanrahan that way. "I don't have to wear your little American flag because in Vietnam I earned a Purple Heart, a Navy Cross, and a Bronze Star so chickenhawks like you could boast about how patriotic they are, but when they had their chance to kill commies they sent guys like me." For once, Hanrahan was speechless. "In fact," continued O'Rourke, "the first legislation I introduce when I get to

Congress will be for universal conscription."

"A draft?" said Hanrahan, looking petrified.

"That's right, Liam, an all-American draft. Everybody goes. Male and female. Rich, poor. Black, white, brown, yellow. Christian, Jew, Muslim, atheist. Out of high school and into the military. No deferments for anyone. It'll give these kids something to do other than smoke dope and jack off. No more elitist armed forces. No more television wars. No more copouts from politicians when they want to invade some horseshit third world country."

"We don't need a draft," said Hanrahan. "That's an outrageous recommendation. It's all academic anyway because you're not going to get elected. I really don't care what you think or stand for—so just shut up!"

"Look, you little wimp," shot back O'Rourke, "we're going to make you chickenhawks ante up to your responsibilities to your country. And for phony patriots like you, Liam," said O'Rourke as he gave a wicked smile, "we're going to have the 'Chickenhawk Amendment'—making the draft *retroactive*."

"You're despicable," said Hanrahan.

"I may be despicable, but I'm no chickenhawk." O'Rourke liked the sound of "chickenhawk" and he used it as a double entendre with Hanrahan: part draft-dodger now willing to get other people's kids killed in stupid wars, part sexual purveyor of young boys. O'Rourke could care less. It was Hanrahan's job to sort out the innuendoes.

"You're nothing but a demagogue," said Hanrahan.

"Don't give me any of that sanctimonious crap," snapped O'Rourke. "You made your bones on demagoguery. If it wasn't for Bill Clinton— the greatest Republican president this country has had since Ronald Reagan— you'd still be a Rush Limbaugh wannabe on that shitty little Long Island radio station." The camera zoomed in on O'Rourke. He couldn't resist. "Fox News. They make it up. You decide!"

"Cut his mike," Hanrahan yelled to the floor director. "I'm not going to dress you down anymore, out of respect for all those *real* Vietnam heroes in the audience. Just shut up and get out of here."

O'Rourke was on a roll, and he couldn't help himself. The floor director was pulling his thumb across his throat in a frantic "cut, cut!" motion, but they were still live. "And, by the way, Liam. I have a special salute for your boss, that great *American* Rupert Murdoch." With that,

O'Rourke gave the finger to the camera.

"Someone call security," yelled Hanrahan from under his desk.

Two black security men, both built like NFL defensive tackles, entered the studio and headed for O'Rourke. They got within six feet of O'Rourke when Clarence Black entered the studio from the other side. "Well, if it isn't Amos and Andy," said Black and the two security men stopped in their tracks. Black was standing, holding his jacket open, showing them his piece. Security did not move and O'Rourke escaped the studio. Black insisted they walk down the seven flights of stairs to the ground floor so they could not be trapped in an elevator. Outside, they found a cab.

"What the fuck was that all about?" asked a frenzied Black, clearly shaken. "There's going to be hell tomorrow. They're going to be all over you."

"I know," smiled O'Rourke. "I know."

23.

O'Rourke and Black met up with McGuire at the Moat.

"I can't believe you just did that," said Sam.

"Neither can I," said O'Rourke, the immensity of the situation hitting him for the first time.

"You guys want a drink?" asked Black.

"Nah," said O'Rourke. "I have a couple of things to do at the office."

After bidding Black goodnight, McGuire and O'Rourke headed for Northern Dispensary Associates down the street. O'Rourke went into his office and McGuire began checking his voicemails.

"Holy shit," O'Rourke heard McGuire exclaim.

Sam was not one for rampant profanity so O'Rourke looked up from the papers he was reading. "What's up, Sam?" he said.

Sam rushed into O'Rourke's office, flushed. "Check this out," was all she said. She played with O'Rourke's brand new phone and punched up his voicemail on the speakerphone.

"This is White House Operator 2403," said the voice. "Stand by for the President of the United States." McGuire's eyes were wide with awe; O'Rourke's eyes were calm in their amusement.

"Tone," said the voice in a pronounced Arkansas drawl, "this is Bill. . . . Bill Clinton. Ah, the President of the United States."

O'Rourke gave a big laugh and was hushed by McGuire. "I think you're in trouble," she added.

"Fuck him," said O'Rourke.

"Tone, how could you?" asked the president. "After all we've been through. After the Good Friday Agreement. How could you do this to me on Fox tonight? You called me a Republican. How could you?" O'Rourke was almost beginning to feel sorry for Clinton.

"Anyway," continued Clinton, "I hope your campaign is successful and Hillary and I would like to talk to you about her senatorial campaign if you have the time." He paused as if thinking if there was anything to add. "Good night."

"Wow," said McGuire. 'Call him back, right now."

"Fuck him," repeated O'Rourke.

"He's right about the Good Friday Agreement. You owe him."

"I don't owe him or Tony Blair or anyone else for doing the right thing," said O'Rourke vehemently. "After eight hundred years of being fucked, you don't just kiss and make up."

"I think you're too hard on the president."

"Simone," said O'Rourke evenly, "love may make the world go round, but hate gives you a reason for living."

"Do you really believe that?"

"What do you think?"

"I think you're a fraud."

O'Rourke laughed. "You may be right."

McGuire shook her head. "How about Hillary's campaign for the Senate? You've got to help her. You can't have Giuliani elected."

"I wouldn't worry about Giuliani," replied O'Rourke. "He's a lousy politician. It took him two tries to beat David Dinkins, and I would not call Ruth Messinger the second coming of Fiorello H. LaGuardia."

"I don't understand your thinking on this."

"Basically, Giuliani is a bully. And most bullies are pussies."

"There's that word again," said McGuire, folding her arms across her chest.

"He's a pussy and a lousy politician," continued O'Rourke. "I wouldn't be surprised if he pulled out of the race, rather than get his ass handed to him by Hillary. The last elected office he'll hold will be mayor of the City of New York."

"I'll believe it when I see it," responded McGuire. O'Rourke looked at her bemused. "You know something I don't?" she added.

"Maybe," said O'Rourke with a sureness that told her Rudy Giuliani would never be senator from New York.

24.

New York Daily News, April 24, 2000

Eye on New York
by Cyclops Reilly

CHICKENHAWKS

A rose is a rose is a rose.

But when is a chickenhawk a chickenhawk a chickenhawk?

Gertrude Stein—help!

I'm confused because I just finished watching *The Hanrahan Debate*.

You've heard of the fox in the chicken coop, haven't you? Well, you should tune in and witness the chickenhawks on the Fox Network. They are something, especially Liam Hanrahan, the bestselling author. To paraphrase Joe Louis, "He can type, but he can't write." In fact, I bet he couldn't tell the difference between a semicolon and an ampersand.

Last night Hanrahan had Wolfe Tone O'Rourke, the well-known politico and candidate for Congress, on his show. O'Rourke is also a Vietnam War hero, winner of the Purple Heart, Navy Cross, and Bronze Star. During the debate, Hanrahan—another one of those guys who always loves a war that other people's kids get to die in—admitted that he was, during our glorious Vietnam experiment, well, AWOL. He had a deferment because of an insidious anal cyst. Well, with that, O'Rourke called him a chickenhawk. A chickenhawk is a description of someone who loves war, but won't be caught anywhere near it.

This is where my confusion begins. I was at a press conference with Declan Cardinal Sweeney the other day—you remember the "I am not a sodomite" press conference, don't you?—and the name of Father Bruce Ritter came up. Father Ritter, who died last year, was the founder of Covenant House, which is supposed to take care of runaway kids, most of whom apparently come to New York from the frozen tundra of Minnesota. You can tell them around the Port Authority Bus Terminal because of their blond hair and purple ears. Anyway, as you may recall, Father Ritter got in trouble because of his great affection for teenage boys. Once

Father Ritter was a big star. Ronald Reagan saluted him at a State of the Union address. Politicians wanted to be photographed with him. Rock stars gave free concerts in order to raise money for Covenant House. But it all came tumbling down in 1990. Ritter was nothing more than a pedophilic megalomaniac. He was, in the parlance of the street, a chickenhawk. (Chickenhawk in this case is sexual—a man who preys on young boys.)

Now I'm totally confused. Liam Hanrahan is a chickenhawk, and so is Father Ritter. But they are different kinds of chickenhawks. Hanrahan is a confessed chicken and Ritter was a very predatory hawk. What's the connection?

You know the only connection I can make? Cardinal Sweeney. Sweeney was a great friend and supporter of Ritter until the hammer fell on the Father. Sweeney is also Liam Hanrahan's favorite prelate. Hanrahan is against abortion, as is the Cardinal. The Cardinal, as you may have heard, has endorsed Jackie Swift, the Blessed Virgin's favorite GOP congressman, because of his strong anti-abortion stand. There is nothing more important to the Cardinal than life itself. Unfortunately, the same can't be said about Congressman Swift and his TV friend Hanrahan. While they are both anti-abortion, they both support the death penalty. Their answer to all crime seems to be "fry 'em first, ask questions later."

I want to know why the Cardinal, the defender of life, is consorting with these two guys? Does the Cardinal value life on two different levels? Is a fetus, a mass of indistinguishable protoplasm, any more important than a flesh-and-blood human being?

Or is the Cardinal throwing us a curveball? Are we looking for the breaking ball when we should be looking for the high, hard one that delineates the pedophiles in the Catholic Church today?

I think the abortion issue is strictly switch-and-bait tactics by the Church to distract us from the likes of the Father Ritters in our midst.

Yes, a chickenhawk is a chickenhawk is a chickenhawk. And apparently the Cardinal is surrounded by them.

You just need a scorecard to tell them apart.

25.

"**D**id you see this?" asked the Cardinal of Monsignor Burke as he discursively waved a hand over Cyclops Reilly's column that sat open on his desk.

"Yes, Eminence," replied Burke, "I have."

"Chickenhawks," said the Cardinal.

"Yes," said Burke. "Reilly makes an interesting point."

"And what might that point be?" asked the Cardinal sharply.

"I think he was referring to how cowardly both types of chickenhawks are."

"His reasoning is flawed," responded the Cardinal.

"But well written," returned Burke.

The Cardinal huffed. "That's the problem with giving a pen to an

Irishman. He starts to crow like a cock and thinks himself some kind of oracle."

Burke wanted to smile at the Cardinal's reference, but did not. "The Irish," he said instead, "are prone to rebellion."

"Rebellion?" the Cardinal said. "I've seen enough of rebellion. There's rebellion everywhere these days—especially in the Church. Gay marriage. Women priests. What's next? Soon they'll be demanding lesbian priests."

"I hold it, that a little rebellion, now and then, is a good thing."

"So you say," snapped the Cardinal.

"I am quoting."

"Who?"

"Thomas Jefferson."

The Cardinal looked warily at Burke. "You are Irish, too."

"As are you."

The Cardinal shook his head. Burke always had a way of agreeing with him while giving him a gentle jab at the same time. "Monsignor," said the Cardinal as he rubbed his fingers across Cyclops Reilly's column, picking up printer's ink in the process, "this is what we're up against."

"Reilly can be tough," said Burke.

"This man has a vendetta against the Church," said the Cardinal before pausing. "And what kind of a name is Cyclops?"

"It's a nickname, Eminence," replied Burke. "He lost an eye in Vietnam. His Christian name is Benedict."

"Do you know this man, this Reilly?"

Burke thought for a moment and answered truthfully, "No, Eminence."

"He's the one who wrote that disgusting story on . . ." The Cardinal suddenly stopped speaking.

"Masturbation."

"Yes," said the Cardinal evenly, "masturbation. Made some Holocaust reference. Everyone was amused . . ."

"Except you."

The Cardinal looked up slowly. "Except me—and Mort Zuckerman," he said, referring to the owner of the *Daily News*.

"Yes," said Burke, "that call you made to Zuckerman put Reilly in his place."

"Yes," said the Cardinal, "but apparently he's back in vogue now." The Cardinal closed the paper and sighed. "We are going to have to be more cunning."

"Cunning?"

"Yes," reiterated the Cardinal, "cunning." The Cardinal plopped down into his chair. "Dr. Costello says we should be more media savvy." The name "Costello" immediately piqued Burke. "We have to know how to manipulate media more than we have in the past. Dr. Costello says we are in a new media age."

"For a simple priest from Niagara Falls," said Burke, "Dr. Costello seems to know a lot about the intricacies of the media."

"I'm not sure I like your tone, Monsignor."

"You are impressed by Dr. Costello, Eminence?"

Burke was making the Cardinal uncomfortable. "Yes," said the Cardinal. "Yes, I am. Dr. Costello knows his way around. He's very experienced."

"Oh," said Burke, "he gave me the impression that he was nothing more than a simple parish priest."

"Not at all," replied the Cardinal. "Costello has friends in high places."

"High places?"

"The Vatican," said the Cardinal matter-of-factly. "He consults frequently with the papal nuncio in Washington." The Cardinal looked up at Burke, who was standing in front of his desk. "He can be trusted."

"Yes, Eminence," replied Burke. He paused, then added, "What does Dr. Costello suggest we do to help the candidacy of Congressman Swift?"

"He suggests that we should take to the airwaves."

"Anything specific?"

"Yes," said the Cardinal as he shuffled papers in front of him. "Costello has come up with a list of 'approved' media that he thinks I should appear on." He handed the piece of paper to Burke.

"Liam Hanrahan," Burke read aloud, "Rush Limbaugh, *Bourne-in-the-Morn*."

"What do you think?"

"They are all right-wing extremists, Eminence."

"And what's wrong with that?"

"Don't you think," said Burke carefully, "that it's too slanted?"

"No," said Sweeney, "these people agree with us."

"Eminence," said Burke with a sudden vehemence, "these people don't agree with you at all."

The Cardinal, surprised, was taken aback. "How so?"

"They are all against your 'working wage' recommendations. They are against unions. They are against the working man. And they are all for the death penalty."

"The abortion question is paramount," said the Cardinal in his own defense. "The Holy Father has made that clear." Burke shook his head involuntarily, but did not respond. "Dr. Costello thinks I should do *Bourne-in-the-Morn* first. He will book it personally."

The Reverend Dr. Costello and *Bourne-in-the-Morn*. What a combination, thought Burke. Burke, by nature, was distrustful of the media, especially media that feigned seriousness while trying to entertain, like Bourne. Bourne was as subtle as an express train. He was famous for his sketches featuring prominent blacks—covering the spectrum from Colin Powell to Jesse Jackson—whom he saddled with slow-witted black voices that would have been familiar in a 1940s Hollywood film. The renditions were nice and funny and racist through and through. Burke thought that Bourne, and those like him, were the new J. J. Hunseckers of the twenty-first century—self-centered, cocksure, and ready to steamroll over anyone who stood in the way of their politics or their paycheck. From Cyclops, he knew about Bourne's drug habit and that they called him "Ricochet" down at Hogan's Moat for the way his eyes would dart to and fro after he had sampled some of Fischbein's Peruvian Marching Powder.

"What do you think of Bourne?"

"Not much."

"Costello says he is a sweet-natured man."

Burke smiled as he thought of Bourne. Then he heard the voice of J. J. Hunsecker in his head: "I'd hate to take a bite of you. You're a cookie full of arsenic."

* * * * *

Sweet Smell of Success was Burke's favorite movie. It was made before he was born, but when he saw it for the first time it brought the old neighborhood back to life. There was the Times Square of his youth in one shot and the Brill Building, just blocks away from his own tenement, in another. But it was the dialogue that had captivated him. Burt Lancaster was brilliant as J. J. Hunsecker on the cusp. "Match me, Sydney," he would say and like magic a light appeared at the end of his cigarette. "I love this dirty town," he would say without embarrassment, and Burke knew exactly what he meant. "You're dead, son. Get yourself buried," came out of his mouth, the words brilliantly chiseled by Clifford Odets. And when Hunsecker declared, "Go now and sin no more," Seán Pius Burke knew he wanted to become a priest.

*   *   *   *   *

"Sweet-natured?"

"Yes," said the Cardinal, "he runs camps for homeless boys."

"He's a man," said Burke evenly, "who laughs at the frailties of people."

"But Dr. Costello says—"

"I don't care what Costello says," replied Burke shortly.

"But Dr. Costello says—"

"Was it Dr. Costello who introduced you to Reverend Cockburn?"

"Yes."

"That was a disaster." The Cardinal nodded. "Why would the leader of the Catholic Church in America—you—want to associate with such a man?"

"It was unfair what Reilly did to him. He ambushed him."

"Reilly told the truth." Burke was getting exasperated. "Eminence," he said slowly, "we have enough pedophiles of our own. We don't need to go importing them from Buffalo."

Suddenly there was a look of desperation on the Cardinal's face, as if a hideous truth had been revealed. "But Dr. Costello says—"

"What's with you and Costello?" asked Burke, his voice rising. "You're a Prince of the Church; this guy's supposed to be a humble Irish priest from Niagara Falls."

"You don't understand," said the Cardinal, his voice suddenly fatigued.

"I understand that he's connected with *Opus Dei*." Burke thought that would get a reaction out of the Cardinal.

"I know. I know," Sweeney said warily, showing no surprise.

Burke was confused. Whatever you might think of Declan Sweeney, whatever you might say, everyone knew he was his own man. "Eminence," said Burke softly, "is there anything you want to tell me?"

"Monsignor," said Sweeney, "I can't tell you. You don't know what a difficult situation I'm in." The Cardinal paused before cryptically adding, "Who will rid me of this meddlesome priest?"

Burke raised his eyebrows then rested his hand on the Cardinal's shoulder in a show of empathy. As he brushed away a few dandruff flakes, he knew it was time to find out a little more about Father John Costello. It was time to call Wolfe Tone O'Rourke.

26.

After his McGuire-mandated exercise trek downtown, O'Rourke took a seat in McCarthy Square, opposite his apartment building. McCarthy Square wasn't a square at all, but a triangle of concrete, surrounded by Seventh Avenue, Charles Street, and Waverly Place. A flagpole, rescued from the 1939 World's Fair, stood in its middle. From his perch O'Rourke could look up Seventh Avenue and had a clear view of the Village Vanguard. As a kid, O'Rourke and his friends used to play stoopball off the monument's front. The pink spaldeen caused havoc as it rose and hit apartment windows six stories up. Back then, in the '50s and '60s, no one thought about who this fellow McCarthy was.

Bernard Joseph McCarthy was a twenty-two-year-old Marine Private First Class when he was killed on Guadalcanal in August of 1942. He was the first Greenwich Villager killed in the Second World War. He was one of the first of sixteen thousand New Yorkers who would give their lives in World War II. There are not many monuments to war in Greenwich Village. In fact, the only ones O'Rourke could think of were the statue of the World War I doughboy in Abingdon Square Park, the Corporal John A. Seravalli Playground over on Gansevoot and Hudson Streets, named for a Village kid killed in Vietnam, and the bronze plaque on the front of St. Joseph's Church over on Sixth Avenue. On that monument were the names of all those in the parish that had gone off to war. The ones with the asterisks did not come back. O'Rourke had double-checked and Private McCarthy was on St. Joseph's list also, marked in death by an asterisk. He had also noticed that, although the names on St. Joseph's "Honor Roll" were alphabetized, McCarthy was misplaced. He was stuck between McCarthy, Charles, and McCarthy, Daniel, who also earned as asterisk. O'Rourke shook his head, hoping that they were not brothers, making Mrs. McCarthy a twin Gold Star Mother.

O'Rourke wondered about this Bernie McCarthy, as his friends surely called him. Like O'Rourke, he was Village Irish and had gone to fight for his country on the far side of the Pacific. O'Rourke was twenty-four when his ass landed in Vietnam and Bernie was even younger. He wondered if Bernie McCarthy had gone to mass in St. Joseph's on Sunday December 7, 1941 or had he lay in bed with a hangover from carousing with his buddies the night before? Probably not, for the missing of mass was a mortal sin and wouldn't sit well in the eyes of his mother. Was he eating dinner when he heard the news about Pearl Harbor, or was he looking at the sports section of the *Daily News*? Maybe he was listening to the football game on the radio that was being played at the Polo Grounds uptown when the announcer broke in with the news bulletin. Did he have brothers and sisters? Must have, because all the Irish had lots of brothers and sisters. And the next morning, what did he do? Did he take the subway to Times Square and enlist in the marines? And did his mother cry when he proudly told her he was now a marine?

And how did he die?

Was it a Jap sniper, or maybe, like in the movie *Guadalcanal Diary,* was he gunned down charging a machine gun nest? Or did he get dysentery and die of the shits?

Although he will be always part of the Village because of this tiny plot of land, it is doubtful that McCarthy ever made it home. They probably just bulldozed him into some mud trap on Guadalcanal.

That was a war different from O'Rourke's war. Many of the GIs killed in Vietnam made it home. Probably even Corporal John A. Seravalli. O'Rourke did not know Seravalli, but both were born in the same year, 1946. He wondered if Seravalli's coffin was closed or if it had one of those Plexiglass windows so the dead hero soldier could be viewed. Was he waked in one of the Irish funeral parlors on West 14th Street or was it in one of the Italian funeral homes over on Bleecker Street?

He wondered if they had a solemn holy high mass for PFC McCarthy in St. Joseph's. Was his mother from the old country, and had she seen the same in Dublin twenty-five years beforehand? Then it was the Black and Tans. Now it was the Japs. Death, as always, was cheap. Did they send useless medals to his mother that just made her cry and cry? Washington gives you medals and a little Gold Star flag to hang in your tenement window, but they take your child forever and you're supposed to be satisfied.

It was a beautiful spring morning and O'Rourke circled the flagpole to see what was written on its base. "Brave Men and Worthy Patriots Dear to God and Famous to all Ages." It also said that it was erected by residents of the vicinity and a local American Legion post. After reading the inscription O'Rourke felt fatigued and went to sit down on one of the two park benches. He was more than fatigued, he was deflated. "Brave Men and Worthy Patriots," O'Rourke repeated aloud. What absolutely cheap crap, he thought. They couldn't come up with something better than Milton's English shit poetry for an Irish-Catholic American marine? Bernard Joseph McCarthy's death fifty-eight years ago had taken the optimism out of O'Rourke's day.

O'Rourke sat looking up Seventh Avenue. Every time he looked at the corner of Seventh Avenue, Waverly Place, and Perry Street—now called Max Gordon Corner in honor of the late owner of the Village Vanguard—he thought of Thomas Merton, because Merton had lived down the block on Perry. For some reason guilt-ridden middle-aged Catholics had taken to the trappist. O'Rourke had read *The Seven Storey Mountain* and had been appalled. It was full of smug pseudo-holiness and flippant remarks about "drunken Irishmen." His inflated ego even went so far as to what kind of rosary beads he preferred. "I used them," he wrote importantly, "in preference to the strong, cheap, black wooden beads made for workmen and old Irish washwomen." O'Rourke wondered what his mother, an old Irish washwoman—with varicose veins like taut wire cables—would have thought of that.

The thing that amazed him so much about Merton, the self-proclaimed Englishman, was how he avoided the three Irish parishes in the Village. He was always going up to Xavier on West 16th Street, Our Lady of Guadalupe on West 14th Street, or St. Francis of Assisi up on West 31st Street, where all the hard cases were supposed to enjoy confessional anonymity. There was no record of him ever venturing over to St. Bernard's, O'Rourke's parish, on West 14th Street. Founded by the Irish who worked on the booming docks after the Civil War, St. Bernard's Church, built in 1870s, had the rare gift of peace and solitude. It was dark, quiet, and beautiful, and even in the hectic New York day you could feel that maybe there really was a God and he just might be listening to you.

Another Irish parish tied to the stevedore trade was St. Veronica's on Christopher Street, established in the 1890s. It had died in the early 1960s as container ships ended the career of longshoremen, who were forced to leave the Village to find new jobs. Now St. Veronica's was a dead parish administered by St. Bernard's and famous for Mother Theresa's AIDS hospice.

The last Irish parish was St. Joseph's on Sixth Avenue, which was the oldest Catholic Church building in New York City. It had once been the home to John McCloskey who was to become the first American cardinal when he succeeded Archbishop "Dagger" John Hughes during the Civil War. To O'Rourke, St. Joseph's reminded him of a ballroom because chandeliers hung from the ceiling. It was all white, antiseptic, and hard, holding none of the grace of St. Bernard's or St. Veronica's. Every time he went by St. Joseph's he thought of his Marine buddy from Vietnam, Kevin Griffin. Griff had taken his mother, Helen—Bronx-Irish hardened by life—to mass there on a Sunday and she was appalled. "What are you taking me to a Protestant church for?" she demanded of her son. "And what," she continued, "do chandeliers have to do with Our Lord, Jesus Christ?"

Like Merton, Dorothy Day had also sowed her wild oats in the Village. In *The Long Loneliness* she speaks of the Village and its importance in her life. She preferred Our Lady of Guadalupe where apparently all the old Commies hung out, but she often went to mass at St. Joseph's after drinking all night with Eugene O'Neill and gang members of the notorious cocaine-sniffing Hudson Dusters at the Golden Swan Café across the way on the corner of West Fourth and Sixth Avenue. O'Rourke was always bemused by the fact that both Merton and Day enjoyed sexual hijinks in their youth—he fathered a child out of wedlock who he abandoned and Day had an abortion—then went on to take stringent views on the morality of others.

They were true believers, possibly because they were converts to Catholicism. Converts are always the most rigid ideologues, rigid because they are secretly afraid what they passionately believe in may be just an illusion. Now there were demands that they both be made saints. Merton and Day, thought O'Rourke. They sounded like a religious vaudeville team. Suddenly, O'Rourke perked up, buoyed by the memory and sacrifice of PFC Bernard Joseph McCarthy, a Marine who died for his country. He could see him in the Guadalcanal jungle cursing as only a Catholic kid from Greenwich Village would. O'Rourke smiled, imaging every third word a heart-felt "fuck," and realized that maybe Bernie McCarthy had more saint in him than either of the Catholic egotists, Merton and Day.

27.

The *Bourne-in-the-Morn* radio studio was in chaos.
The Cardinal was due within the half hour, and Bourne was slumped forward in his chair, his head on the console, hidden by his oversized cowboy hat. "His man," Barrymore—big, black, and disgusted—took the hat and flung it into the corner. He grabbed Bourne by his long, stringy hair and pulled him up so he could see his eyes. They were open, but weren't seeing a damn thing. Bourne was something to look at in his present state—stoned out of his mind, yet resplendent in his jodhpurs, buckskin coat, and cowboy boots with

spurs. He looked like a gay Marshal Sam McCloud after a bad night.

"Where's his shit?" said Barrymore to no one in particular as he dropped Bourne's head back on to the console. He ran his hand through Bourne's coat pockets with no success. Then he pushed his fist into Bourne's right pants pocket. He came away with one of Fischbein's aluminum packets, which he opened, dumping its entire contents on the desk in front of Bourne. He frisked Bourne's shirt pockets until he found his straw, then shoved it up his nose and barked in Bourne's ear, "Hoover left!" Obediently, Bourne vacuumed half the cocaine off the desk. Barrymore moved the straw to the other nostril and commanded, "Hoover right!" Pavlov's dog couldn't have done it better. The desk was clean in seconds.

For the first time since Barrymore had found him unconscious in the back room of Hogan's Moat, Bourne's eyes flew open. Then his nose started to twitch, and eyes started darting about separately in random directions, which is how he came to be known as "Ricochet" down at the Moat. With a tremendous sneeze, a small cloud of cocaine billowed up in front of Bourne's face, as though announcing a papal election. Barrymore relaxed because he knew Bourne was going to be all right.

* * * * *

Bourne thought he was a kingmaker. The kingpin of political radio. The man who could make or break politicians as they came, hat in hand, to be on *Bourne-in-the-Morn*. They came to trade barbs with "The B-Man," but they prayed for his benediction. It had started with Bill Clinton back in 1992 trying to reach out to a segment of voters that had until then been ignored. That was Bourne's demographic: young, hip, affluent, spoiled. If you loved politicians, *Bourne-in-the Morn* was a must-listen. On any given morning there would be the future heroes: Giuliani, the mayor with two girlfriends and one pissed-off wife, or Pataki, the clueless governor. There would be boring senators from Connecticut and obscure congressmen from Nevada, all trying very hard to show their wit and their concern, to convince America that they were just, well, regular guys.

Clinton's election had signaled a rebirth for Bourne. For years

Bourne had been radio's original bad boy, the man for whom the term "shock jock" was invented. He had jolted New York awake back in the 1970s upon his arrival from Cedar Rapids. There had been stunts, suspensions, and annual visits to Betty Ford, but he never actually sobered up. It was all for show. "Yes," he would say, "January 11, 1991, was the most important day of my life, the day I stopped using drugs and alcohol." He had been clean for about a month when he ran into Fischbein one morning in the men's room at the Moat. He had been out all night and had to start his show in about two hours. One Fish-pack kept him awake, two made him funny, three had him screaming to get Cokie Roberts on the phone "right this minute." When she sweetly cooed, "Good morning, B-Man," Bourne would wax poetic like Robert Duvall in *Apocalypse Now*, "I love the smell of Cokie in the morning."

* * * * *

By 7:20, Bourne was functioning. He had Dan Rather on the line talking about the appearance of Our Lady of Greenwich Village. "If this appearance is legitimate," said Rather in that voice that signaled that he was so excited he was about to have an asthma attack, "it could be a devastating blow to the Democrats."

"Geez, Dan," said Bourne, "you mean the Virgin Mary is a registered Republican?"

"I'm not saying that, B-Man, but the consequences to such an appearance can't be overestimated."

"Dan," replied Bourne, beaming after his second Fish-pack, "is there any hope you could get Our Lady of Greenwich Village on *60 Minutes* next Sunday?" Rather never got to reply because Bourne pulled his thumb across his throat, and Rather disappeared from the airways. "Guess the Virgin must have gotten Dan on his cell phone," said Bourne as the Cardinal walked into the control booth, along with Dr. Costello and Father Dowd. "We'll be back in a minute," said Bourne, "with a very, very special guest."

Bourne shook the Cardinal's hand then helped seat him in front of a hanging microphone, which he adjusted in front of the Cardinal's face. Bourne noticed Costello in the control booth and waved to him. Bourne wondered what made Costello tick. He had first contacted Bourne about making a contribution to Bourne's Bivouac for Boys, where homeless children got to spend the summer. Costello had sent a check and had even come up to the Catskills to bless the camp and told Bourne how it reminded him of Reverend Cockburn's GodScou✝s. As long as the checks kept coming, Bourne thought, what the hell.

Dowd took a seat in the control room next to the engineer and watched Costello. The good doctor was beginning to come out of his shell. He reached into his ubiquitous briefcase and took out a stack of bumper stickers that said SAVE THE FETUSES and a brown bag of campaign buttons that declared SWIFT FOR CONGRESS. He pinned a Swift button in the lapel of his black suit and offered one to the engineer and Dowd. The engineer took one, but Dowd declined with a slight smile. As the media spokesman for the archdiocese, he had no intention of playing the partisan.

"Our guest this morning," said Bourne after the station break, "is Declan Cardinal Sweeney, the archbishop of the Diocese of New York. Good morning, your Eminence, how are you this morning?"

"Bourne, I feel like a million bucks."

"That's not surprising, Eminence," said Bourne, laughing, "considering the vast real estate holdings the Church has in New York City."

The Cardinal gave Bourne a perfunctory smile that said, "Move on."

"So, Cardinal, what do you really think about Our Lady of Greenwich Village?"

"I think, Bourne, it is an important sign from God."

"A sign?"

"Yes, Bourne. Who is the most important person in God's life?"

Bourne laughed, imagining what kind of a life God might lead. "I don't have a clue, your Eminence."

"His mother, Bourne, his mother."

"Oh."

"Yes, this is a sign from God that abortion must stop now."

"Now, Cardinal," said Bourne, "you upset a lot of people—mostly Catholic politicians—last week when you had your little press conference with that fruitcake Cockburn."

The strain showed on the Cardinal's face as he gave a little laugh that signaled he didn't want to get into Cockburn. "Oh," said the

Cardinal, "let's give the Reverend Cockburn the benefit of the doubt. The press ambushed him."

"Well, Cardinal, a lot of Catholic politicians wish that you'd give *them* the benefit of the doubt on this Wafer Watch you've imposed."

"Bourne," said the Cardinal severely, "you should not reduce the Holy Eucharist to such a frivolous term as 'Wafer Watch.'"

Trying to get a straight answer—or a funny one—out of Sweeney was beginning to grate on Bourne. He went right after the Cardinal, saying, "You've been accused of politicizing the Eucharist."

The Cardinal shifted in his chair and turned reflective. "You know, Bourne, maybe you're right. Maybe we should all take a breath and reflect on the events that have taken place in the last week."

Bourne was so surprised by the answer that he stammered, "Are you apologizing, your Eminence, or perhaps flip-flopping?"

The Cardinal would not be baited. "You know, Bourne, you made a good point. Maybe we have become too combative with each other. Maybe all of us should allow each other 'the benefit of the doubt.' It couldn't hurt."

"What's wrong with him?" said Costello through clenched teeth as he bolted from the booth, ran into the studio, and pulled a chair up alongside of the Cardinal, startling the old man. Dowd was shocked and his mouth dropped open in surprise. Bourne frowned on the interruption, but there was nothing he could do. "We've been joined by the Reverend Dr. John Costello, an old friend of the *Bourne-in-the-Morn* program. How are you today, doctor?"

"I'm fine, Bourne," Costello replied with a canned affability. "Could I interest you in a SWIFT FOR CONGRESS button or a SAVE THE FETUSES bumper sticker?" For some reason, all Bourne could think of was Flipper.

"Sure, Doctor," said Bourne without enthusiasm, "anything you say." In the control booth, Dowd wondered what made Costello tick. He was pushy, but his answers to difficult questions were platitudes printed on bumper stickers and campaign buttons.

Costello was about to insert a little backbone into Declan Sweeney. "I just want to reiterate," said Costello, commandeering the Cardinal's microphone, "what the Cardinal said the other day about denying the Eucharist to politicians who flout the Church's teachings."

"Dr. Costello," said the Cardinal, placing a hand on Costello's right arm.

Costello ignored the Cardinal. "It is objectively dishonest for Catholics who publicly dissent with the church's pro-life teachings to receive Communion," said Costello. "No one has an absolute right to the Eucharist."

"Are you saying—" said Bourne.

"John," said the Cardinal gently, tugging on Costello's sleeve.

Costello ignored both of them and continued, "Any Catholics who vote for candidates who stand for abortion, illicit stem-cell research, or euthanasia suffer the same fateful consequences. It is for this reason that these Catholics, whether candidates for office or those who would vote for them, may not receive Holy Communion until they have recanted their positions and been reconciled with God and the Church in the Sacrament of Penance."

"Cardinal Sweeney," said Bourne, "do you agree with that?"

"We should all strive for some middle ground," said the Cardinal, before Costello cut him off.

"Anyone who professes the Catholic faith with his lips," said Costello, quickening the pace, "while at the same time publicly supporting legislation or candidates that defy God's law, makes a mockery of that faith and belies his identity as a Catholic. On the basic moral teachings of the church, there is no wiggle room."

Dowd wanted to reach out and grab Costello by the neck. The Cardinal sat there, resigned, as Costello, his voice rising by the second, continued his rant as he found his cadence. "Abortion is an act of violence!" said Costello, slamming his open hand on the desk. "Violence never corrects violence." Another hand slam. "A woman has been raped." Hand slam. "I can understand the desire for an abortion, but then she is inflicting violence on the unborn and she's inflicting further violence on herself. And the violence is never dissipated," he said as both hands hit the table hard, causing the Cardinal to jump in his seat.

"So," asked Bourne, surprised and suddenly tentative, "you are against abortion even in cases of rape and incest?"

"I am," said Costello, spittle shooting out of his mouth. "I always compare the killing of four thousand babies a day in the United States, unborn babies, to the Holocaust. Now, Hitler tried to solve a problem, the Jewish question. So kill them, shove them in the ovens, burn them. Well, *we* claim that unborn babies are a problem, so kill them. To me it really is precisely the same."

"Surely," said Bourne, "you're not equating an abortion on an incest victim to the Holocaust?"

"Of course not," said the Cardinal.

"I am!" said Costello. "What's the difference?"

Dowd was red in the face. He took his hand and slammed it on the control room glass, which caught Bourne's attention. "We'll be back," said Bourne, signaling for his engineer to cut to commercial, "after these messages."

Dowd bolted into the studio. "You have no right," he said sticking his finger under Costello's nose, "to put words into the Cardinal's mouth. No right."

"I was only," said Costello, "trying to clarify what the Cardinal meant."

"You were only," shot back Dowd, "making matters worse."

"Gentlemen, gentlemen," said Bourne, maybe the only sane man in the room.

"Fathers," said the Cardinal, "please."

"The interview is over," Dowd told Bourne. "The Cardinal has other appointments this morning." Dowd helped the Cardinal out of his chair.

"You better watch your step," Costello finally said to Dowd. "I know important people in Rome."

Amid the havoc, the wide-awake Bourne didn't miss a beat. "We'll be right back with Tim Russert of *Meet the Press* and his take on Our Lady of Greenwich Village."

28.

"*Bourne-in-the Morn*," sang the jingle as the commercial ended. A deep announcer's voice boomed, "Welcome to *Hide the*

Eucharist, the game show where the Cardinal has the host and the Democratic politician has to find it! And here's our M.C., Declan Cardinal Sweeney!"

"Ah, good mornin' Bourne, and God bless," said one of Bourne's actors in an Irish accent that would have embarrassed Barry Fitzgerald.

"Ah, good morning, your Eminence," said Bourne with a chuckle. "It's great to have you back on the show two days in a row."

"Ah, it's grand to be back here, Bourne."

"So, your Eminence," said Bourne playing the straight man, "where have you hidden the Eucharist?"

"That's for me to know and you to find out, you worthless bag of shite."

"Your Eminence," said Bourne in a mock shock, "watch your language."

"Ah, ya enema bag, ya."

"Cardinal!" said Bourne. "Now let's get back to the show. Where have you hidden the Eucharist from the pro-abortion Democrats?"

"That's for Our Lady of Greenwich Village to know, and you to find out."

"I don't think you want to go in that direction, Cardinal," said Bourne in ersatz admonition.

"In that case," said the Cardinal, "is it in altar boy number one? Altar boy number two? Or altar boy number three?"

By this time Bourne was laughing so hard that he couldn't go on. "We'll be back tomorrow to see in which altar boy's hide we've hidden the Holy Eucharist," said Bourne, still enjoying the effect of his third Fish-pack.

"God bless ya, Bourne," said the ersatz Cardinal and a commercial ended the charade.

* * * * *

Monsignor Burke walked into the kitchen where the Cardinal and Father Dowd sat at opposite ends of a table, listening to the radio. Dowd turned it off.

"I'm ruined," said the Cardinal. "My God, I ruined it for everybody."

"Did you hear Bourne?" Dowd asked Burke.

"I did."

"What are we going to do?"

"The first thing we're going to do," said Burke, "is stop taking advice from Father Costello."

"You're right, Monsignor," the Cardinal said. "I should have listened to you."

With that Father John Costello entered the kitchen. "You've ruined us," the Cardinal told him.

"What are you talking about?" said Costello.

"Did you hear your pal Bourne this morning?" said Dowd.

"No, I didn't."

"He made a mockery of the Cardinal," continued Dowd. "They invented a game show skit called *Hide the Eucharist*."

"Oh," said Costello with a discursive wave of his hand, "it's only Bourne having a little fun."

"He insinuated," said Burke in a frozen voice, "that the Eucharist is hidden in the rump of an altar boy."

"It's only harmless fun," repeated Costello.

"I don't find it funny at all," said Burke. "And I don't want you bothering the Cardinal anymore. If you have anything to say to the Cardinal, come through me. Maybe it's time to go back to Niagara Falls—or wherever you're from."

"But Eminence," said Costello, ignoring Burke completely, "I have you booked on Rush Limbaugh later in the week, and Liam Hanrahan next Monday."

"There will be no more bookings," said Burke.

"I want to know what his Eminence thinks," said Costello, heading towards the Cardinal, who was still seated at the table. As Costello approached, the Cardinal shifted away, as if in fear.

Seán Pius Burke put his powerful body between Costello and the Cardinal. "Get out," he said to Costello. "I don't know what your game is, but I want you out."

"My work here is not done," insisted Costello.

"You mean *Opus Dei*'s work, don't you?"

Costello was taken by surprise. A smirk came over Costello's face and he fingered the crucifix that hung around his neck. "I'll go when the nuncio says my work is done—and only when it's done. I take my orders from the nuncio, and the nuncio takes his orders—"

"The pope," Burke interrupted.

"You're very bright, Monsignor. Maybe too bright. If the Cardinal will excuse me," said Costello with the conceit of the well-connected. "I'll take my leave now."

After he was gone, the three priests were silent.

"He's a bugger," was all the Cardinal could muster.

"What can we do?" Dowd asked.

The Cardinal held his hand to his jaw, as if he had a pounding toothache. "Maybe Congressman Swift can help?" the Cardinal said without too much hope.

"The last person to deal with Costello, I think, is Jackie Swift," said Burke. "I'll think of something."

Burke wasn't too concerned. He had already asked Tone O'Rourke to find out what he could about Costello. A sweet smile of conspiracy crossed Burke's face. "This," said the Monsignor, "just might be a job for the Fenians."

29.

"It's Stinky!"

"What?" asked O'Rourke.

"You don't want to know," said Baroody laughing.

"Oh, yes I do," said O'Rourke emphatically as he pulled the snapshot of Costello out of Baroody's hand. "You sure?"

"Positive."

"Where?"

"Paris in the late '70s," replied Baroody.

"What's his MO?" asked O'Rourke.

"Bagman."

O'Rourke was silent for a minute. "For whom?" he said deliberately, the two words stretched wide apart.

"Back then," said Baroody, "it was Solidarity in Poland. His bank in Madrid wired the money into the papal nuncio's account in Paris."

"The nuncio, your boss?" interrupted O'Rourke.

"Yeah," said Baroody. "The nuncio would withdraw it, then carry it to Wojtyla in Krakow who made sure Solidarity got it."

"*Karol* Wojtyla?"

"That's right," smiled Baroody, "the present pope."

"Son of a bitch," was all O'Rourke could muster.

"But that's not why they call him Stinky," said Baroody, with a gleam in his eye.

"Let me guess."

"You got it."

"You guys," said O'Rourke, trying to be diplomatic, "hang out together?"

"No," said Baroody, "I'm not into that."

"Good to hear."

"Well," said O'Rourke, "we know why he's here."

"Money?"

"Exactly. This guy likes to spread the *Opus Dei* wealth around. Right now I think he's spreading it around this congressional district."

"You get yours yet?" said Baroody, trying at humor.

"No, I didn't," replied O'Rourke, "and I don't think I'm going to get any of that money. But I bet Lamè is getting it, and I'm sure Jackie Swift is stuffing his safe deposit box with cash. If we don't remove Costello from the equation, we're in trouble."

"How you do that?"

O'Rourke hesitated for a second. "Maybe," he said, breaking a smile, "a little Belfast justice is in order."

30.

"Did you get my check?" was the first thing that O'Rourke said to the monsignor when he heard his voice on the phone.

"I did indeed," said Burke, "but that's not what I'm calling about."

"Costello?"

"That's it."

"Meet me."

"Where?"

"Union Square. Under General Washington's balls. Three o'clock. Lose the collar." Before Burke could ask what the hell he was talking about, O'Rourke hung up on him.

O'Rourke, Burke knew, loved being cryptic. Burke, dressed in civilian clothes, left the chancellery and walked over to 51st Street and Lexington where he took the downtown local to Union Square. He emerged across the street from what was, in his youth, "S. Klein on the Square," the renowned department store for the working stiff. Burke smiled. He could still envision those large tables on the ground floor where twenty or thirty women would fight and pull and scratch as they grabbed for that perfect brassiere. It was Bloomingdale's for the poor. He also recalled that there was an Automat around the corner on East 14th Street between Fourth Avenue and Irving Place. He remembered it was there that he had his first sampling of creamed spinach—fresh from its little glass ten-cent door. That was the New York that Burke grew up in and loved. Now Klein's and the Automat had been replaced by a tall, spiritless structure that annoyingly blocked his view of the clock in the Con Edison tower on East 14th Street.

General Washington's balls. Some clue. He walked along 14th Street to Broadway and looked across into Union Square. He saw a man on a horse and went to see who it was. It was George Washington all right. Burke went behind the statue and saw Wolfe Tone O'Rourke sitting on a parapet staring into a manila folder.

"Hello, Congressman," said Burke.

O'Rourke, his focus broken, looked up to see the monsignor. "And how is the *sagart* of Hell's Kitchen today?" he asked, using the Irish word for priest.

Burke laughed. "Tone," he said, "the *sagart* of Hell's Kitchen is in big trouble." O'Rourke pointed to the parapet, and Burke took a seat. "Where are they?"

"What?"

"Washington's balls?"

"Washington ain't got any balls," said O'Rourke with a smile, then pointed under the tail of Washington's horse.

Burke laughed. "So they're not really George's balls."

"Technicality."

It was time to get down to business. "I know you're busy, Tone, with the campaign and all, but I had to talk to you about this guy Costello."

O'Rourke stuck his hand out and wiggled his fingers downward, telling Burke to lower his voice. "I had Clarence Black, my investigator, take a look at the life and times of the Reverend Dr. John Costello," said O'Rourke, almost in a whisper, as he held up the folder for Burke's inspection. "He's a busy man. That him?" said O'Rourke holding out a photo of Costello for Burke to identify.

"That's him. He isn't from Dublin, is he?" queried Burke.

"Nope," said O'Rourke. "An orphan lad from Leitrim. Brought up by the Irish Christian Brothers."

"Maynooth?"

"In his dreams," laughed O'Rourke, "and part of his legend. Spent his vocation in England where he was ordained. Been with *Opus Dei* since his teen years. He's spent a lot of time in Spain, home of *Opus Dei*. When Wojtyla became pope, he moved to the Vatican. He has an apartment in Niagara Falls, on the Canadian side, but he spends a lot of time in Washington with the papal nuncio."

"He's not even affiliated with a church up in Canada?"

"No," said O'Rourke. "He's a free agent. If we were talking spies, I'd call him a 'sleeper.'"

"What's his game?"

"Money," replied O'Rourke. "Very active Canadian bank account."

"That's it," said Burke, snapping his fingers. "The son of a bitch is *Opus Dei*'s bagman in this country."

"You learn fast," said O'Rourke with a smile.

"It's coming together now," said an animated Burke. "He's making all these contributions to Cockburn's GodScou✞s, to Bourne's Bivovac for Boys. He's buying media attention to fight Free Choice. That's got to be it." O'Rourke started laughing. "What's so funny?"

"He's trying to fuck me, too," said O'Rourke. Burke smiled. Others always cleaned up their language around the monsignor, but not Tone O'Rourke.

"How so?"

O'Rourke waved a paper in front of Burke. "Take a look."

The numbers meant nothing to Burke. "I don't get it."

"But my opponents do," said O'Rourke. "Checks were written to the campaigns of Thom Lamè and Jackie Swift. A little double-barreled action for the peripatetic Father Costello."

Burke shook his head. "This guy plays hardball. The Cardinal's frightened of him, you know."

"I thought the Cardinal loved this guy."

"He did, until he started pushing him into the Reverend Cockburn and then *Bourne-in-the-Morn*. Costello is a walking disaster—and he's just warming up. He's got the nuncio and the pope in his corner, and he ain't afraid to push. Lot of hubris there." Burke paused. "What did you mean by that 'Belfast justice' comment the other day?"

O'Rourke laughed. "This guy's wired," he said. "He has three passports, Canadian, Irish, and Vatican. He lives in Canada, but his work is in Washington. He has no work permit here. He shouldn't be allowed to conduct business in this country. I don't like him sending money to my opponents, and I think I have a way to stop him from doing it."

"Belfast?"

"What if he was a terrorist on the run?"

"What if?" replied Burke.

"You think MI5 might be interested?" Burke nodded. "See that Virgin record store?" Burke nodded again. "Well, they sell disposable cell phones. Go buy one." Burke got up to leave. "And don't use a credit card," added O'Rourke.

Ten minutes later Burke returned with the cell phone and gave it to O'Rourke. Burke dialed *Sinn Féin* HQ in Belfast. "Tubby Cuddihy," he said.

"Who should I say is calling?"

"Skin-the-Goat."

Tubby Cuddihy came on the line. "And how is my favorite New York Invincible?"

O'Rourke laughed. "Fine, and how are things in *Béal Feirste*?"

"Quieter."

"I bet," said O'Rourke. "How's the waistline?"

"They still call me Tubby."

O'Rourke laughed. "Should we speak in Irish?"

"Why bother?" asked Cuddihy. "MI5 has plenty of Gaelic speakers if they're listening. What can I do for you?"

"Jack Costello still missing?" O'Rourke was referring to IRA Jack Costello who was still in hiding years after winging a shot at Margaret Thatcher. He was one Fenian there would be no amnesty for.

"Missing, but not lost," said Cuddihy cryptically.

"I see. What if he were to be caught in Washington?"

"Jack could use the diversion, if you know what I mean."

O'Rourke knew exactly what Cuddihy meant, and he would be happy to supply Jack a distraction so he could walk the other way.

"I have a candidate."

"But won't they know?" asked Cuddihy.

"They will eventually," replied O'Rourke, "but it still helps Jack. And it will help someone prominent here—and embarrass the English when they discover they've plucked the wrong Costello"

"Sounds grand."

"I have your permission?"

"Yes, you do," said Tubby Cuddihy and he hung up the phone.

O'Rourke turned to Burke. "We're in business."

"Is it going to be alright?" asked Burke, now concerned for the first time.

"It will be fine," said O'Rourke. "Tell the Cardinal he owes me one." The look of nervousness on the monsignor's face did not dissipate. "Have time for a drink?"

"No," said Burke. "I have to get back to the chancellery."

"I'll see you then," said O'Rourke.

"Thanks, Tone, I really appreciate it."

Burke wondered if he had done the right thing. He kept his eye on

O'Rourke as he crossed 14th Street. Burke watched as O'Rourke came to the curb and casually threw the cell phone into the sewer, before innocently walking away as if it was something he did every day.

31.

"So, what are we going to do about Thom Lamè?" O'Rourke asked McGuire, Black, and Nuncio Baroody.

"Do you want to challenge his petitions?" asked McGuire.

"No," replied O'Rourke. "He's been down the petition road before. He knows what he's doing."

"How about his finances?" Clarence Black offered.

"That," said O'Rourke, "is a worthy start."

"Background check?"

"Definitely."

"What exactly are we looking for?" McGuire asked.

"I don't know," admitted O'Rourke. "Look at his finances. Are they in order? Is he paying money to someone he shouldn't be? Does he have any bad habits that cost money? Things like that. Anyone have any other things we should check out?"

"This may seem crazy," said Baroody, "but I think you should see if he has a video rental account."

"Why?" asked Black.

"As the boys as Julius's like to say, Lamè might be a 'fauxsexual.' Let's make sure he's the fag he professes to be," said Baroody, "if you know what I mean."

"I don't know what you mean," replied Black, "but I'll look into the probability."

"Yes, Clarence," seconded O'Rourke, "check it out."

"What's all this supposed to get us?" asked McGuire in a voice that said she wasn't that happy with the sleaze factor entering into the race.

"Something," replied O'Rourke. "Maybe nothing."

"I think you're wasting your time," said Sam.

"Do you remember Edwin Edwards, the former governor of the great state of Louisana?"

"Yeah," said McGuire, "I think he's still doing time."

"Well," said O'Rourke, "he once said that the only way he could lose an election was 'to be caught with a dead girl or a live boy.' That's what we're looking for."

"And in this district," added Baroody ominously, "I hope it's not a live boy."

32.

New York Daily News, May 3, 2000

Eye on New York
by Cyclops Reilly

VIETNAM COMES TO 72ND STREET

Vietnam came to 72nd Street today.

Wolfe Tone O'Rourke, who is seeking the Democratic nomination in the 7th Congressional District, was shaking hands with early morning commuters who were heading for the subway to take them downtown to work.

The sun was brilliant and the Ansonia Hotel, in the background, stood out as a New York jewel.

O'Rourke is one of those candidates that the establishment hates—because he says what he believes, not what the pundits and the main stream media want to hear. He's been called dangerous, ingenuous, and idealistic. Along with Charlie Rangel and Chuck Schumer, he might be the best politician alive in New York City today.

It was your typical "meet and greet." O'Rourke shook the commuters' hands as they headed into the ground. Some recognized him from his little tête-à-tête with Liam "Anal Cyst" Hanrahan on the Fox network last week.

The greetings were friendly until a terrible sound brought O'Rourke back to his days as a Navy medical corpsman in Vietnam. O'Rourke turned around and saw an 18-wheeler turn a messenger's bicycle into a twisted paperclip. The tractor-trailer driver slammed on the brakes as quick as he could and the only sound on West 72nd Street and Broadway was the screams of the young black man under the cab's right wheel.

O'Rourke broke away from the subway commuters and ran to the injured man. In one motion he grabbed him by his belt buckle and pulled him out from under the truck and into Broadway. O'Rourke then pulled his own belt off and ran it under the messenger's left leg, up by the groin. By this time blood was shooting into O'Rourke's chest because the main artery had been severed. O'Rourke pulled the belt tight and the messenger left out a scream that echoed all the way down 72nd Street. O'Rourke pulled tighter and the blood flow slowed.

O'Rourke knew the messenger might bleed to death.

Sirens in the background became louder as the FDNY ambulance pulled up. O'Rourke instructed the paramedic to the situation and the young man took over.

O'Rourke dropped to sit on the sidewalk as the medics worked on the messenger. Simone McGuire, his campaign manager, came over and hugged O'Rourke. Soon she too was covered with the messenger's blood. O'Rourke looked dazed as he tried to hail a cab to get downtown to his office in the Village. Seeing the blood covered O'Rourke, cabbies accelerated and passed by.

O'Rourke's performance had to be seen to be believed. It was a once-in-a-lifetime action drama that probably took all of two minutes. He did what every Navy corpsman's is trained to do—give the patient a chance to survive.

Somewhere, I had seen it before.

Yes, it was the day in Vietnam when a Navy medic named O'Rourke saved my life.

33.

"You're in trouble," said Vito Fopiano, holding up the *Daily News* in front of Jackie Swift. There was O'Rourke, in glorious color, tending to the injured bicycle messenger, covered with his blood. The headline said: TONE SAVES. The story was on page three along with Reilly's column.

"Yes, you are," seconded Madonna-Sue.

They both seemed to be enjoying Swift's misery. Swift wished they would all go away.

"O'Rourke's a fucking war hero, for Christ sakes," continued Vito. "What are you going to run on? That you introduced a bill to ban pornography from the Internet?"

"If I recall," spoke up Peggy Brogan, "that Ban-the-Porn idiocy was your idea, Vito. You called it playing to the base." Vito looked at Brogan's ass and wanted to talk about anything but porn.

"Yeah," put in Madonna-Sue as she rubbed her pregnant belly, "that was your idea, Daddy."

"As a Korean War veteran—" said Vito as he launched into his "I-have-seen-the-face-of-war" speech.

"Cut the shit, Vito," said Swift, showing some life. "You were a fucking quartermaster in Tokyo, handing out underwear. You never saw a shot fired in anger. Save your crap for those old guineas at the VFW."

Vito was quiet, and did not speak for a good minute. "You've got to win, Jackie," he said quietly. "If you lose, Madonna-Sue will be a target next and she'll never have a chance to be Speaker of the House."

"The only Speaker of the House here," said Swift, "is you, Vito. You have more input into our marriage than I have."

Brogan was exhilarated that Swift had finally stood up to Vito. She especially loved the jab about "those old guineas at the VFW." The Irish had spoken. "Okay," she finally said, "we're in a fix. But I think it's something that can be fixed."

"Who really is this guy O'Rourke?" and everyone knew that Madonna-Sue had asked the most important question of the day.

All eyes turned to Swift because he knew who O'Rourke was better than anybody. They had been through the political wars together, going back to 1968 when Bobby was running for president and Paul O'Dwyer was trying to unseat Jack Javits in the Senate. By June, Bobby was dead and in November Javits put an end to O'Dwyer's dream. 1968 was a loser's year for both O'Rourke and Swift. Yes, Swift knew who O'Rourke was, but he didn't particularly want to go there.

"Who is that negress who's always with him?" asked Vito, holding up the *Daily News* open to page three and pointing at the picture of McGuire embracing O'Rourke.

"That's his campaign manager," Swift said quietly. "Simone McGuire. Used to work for Schumer."

"Anything more to it?" put in Vito.

Swift knew there was more to it, but didn't want to dabble in the domestic affairs of O'Rourke. Besides, Swift's house was 100 percent glass.

"They're lovers," said Brogan suddenly.

"Lovers?" said Vito, and the three other people in the room began to feel uncomfortable.

"That's the word on the street," said Brogan.

"Interesting," was the only thing Madonna-Sue could muster as she searched the bottom of her handbag for a cigarette. Swift and Brogan looked at each other ominously. It was generally not a good sign when Madonna-Sue, out-of-the-blue, started lighting up for no reason.

"A negress," said Vito with just a trace of a smile crossing his face. "Anything else on O'Rourke?" he added. "Drugs? Boyfriends?"

Jackie had absolutely nothing to say about drugs of any kind. He just wished this meeting would end. "He's never been married, I believe," said Madonna-Sue. "Middle-aged Irish guy. What's up with that?" Madonna-Sue obviously didn't understand the Irish and Swift was not about to help her out.

"You sure he's not a homo?" asked Vito hopefully, suddenly turning O'Rourke into some kind of all-gender sex machine.

"Even if he was gay, that's not a negative in this district, Vito. You're not on Staten Island now," Swift said, reminding Vito that the political tricks of Richmond County did not apply on Manhattan Island.

"How did he make his money?" Vito wanted to know.

"Political consultancy," replied Swift. "He gets paid handsomely to beat some of the dunces you guys at the Republican National Committee pick to run for office. He was one of the guys—don't you remember, Vito?—who took Alphonse D'Amato out." Vito was silent. D'Amato was Vito's meal ticket and now he was gone. Vito noticed that people were not as in awe of him without D'Amato in the United States Senate. It was all the more reason to hate Wolfe Tone O'Rourke.

"So, let's see," said Madonna-Sue. "He's a millionaire war hero who daily saves bicycle messengers from certain death just for the fun of it. You *are* in trouble."

"Didn't he have some trouble with the navy?" queried Vito. "Sometimes you can turn a negative into a positive."

"Didn't he have to leave the country or something?" said Madonna-Sue as smoke rushed from her nose.

Jackie Swift knew O'Rourke's story intimately, but he kept his mouth shut.

"He wasn't connected with the IRA, was he, Jackie?" asked Brogan. Swift gave Brogan a look that said "don't go there," but it was too late.

"Wasn't he involved in getting Clinton to give Gerry Adams a visa to get into the U.S.?" added Madonna-Sue.

"Yes, he was," said Vito, his voice rising with new hope. "Why, this guy's nothing more than an IRA terrorist. Let's find out for sure."

"Might be something Wellington Mulvaney might be interested in," added Madonna-Sue.

"Great idea," said Vito, and the two Fopianos were now actually smiling. Brogan looked at Swift and wished she had kept quiet.

Jackie Swift looked ahead in glum silence, hoping that the ghost of Paul O'Dwyer would forgive him the ultimate Irish betrayal, that of unintentional informer.

34.

"It's a girl!" Clarence Black said triumphantly as he walked into O'Rourke's office.

"What?" said McGuire and O'Rourke simultaneously.

"You know you were talking about a 'dead girl or a live boy?' Well, it's a live girl. In Illinois, where Lamè went to graduate school. Pays her $967.35 every month in child support. This guy's straight."

"Or a switch-hitter," added O'Rourke.

"And Nuncio was right," continued Black.

"What?"

"About the movies he rents. He never rents gay porn. He only rents straight porn. He's a big fan of Buttman's movies."

O'Rourke laughed, as did Black. "Buttman? Who's Buttman?" asked McGuire.

"Let's just say he's the Federico Fellini of porn," said O'Rourke.

"How do *you* know?" asked McGuire sharply.

"Well . . . well," stammered O'Rourke.

McGuire cut him off. "So you like to watch dirty movies about women's behinds." O'Rourke had been found guilty and knew he was headed for the gibbet. "I don't understand men and their porn." She dropped herself into a chair and just stared at O'Rourke who looked and felt as guilty as that day when his mother had caught him stealing that peapod. "Well," said McGuire, "at least you won't have to watch Buttman movies anymore." O'Rourke felt he had been reprieved at the last minute by the governor. "What are you going to do with this information?"

"What's the woman's name in Illinois?"

"Sarah Fineman."

"Sam," said O'Rourke, "get Thom Lamè on the phone. Tell him we have some news for him."

"News?"

"Yeah, tell him we know who Sarah Fineman is, his HIV has taken a turn for the worse, and he's not running for Congress this year."

35.

"Whatdaya think?" asked O'Rourke as he admired his medals in the mirror. Baroody and Black looked on, but didn't say a word.

McGuire, a late arrival to the office, stood in the doorway, a look of disgust on her face. "You look," she said, "like Leonid Fucking Brezhnev."

"And Happy Mother's Day to you, too," said O'Rourke as Black and Baroody stepped aside allowing McGuire to enter.

"And what's so good about it?"

"We were just seeing what kind of American insignia Tone should wear on the talk shows," said Baroody.

"God," said McGuire, "don't wear those bulky medals. You look like a refugee from the politburo. Got any Alka-Seltzer?" O'Rourke unpinned the medals and carefully put them back in their cushioned box. "Try an American flag," she suggested.

"Like the rest of the phoneys?" said Black.

"It's your flag too, you know," countered McGuire.

"Good point," conceded Baroody. "What's the matter with your stomach?"

"Upset," replied McGuire. "Must be food poisoning or something. Tone did scallops last night."

"I'm okay," replied O'Rourke.

"It would be impossible to poison you," McGuire shot back, "after all the scrap you put in your body over the years."

O'Rourke did not want to get into a fight this early in the morning and tried to change the subject. "You up to making the trip with Clarence and me to D.C. for *Sunday Press Box*?"

"That's my job. I'll be with you," she said as she fished in a glass container on the windowsill. "I'm still your campaign manager." She threw a pin-on American flag at O'Rourke. "Put that on."

O'Rourke stuck it in his lapel and looked at himself again in the mirror. He shook his head. "Give me another one of those things."

McGuire flipped one across the room and O'Rourke caught it. He stuck it in his other lapel and smiled. "That's the statement I want to make."

"You look like a fool," said McGuire.

"That I am," replied O'Rourke. "Let's go over a few things before we head for the shuttle."

The four of them sat down and O'Rourke stared at a list he had on a legal pad. "First, Sam, great job getting me on *Sunday Press Box*."

"Thanks," said McGuire, and her sweet smile returned. "Dan Dorsey and I go back a while with Senator Schumer."

"Yeah," cut in O'Rourke, "they both love the sound of their own voices. Okay, let's see where we are. The 800-number and cheap sign?"

"Got it."

"What's the latest on Lamè?"

"He's still thinking about it, he says," said McGuire.

"Thinking about what?" said O'Rourke with a touch of exasperation in his voice. "I'm about to ruin his career." McGuire shrugged her shoulders. "Get him on the phone," ordered O'Rourke. McGuire took out her cell phone, dialed, and handed the phone to O'Rourke, who was surprised when Lamè answered this early on a Sunday morning. "Thom, Tone O'Rourke here." McGuire reached over O'Rourke and set the phone to speaker mode.

"Getting ready for *Sunday Press Box*?" There was a touch of honey in Lamè's tone. "Yeah, Thom," said O'Rourke, "we're about to head out to LaGuardia to catch the shuttle."

"Well," said Lamè, "we may be talking later." O'Rourke looked at McGuire, and they both realized that they were about to be set up by Danny Dorsey.

"Thom," said O'Rourke, "what's your answer to the proposition that Sam McGuire had for you earlier this week?"

"I don't know," said Lamè. "I'm reconsidering. After all, it was just a youthful indiscretion."

"Hey, Thom," said O'Rourke in a tough north Village voice, "you were twenty-nine at the time."

"And what gives you the right to tell the world about me?" said Lamè.

O'Rourke had had enough. "Look, you pseudo-cocksucker, either you pull out of the primary or I'll drop this paternity suit on you like a ton of bricks. Do you understand?" There was silence at the end of Lamè's line. "If you fuck with me, your political career is over. 'Sodomy on demand' won't help you ever again." Still silence. "Thom," said O'Rourke, "I'm going to give you a little free political advice. Retreat now and live to fight another day." O'Rourke did not wait for an answer as he snapped the cell phone shut. "Let's get out to LaGuardia," he said and the meeting ended.

*   *   *   *   *

His name was Danny Dorsey and he was the kind of Irish that O'Rourke hated. Out of a working class family in Syracuse, New York, he had made it in politics by being the perfect vehicle, Sunday after Sunday, for the Republican Party. If they had a point to get across, they just went on *Sunday Press Box*, confident that good old Danny Dorsey would seamlessly get their talking points across to the American people. If he had John McCain on one more time, they were going to have to get married.

Dorsey panted as he waited to ask questions and was famous for the inevitable "gotcha" quote from forty years ago. He always brought up that he worked for Bobby Kennedy as a way to show his Democratic bona fides, but he was firmly in the pocket of the Republican Party. He was, O'Rourke knew, a political fraud.

He gave O'Rourke a big smile as they both sat down. Dorsey shifted in his seat, then looked down at the American flag in his lapel and straightened it for the camera angle. That was a new one, even for Wolfe Tone O'Rourke. "This is Dan Dorsey, and welcome to *Sunday Press Box*. Our guest today is Wolfe Tone O'Rourke, Democratic candidate for New York City's 7th Congressional District. Tone," said Dorsey, "nice to have you back on *Sunday Press Box* after all these years."

"Dan," said O'Rourke, "Happy Mother's Day and it's always a pleasure to be in the box." O'Rourke looked at McGuire in the control room and saw a small smile. Clarence Black looked away. And it went right over Danny Dorsey's well coiffed head.

"Tone and I go back a long way," Dorsey said into the camera, "First, Tone, why are you wearing two American flags?"

"Because I'm twice the American you are, Dan."

Danny, his head still down, pounded away. "When we were working together on Bobby Kennedy's last campaign—"

O'Rourke cut him off. "You were a gofer, Dan. I was the senator's advance man."

"Yes," said Dorsey, "on that fateful night—"

O'Rourke again cut in. "On that fateful night I led the senator right into the arms of Sirhan Sirhan and changed the history of this country."

"How so?"

"Without Bobby Kennedy, this nation changed. We had already lost Dr. King. All you had left was Hubert Humphrey, another bloated has-been. The likes of Nixon, Reagan, and Bush. Now we have Bush the younger and dumber running for president. Democrats and Republicans without style, class, or courage. You get an excellent pol like Clinton, although a man without conviction, and he can't help but pull his thing out of his pants and wave it at interns. And Democrats lose years defending this guy who robbed the American people of so much. An absolute criminal waste."

"Ah, Tone," said Dorsey in a hushed tone, "this is a family show."

"Well, Danny," said O'Rourke, knowing full well that Dorsey hated being called Danny, "you and your cohorts in the media had no problems talking about Bill and Monica during the impeachment hearings. I recall you also had a fascination with the cum-stained dress that Linda Tripp was so fond of." O'Rourke thought Dorsey might pop a blood vessel at the mention of presidential cum.

"Come on, Tone," began Dorsey before he realized what he had said. O'Rourke was getting under his skin. "But," said Dorsey forcefully, "we were only doing our journalistic duty during the Clinton impeachment hearings."

"Danny, let me be blunt. You wouldn't know your 'journalistic duty' if someone put it on a plate in front of you."

"Tone, I must disagree."

O'Rourke cut him off. "One of the problems with this country is guys like you who think they're important and never shut the fuck up." Danny hopped in his seat in indignation. "Calm down, Danny, it's still a free country."

"Watch your language," warned Dorsey.

"I'll watch mine, if you watch yours." O'Rourke was just getting going. "As I told that imbecile over on Fox, the people own these airwaves, not you, not Murdoch, not General Electric. You and the rest of the journalistic frauds couldn't wait to air Clinton's semen story, but when the language gets a little raunchy, you're like Claude Rains in *Casablanca*—'shocked, shocked'—that such filth could be going on the airwaves."

"Let's move on," said Dorsey. "Right now on the phone from New York City we have City Councilman Thom Lamè, also a candidate for the Democratic nomination in the 7th Congressional District. Mr. Lamè, welcome to *Sunday Press Box*." Lamè was now in the big leagues and he hardly could believe it. "How's your campaign going for Congress against Tone O'Rourke?"

There was silence on the other end of the phone as they put a picture of Lamè on the screen. O'Rourke was psyching himself up also, for he knew he was about to do something he didn't want to do: destroy a fool named Thom Lamè.

"Are you there, Councilman Lamè?"

"Yes, Dan," Lamè finally said.

"How's the campaign going?"

"Well, Dan, I have something very important to say about the race for the nomination of the Democratic Party in the 7th Congressional District." Lamè used the pregnant pause well and O'Rourke's face remained a stone. Lamè cleared his voice. "At this time, Dan, I am withdrawing my name from consideration and endorsing the candidacy of Wolfe Tone O'Rourke. Clearly, Tone O'Rourke, with his long service to the district, is the right man for the job."

Dorsey looked disappointed, and O'Rourke forced himself to look surprised. "Thanks, Thom," O'Rourke said, "that was very generous of you, your endorsement. I look forward to working with you from Washington and helping you in your future campaigns. And a happy Mother's Day to you and yours!"

Lamè wanted to reach through the television screen and strangle O'Rourke, but he went with the flow, knowing the political game is a long one and the first one out of the gate doesn't necessarily win the race. He knew that O'Rourke had already helped him in more ways than he could ever imagined, "Thank you, Tone. And you can be sure that someday I will cash in that IOU."

O'Rourke nodded for the camera and smiled at Danny Dorsey, who looked like they had just taken away his dog bone. "This will save you a lot of money," was the first thing that popped out of Dorsey's stunned mouth.

"Well, Dan, I'm still up against the Fopiano machine, that well-oiled juggernaut of Family Values." O'Rourke smiled, and, back in New York, a shiver ran through Vito, Madonna-Sue, and Jackie Swift. "However, Dan, I will need to raise bribes—I mean, campaign contributions. I will accept nothing larger than twenty-five dollars, and for that you will get a T-shirt, a dirty campaign button, and my everlasting gratitude." Tone held up a piece of cardboard, the kind that comes when you get your shirts back from the dry cleaners. On it was his new 800 number, written in black magic marker. "Call '1-800-BRIBE-ME' to contribute to the Tone O'Rourke for Congress campaign."

O'Rourke smiled for the camera as he held the piece of cardboard up with both hands. Dorsey, defeated, offered no admonition. "We'll be right back after these important words from our sponsors," was all he could muster.

36.

Back in New York and back in the office it was *déjà vu* all over again. "This is White House Operator 1524," said the voice, "stand by for the President of the United States."

"Oh, no," said McGuire, "not again."

"Tone," said the voice, hard and petulant, "this is Bill Clinton. I can't believe you just threw me under the bus again on Danny Dorsey's show. What did I do to you? Hillary's all upset."

"Yeah," interjected O'Rourke, "I'm sure she is." McGuire hit

O'Rourke on his Vietnam arm and O'Rourke winced.

"Sorry," she said sheepishly.

"I did my best for this country," the president said, "and I did well for Ireland too. Next time you're in Washington, stop by." With that the president hung up.

"I think he's pissed at you."

"No shit," said O'Rourke. "If he'd get pissed at the Republicans as often as he gets pissed at me, he'd be a better president. The Clintons are to the Democratic Party what the British are to Ireland—all they leave is their stink."

"Come on," said McGuire, wincing at O'Rourke's words, "cut him some slack."

O'Rourke shook his head. "Never," he said, and McGuire knew he meant it.

37.

"I'm late," said Sam McGuire casually, and O'Rourke instantly knew what she meant. He had probably missed more periods than most women. He remembered that Rebekah, out of a well directed guilt, used to miss a period every couple of months just for the fun of it. Grace usually had no periods because she drank so much. But eventually the blood would begin to flow again and O'Rourke had always assumed he was just shooting blanks.

"You take one of those pregnancy tests?" asked O'Rourke.

"Yep."

"Well?"

"It was the right color."

"So, it wasn't my scallops."

"No, that was morning sickness on Sunday."

"But you were using an IUD, right?"

"They work 99 percent of the time," said McGuire.

This must have been the one-hundredth time, thought O'Rourke, and the IUD had turned into an IOU. O'Rourke was fifty-three, going on fifty-four, and he couldn't believe what he was hearing. "How are you feeling?"

"Just wonderful." So was O'Rourke. He took Simone McGuire in his arms and hugged her like he had never hugged a human being before. Then they fell on the bed they had conceived their child in and the three of them hugged for the first time as a family.

38.

"Tone, I don't know what to say," said Clarence Black. "What's the matter?"

"You know Doodles Carney?"

"Doodles from Mayor Koch's security detail?"

"Yeah," continued Black, "he's retired and works for me once in a while. I have him keeping an eye on this Costello fellow you're interested in down in D.C."

"So?"

"Well, Doodles says Costello was meeting with a FBI agent by the name of Robert Hanssen?"

"Are you getting a red flag here?"

"My investigator says that Hanssen is a fanatical Catholic."

"You mean he belongs to *Opus Dei*?"

"Yes," replied Black, "he's been known to try to recruit young FBI agents into *Opus Dei*."

"So how's he involved with Costello?"

"Costello, Hanssen, and the papal nuncio," said Black, "had a meeting last night at eight o'clock."

"Why is Doodles so amazed?" O'Rourke asked.

"Well, he's worked with the FBI a lot in New York, and he ran into the FBI while tracking Hanssen."

"So we're tracking Costello," said O'Rourke, "and the FBI is tracking Hanssen, and we're all bumping into each other at the papal nuncio's residence in Washington, D.C."

"Doodles," said Black, "was told to steer clear. That this was heavy stuff."

"How heavy?"

"Espionage heavy," said Black.

O'Rourke was quiet. "I don't know what to say. I was going to drop a dime on Costello any day now. You know, the IRA angle. Say he's Jack Costello, the boyo who took the shot at Maggie Thatcher years ago." O'Rourke was pensive. "Don't know what to do now. Do you think Costello knows he's in this deep?"

"I think Costello is a politician," said Black. "I think he is a money man for the Vatican. But I can't believe he's involved in espionage."

"I agree," replied O'Rourke. "Is there any kind of arrest for Hanssen imminent?"

"I don't think so."

"Well," said O'Rourke, "maybe Cyclops Reilly might want to know about the Reverend Dr. Costello and why he's hanging out with all these very proper, very upright, and very sleazy Catholics."

* * * * *

O'Rourke, Reilly, and Black were at the end of the bar when Séan Pius Burke arrived. "Why do off-duty priests always dress like plain-clothes cops?" said Reilly in greeting his cousin.

"Yeah," agreed O'Rourke, "right down to the white socks and black shoes."

"And how are you fucking guys?" said the Monsignor and all four of them laughed.

"Let's go in the back," said O'Rourke. "We can sit at Bobby's table." The cousins looked at each other but said nothing. O'Rourke, they knew, was very sensitive about Bobby Kennedy and rarely brought up his name without provocation. They went straight to Table One, left, in front of the window.

"Can I get you guys anything?" the waitress said.

"Refill," said Reilly. "Vodka rocks."

"I'd like a Jamey 12," said the priest.

"Same here," said Black of the Jameson.

"I'll be a good lad and stay in dry dock," said O'Rourke.

"Where's Sam?" asked Reilly.

"I don't want to get Sam involved in this. Do you understand?" The cousins and Black all nodded.

"Shoot," said Reilly.

"I called a friend at the Justice Department," began O'Rourke. "He's one of Bobby Kennedy's old boys, one of the last, about to retire. I asked him about Costello and that Robert Hanssen character who Doodles stumbled upon at the Nunciate and he said he'd have to call me back. Well, he called me back from a friend's house because he didn't want to be heard talking about either of those two guys."

"It's that serious?" asked Burke.

"My friend said he had only two words for me: 'national security.' He told me not to get involved and that there was an ongoing investigation."

"Is that all?" asked Reilly.

"He said," added O'Rourke seditiously, "that we'll be reading about it on the front page of the *New York Times* very soon."

"Fuck him," said Reilly with sudden vehemence. The drinks were brought and the conversation ceased for a moment. "Fuck him and the FBI," Reilly repeated. He was beginning to see the front page of the *New York Daily News* with his byline on it.

"Be careful, Cyclops," said O'Rourke. "This is *very* serious stuff. If you write anything, do not mention Hanssen."

"Why?"

"Because you'll find yourself in front of grand jury—or even worse!"

"They can't frighten me," said Reilly.

"Yes, they can," said O'Rourke. "Costello is a player in this, but I don't know what kind of a player."

"So what do you want me to do?" asked Reilly.

The monsignor and O'Rourke looked at each other. Burke cleared his throat and spoke first, almost in a whisper. "Father Costello, I happen to know, is the pope's bagman in this country. He is trying to affect the outcome of elections this year with money."

"I'm shocked," said Reilly, and O'Rourke cracked a smile.

"He's giving money to my opponents," said O'Rourke. "So I'd like to embarrass him."

"He's putting the arm on the Cardinal," said Burke, his voice in such a tight whisper that it could cut like a razor, "and I'd like to see him removed *permanently*."

"So you want me to write something?"

"Like you *don't* want to write something?" teased O'Rourke.

"Fuck him," said Reilly. "We'll see what kind of juice he has." For a second he was quiet. "Putting the arm on the Cardinal?"

"Big time," said Burke.

"Who can help me?" asked Reilly.

O'Rourke pointed across the table at Black.

"There's something else you should know, Cyclops," said Black.

"Yeah?"

"There was another man of the cloth at that meeting with Hanssen, Costello, and the nuncio."

"Like who?" said Reilly.

"Like New York City Councilman Menachem Mandelstam."

Reilly pounded his fist on the table so hard that the sound echoed up and down the empty room. The waitress checked to see if anything was wrong. "Well, gentlemen," said Reilly in a subdued voice, "we got the cocksuckers."

"Because of Rabbi Menachem Mandelstam?" asked Burke.

"No Hands Mandelstam!" corrected Reilly, and a devious smile spread across his face.

Monsignor Burke looked at O'Rourke and said, "What's the connection?"

"The connection, I think," said O'Rourke, "is that it's the beginning of the end for the Reverend Dr. Costello."

* * * * *

"Madonna-Sue Fopiano learned the political trade working for Manny Mandelstam," said Reilly, shedding some light on the connection between Mandelstam and the Fopianos. "When Vito got elected to Congress and moved to D.C., he left Manny to show

Madonna-Sue the ropes. Mandelstam is a piece of work. Always loved having his picture taken with Meir Kahane or Ariel Sharon. He loves those Jewish Nazis."

"Where'd that 'No Hands' stuff come from?" asked O'Rourke.

Reilly started laughing. "I was a kid reporter about twenty-five years ago when all those massage parlors were opening in Times Square. The cops were going to bust them, so we went along with them for a story. We burst into this place on 42nd Street, go in the back room, and there's this black chick standing next to this guy who looks like a Hassidic rabbi."

"She blowing him?" suddenly asked the monsignor and six eyebrows shot up in surprise.

"No," said Reilly, smiling at his cousin with new respect, "that's the thing. He won't let her touch him. Won't touch himself either! Got his hands clasped in the air and he shoots without touching himself."

"No hands!" said O'Rourke, laughing.

"That's it. 'Why, Councilman Mandelstam,' says this big mick police captain, 'I'm shocked by the behavior of a man of the cloth such as you!' And I see it's Mandelstam who's always saying the most terrible things about the *schwartze,* and he's there with this black chick."

"Shit," said O'Rourke.

"Well," continued Reilly, "the photographer gets a real good picture of the good rabbi and the black hooker, and Mandelstam falls off the massage table and lands on the floor. His yarmulke floats after him like a parachute, lands on his hard-on. Another picture. He's desperate. He doesn't know what to do. So the Irish captain winks at me. 'Maybe we should just overlook this, Cyclops,' says he. 'A man of the cloth and a New York city councilman to boot!' I look at Mandelstam, and he says, 'It's not a sin—no hands!'"

"You're shitting us," said O'Rourke.

"God's honest truth. I let him ride. He's been in my pocket ever since."

"Holy shit," said O'Rourke. "So, he's your GOP mole."

"I told him I'd snap him in half if he doesn't come through," said Reilly. "Cheap bastard, too. The cop goes to arrest the hooker, and she says, 'For what? I never touched the motherfucker. Comes in here three times a week, pulls out his weenie, waves his arms, and comes on himself. Tips me with a stiff one dollar bill.'"

"What does it all mean?" asked Burke.

"It means we know how Costello, Hanssen, and Mandelstam are connected," said O'Rourke. "And because we know Mandelstam is involved we know that the Fopianos and Swift are connected. This is dangerous stuff. We'll have to be *very* careful."

39.

New York Daily News, May 24, 2000

Eye on New York
By Cyclops Reilly

Oops, It's *Opus Dei*

Get a load of this.

What if I told you that I knew people who liked to get their buttocks beaten as a way to get closer to God?

What if I told you these guys were really into wearing haircloth shirts so it could rub their skin until it was raw?

What if I told you I know guys—and a few ladies too—who like to take instruments of mortification and flog themselves on the back until they bled?

Hey, most people would say, "Whoa! That's kinky stuff—and I'm not into that."

Yeah, I think the Marquis de Sade invented a name for it—Sadomasochism.

Some people get off that way. Hey, me? Whatever floats your boat pal, just so long as you don't bother anyone else.

But these folks don't do these weird things—so they say—to get a sexual kick. They do it for the love of God.

I ain't lying.

They belong to an extreme right-wing organization of the Catholic Church called *Opus Dei*. *Opus Dei* is Latin for "the Work of God." They think of themselves as being elite. Kind of like the marines of the Church.

There are a lot of rumors swirling around New York and Washington, D.C. right now and they involve an *Opus Dei* priest named John Costello. When last seen, he was going into the papal nunciate in Washington for a meeting. Also seen entering the building was New York's own councilman extraordinaire from Crown Heights, Rabbi Menachem Mandelstam. There were other guys going into the nunciate also, but that's a story for another time.

Father Costello has also spent a lot of time in New York lately. He's been staying at the Cardinal's residence on Madison Avenue, behind St. Patrick's Cathedral. Rumor has it that he has been advising Declan Cardinal Sweeney on Vatican Politics 101—how to get anti-abortion candidates, like Jackie Swift, elected to Congress with the blessing of Holy Mother Church.

My sources tell me that Costello, who is not even an American citizen,

was the man behind bringing the Reverend Chester Cockburn to New York so he could deny he was a sodomite. I'm also told that he insisted that Cardinal Sweeney appear on the *Bourne in the Morn* radio program, which turned into another disaster for the Cardinal.

Now, Cardinal Sweeney and I don't always see eye to eye. In fact, we never see eye to eye. But the Cardinal is a good and decent man. The Archdiocese of New York, under his intimate direction, ministers to the sick, runs orphanages, has one of the best independent school systems in the nation—and they let everybody in because they don't care if you're a Catholic or not. Cardinal Sweeney is a direct descendent of Archbishop Dagger John Hughes, who was instrumental in setting up these Catholic institutions to minister the Irish who came to America during the potato famine.

I want to know what the Reverend Dr. John Costello, who is not an American citizen, is doing in the United States of America trying to interfere in the election this November that is going to take place in New York's 7th Congressional District between Wolfe Tone O'Rourke and Jackie Swift?

And here's the kicker. I want to know what Councilman Mandelstam was doing at the papal nuncio's house in Washington, D.C. He went in with nothing and was seen leaving with a shopping bag, bulging at the sides.

I called Mandelstam for a comment today—we're old friends going back to the early 1970s when we first met in Times Square, of all places—but he didn't return my call.

Geez, Manny. Give me a ring. Maybe we can talk about old times.

40.

Séan Pius Burke entered the Cardinal's study and stood before the Cardinal, who had the *Daily News* opened to Cyclops Reilly's column on *Opus Dei*. "What does it mean?" he asked Burke as he looked up.

"It means, I think, that you won't be seeing the Reverend Dr. Costello anymore."

"Why would Reilly do this for me? Does he want anything?"

"He wants nothing but a good story," replied Burke. "He did it because I asked him to do it. So did Wolfe Tone O'Rourke."

"O'Rourke," said the Cardinal, "that heathen."

"That 'heathen' donates over six figures a year to the Archdiocese of New York," said Monsignor Burke, his voice rising. "What this archdiocese needs, I would say, are more 'heathens' like O'Rourke."

"Six figures," said the Cardinal. "You must be joking."

"Do you consider St. Bernard's School down on West 13th Street in the Village a joke?"

"No, of course not. It is one of our oldest parishes."

"Well, O'Rourke is the benefactor that keeps that school open."

"I didn't know," said the Cardinal softly.

"He wanted no publicity," said Burke. "I probably shouldn't have told you that."

"What does he get out of it?" asked the Cardinal.

"Nothing," said Burke. "O'Rourke has been very fortunate, financially, in his life, and this is his way of repaying the Church for his education at St. Bernard's. He is a true philanthropist."

"Hmmm," mused the Cardinal. "Maybe I should meet with this O'Rourke, if that's possible."

"I'll see what I can arrange," said Monsignor Burke. "How about Cyclops Reilly?"

"I think," said the Cardinal with some amusement, "that I can work only on one Irish devil at a time."

41.

Everyone had their eye on the door of the city council minority leader, Menachem Mandelstam. Reporters stood down the hall and waited to see who would show up this morning. They could tell something was up when Swift himself arrived at the unearthly hour of 9 a.m. Peggy Brogan was with him, looking mildly ruffled, her long blonde hair stuffed inside an oversized cap. The watch continued as everyone waited for Menachem Mandelstam and Vito Fopiano. And they weren't disappointed. Mandelstam and Fopiano showed up together. Both had their chins cemented to their chests, looking like a couple of mobsters doing a perp walk.

"Vito, Manny. Any comment on Cyclops' column this morning? What's your connection to Costello? Did any money change hands?" There wasn't even a "no comment" from the two of them as they sought the shelter of Mandelstam's office.

"Hey, Manny," Abe Stein called out as Vito pulled the door closed, "did you forget your shopping bag?"

"Fucking press," said Mandelstam when he was inside the safety of the office.

There were no formalities. "Where's the money?" asked Fopiano.

"In the safe at my district office in Crown Heights," replied Mandelstam.

"Jesus H. Christ," replied Fopiano. "Get it out of that fucking office."

"But where?" asked Mandelstam.

"I don't care where," said Vito, "just somewhere away from here. If the Feds go looking—"

"You're toast," interrupted Brogan.

"Toast," Fopiano repeated.

"How much?" asked Swift.

"One hundred thousand in unmarked twenty-dollar bills," replied Mandelstam.

"Good Jesus," said Brogan.

Fopiano grabbed Mandelstam by the arm. "Go," he commanded. "Get out of here and get rid of that money." Vito practically pushed Mandelstam out the minority leader's door, into the arms of the waiting press corp. "Jesus Christ" was all Fopiano could muster for Brogan and Swift as the press surrounded Manny like wolves that hadn't eaten for a week.

"What do we do now?" asked Brogan.

"Keep our mouths shut, stay out of sight, and hope this blows over," replied Vito.

Jackie Swift looked at his hands and saw they were shaking. So did Brogan. Swift smiled at Brogan, and she was relieved by his brave front. But there was only one thought going through Swift's nervous mind at the moment: He needed a Fish-pack.

42.

It ended quietly. O'Rourke got a call from his friend at the Justice Department, who told him that the papal nuncio had decided to cooperate with the FBI investigation into Robert Hanssen and had turned over the Reverend Dr. Costello to the Immigration and Naturalization Service, who in turn took him to Reagan National Airport and saw to it that he made his Air Canada flight to Toronto, with a connection to Niagara Falls.

McGuire arranged a conference call between Monsignor Burke, Cyclops Reilly and Clarence Black. "It's over," said O'Rourke into the speakerphone. "Costello is on his way back to Canada."

"It's not over," replied Reilly with vehemence. "What about that shopping bag full of money that Mendelstam ran off with?"

"Let it drop," said O'Rourke. "We accomplished what we wanted to accomplish."

"I'm not going to let it drop," insisted Reilly.

"Benedict," said the monsignor, pulling rank, "it's over."

"No, it's not," said Cyclops as he slammed the receiver into its holder and got the attention of the entire city room at the *New York Daily News*.

43.

New York Daily News, May 30, 2000

Eye on New York
by Cyclops Reilly

I AM YOUR WORST NIGHTMARE

I am your worst nightmare

Yesterday, I got home and there was a message on the answering machine. It said, "If you know what's good for you and your [relative] you'll take your nose out of other people's business. Have a nice life. You know, short and sweet."

Well, let me tell you something, whoever this sleazebag is. I am Irish and the worst thing you can tell an Irishman is *don't* do something. If you wanted the Irish to stop drinking you'd just say "drink as much as you want, it's on the house." The ensuing sobriety would be such that AA would be out of business.

My relative in question and I grew up together. He is a very important person in this city and by targeting him they are targeting an even more important person.

In a recent column I wrote about how this money-grubbing *Opus Dei* priest, one grandly named the Reverend Dr. John Costello, was running around New York City with a briefcase full of money. Last seen, he was at the papal nunciate in Washington, D.C. stuffing councilman Menachem Mandelstam's big brown shopping bag with said money.

I asked my old pal, Manny, to give me a ring, but, so far, he hasn't. Manny and I go back a long way. Funny, when I heard that threatening message on my phone machine I thought immediately of Manny. It wasn't Manny, but the guy I hired to find out who called me, said the call was from Florida. And I know Manny has a lot of friends in Miami Beach.

Last I heard about the Reverend Dr. Costello he was put on an Air Canada flight by the FBI. I assume that he won't be coming back for a while.

Since I've been warned I guess now it's my turn to do the warning. If anything happens to my relative, or the man he works for, I'll be calling on you, Manny Mandelstam. And I'll be calling on some of your important friends on Staten Island. You know who I'm talking about. Yeah, I'll be calling. And it won't be to say hello.

44.

Monsignor Burke led O'Rourke to the Cardinal's study and knocked. "Yes," said the Cardinal as Burke opened the door and allowed O'Rourke to pass into the room before him. The Cardinal stood there, impeccable in black suit and Roman collar, glaring at O'Rourke while he fingered the gold crucifix that hung from around his neck.

"Eminence," said Burke, "Wolfe Tone O'Rourke."

O'Rourke walked across the room and without warning or embarrassment fell to his knees in front of the Cardinal, his head bowed, and waited. The Cardinal was surprised. He stood over O'Rourke, who did not move, then slowly extended his hand.

O'Rourke kissed his ring, then stood and shook the hand the ring was attached to. "Your Eminence," he said, "it is an honor to meet you."

"Thank you," said the Cardinal, not sure that this was the same wild man he had seen on television. "Would you like some coffee?"

"Yes, I would," said O'Rourke.

"Would you ask Maggie, Monsignor," said Sweeney with a gesture of his hand that served as a dismissal, "to bring us some coffee?" Burke bowed and exited.

"Dagger John," said O'Rourke with excitement as he pointed to the portrait of John Joseph Hughes on the wall.

"You recognize the first Archbishop of New York?" said the surprised Cardinal.

"He's one of my heroes."

"Why?"

"Because he didn't take any—" O'Rourke stopped himself just before he said it, "Guff."

The Cardinal smiled. "He was a hard man," he said.

The archbishop was called Dagger John because, according to legend, the cross he always made after his signature looked like a dagger. Others said the name emanated from the long stiletto-like crucifix he liked to fashion.

"He was a very good man," said O'Rourke. "He was basically a Fenian in vestments."

"You make him sound like an extremist."

"For his day, your Eminence," said O'Rourke, "he was. His extremism built St. Patrick's Cathedral on the coppers of Irish scrubwomen. His extremism in defense of our people in the face of Protestant hegemony led to the creation of the Catholic school system, the hospitals, and the universities."

"Fordham University was his," agreed the Cardinal.

"I love the story about those Catholic bigots," said O'Rourke, "the Know-Nothings coming to New York City in the 1840s, thinking arson."

"Archbishop Hughes," said the Cardinal proudly, "knew how to handle them."

"Yes," said O'Rourke, "he said if one Catholic church was torched, he would burn the city to the ground, à la Napoleon, making New York a second Moscow. He put the fear of Jesus into the Protestant hierarchy."

"The fear of Jesus," replied the Cardinal with a smile, "can be truly marvelous to observe."

There was a knock on the door, and an older woman entered with a tray holding a silver coffeepot and cups. The Cardinal gestured to a couch and the coffee was put on a table in front of it. "Thank you, Maggie," said the Cardinal as she poured their coffee. Finished, she quietly exited the room. "He was a good looking man," said Sweeney, "with a fine head of hair."

"Did you know he wore a toupee?" O'Rourke asked before taking his first sip.

"Who?"

"Dagger John."

Sweeney raised his eyebrows in surprise. "No!"

"Yes!"

"He must have been a vain man," said the Cardinal.

"No," said O'Rourke, "he was just a man."

The Cardinal stared at O'Rourke in response to his cryptic answer. "It's a shame," he said, "that I am to be put in charge of disassembling Archbishop Hughes's work." O'Rourke nodded. "With the faith of our fathers dwindling, I am forced to close some of Archbishop Hughes's churches and schools. That is why I wanted to meet you. To thank you for your help."

"Help?"

"For your support of St. Bernard's School down in the West Village. It was a generous endowment. Without your money I would be forced to close that wonderful old school."

O'Rourke turned red. "You weren't meant to know about that."

"I know," said Sweeney, "but Monsignor Burke let it slip. He did not mean to betray your trust. It just happened."

"I may have to take a little Fenian justice to the good monsignor," said O'Rourke lightly.

The Cardinal felt comfortable with this man, whom he expected to dislike. "I want to thank you for these columns," said the Cardinal, holding two recent "Eye on New York" clippings out for inspection: Reilly's "Oops, It's *Opus Dei*" and "I Am Your Worst Nightmare" columns.

"Cyclops did those," said O'Rourke, "not me."

"But I understand you were the man behind it, using a private detective to find out about Father Costello."

"The Reverend Doctor Costello," corrected O'Rourke.

"Yes," said the Cardinal with a chuckle, "how august. I should never have taken Costello's advice and done that man's radio show," said the Cardinal. "I was such a fool. Monsignor Burke was right. Bourne is a bigot."

O'Rourke nodded. "You should listen to Johnny Pie more. He is a man with his finger on the pulse of this great city."

Johnny Pie, thought the Cardinal with a smile. "I also want to ask you for your forgiveness."

"Forgiveness for what?"

"Because I judged you without knowing you. It was hubris on my part," confessed the Cardinal. "Perhaps, knowing now what I know, I shouldn't have endorsed Congressman Swift."

"There are worse people than Jackie Swift in this world, believe me," said O'Rourke. "Anyway, your endorsement only helped me."

"How so?"

"Your condemnation might seem like a negative, but it's really a positive."

"In what way?"

"With gays, liberals." The Cardinal nodded. "If they knew I was here, it would cost me votes."

"You are a manipulator of people," said the Cardinal.

"As are you," replied O'Rourke, though not in a threatening way.

"We share a profession, I think," said Sweeney, as if something was bothering him.

"What is it, Eminence?"

The Cardinal shrugged. "I get such bad advice sometimes."

"Like I said, listen to Monsignor Burke."

"You're right," said Sweeney. "Unfortunately, I've been listening to Father Costello and Vito Fopiano."

"They are frauds of the same stripe. They have no respect for anything that is just or decent."

"The same has also been said about you," said the Cardinal squarely, but not sharply.

O'Rourke measured his words carefully. "Your Eminence, I have tremendous respect for you and the Holy Mother Church." The Cardinal nodded. "We are in very traumatic times. The country is in the hands of people like Jackie Swift and Rupert Murdoch and *Bourne-in-the-Morn* and I, as a Catholic and a Democrat, have a duty to challenge them and their philosophy. These are the new Know-Nothings, Neo-Know-Nothings, if you will." O'Rourke gave a little laugh, then the smile left his face. "I wish you would put *their* feet to the fire sometimes."

"What do you mean?"

"You take great delight in dropping the hammer on politicians like me," he said quietly, "but you give reactionary Republicans a lot of rope."

"That's not true," replied the Cardinal.

"Yes, it is," said O'Rourke.

"Give me an example."

"You always jump on politicians who are pro-abortion, but you never condemn politicians who are pro-execution."

"Give me an example."

"George W. Bush. He's fried 152 souls as governor of Texas."

"I didn't realize it was that many," replied the Cardinal.

"Does the number matter?" Sweeney shook his head vigorously. "Half may have been guilty, Eminence, but I'll guarantee that at least a quarter were innocent and another quarter were imbeciles. And my calculations are conservative."

"Maybe I should have been more robust in my defense of life," admitted the Cardinal. "But that does not prove your point about me being prejudiced against politicians like you."

"How about when George W. Bush went to Bob Jones University, desperate after he lost the New Hampshire Primary to John McCain earlier this year?" asked O'Rourke. "I didn't hear you say a word. You gave comfort to the enemy."

"Why is Bush the enemy?"

"Because of anti-Catholic moves like Bob Jones University," said O'Rourke.

"Perhaps we should move on from Bob Jones," replied the Cardinal.

"Just remember, Eminence, that these Neo-Know-Nothings are the same group that Dagger John Hughes fought. They haven't changed in 150 years. They still hate us."

"Isn't *hate* too strong a word?" asked the Cardinal.

"I don't think so," said O'Rourke. "The only thing these guys worship is money, plain and simple. I may not be much of a Catholic, but nevertheless I was born one, and I'll die one."

"What does your Catholicism have to do with your politics?"

"Everything," said O'Rourke with a small smile. "At my advanced age, I finally realize that being a Catholic has been the most awesome influence of my life."

"How can that be?" asked the Cardinal incredulously. "A good Catholic can't be for abortion."

"I am not for abortion," said O'Rourke, and he thought of Sam and their baby. "Being pro-choice does not mean I'm pro-abortion. Personally, I find it abhorrent, but I also believe in the strict separation of Church and State," he said firmly, but quietly.

"But the Church teaches against abortion."

"Yes," said O'Rourke, "but the Church also teaches the sanctity of free will."

"Then free will has taken you in the wrong direction."

"That is for God to decide," said O'Rourke, standing his ground.

The Cardinal remained silent for a second. "You are a difficult man," said the Cardinal. He looked at the coffee in his cup, which he held like a chalice. Unconsciously, he swirled the remaining coffee around in the bottom of the cup like it was sacrificial wine. Finally, he spoke. "Yes, you are a difficult man, a difficult Catholic, even. But I think, perhaps, that you are a good man, too." He stood up. "I've enjoyed our meeting."

"I've enjoyed it also," said O'Rourke as the Cardinal softly touched the back of his jacket, moving him toward the door.

"May God protect you."

O'Rourke looked at Dagger John's portrait one last time and smiled. "Isn't it is a terrible thing, to fall into the hands of the living God?'" he said.

The Cardinal stared at O'Rourke then opened the door. "Monsignor Burke," he called down the hall. "Could you show Mr. O'Rourke out?" With that he turned and reentered the study. He walked up to the painting of Dagger John Hughes and exhaled. The eyes of the Cardinal locked on the painting and he wondered if the Archbishop actually had worn a wig 150 years ago. Then the Cardinal began to laugh—hard.

"Your Eminence," said Burke, rushing back into the room with alarm. "Is everything alright?"

"Yes—" The Cardinal stopped because he had almost called the monsignor "Johnny Pie." "Yes, Seán Pius, everything is alright."

Burke raised his eyebrows because the Cardinal almost never called him by his Christian name. "What did you think of him?"

"It is a dangerous man," said Declan Cardinal Sweeney, "who knows history and can quote scripture." He looked up once more at Dagger John Hughes. "I think, Seán Pius, I may want Wolfe Tone O'Rourke on my side."

* * * * *

After his meeting with the Cardinal, O'Rourke came out of the chancellery on Madison Avenue and started walking west to catch the Sixth Avenue subway down to the Village. As he passed the cathedral's side door on 50th Street, he stopped. He hadn't been in the cathedral since Bobby Kennedy's funeral and he didn't want to visit now. It was a place filled with bad memories, but for some reason he couldn't tear himself away. He stood looking at the cathedral's bronze door, afraid to go into St. Patrick's because of what might be waiting for him. Finally, as if being beckoned by some siren, he walked up the few steps and into the church that had meant so much to so many New Yorkers, including himself.

He stood in the back, thinking about his last time here. It was in the early morning of June 8, 1968, hours before Kennedy's funeral mass was to begin. He was an honor guard, standing silently by the coffin that was draped with the American flag. He was waiting to be relieved so he could catch last call at Hogan's Moat. The Irish are supposed to embrace death. Laugh at wakes and sing the praises of Tim Finnegan, dead until a noggin of whiskey—from the Irish *uisce beatha*, water of life—brings him back to life. But O'Rourke wanted nothing to do with death and he hated wakes and funerals with a passion. To him they were an embarrassment because he never knew what to say. And how do you say you're sorry to the pregnant widow because you took the wrong turn and her husband had his brains blown out? O'Rourke, that Saturday morning, had closed his eyes as if trying to deny the reality that had claimed him and the nation. Unconsciously, he had begun to nervously rock on his heels, back and forth. Then he heard the creak. He opened his eyes, but there was nothing amiss. He closed his eyes again and there was another creak. His eyes flew open and he saw there was no one near the casket but him. He could not take his eyes off the box and his mouth became dry.

The coffin squeaked again, and O'Rourke thought he was going insane. Was the Senator alive inside the box, trying to get out?

O'Rourke placed his hand on the box, as if to steady himself, and he felt the coffin move to one side. He put his hand on the other side of the casket, and the box shifted the other way.

O'Rourke then saw it was the old catafalque's fault. It wasn't level and the box was able to move when a hand gently touched it. He smiled. It was just Bobby having a little fun with him.

Now, inside the cathedral, O'Rourke could see that there was no box occupying the center aisle and somehow he felt better. He walked down to the high altar and then sat in a pew close by. Underneath the altar, O'Rourke knew, were the tombs of all the archbishops of the Archdiocese of New York. From the great ceiling of the cathedral, on long wire-strings, red hats called *galeros*, represented New York's dead archbishops, ten in all. O'Rourke stared at each and every one of them, wondering which one was Dagger John's.

As he sat there, he saw a man in a black suit enter the pew in front of him. He could see it was the Cardinal, strangely anonymous in his own church. Sweeney stiffly kneeled and with the purity of a young boy on the day of his First Holy Communion, placed his hands together, fingers pointed to the ceiling in prayer. Then he started to look up at the ceiling above the high altar. He was also looking at the *galeros*, very conscious that some day very soon, his own red hat, number eleven, would be among them. The legend in the Church had it that when a red hat fell from its mooring, a soul had ascended into heaven. "In that case," thought O'Rourke with a small smile, "looks like all the Archbishops of New York are still doing time."

O'Rourke felt a special contentment for he knew that he had piqued the Cardinal, just as he had been piqued by the ghost of Bobby Kennedy on that June day so long ago. Then O'Rourke also smiled, for it was obvious that Declan Cardinal Sweeney was searching for the *galero* that belonged to his ancient predecessor, the irascible archbishop, Dagger John Hughes.

45.

O'Rourke was in a daze. He stood outside his apartment building on Charles Street on a beautiful summer's day and felt as if someone had sucker punched him in the stomach. Slowly, like an old man, he started to walk west towards the river.

The note had been succinct. "I have to think the baby over. I'm going to my mother's in Tortola. I'll call you."

O'Rourke got it: Don't call me, I'll call you.

Think the baby over. My God, what a way to put it.

Since O'Rourke won the Democratic primary on June 19th, their silences had been loud. Two bodies in the same space doing their best to ignore each other. The pregnancy had changed McGuire. She was sick every morning and she placed the blame squarely on O'Rourke. She had become depressed and silent. There were no smiles and no smart-ass asides to keep O'Rourke in his place. O'Rourke could actually physically feel them drifting apart from each other.

"Is it the baby?" he asked.

"What do you think?" McGuire responded curtly.

"I think it's the baby."

"Well, you're right."

"Doesn't the baby still make you happy?"

"I'm not sure," she said. "I'm not sure at all about this child."

"What are you not sure about?"

"That this child should be brought into this world."

"Don't talk like that."

"Don't *you* talk like that," she snapped, and O'Rourke knew it was not the time to have a drag-out with her.

* * * * *

Then this afternoon, after work, the note.

He walked along Charles and passed the synagogue near the corner of West 4th Street, the Congregation Darech Amuno. O'Rourke's father used to do free plumbing for the rabbi back in the 1950s. One of his fellow Irish supers asked O'Rourke's father why the freebie and the response was classic O'Rourke Senior: "Because the rabbi's a fucking good guy and he's also a man of God." O'Rourke walked past the house of poet Hart Crane, who had committed suicide by jumping off the stern of a boat, and envied him. He continued on Charles past Bleecker Street, past the back of the Sixth Precinct and the Bomb Squad and came to a stop on the corner of Charles and Hudson. He crossed over to the Sazerac House restaurant where his friend Nick Pinto used to work, then turned south and headed in the direction of the World Trade Center.

He walked on Hudson past Ruby Fruits lesbian bar and the

Cowgirl Hall of Fame. Past Christopher Street, he found himself in front of St. Luke's in the Fields, the oldest church in the Village. Well, finally, the Episcopalians seemed to have something on St. Joseph's over on Sixth Avenue—they were the oldest. He was drawn to the side yard which was surrounded by wonderful brick buildings built in the 1820s. There wasn't a soul in sight and he found himself face-to-face with the statue of the Blessed Virgin, glorious in her patina, except for her prayerful hands and nose, which glistened like silver from all the hands that had rubbed her throughout the years. This Virgin was the opposite from the ones that had been tormenting him in his dreams. Although her face was uncovered, he could not see this Virgin's eyes. It was weird. They were open, but they were blanks; there were no eyes. But unlike his dream Virgins, she had a wonderful smile. No teeth, just a line of a warm smile. It reminded him of Rosanna's smile. And she had a big bust like Rosanna. Then O'Rourke noticed something very strange about this Virgin: she had patina streaks under her eyes, as if she had been crying. Crying, but smiling at the same time. At the base of the statue was a plaque which called Mary, "the Blessed Mother of Christ." There was a veneer of begrudging Protestant respect there somewhere, mused O'Rourke.

O'Rourke placed his hands on the Virgin's clasped hands and made a simple prayer. "Please save my baby."

The Virgin and O'Rourke were surrounded by the sounds of the city—cars and horns and the laughter of kids returning from school with their mothers. He looked up behind the Virgin and saw the mitered edge of the huge former Federal Archives Building, now just known a little too grandly as The Archive. When he was a kid, he had played stickball off it. Now Monica Lewinsky lived there.

He caught a whiff of the PATH across the way on Christopher Street. For some reason the PATH—O'Rourke still thought of them by their old name, the Hudson Tubes—still had that strange smell of its own. It didn't smell like the subway or any other thing in New York. It smelled like a city full of moldy sweat socks. It was as if New Jersey was exporting an aroma on New York in revenge for some wrong.

"Please save my baby," he said again.

The Virgin stood upright, as if she was noncommittal. O'Rourke wondered if the Virgin was listening to him. Then it came back to him from his childhood. His mother had taught him all his prayers in Irish, just as she had been taught her prayers in Irish by the nuns in the orphanage in Sandymount. O'Rourke knelt in front of the Protestant's Mary on one knee and it flowed out of him, nearly fifty years after he had learnt it:

> *Sé do beata Muire atá lán grásta*
> *Tá an tiarna leat,*
> *Is beannaigh tú tar na mná*
> *Agus is beannaighe toradh du broinn Iosa.*

O'Rourke stood up and clasped the Virgin's hands with his. "*Agus is beannaighe toradh du broinn Iosa,*" he repeated. "And blessed is the fruit of thy womb, Jesus."

He looked the Virgin in the eye. "Womb," he repeated. "The fruit of Sam's womb." O'Rourke stood back and said, "You must save my child. For if you don't, who will?"

Still feeling deflated, O'Rourke exited St. Luke's yard and walked to the corner of Christopher Street. He could see the twin spires of St. Veronica's across the street, one of the old, dead Irish parishes that was established to care for the Irish who worked on the docks, now also dead. In its heyday it must have been one of the noisiest parishes in the city because it was stuck between the old 9th Avenue Elevated Line on Greenwich and the Highline running down Washington Street.

A.D. 1890, the cornerstone read. A century and a decade ago. He entered through a side door and found himself beside a plaque for the Reverend Daniel J. McCormick, who had built "this beautiful temple."

The brass plaque said that "he was born in this city November 29, 1852." O'Rourke smiled. No immigrant McCormick—he was proud to be a native New Yorker—but it was obvious that he was a famine baby. Did his parents meet on a coffin ship escaping Black '47? The young Dan McCormick had been ordained a priest in St. Joseph's Seminary, Troy, New York, on December 22, 1877. He died around the corner, in the parish rectory, now Mother Teresa's AIDS Hospice, on January 23, 1903. An old fifty-one.

Father McCormick had built a fine church. Now catering largely to the Ecuadorian community, there were still signs of the Irish it had originally been built for. In the back, left over from World War II, was a listing, by street, of all who had served in the armed forces. Of the nearly five hundred names, almost all were Irish. St. Veronica's Parish, according to the list, ran all the way up to Abingdon Square, where St. Bernard's took over. St. Veronica's was the start of the Irish-Catholic West Side, which extended all the way up to Hell's Kitchen in the West 50s, where many of the Irish had become Westies, like the fathers of Cyclops Reilly and Séan Pius Burke. O'Rourke remembered the last of the Village docks, before the container ships, from the early 1950s, but wondered what it was really like just before and just after World War II. Irish babies galore with Baptisms, First Holy Communions, and Confirmations by the truckload. It must have been something. O'Rourke thought of his own baby and envied the long departed St. Veronica Irish because he feared he might never see a child of his own receive the sacraments of the Church.

O'Rourke remembered that his mother used to take him here when he was a child. At that time, the family had lived on Bethune Street, just three blocks away. He remembered one mass when he was being rambunctious. "Mammy, why is that man wearing a petticoat?" he asked loud enough so the whole church could hear. That man was the priest and the petticoat was his alb. She hushed him, and when that did not work, she said the magic words, "No Li-Lacs." Young Tone got the message and shut his trap. Duly, he was delivered to the chocolate emporium for his lollypop. O'Rourke looked around St. Veronica's and saw that they had not removed the confessionals like a lot of the Catholic Churches had. The four confessionals, two to a side, stood adamant. Thinking back nearly fifty years to the alb caper, he realized he had finally confessed one of his long lost sins.

Above the left front altar O'Rourke saw the Virgin Mary. She was a giant version of Rosanna's statue. He did not go to her, but stared at her from the back of the church. He had just had a long chat with her across the street. She knew what he wanted, but O'Rourke did not feel confident that she would respond.

In the back, near Father McCormick's plaque, was another Virgin, *Nuestro Senora del Quinche*—Our Lady of Quinche. Ecuadorians surrounded her glass case and it was easy to see that she was a people's

Madonna, an adored protector. Children were held up by their parents to touch the glass of the Madonna and her child. O'Rourke was proud of what was happening before him, as if the Irish had handed the church over to a new generation of immigrants, the new Americans. O'Rourke smiled because the politician in him was coming out. He wondered if the worshipers were citizens and registered Democrats.

He started to leave, when he spied the statue of St. Patrick. O'Rourke was delighted. The Ecuadorians may have commandeered this parish, but Patrick would not leave. O'Rourke placed five bucks in the slot and lit an electric candle. There was a handwritten note by the coin slot that read "Pray for my son John" and O'Rourke did. There were a few old Irish left in the parish and O'Rourke wondered if John's mother was one of them, perhaps living in a rent controlled apartment on Weehawken Street.

O'Rourke got up to leave when he was overcome by it all. The 500 Irish World War II veterans, Father Dan McCormick, the Catholic Virgin up above, the Protestant Blessed Mother of Christ over at St. Luke's, and now *Nuestro Senora del Quinche*. And, of course, St. Patrick. And John's Irish mother, God bless her. For in this church of death for an Irish culture that no longer existed, O'Rourke suddenly felt hope because, for the first time, he knew what he had to do.

"Go," Father McCormick commanded.

"Go," said St. Patrick, the three Marys, and John's Irish mother.

"Go to Ireland," they all said.

And O'Rourke knew that the answer to the survival of his unborn baby awaited him in the land of his birth.

46.

Sam McGuire had always been proud of her breasts. She had gotten them early and by the time she was thirteen, she was already a B-cup. Even at that young age she loved to stand naked in front of the mirror, her hands interlocked behind her head and watch her young, taut boobs. They stood out as if defying gravity. As she had matured her breasts had changed. They were no longer pert. There was a majestic sag now and, unharnessed, they swayed provocatively. O'Rourke had watched her arouse him once by just standing there naked, her hands on her hips, her tits ripe, and all he could do was shake his head and say, "Shit."

"I wish I had bigger tits," said McGuire.

"Jesus," said O'Rourke, "what are you talking about?"

McGuire grabbed a breast with each hand and held them in front of O'Rourke's face. "I want *really* big tits."

"You're insane," said O'Rourke laughing.

She loved it when O'Rourke kneaded them and licked them and pulled on her nipples with his front teeth. "Jesus, Tone," was all she could say.

Now that she was pregnant, they had in fact become bigger. Her aureoles were almost the size of pancakes. The House of Aureoles, she thought. As always, she liked to touch her breasts and rub them when no one was looking. Now she stood naked in front of a mirror in her bedroom in her mother's house in Tortola and surveyed her rapidly changing body. At four months plus, she could see her stomach protruding, almost like a little old man's potbelly. As she turned to the side, she could see her ass was getting thicker, sticking out back like a bay window. She knew she would have to decide soon.

* * * * *

McGuire was desperate for a smoke.

Her mother forbade her to smoke in the house. "Think of the baby," her mother, Amanda McGuire, would say in her gentle West Indian accent. Amanda was divorced from McGuire's father, who still lived in New York. Her parents had met when he was sent by his corporation to open an office in Tortola. McGuire was the first born and wondered if she wanted to be the conduit of another black child, parented by another black woman and Irish-Catholic father. It wouldn't be fair, something in her psyche repeatedly warned.

McGuire walked to the beach, just a few blocks from the house. As she lit up, she felt guilty because of the baby. "Fuck the baby," she thought as she inhaled deeply and could feel a lovely faintness to her head. She wanted to close her eyes and sleep. Sleep for a long time. That was the toughest thing about the pregnancy, the immense feeling of exhaustion that would not leave her. It seemed all she did was sleep and pee, pee and sleep.

She sucked the smoke into her lungs and watched the sea before her. Out of the corner of her eye she saw a tiny blue figure in the distance. It looked like a nun walking towards her. She was wearing a blue dress with blue stockings and blue shoes. She even had a blue floppy sun hat covering her very fair features. And as she got closer what stood out was how pink she was. Under the hat McGuire could see white-ish blonde hair. Maybe in her day she had been a blazing redhead, but that would have been a while ago because this woman must have been in her late sixties. She was getting closer, this blue nun of hers.

"This heat will be the death of me yet," she said to McGuire in a lilt, as if they were old friends. "Where I'm from, we don't get heat like this." McGuire looked at the woman like she might know her from New York. "Jesus," said the woman, "I'd love a fag," not really asking, but demanding a cigarette from McGuire. Without saying a word, McGuire, in a real New York gesticulation, banged the bottom of the pack of cigarettes on the top of her hand, and three popped up to surrender. "Ta," said the woman, "give me a light." Before McGuire could move, the woman gently pulled the cigarette out of McGuire's mouth and put it to her unlit fag. A flame shot into the air, startling McGuire, who pulled away. "Ah ha," said the woman, delighted. "I love the fire! Thank you." She replaced the cigarette in McGuire's mouth as nimbly as she had removed it.

"You're welcome," said McGuire, still stunned. She didn't know if she even wanted to have a conversation with this woman, but she couldn't help but blurt out: "Where are you from? I haven't seen you before."

"I'm Brigid Dillon from the land of saints and scholars—although they sin there as much as anywhere else," she said.

"Ireland?"

"Indeed, from Dundalk in the county of Louth, the Wee County."

"Simone McGuire," Sam said, using her proper moniker. "I like your name. Brigid has a wonderful flow to it."

"I'm named after the saint, not that naked French movie star," she said, laughing. "McGuire? Are you one of us?"

"One of us?" asked a confused McGuire.

"Irish."

"On my dad's side," replied McGuire. "My mother is from the island."

"Simone is a lovely name, too," said Brigid.

"But Brigid has panache," countered McGuire, letting the word roll off her tongue. "We even have a St. Brigid's cross in my mom's house down the road here."

"St. Brigid is everything to everyone," said the woman in blue. "It is said that if you put your Brigid's cross outside the window at night, she will come and bless it herself."

"I'll have to try that some time," said McGuire, not sounding convinced.

"You should," Brigid Dillon said with conviction. "Would you like to see mine?" With that she rolled up the sleeve of her blue dress and pointed to the blue tattoo on her forearm. "If Brigid comes to bless this cross I'll be able to say 'how do you do!'"

Both McGuire and Dillon broke out in laughter. The tattoo was a shock to McGuire. Women today were always decorating their bodies with piercings and tattoos, but Brigid Dillon did not fit the mold and Brigid noticed. "What's the matter, my dear?"

"Oh," said McGuire, "I'm just surprised that a woman of . . ."

"My age?" interrupted Brigid.

McGuire blushed, giving her an imperial glow. "Yes," she continued, "your age would have a tattoo."

"Well," said Brigid, "you should see the one on my bum!"

McGuire didn't know if she was joking or not, but could not help laughing and liking this unlikely tourist.

"And it is said," said Dillon as she pulled her sleeve back into place, "that if you carry St. Brigid's Cross with you, you will never die in a violent accident."

"Really?" said McGuire, unconvinced.

"You should try it for the safety of your baby."

McGuire felt a chill and turned defensive. She thought her baggy clothes hid her secret. "How do you know?"

"I had fourteen of the little ones myself. Sure there's nothing like a bab-bee, is there?"

"I wouldn't know."

"Sure you will do well with your bab-bee," Brigid continued, "and it will be a wonderful child who will bring great pride to both you and your husband."

"I'm not married."

"You will be," said Brigid, laughing again.

"I doubt it."

"But your husband loves you."

"He is not my husband," replied McGuire tautly, "and I don't know if he loves me or not."

"He has proven it already, hasn't he?" McGuire shook her head. "By giving life to your child."

McGuire was getting exasperated. "How do you know all these things?" she snapped.

"After fourteen, Simone, I know about these things. Now the best part," said Brigid almost conspiratorially as she put a hand to McGuire's arm, "is the breastfeeding. It's like being close to God. Once you get over the pain, there's a lot of pleasure, both psychic and physical, in nursing a baby, but also exhaustion if you have one who doesn't sleep at night and wants to feed every couple of hours. Nursing also makes you incredibly thirsty. You get really hungry, but you can eat almost anything you want without getting fat." With that she tapped McGuire on her ample bottom. "*If* you know what I mean." McGuire smiled, totally disarmed. "And with those grand Picassos," added Brigid, pointing to Sam's breasts, "you'll do well!"

Brigid turned to the sea. "My God, what a beautiful little boat," she said.

"Where?"

"Right out there. Don't you see?"

"I'm not only pregnant, fat, and dowdy," said McGuire, "but I can't see a damn thing without my contact lenses. Where?"

Brigid took her left hand, waved it in front of McGuire's eyes, snapped her fingers, and pointed again, "There."

McGuire look out and saw the boat as clear as morning. "My

God," she said, "I can see it."

"Of course you can," was all Brigid said. She took the last drag from her fag, declared it "heavenly," and turned to leave. "You will be a wonderful mother and your husband will love this child more than anything else in the world." She threw the cigarette to the ground and pivoted her foot on it, killing the fire. "I think I'll take a stroll on the strand now. Take care, Sam, and may God be with you and your child." Then without another word, she turned towards the beach and headed straight for the water. Sam watched as Brigid plopped into the sand and removed her shoes and stockings. Then, oblivious to the tourists sunning themselves around here, she began to disrobe. The blue skirt dropped to the sand, followed by her bra and panties. She perfunctorily brushed a hand over her pubic hair, raised her arms in the air as if in triumph, and ran into the water. The last thing McGuire noticed was that there was, indeed, some kind of tattoo on Brigid's left buttock.

McGuire was still in awe at Brigid's uninhibited performance, when it hit her hard. "She called me Sam," she said aloud. "How did she know?" But when she turned back towards the beach, there was no sign of her benefactor. McGuire shook her head and punched another cigarette out of the pack. Her hands were shaking as she lit it. There was no burst of Brigid's flame this time and she was relieved. She took a deep drag that she had first learned to do at The Mary Lewis Academy in Queens when she was fifteen. She looked out again at the sea, still hoping to see her new friend Brigid. Then she felt her shirt, which was wet. She looked down and there was a huge stain. She pulled the front of her T-shirt away from her and looked down at her pieced left nipple, where milk was dripping out of her steadily—like a stigmata—as if demanding an infant to nurture.

* * * * *

For the rest of the day McGuire couldn't get Brigid Dillon out of her head. She stood again in front of the mirror in her room and began undressing. Soon she was naked and she placed both hands on the side of her stomach and just stared at her reflection.

"So I hear you're going to make me and your daddy happy," she said aloud to her belly. It was the first time she had used the word *daddy*, and it sounded very strange. She massaged her mass and thought for a second that she could feel a response. "My God," she said, "how did I ever get myself into this mess?" Exhaustion overcame her. She went to turn off the light and noticed the Cross of St. Brigid. She took the cross off the wall and brought it to the window, leaving it on the sill, still without conviction. "Do your magic, Brigid," she said, heading naked to her bed.

Her sleep was deep, but troubled. All she thought of was O'Rourke. She could see him in the distance, but she couldn't get to him. Oh, how she missed him. They hadn't spoken in weeks. She knew him; he was probably brooding, wondering what he had done wrong. Probably drinking again. It wasn't his fault at all. And it really wasn't McGuire's fault either. It was just the collision of two human beings who loved each other, but who lived in confusion and the strange hopelessness that always seemed to find the Irish in a state of love.

She awoke in the middle of the night in a sweat. The sheets were wet and her breast was still dripping like an old faucet. She would have to get to the doctor in the morning. "Oh, Christ," she said, realizing that she had to get up and take a pee. As she pulled herself in a daze up to the side of the bed she thought she saw something outside her window. A pink hand coming out of a blue dress, making the sign of the cross over her St. Brigid's Cross.

47.

Up early Sunday morning, O'Rourke left Clarence Black to sleep in and walked down from the Shelbourne Hotel via Kildare, Nassau, and Grafton Streets to catch the number nineteen bus at College Green. He was on his way to Glasnevin Cemetery. For a man who hated wakes and funerals intensely, he had a strange affinity for cemeteries.

Dublin was always a slow-starting town, especially on Sundays.

There was simply no comparison to New York. New Yorkers took pride in their hustle. Dubliners were more gentle with time. What did O'Rourke's father like to say? "When God made time, he made plenty of it." And after a few days in Ireland O'Rourke noticed that he had a hard time pulling himself out of bed, even by 9 a.m. Sometimes he just had to finish that old *Ironsides* rerun on RTE. The old man, thought O'Rourke, was proven right again.

O'Rourke went to the top of the bus, which was empty, and sat in the front seat. He gazed at the empty streets as the bus swept through O'Connell Street and swung up Parnell Square West. To his right was the Garden of Remembrance, the place where the GPO rebels had been rounded up and camped before the British figured out who they were going to shoot. Looking out to his left, O'Rourke smiled as he spun by #29, Vaughan's Hotel back in the early 1920s, unofficial HQ to Michael Collins and his squad. The bus passed the Black Church on the way north. The Black Church was the most sinister and inhospitable looking church in the world. Legend declared that if you ran around it three times the devil would appear. O'Rourke smiled at the thought that the British could find the devil, Collins himself, at #29, *sans* the exercise.

O'Rourke was daydreaming when the bus came to a stop with a jolt in front of the old Broadstone railroad station. There she was, just below him, as if she had been waiting for him. Only in Ireland could the Blessed Virgin Mary be propped up almost at double-decker eye-level like a traffic cop and no one thought it odd. She had been there for years, O'Rourke remembered, even going back to the 1970s when O'Rourke was "on the run" living down on the South Circular Road, still stewing about Vietnam and its personal carnage. He had been told by his cousin, Monsignor Vincent Bartley, that she was erected in the Holy Year of 1950—the year the O'Rourkes had left for New York. Vince, then a choir boy, sang at the installation. She was called Our Lady Queen of Peace. After a half century of rain and damp she still looked serene, although pollution had rendered her a permanent dirty Dublin gray. O'Rourke could see that she had averted her eyes, strangely annoying him.

She was being coy this time, thought O'Rourke. Not like in the dream when she covered her face up and only showed him her eyes, which were the eyes of his dead mother. O'Rourke was beginning to feel resentful toward this piece of plaster. "What do you want of me?" he asked out loud. There was no response from the statue. "What's the game here?" Whatever the game, it was her game and O'Rourke was playing it, but he did not know the rules. He didn't know what she wanted, but she wanted something. He was biting his lip in frustration when the light changed and the bus went up the road toward Phibsborough.

O'Rourke got off the bus in Glasnevin and walked up to the main gate, where he bought two roses. Inside he walked to the right, past the office, to the grave of General Michael Collins. Although Collins was buried in 1922, he didn't get his headstone until 1939. A sort of delayed grant, after many negotiations with Collins's brother Johnny, from the *Taoiseach*, Eamon DeValera. DeValera, petty to the last, decreed that the back of the headstone, the first thing one sees, be written in Irish, clearly to vex those not up on their Erse.

O'Rourke went to the front of the grave and was surprised to see that, for once, it was covered in flowers. Usually the barrenness annoyed O'Rourke, but this time the grave abounded in color. He left the rose in a vase and said a prayer for one of his two heroes, Bobby Kennedy being the other one. Two Irish revolutionaries with different methods who came to the same ending. O'Rourke shook his head at the waste and said a prayer for all the young Irish soldiers, mostly killed in the Congo while on UN patrol, who surrounded Ireland's premier general.

O'Rourke walked past the appropriately named Republican Plot, home to John Devoy, Jeremiah O'Donovan Rossa, Harry Boland, Cathal Brugha, and all the other ancient Fenians. At Parnell's grave boulder, he took the first right and started the walk towards St. Brigid's, where his mother and her parents were buried. There were many Blessed Virgins along the way. Some pristine above the grave, others with an arm or a shoulder missing after all the years in the rain. He stopped to look at one whose features had been eroded. She looked at him fully, but with really no face. No eyes, just a bump for a nose, two lumps for ears. O'Rourke stood in the early morning quiet and felt serene. The irritation that the polluted Broadstone Virgin had caused him was now gone. This Virgin wasn't giving him any clues either, but at least she stood before him without intimidating him. Maybe they could work this out. Then O'Rourke jumped as a rat—no, it was only a squirrel—ran across his path. O'Rourke realized that there would be no détente between himself and his celestial mother.

He saw the wall and resurrectionist tower near his mother's grave and was forced to smile. His mother had been cremated, and when O'Rourke had returned with her ashes to bury them, the gravedigger had said, "This is a grand spot to be buried in." O'Rourke, frustrated and depressed by the whole ordeal, had turned on your man curtly: "And why might that be?"

"Do ya see that wall there?" O'Rourke nodded. "Well, beyond it is the Botanical Gardens." O'Rourke was forced to smile at the Dublin-in-the-rare-ould-times moment and he was sure that his mother would have been delighted too. He gave your man an extra ten *punts* for his digging and his philosophizing.

It only took O'Rourke a moment to find the stone. It had been replaced by his altar-building Uncle Dick in 1961. Since he was the last Kavanagh, he owned the plot that contained what was left of his mother's family. There was young Charlie who was planted here in 1914. Grandmother Rosanna was next in 1915. Grandfather Joseph followed in 1924, followed by young Joe in 1961. O'Rourke's mother was the last—until O'Rourke was ready—in 1989. The only two missing were Dick and Frank, who both died in America and were buried in the Bronx.

Here was a family that O'Rourke was clueless about. He had only the fractured stories of his mother. The grandfather was a hairdresser, a barber, who had a shop in Aungier Street. He was a former alcoholic, a turf accountant, and a revolutionary in his time. He knew little of the grandmother who died just before his mother's eighth birthday, landing her in an orphanage in Sandymount. Yes, there was one other thing about Rosanna. She was the original owner of the statue of the Blessed Virgin that O'Rourke now possessed. Charlie was the mystery boy, who choked on a fishbone on a Friday. Joe was the first child in 1901, Frank the second in, maybe, 1902, both bitten by the revolution bug. Just children, like so many of Michael Collins's "men." Charlie's birth year looked like 1904 (he died in 1914 and the stone said "ten years of age"). He knew his mother was 1907 and he assumed Dick was just after her.

Worthless numbers, all of them. A dead family that no one cared about anymore. He dropped the rose on the grave and said a prayer. O'Rourke always believed that if you thought of the dead it was like a prayer. Who knows? Maybe someone still needed help getting out of purgatory. It was beginning to rain and O'Rourke pulled his New York Mets baseball cap out of his jacket pocket for cover. He was saying the Act of Contrition in Irish, as he mother had thought him.

A Dhia, tabhair cúnamh dom

chun faoistin mhaith a dhéanamh.
A Dhia, cabhraigh liom
mo pheacaí a aithint,
fíordhólás a bheith orm fúthu,
iad a admháil gan ceilt san fhaoistin,
agus rún daingean a bheith agam
gan peaca a dhéanamh arís.

As he finished the prayer, he looked out over all the gray graves and the barren soil—he wondered when was the last time a single blade of grass had actually grown here—and in the distance he could see her—a brand new Virgin Mary, probably on top of a fresh grave. She was in vivid color, with blues and whites and that ruddy Irish complexion. She was way up there, over in the next plot from where his mother was. In the starkness of the cemetery on a rainy Sunday morning, she seemed alive and animated. She was a good distance from O'Rourke, but she looked like she was smiling at him.

O'Rourke looked at the mother's gravestone again, then took out his notebook and jotted all the information on the stone down, about the grandparents and the two uncles he never knew. He didn't know what he was going to do with them, but he knew he had to write it down.

The rain was getting harder and the pages of his notebook were turning limp when he closed it and put it in his pocket. "I won't forget you. I promise," he said to the slab of marble in front of him. Then amid all the dead, he saw life. A snail was making its slow way up his mother's gravestone. "*Seilide,*" O'Rourke addressed the snail in its Irish name. He reached down and plucked it off the stone and the *selide* immediately sucked its head and horns and legs into its little shell, giving O'Rourke a smile. O'Rourke gently placed the snail back on the headstone. "Welcome to the family."

It was time to get out of the rain. He looked up to say goodbye to the brilliant Virgin in the next plot and realized with a jolt that she did not exist.

48.

O'Rourke did not sleep well, and he woke up agitated. He had been pestered by two of them this time. They had double-teamed him.

He was first confronted by the Broadstone Virgin, the one stuck up in the air like a traffic cop. This time she had turned her back on him, as if showing him her rump, not in a provocative way, but more as a way to scorn.

In the dream he was alone again in the top of the double-decker. Although there was no one about, he could hear the chorus all around him:

Hail Mary, full of grace
The Lord is with you
Blessed art thou amongst women
And blessed is the fruit of they womb, Jesus.

"And how is the fruit of your womb, Jude?" the Virgin asked O'Rourke.

She called him by his Christian name, which no one knew. O'Rourke had been called Tone since the day of his birth.

"I don't have a womb," snapped O'Rourke. "I'm a man!"

"You do have a womb, Jude," she replied.

"What womb?"

"You know what womb I'm talking about."

O'Rourke thought of Sam. "Is it going to be alright?"

"That's up to you," said the Virgin as she began to slowly turn toward him. He couldn't catch her face because the bus pulled away, past the Broadstone Station, on its way to Glasnevin.

Next he found himself in Glasnevin standing before the Virgin with no features. Lumps for nose and ears and a couple of sinkholes for eyes. No mouth at all.

"Your womb," she said to O'Rourke, as if continuing the conversation of the Broadstone Virgin.

"Womb?"

"You know what I mean," she replied.

"Sam's womb?"

"It bears fruit," said the Virgin.

"My child."

"Yes, your child," reaffirmed the Virgin. "She is lonely for you."

"She," repeated O'Rourke softly, and for the first time he knew he had a daughter. "I think of her all the time."

"The child knows that."

"She does?" said O'Rourke with surprise.

"I reassure her," said the Virgin, "of the love of her parents, but she does not believe me."

"Well," said O'Rourke, "I love her like I loved my mother."

"I know," replied the amorphous Virgin.

There was silence and suddenly it began to rain heavily and Glasnevin Cemetery became even more gloomy than it naturally was. Through the rain, he thought he could see a fine line forming for a mouth on the Virgin's statue above him. It was the long-lined mouth of the Conways, his grandmother's people. And then eyes filled the two sinkholes and he swore they were the eyes of his mother. He excitedly wondered what would happen next to unlock this mystery, but then the dream failed and he awoke drained and disappointed.

O'Rourke rose naked and walked to the window of his Shelbourne Hotel suite. Below him, St. Stephen's Green was splendid in its summer dress, so green and full that it was impossible to really see anything in the park except for the pond. But the luxury of the Shelbourne suite and the park did not raise O'Rourke's spirit. This morning he had grim work to do and it was time to get moving.

* * * * *

O'Rourke came out of the Shelbourne, turned left, and headed down Merrion Row on his way to Merrion Square. O'Rourke loved walking around Dublin because he was always touched by its history. At Merrion Square, across from Clare Street, he surveyed the colorful reincarnation of Oscar Wilde. This statue was joyful, coy yet cheeky as he flirted, provocative in repose—well befitting its Dublin sobriquet, The Quare in the Square.

Dublin was a city of history that jumped out at you. Just over there, on Merrion Square South, were the houses of Yeats and George Russell and right in front of him was Oscar Wilde's father's townhouse. O'Rourke looked down Merrion Square towards Hollis Street Maternity Hospital where he was born in 1946 in near poverty. America and its filthy politics had been good to O'Rourke—he could buy one of these beautiful buildings on Merrion Square if he so desired. Maybe that would impress Sam. Maybe not.

He swung around Fenian Street and passed into Westland Row. He walked passed St. Andrew's Church, where he was baptized, toward the Westland Row railroad station. He crossed Pearse Street to Lombard Street and went into Joyce House, the Registrar's Office. He was directed to the second-floor research department in his quest to find out about his dead relatives. He got there early enough so that the place was not yet packed with vacationing Americans trying to find clues to their exiled existences.

His task was grim and he was depressed at what he might find. Yet he was nervous in anticipation, kind of like the nervousness one would get on a first date. He had his notes from the gravestone up in Glasnevin and he was going to find out as much as he could about this lost family of his mother's that, for some reason, had been dogging him now for months. His list was small:

Joseph Kavanagh, grandfather

Rosanna (née Conway) Kavanagh, grandmother

Joseph, Francis (Frank), Charles (Charlie), Mary, Richard (Dick), the children.

Uncle Charlie was first. O'Rourke went to the front desk and was given the index book for deaths in 1914. There Charlie was in the book in the first quarter of the year. It was easy work. O'Rourke filled out the form and gave it to the clerk. Within ten minutes some of the answers were horribly revealed.

Dáta agus Ionad Báis/Date and Place of Death: 1914, 10 March. 1 Piles Buildings. The first surprise: 1 Piles Buildings. What where they? O'Rourke thought the family home was on Aungier Street. Also, a mention of Arthur's Lane. And what and where was Arthur's Lane?

Aois an lá breithe is déanai/Age last Birthday: 10 years. Bachelor, the paper said. O'Rourke had to smile at the obvious.

Cúis Báis Dheimhnithe agus fad an tinnis/Certified Cause of Death and Duration of Illness: Paralysis of heart following diphtheria. Sudden cardiac failure per medical attendant on way to Adelaide Hospital.

Diphtheria. Who in God's name dies of diphtheria anymore? But this was 1914, just before the beginning of the Great War and there were no tetanus shots. So Charlie died on his way to the Adelaide Hospital. Did Charlie feel the bump of the cobblestones as the horses panted and pulled to save his little life? It said his father was with him at the time of death. Where was his mammy? Back with the other kids? Did he cry out for his mammy at the end? And did Rosanna know that this was the beginning of her own end? Was the grief of Charlie's death going to be responsible for her own death only eleven months later?

O'Rourke had a special affinity for his Uncle Charlie. Maybe because he was next to his mother in age and maybe because he had never seen a picture of him. He had photos of Rosanna and the grandfather. He knew his Uncles Dick and Frank in New York and he had seen photos of Joe Jr., taken on the windy plains of Portrane, the lunatic asylum ten miles north of Dublin. So Charlie was the mystery. The ten-year-old ghost who must have been terribly sick and terribly frightened by it all. How does one get diphtheria? From lousy sanitation? The poor always have lousy sanitation. They always get to die in their own shit. Did Charlie know he was the harbinger of destruction for the Kavanagh family? Did he know he was lucky to be the first one to die because it saved him from becoming an orphan?

But there was no mention of a fishbone in Charlie's throat so his mother must have been mistaken. Maybe that's what the parents told the children, to assuage the queer feeling the instant disappearance of

Charlie would surely cause.

Grandmother Rosanna was next.

Dáta agus Ionad Báis/Date and Place of Death: 1915, 23 February. 8 Piles Buildings. That name again: Piles Buildings. But this time number 8. O'Rourke was mystified. No sign of Aungier Street anywhere in sight. Had they moved after Charlie's death?

Aois an lá breithe is déanai/Age last Birthday: 37 years. She was so young. The math was quick, she was probably born in 1877 or 1878.

Cúis Báis Dheimhnithe agus fad an tinnis/Certified Cause of Death and Duration of Illness:Tuberculosis, about 12 months. Cardiac disease certified.

O'Rourke was horrified. Tuberculosis. He couldn't believe it. No one died of TB anymore. It was a disease out of the damp history of this island. Thirty-seven, leaving five children, some of them near babies, and an overwhelmed husband.

Síniú, Cáilíocht agus Ionad Cóonaithe an Fhaisnéiseora/Signature, Qualification and Residence of Informant: Joseph Kavanagh, widower of deceased, present at death. 8 Piles Buildings. So his grandfather was with her at the last, perhaps holding the hand that did not contain the rosary? Was the priest there to anoint her? To pray for us sinners now and at the hour of our death. Amen. And where were the children, including O'Rourke's mother? Big sinner, thought O'Rourke, this Rosanna Kavanagh.

First diphtheria, now tuberculosis. Did you ever hear of two people in one family unit dying from diphtheria and TB within a year? What was going on here? A fourth of the family dying from stupid diseases in the Piles Buildings. The Piles Buildings, another joke gone flat. O'Rourke, the reluctant millionaire, finally realized that his mother's family had been murdered by poverty.

Joseph Kavanagh.

Dáta agus Ionad Báis/Date and Place of Death: 17 January 1924. Aungier Street Dublin. Well, finally, the street his mother always talked about.

Aois an lá breithe is déanai/Age last Birthday: 51 years. That would bring his birth date to 1872 or 1873.

Cúis Báis Dheimhnithe agus fad an tinnis/Certified Cause of Death and Duration of Illness: Chronic nephritis certified. Bad kidneys. A gift from the Black and Tans because he would not tell them where his IRA sons were?

Joseph Owen Kavanagh. Joe Jr.

He remembered his death date well, just before Christmas 1961. His mother tried to get home to Dublin but couldn't because of all the holiday bookings. Not many Aer Lingus flights in those days. Travel was a big deal. Uncle Joe would be buried without immediate family. Another lonely Kavanagh funeral at Glasnevin.

*Dáta agus Ionad Báis/*Date and Place of Death: 1961, 21 December. St. Ita's Hospital, Portrane. 26 Temple Lane off Dame Street, Dublin. A new address. Temple Lane in the now hip Temple Bar district. O'Rourke knew it well. It was just an alley running off Dame Street, where George's Street begins. A short jog from the Olympia Theatre. Just across the street from his favorite pub, the Stag's Head. He was told by his godfather, way back in the 1970s, that some of his mother's people had lived there. Was this a clue?

*Aois an lá breithe is déanai/*Age last Birthday: 60. Joseph would live to be the oldest of the Kavanagh men, a mere sixty years, two months. Was this a warning to O'Rourke?

*Cúis Báis Dheimhnithe agus fad an tinnis/*Certified Cause of Death and Duration of Illness: Myocardial degeneration, 6 months, arteriosclerosis certified, 1 year.

A bad ticker from all the smokes—every photo O'Rourke had ever seen of his Uncle Joe had been punctuated by the blazing faggot in his hand. O'Rourke's mother used to send him money religiously to keep him in smokes. Tobacco and the Irish diet of grease encased in grease suffocated Joe's poor heart.

So that was the history of the gravestone up in Glasnevin. The research room was beginning to fill up with Americans. O'Rourke sat, utterly deflated. He couldn't get his grandmother, Rosanna, out of his mind. He could see the picture he had at home of her. There she sat in sepia at a table with the grandfather. She was on the right. A book in her hand. Looking at the camera. She had that wide Conway mouth that his mother had inherited. There was no smile, just a line. But she was not cross in the photo, which was obviously taken in a studio. Her eyes smiled and you could see that they must have lit up when she was happy. The grandfather, with the splendid handlebar mustache, sat to the left, his mouth slightly ajar. O'Rourke guessed it was about 1911. She had four years to live. O'Rourke thought about Patrick Pearse, who lived yards from this very office, and the Dublin of his grandmother came into focus.

Rosanna died in 1915, a pregnant year for Ireland. In May, the RMS *Lusitania* sets sale from Pier 52 at the foot of West 12th Street—oddly enough, the border separating the parishes of St. Veronica's and St. Bernard's. The queen of the Cunard Line meets the U-20 off the Old Head of Kinsale in County Cork. Kapitänleutnant Walter Schwieger peers through his periscope, shouts "Torpedo loose!" and the grave-diggers work overtime. Dublin is a city full of revolutionaries waiting for the next Easter. Big news that summer was the death of Jeremiah O'Donovan Rossa, the mad Fenian who had died on Staten Island in June. On Tom Clarke's order, the indefatigable John Devoy dug Rossa up and sent him home for show. "The fools, the fools, the fools!" said Pearse—who would face the wall at Kilmainham and earn a quicklime grave himself within nine months—"they have left us our Fenian dead." But Grandmother Rosanna did not hear Pearse, for she had already made Glasnevin the previous February. She lived somewhere on Aungier Street, according to his mother. But that was not true. She lived and died in the scatologically named Piles Buildings, Arthur's Lane. She had four sons in addition to his mother. Joe and Frank would be IRA gunmen, one boy, Charlie, his mother had repeatedly misinformed him, would choke to death on a Friday fishbone and the other one, Dick, would grow up in an orphanage, like O'Rourke's mother. Did Charlie's death grieve Rosanna into tuberculosis? Did she give up hope? Did she stop believing in the Virgin Mary? When she was dying did she wonder if she would ever see summer again? Did she wonder who would take care of her children? Did she wonder, "why me?" Did she ask why her Blessed Virgin had deserted her?

It was time to get moving, but O'Rourke had a hunch. Because his mother always made a big deal out of Uncle Joe's birthday—October 10, 1901—he decided to try and find his grandparents' marriage certificate. If there was one thing the poor the world over did for nothing, it was fuck and fuck often. O'Rourke made a wild guess and asked for the marriage index for 1900. He immediately went to the quarter beginning July 1 and searched. A Kavanagh showed up on

September 17, marrying a Conway. He filled out the slip and waited for the verdict.

Ainm agus Sloinne/Name and Surname: Joseph Kavanagh. Rosanna Conway.

Sollúnaíodh an Pósadh/Marriage Solemnized at: the Catholic Church of St. Michael & John. On Wood Quay, facing the Liffey.

Staid/Condition: Bachelor. Spinster. O'Rourke smiled at the spinster notation. It was a word that, pronounced viciously enough, could stick in the craw of an unmarried Irish woman.

Gairm Bheatha/Rank or Profession: Hairdresser for him. Blank for her. Rosanna must have done *something*, but the state, British at that time, thought it unimportant.

Ionad Cónaithe/Residence at the time of Marriage: the groom, 40 Camden Row. The bride, 26 Temple Lane. There was the Temple Lane reference again, just as in Uncle Joe's death certificate. That must have been Rosanna's home. Camden Row was only blocks away from Temple Lane. This was beginning to sound like a neighborhood romance.

Ainm agus Sloinne an Athar/Father's Name and Surname: Joseph Kavanagh (deceased). Richard Conway (deceased). So that's how Uncle Dick got his name. And for the first time O'Rourke knew his great-grandfathers' first names.

Gairm Bheatha an Athar/Rank or Profession of Father: Kavanagh was a Labourer; Conway a Cabinet Maker. Not only did Uncle Dick get his name from his grandfather, but he also inherited his grandfather's carpentry skills which he used to make altars dedicated to the Virgin Mary.

In ár bhFianaise/in the Presence of us: John Kavanagh was best man; Elizabeth Reilly was maid of honor. O'Rourke knew his grandfather's brother, Jack, lived in Dun Laoghaire and had lived into his 80s, dying in the 1950s after the family had immigrated to America. He was clueless about his grandmother's friend, Elizabeth Reilly. He made a note to tell Cyclops.

So many of the family secrets had been revealed and O'Rourke, after only an hour's work, felt exhausted, but in a way exuberant. He now knew where he had come from. He didn't know if it helped him in any way, but he felt more complete. There were literally hundreds of relatives on the O'Rourke side, stretching from Dublin into Meath and

Louth and down to Wexford, but it was this little Kavanagh family of seven that had caught his fascination. Now all dead, but not forgotten. At least not in this moment.

49.

The following morning O'Rourke was back at the Registar's Office in Lombard Street. He started collecting birth certificates for the Kavanagh children. He knew both Uncle Joe's and his mother's birthdays and got the certificates. He backtracked with Charlie the ten years the gravestone said and sure enough found him in January 1904, the year of Joyce's *Ulysses*. Did Joyce and Nora Barnacle ever come across the Kavanagh clan as Rosanna wheeled Charlie's pram across St. Stephen's Green? Did Nora see little Joseph clutch onto his mother's skirt or hold his da's hand in the Bloomtime summer of 1904?

He knew his Uncle Frank was born on November 2nd, All Souls Day. O'Rourke searched the index books for 1902 and 1903 and only came up with a Myles Francis Kavanagh. He got the certificate, but it was not the right Frank. "Myles," laughed O'Rourke. Boy, was that the wrong fucking name for Frank Kavanagh, the meanest son-of-a-bitch O'Rourke had ever encountered in his life—and that was saying something.

Frank Kavanagh, after his IRA troubles, somehow got to America in the early 1920s, probably illegally, probably as a seaman. He had Hollywood good looks that would put Clark Gable to shame. He loved booze and women and plenty of both. His habit was to work for six months at sea, come back to New York and drink and whore until his money ran out, and then go back out to sea. During World War II he shipped out with the merchant marine and his ship was torpedoed by the Japanese in the South Pacific. He spent nearly three years in a Japanese prisoner of war camp. He lived on rice and fishheads. Then it was POW bait. Today they call it *sushi*.

The only thing Frank hated more than the Japanese were the British, who had, in effect, chased him out of his own country. One of the great indignities of his life was being liberated from the Japanese by the British army. Even after twenty-five years, the IRA man inside remained belligerent. As he came out of the camp, dressed in a thong, a British Tommy in sympathy said, "How are ya, mate?"

Frank Kavanagh took one look at the soldier and let out a well directed, "Go fuck yerself, ya British cunt!" The Tommy almost collapsed, he was so shocked. Frank may have weighed only ninety pounds, but his malicious Irish memory was perfect.

After the war he lost a leg at sea in an accident and moved to Greenwich Village—in St. Veronica's Parish—to be close to the O'Rourkes. He expected young Tone to come and do his grocery shopping every day after school. Tone wanted to play ball like his hero Willie Mays of the New York Giants. He wanted to perfect the basket catch that Willie used at the Polo Grounds uptown. Tone stopped showing up to do the grocery shopping. Frank got madder than usual. When Frank passed away a few years later, Tone was out of Frank's substantial will. O'Rourke smiled, thinking of the hard life lesson that Frank Kavanagh had taught him early on.

As usual, Frank was continuing to be difficult. O'Rourke was sure of his birthday, November 2, but could not find him in either 1902 or 1903. Charlie was 1904 so O'Rourke went to 1905—and there was Frank. The first surprise was that Charlie was between Joe and Frank.

O'Rourke's mother was next in 1907 and then he had to look for Richard, his Uncle Dick, after her. He went to 1909 to give Rosanna a year's break and found Richard on October 16.

The only difference in all the birth certificates was that Dick was the only one not born at 40 Camden Row. It was the grandfather's home when he got married and apparently, Rosanna had moved there and raised the family. Dick was born in the Rotunda Hospital in Parnell Square. O'Rourke wondered at the reason. Was it a tough pregnancy or was it becoming the fashion to have babies in hospitals by 1909?

The family was complete and O'Rourke felt rather proud. Rosanna and Joseph had been prolific the first nine years of their marriage:

Joseph, October 10, 1901

Charles, January 17, 1904
Francis, November 2, 1905
Mary, March 18, 1907
Richard, October 16, 1909

O'Rourke was one of those people who looked for significance in everything. He truly believed that serendipity meant something. The dates jumped out at him. His mother was born on March 18, the day after St. Patrick's Day. St. Patrick's Day was always a two-day celebration to O'Rourke because of his mother. He also noticed that his Uncle Dick was born on October 16. He shared his birth date with Michael Collins. O'Rourke smiled. Somehow, he couldn't see Michael Collins building temples to the Virgin Mary in each room of his apartment.

Charlie's birthday was the oddest. January 17. It must have been a date of immense joy in 1904 when he was born. And O'Rourke wondered if his grandfather was aware of it when he died 20 years to the date of Charlie's birth in 1924?

In a strange, benign way O'Rourke was suddenly curious about the mating habits of his grandparents. Kids in 1901, 1904, 1905, 1907, and 1909. What the hell was going on in 1902 and 1903? He doubted they had come up with some amazing form of birth control, which left the question, was there a miscarriage or an infant death, or even a stillbirth? It was a distinct possibility considering the fertility of this young, robustly sexual couple. O'Rourke thought of going through the birth and death books one more time, but he just wasn't up to it. For now, at least, he would let his imagination dictate what was going on over at 40 Camden Row.

O'Rourke left Joyce House and walked down Pearse Street to the Dublin City Library and Archive. He had used it before when he was working on Mary Robinson's campaign for the Irish presidency in 1990. He went upstairs and headed for the Thom Directories, a great source of information on Dublin going back to the mid-nineteenth century. It listed every business in the city, by street name. He decided to look in the 1900 book and searched for Camden Row, #40. There it was: Joseph Kavanagh, hairdresser. He continued going backwards until he got to 1893 and found another barber had the business in that year. Did O'Rourke's grandfather buy that business? Now O'Rourke went forward. Nineteen-ten was the last listing for Joseph Kavanagh at 40 Camden Row. Since all but one of the children were born there, they must have also lived in the building. After sixteen years of business on Camden Row why did he suddenly move? Why the economic downturn? Too many mouths to feed?

The librarian directed O'Rourke to some maps of Dublin City and he immediately checked the key for the Pile's Buildings. To his astonishment, they were there in postal code Dublin 8, and it also gave the street name Golden Lane, which was just to the south of Aungier Street, very near St. Patrick's Cathedral. On the map he could see Golden Lane, right next to Arthur's Lane. And the Adelaide Hospital was just around the corner. On the map, O'Rourke could see it was only a block from the beautiful park at St. Patrick's. He wondered if Rosanna ever took the children to romp in the park on a sunny summer's day. He rechecked the Thom's Directory and found that #1 and #8 Golden Lane were tenements, worldwide nomenclature for the poor.

O'Rourke had one more thing to do. Sam had not been a complete failure teaching him about strange technologies—like cell phones and the Internet. She showed him how to use Google by putting his name in the search engine. He was surprised by the number of items that came up with his name on them.

"How do you like being Googled?" she asked.

"Feels good," replied O'Rourke.

"Is that all you think of?" replied Sam, not all that upset at the innuendo.

O'Rourke loved Sam's humor and was a bit surprised to catch himself laughing out loud as he typed in "diphtheria" into the search engine. The description was surprising: "Diphtheria is a very contagious and potentially life-threatening infection that usually attacks the throat and nose. In more serious cases, it can attack the nerves and heart."

Throat and nose. O'Rourke's mother had been right, in her own way. As Charlie succumbed to the diphtheria, O'Rourke's mother thought he had choked on a fishbone. Nineteen-fourteen. Eighty-six years ago. It was strange. O'Rourke worked in a profession—politics— where truth was never spoken and seldom thought. Yet his mother spoke her version of the truth to him about Charlie's death, so long ago. And that tombstone up in Glasnevin spoke the truth too, giving clues to a family that had been forgotten for almost a century.

O'Rourke came out the Pearse Street Library and started walking back towards City Centre. He thought of the Kavanagh family gravestone up in Glasnevin and how that new statue of the Virgin Mary seemed to be stalking him from over in that other plot, as if beseeching him to write down the information that was chiseled into the stone. It was all so curious.

When he got to Westland Row, he stopped. He made a left and, for some reason, headed for St. Andrew's, the church where he had been baptized as Jude Wolfe Tone O'Rourke. Life had taught O'Rourke's mother many lessons and she was a big believer in St. Jude, the saint of hopeless causes. It was as if the church, which would have saved him from the nothingness of limbo if he had died in infancy, was inexorably pulling him towards it.

In *Ulysses* it was called "All Hallows" as Mr. Bloom paid a visit. He saw a woman coming out and decided to go inside for the first time in nearly thirty years. He genuflected and took a seat in a pew in the almost empty church. Up ahead was the baptismal fount where his christening into the Catholic Church had taken place. He didn't know it for a fact, but he assumed that this was also the place where the revolutionary Pearse Brothers, Padraic and Willie, had also been baptized. They were born only paces away in Great Brunswick Street, which was now named after them. And they had gone to the Christian Brothers School next door. He still didn't know what to make of Patrick Pearse, the wall-eyed poet. He was a lousy revolutionary, a miserable politician, and, by all accounts, a terrible businessman. Someone had even written a book about him called *The Triumph of Failure*. He was an odd duck who ran a school for boys, which sent a red flag up for O'Rourke. But he was an excellent motivator. First at the grave of O'Donovan Rossa in 1915, then later at the GPO on Easter Monday as he read the declaration of independence he had authored, *Poblacht Na h Eireann*. Next to Yeats, he might be one of the oddest people ever to join the Irish Republican Brotherhood. Collins observed Pearse in the GPO and took notes on how *not* to run a revolution. Whatever he was, he somehow succeeded in getting the Irish off their asses after seven hundred years of obsequiousness to Britain.

The baptismal fount reminded him not only of his own beginning, but what was going on with Sam and the baby. There hadn't been a word out of her for the last month. He had called her a few times in Tortola, but she never returned his voicemails. The Luddite in O'Rourke scoffed at the notion that all the new technology was helpful. If it was so fucking helpful, why didn't Sam call him? What was to become of their baby? O'Rourke didn't know what to do. Time was becoming tight for the baby's survival. Maybe he should go straight to London and hop a flight to the British Virgin Islands?

Then he thought of the other Pearse brother, Willie. Pearse the sculptor and occasional revolutionary. He went into the Mortuary Chapel and looked at his *Mater Dolorosa*, Christ's sorrowful mother, standing. Our Lady of Sorrows. O'Rourke grunted. This was getting personal. His mother had been married at Our Lady of Perpetual Sorrow in Foxrock in 1945. Ireland's "emergency" over—and hers about to begin. If there was ever truth in advertising, thought O'Rourke, it was his mother getting married in Our Lady of *Perpetual* Sorrow. His parents' marriage still served as a warning to O'Rourke, the eternal Irish bachelor.

O'Rourke looked at Willie Pearse's sculpture and wondered how it had affected his mother, the very political Mrs. Margaret Pearse, in the years after his execution. The Via Dolorosa was the route Christ took to Calvary after Pontius Pilate washed his hands of him. It was where St. Veronica wiped the sweating face of Christ and was rewarded with his image on the cloth. It must have been difficult for Mrs. Pearse. Although she didn't live on Pearse Street after the Rising, she probably came to mass at St. Andrew's on the occasional Sunday, and the old church must have been a constant reminder of her dead sons. They were baptized here and they should have been buried out of there, but the British were not about to have any more Fenian extravaganzas, like Rossa's funeral. It must have been agony for Mrs. Pearse to stare at the *Mater Dolorosa* and think of her two sons. It was the grief of an earthly mother, sharing in the pain of the Blessed Virgin.

He thought of his own mother and how it must have hurt her when Rosanna died in 1915. Then the horror of being taken out of her own house and moving to a strange orphanage. O'Rourke was a menopause baby, and as a child, he worried about what would happen to him if his older parents died. The bond with his mother was extraordinary. Would he ever have a child? If he did, would the bond be as powerful? He couldn't believe his predicament. He was now nearly fifty-four-years-old and about to become a father. Or would he? He wondered about Sam and his daughter. A daughter according to a dream. He didn't know what to do. In front of the *Mater Dolorosa* he knelt and said a prayer for Sam and the baby girl. Then he said a prayer for his newfound family, the Kavanaghs, late of Camden Row, Dublin City.

50.

His dreams had changed. The Virgin was gone, replaced by the toddler. A little girl with wonderful golden, curly hair. She was so young she couldn't possibly talk yet, yet O'Rourke instantly knew her name. It was baby Rosanna, his aunt, the sister his mother had never known about. She reached her arms out to him, but they would never touch. For O'Rourke knew this was another Dublin ghost.

"Hello, Tone," she said. She was too young to talk, but she was talking as if she was maybe six or seven. O'Rourke didn't know what to say. "Don't you want to know my name?" she asked?

"I think I know it," said O'Rourke. "It's Rosanna, isn't it?"

"Yes," she responded. "Joe was named after da and I was named after mammy. I, too, was born at 40 Camden Row. After Joe and before Charlie. They said 1903." Then her voice turned sad. "But I had to die."

"I'm sorry," said O'Rourke.

"That's all right," she replied evenly. "But remember I existed as sure as your mammy did."

"I knew you were missing," he said, "from the records in Lombard Street."

"But you didn't search for me."

"I will. Today. I promise."

"They never talked about me, you know."

"Who?"

"Mammy and da. I think when I died they felt so sad. Only my brother Joe knew. I think Charlie was too young."

"I will find you today."

"Don't forget me, please. I'm a Kavanagh too, just like the rest of them. Just like you. Think about me so your mammy, my sister Mary, will know I existed. Please."

O'Rourke awoke and bolted upright in his bed at the Shelbourne. The summer dawn was upon Dublin City and he could hear the birds nosily awaken in St. Stephen's Green below him. He got out of the bed naked and fell to his knees to say a prayer for little Rosanna Kavanagh who left this world almost a century ago. He could feel her loneliness and her need to feel loved and wanted, just like everyone else in this terrible world.

The Virgin was changing tactics, thought O'Rourke. O'Rourke admired her for the effective politician she was, moving O'Rourke closer to another lonely little girl who resided in Sam McGuire's womb halfway around the world.

51.

Now he was taking orders from a ghost. Did he really dream about a child named Rosanna? Or was it some figment of his imagination buried down deep that had come to the surface of his conscience because of the guilt over McGuire and the baby? Still, he had promised the child he would look for her, so he dressed and once again headed over to Lombard Street to search for this little girl, who may never have really existed.

He came out of the Shelbourne Hotel on a warm, sunny late July morning and started to head to his left when he stopped in his tracks. No, he decided, he was going the wrong way. He crossed over to St. Stephen's Green, said hello to the statue of his namesake Wolfe

Tone, before heading toward Grafton Street and the Traitors Gate at the entrance to the Green. Around Stephen's Green West he went by the College of Surgeons and made a left into York Street on his way to Aungier Street. From there he made his way to Bishop Street where the massive façade of the Dublin Institute of Technology stood before him. It was the location of the old Jacob's Biscuit Factory, where Thomas MacDonough and Sean MacBride would earn their 1916 death sentences. The school's curved front, like Jacob's before it, always reminded him of the rotunda of Ebbets Field, of all things.

Down Bishop Street, to the left of the college, O'Rourke went until he came to the National Archives of Ireland at #8. He was photographed and issued an ID card then went upstairs to look at the 1911 Census. It was on microfiche and first he worked all of the Piles Buildings on Golden Lane, but could find nothing about the Kavanaghs. If anything, O'Rourke had surmised about his grandparents, they were creatures of habit. They had spent most of their lives surrounded by the same streets and buildings. Rosanna must have grown up in Temple Lane and her husband lived only five blocks away on Camden Row. He bet they must have met at church, at Michael's and John's. This was their neighborhood, the Strumpet City of James Plunkett, ripe with poverty and unrest, but they would never leave it. They were real Dubs. They had left Camden Row in 1910 and they had not arrived in the Piles Buildings until at least 1914. He just knew they lived around here someplace. He pulled out his map of Dublin and ran his finger down Camden Row to the west and the next street, an extension of Camden Row, was Long Lane. He went back to the desk and got the census for Long Lane.

One by one he went through them until he came to #36 Long Lane. A chill ran down O'Rourke's spine, for there they were, all seven of the Kavanaghs, including his mother. And for the first time he saw the signature of his grandfather, Joseph Kavanagh. It was strong and clear and it never wavered below the line that said, "Signature of the Head of Family." The census had been filled out all over Ireland on Sunday, April 2, 1911. After all these years and all his mother's stories, it was there for all to see, not on a sad gravestone, but on an official British government document, proof that the Kavanagh family existed in the eyes of the government. The grandfather was older than O'Rourke had thought, it seemed, because the census said he was forty, which would have put his birth year at 1870 or 1871. He was six years older than Rosanna. Joseph, Rosanna, Joe Jr., and Charlie could all "read & write." The other children, Francis, Mary, his mother, and Richard, "cannot read & write." The three older boys were "scholars," and O'Rourke's mother and his Uncle Dick obviously didn't go to school yet, but stayed home with Rosanna, who still was not assigned a profession by the government.

There was no sign of another child, perhaps a daughter named Rosanna, but then he saw it. "Total children born alive: 6; children still living: 5." There was a missing child and O'Rourke's heart began to race. He printed out a copy of the document and ran out the door into Bishop Street.

* * * * *

He hailed the first taxi he saw—that was one of the great things about the new Dublin, you could actually find a cab when you needed one—and minutes later was at Joyce House on Lombard Street. Up to the second floor he went and pulled the birth indexes for 1902 and 1903.

He started looking for a female child born in South Dublin. He looked for a Rosanna, but she was not to be found. He then searched for familiar names. He knew his mother had a sister named Nellie, which in Ireland at that time was short for Ellen. He found an Ellen and his heart raced. When they called his name out with the information slip, he thought he had solved the mystery.

"I'm sorry," informed the woman clerk, "there seems to be a mistake in the book. I checked twice and this Ellen does not exist."

O'Rourke went back to the books and searched again. He tried to limit his search from late 1902 until early spring 1903. Those were the parameters, because young Joe was born in October 1901 and Charlie was born in January 1904. He tried Mary Anne, which he thought might be his grandmother's name. No luck. He tried Eileen. Nothing. He tried Annie, Kathleen, and Frances and all the other girls names in South Dublin within his parameters and got nothing.

Maybe he was wrong in what he was looking for. Maybe it was a boy. Maybe Baby Rosanna was a ghostly curveball. First he tried John because that was his grandfather's brother's name. Nothing again. Then he tried James and James Leo and James Patrick and there was a John

Joseph and Patrick and he came up totally empty. This child—he was positive she was a girl—was beginning to depress him.

He abandoned the birth books and worked the death books for 1903 and 1904. The age was listed for every entry. He choose zero to one and searched for South Dublin deaths. There was a "Nellie," the same name as Grandmother Rosanna's sister. He handed in the paper and awaited the verdict. Little Nellie Kavanagh, spinster, read the document, was a child of a servant, and had lived nine hours in 1903. The only trouble was, she was not Rosanna's and Joseph's daughter. It was the wrong child.

O'Rourke explained his situation to the clerk who said that not all births and deaths had been religiously registered. Perhaps, if the child died in the first few days after birth no one had bothered to register it.

In his mind's eye O'Rourke could see Baby Rosanna and he knew she was beseeching him to keep searching for her. He kept checking randomly, anything close to what "qualifications" Baby Rosanna presented to him. He kept coming up with babies who had died at six months of bronchitis, pneumonia, and other diseases that today antibiotics would wipe out in days.

"You look depressed," the clerk said to O'Rourke.

"I am," he replied. "I can't find this child who I know existed from the census of 1911."

"Sounds like a Holy Angels Plot baby to me," said the clerk. She went on to explain that the Holy Angels Plot was up in Glasnevin and that babies that died in infancy were buried there.

Poor Baby Rosanna. Forgotten and abandoned. All O'Rourke knew was that she was not in the family grave in Glasnevin, he couldn't find her in the birth/death records, and maybe she was in Holy Angels with all the other little dead Dublin babies. No wonder she felt abandoned. When he went to visit his mother up in Glasnevin, O'Rourke was always moved by the graves of infants and young children. There was sometimes a picture of a beautiful child and on the stone would be written: "Love you always from your heart broken Mammy and Daddy." He knew this baby had broken his grandparents hearts. He also guessed that she died before his mother was born because his mother never mentioned she had a sister. The pain of a century passed was drilling O'Rourke in his chest.

O'Rourke sat alone looking out the window onto Lombard Street. O'Rourke thought of this young child who was not even remembered on the family gravestone and to his utter surprise, began to cry, tears silently running down his cheeks and onto the 1911 census certificate before him. Baby Rosanna had been found, but not found. O'Rourke wanted to comfort this little ghost that so much wanted to get back into the dead Kavanagh family. O'Rourke knew he had failed Baby Rosanna, but he had done his best. He could see her in his mind's eye awaiting the verdict. Right now there was nothing he could do. Soon, he promised, he would make it right.

"I won't forget you, Rosanna," he whispered. "I promise I won't forget you."

52.

"Where is he?" McGuire snapped into the phone at Winthrop Pepoon. "All I'm getting is voicemail at the office and at home."

"Sam, is that you?"

"Where is he, Winnie?"

"He's in Dublin."

"With another woman?"

"No, no, Sam," said Pepoon. "He's with Clarence Black."

"What the hell is he doing in Dublin?"

"I think he needed to get away."

"I bet," countered McGuire, "he really needed a drink."

"That too," Pepoon chuckled, and then turned serious. "You know you're the reason he stopped drinking. Without you, there is no reason not to drink."

"Oh, Winnie, what am I going to do?"

"Why don't you call him?"

"He still doesn't own a cell phone," reminded McGuire.

"But Clarence does. They're five hours ahead of us. Give him a buzz."

"I will," said McGuire. She then paused before saying, "Oh, Winnie, I'm so confused."

"He misses you, Sam."

"Does he?" asked McGuire, brightening a little.

"He misses you with all his heart," said Pepoon. "You know he's that kind of man."

"Yes," said McGuire, "I know he is."

53.

O'Rourke and Clarence Black were sitting at the bar of the Stag's Head, just off Dame Street. O'Rourke had been coming here since the 1960s, when he was a college student at CCNY and he had first returned to Dublin to visit his family. At night it was an asylum, dense and loud, but by day the quiet reminded him of what Joe Flaherty had once written: "The warmth of the room appealed to my Irish heart; it seemed like a blend of wood and whiskey, combining the best aspects of the womb and the coffin."

The bar dated from Victorian times and had lived through every major event in modern Irish history. According to legend, every remarkable Irishmen, including Joyce and Collins, had bellied up to this bar. He could just imagine Collins, hunched in a snug, conspiring with one of his spies from Dublin Castle, which was just a five minute walk away. In the great James Cagney movie, *Shake Hands with the Devil*, the Black and Tans come into the bar from the Dame Lane side entrance looking for IRA man Michael O'Leary and have the tables turned on them by the hard-drinking, quick-thinking clientele.

And now the bar meant even more to O'Rourke because of the information that he had just learned about his grandparents from the archives in Lombard Street. If you walked out the door and slid through the alley to Dame Street and crossed the road, you would find yourself in front of 26 Temple Lane, Rosanna's childhood home.

Temple Lane was more alley than lane and the brick façade of #26 had been altered, but there was an atmosphere that hadn't changed much since 1900 when Rosanna left here to marry O'Rourke's grandfather. And O'Rourke wondered, when they were courting, did his grandfather drop off Rosanna at her mother's house, then proceed across the street to the Stag's Head for a pint before heading down the road for his home in Camden Row? Did he sit right at this bar, in this spot, and wonder about Rosanna, her scent, and what her wonderful breasts might look like? Could he ever imagine that a century later, his grandson, an American multi-millionaire, would sit at the same bar and wonder about him, Rosanna, and another woman with marvelous breasts?

The quiet of the afternoon was broken by the ringing of Black's cell phone. Black listened, then handed the phone to O'Rourke. "It's for you," he said with a small smile.

"Tone O'Rourke here."

"Tone, it's Sam. I miss you," she said.

"I miss you too," he replied, trying to swallow the sudden lump in his throat.

"Tell me about St. Brigid."

"What?"

"St. Brigid," insisted McGuire. "You know about all the Irish saints. I know Colmcille is your favorite, but tell me of Brigid."

"Well," said O'Rourke, staring at Black with a look of puzzlement on his face, "she is one of the three prominent saints of Ireland, along with Patrick and Colmcille. I believe the name Brigid derives from 'fiery arrow.'"

"Fire!" said McGuire.

"Yes, fire. Fire has always been associated with her for some reason. She is the patron saint of milkmaids—"

"Milkmaids!" said McGuire holding her breast. "What else?"

"Eye ailments."

"Stop it!" said McGuire excitedly. "What else?"

"I think sailors and, of all things, bastards."

"Bastards!"

"Yes," said O'Rourke, "bastards."

"Tone," McGuire said excitedly, "we have a bastard."

"Well, you know, Sam," O'Rourke almost whispered into the phone, "we can change that."

"You're damn right we can."

"Suits me," said O'Rourke. "When can you get here?"

"Oh, Tone," replied McGuire, "you've made me so happy."

"What changed your mind?"

"Oh, I met this wonderful woman at the beach yesterday, who predicted we'd have a child and would be happy. You can't image what has been happening to me. Brigid Dillon knows all about children—she had fourteen of her own—and she says we're going to have a baby that will fill us with joy."

"Brigid Dillon?"

"Do you know her?"

"Yes—and no."

"What are you saying?"

"Well," started out O'Rourke slowly, "my paternal grandmother was named Brigid Dillon and she married my grandfather, Seán O'Rourke, and they had fourteen children, including my father. But I never met either of them. They died way before I was even born."

"Where were they from?"

"County Louth."

"The Wee County!"

"Yes, how do you know that?"

"Your grandmother told me."

54.

O'Rourke and Black waited for Sam McGuire to clear Irish customs. She had flown from Tortola to London on British Airways and then popped over to Dublin on Aer Lingus. O'Rourke waited for the first black face to appear, then ran to it.

"*Fáilte go Éireann*," said O'Rourke as he embraced McGuire.

"Welcome to Ireland."

She wrapped her arms around his shoulders and hugged him as hard as she could. "I thought I'd never see you again," she said then hugged O'Rourke again. "I never want to let you go again," she confessed. She then started to cry.

"Jesus," said O'Rourke, "don't cry or I'll be howling too."

"Hey," said Black, "doesn't the hired help around here get a kiss too?"

"Oh, Clarence," said McGuire, pecking him on the cheek, "I'm so happy to see you guys."

"You mean this guy," said Black, pointing a thumb at O'Rourke.

"Especially this guy," agreed McGuire.

"Let me look at you," said O'Rourke and for the first time he could see McGuire's protruding belly. "You both look great!" was all he could say.

"Well," said Black, "I got a plane to catch."

"Where you going?" asked McGuire.

"Back to New York," replied Black, "taking the 10:30 Aer Lingus flight."

"Do you have to go?" asked McGuire.

"Hey," said Black, "if I want to sit around with a bunch of harps in bars, I can do that at Hogan's Moat!"

McGuire laughed, but then frowned. "I thought you weren't drinking," she directed at O'Rourke.

"I wasn't," he replied, "until you left me."

"Well," McGuire replied, "I'm back, and I'm staying."

"Okay, you guys," said Black. "I'll see you back in New York. We have a busy fall ahead of us." Black looked up at a television monitor where CNN International was playing. "Holy shit," he said, then began laughing. It was Jackie Swift, Madonna-Sue, young Vitoessa, and the newest member of the family, just weeks old, whom they were waving around as the newest product of their family values beliefs.

"What's going on?" asked O'Rourke.

"The Republican National Convention," replied McGuire.

"I see they have the new kid working already," said O'Rourke, shaking his head.

"You know what they call her?" queried McGuire. Both Black and O'Rourke shook their heads. "Julie-Annie."

Both men started laughing. "No fucking way," said O'Rourke.

"It's true," said McGuire, "they named the kid after Mayor Giuliani."

"Well, I'll be damned," was all Clarence Black could say.

"That's why I love Dublin," said O'Rourke, "you get to miss all this disgusting shit."

They said goodbye to Black one more time, then left the terminal, and O'Rourke waved his limousine to the curb. "My God, Tone," said McGuire, surprised and cheeky all at once, "you sprang for a limo. You actually spent some money!"

"Hey," said O'Rourke, "you make me sound cheap. I'm not cheap," he protested.

"Not much!"

"Shaddup and get in," and McGuire hopped in, helped by a tap on the bottom by O'Rourke.

"Some things never change," she said, not really protesting.

"Let's go down O'Connell Street, then work your way to Wood Quay," O'Rourke told the driver. "Use the city streets on the North Side." Soon they were driving through Phibsborough and down North Circular Road. "That's Mountjoy Prison," pointed out O'Rourke. "This is O'Casey territory," said O'Rourke, indicating Sean O'Casey's birthplace on Dorset Street. McGuire nodded, groggy from the trip and excited to be seeing Dublin for the first time on such a beautiful summer's day. Then they were driving down Parnell Square, zipping past the birthplace of Oliver St. John Gogarty, Joyce's Buck Mulligan.

"There it is," said O'Rourke, pointing out the General Post Office in O'Connell Street. "That's where the revolution started. Doesn't the tricolor look beautiful today?" His pride in Ireland was evident in his voice. The limo swung onto the south quays and soon they were in front of Sts. Michael's and John's. They got out of the limo, and O'Rourke took McGuire's hand. "Take the bags to the Shelbourne," he told the driver. "We'll walk back from here."

"The Shelbourne," repeated McGuire. "So you are spending some bucks."

"Yeah," deadpanned O'Rourke, "I'm trying to impress this broad I know." McGuire gave him a solid whack and O'Rourke knew they were one again. "Come on," he said, pulling her by the hand. They climbed the steps to the church and surveyed the River Liffey before them. "That's the Four Courts," said O'Rourke, pointing to the left, "and that's the Ha'penny Bridge," he said, thrusting an arm to his right. O'Rourke had his left arm around McGuire, holding onto her hip and buttock.

"Still like that ass, I see," she said.

"I see there's more to like."

"I should whack you."

"But you won't."

"But I won't." He kissed her gently on the lips and then just licked the tip of her nose with his tongue. "You're going to get me in trouble," she said.

"I already got you in trouble!" he returned, and they both broke into laughter. "This is Saints Michael's & John's Roman Catholic Church, now, sadly, defunct. A historic Dublin landmark. First Catholic chapel in Ireland to peal a bell after the passing of the Catholic Emancipation Laws in 1829."

"As usual," replied McGuire, "you know your history."

"Do you know what happened here on Monday, September 17, 1900?"

"I don't have a clue," she said.

"My mother's parents were married in this church," he said. "If that hadn't happened, I wouldn't be here, and neither would that baby." They remained silent and watched as a bird swooped down on the Liffey and plucked a fish from the river before flying off in the direction of Chapelizard.

"Wow," said McGuire quietly. "Nineteen hundred—a hundred years ago next month."

"Yeah," said O'Rourke. "Long time ago. Queen Victoria's last visit to Dublin. I bet the old Famine Queen must have driven right by here on her way to the Vice Regal Lodge in Phoenix Park."

"The Famine Queen?" asked McGuire.

"The Irish never forget," laughed O'Rourke.

"Tell me about it!"

"So right here," continued O'Rourke, "my grandparents, Rosanna Conway and Joseph Kavanagh, were wed. And I can't think of a better place to ask you this: Will you marry me?"

McGuire stood mute, she was caught so off-guard by the question.

Then tears filled her eyes. "Yes," she said. "Yes, Tone. Yes, I will marry you." They embraced each other and she sobbed heavily into his shoulder, totally overcome, this time with overwhelming joy.

* * * * *

O'Rourke and McGuire walked back to Dame Street then cut up Church Lane and across Suffolk Street where it became Nassau. They stopped by Molly Malone's statue at the foot of Grafton Street. "She is known," said O'Rourke, "as the Tart with the Cart."

McGuire laughed. "I think I love Dublin," she said.

The most prominent thing about Molly Malone were her fabulous breasts. McGuire pointed to them, then at all the cleavage coming at them from Grafton Street. "I've seen more boob here in fifteen minutes than I've seen in New York all year."

O'Rourke laughed. "Yeah. When the temperatures go up, the tops go down."

"No kidding," laughed McGuire.

"Something to do with dairy, I believe," said O'Rourke as he pulled Sam by the hand. "Come on, I have to get you something." Just in from Grafton Street was the College Jewelers. He took McGuire by the hand and led her into the store. "You'll need an engagement ring and a wedding ring, Sam. Go to it." O'Rourke stood back and watched McGuire, who was like a kid in a candy store.

"Oh boy," she said. "Oh boy!" She tried on several engagement rings, found what she liked, then looked for a matching set of gold wedding rings. "Come here," she said. "Let's get a fitting."

"For me?"

"Who else?"

"Well, my father never wore a wedding ring."

"Well," she said, "you're going to wear a wedding ring. I'm not letting you wander all over New York like a dog without a license."

"Gee," said O'Rourke, "great analogy."

"You know what I mean," McGuire said, seriously.

"I know what you mean," he replied. "But I don't think you'll have to worry. You're the last woman I'll ever belong to."

"You only have one other choice if you break that promise."

"What?"

"Death."

"Gotcha."

It took forty-five minutes, but McGuire found what she wanted. The bill was nearly fifteen thousand dollars. "Can we afford this?" she asked, concerned.

"Yes," was all O'Rourke said in response.

They came out of the jewelry shop and walked along Nassau Street hand in hand. They turned right on Kildare Street and walked toward St. Stephen's Green. At the corner they turned and entered the Shelbourne Hotel. In their suite, McGuire was blown away by the view of the Green. "It's so, so . . ."

"Green?" replied O'Rourke.

They both laughed, then they kissed, and O'Rourke's hands were all over McGuire's ass and he was rubbing her belly and he was as hard as he could be. McGuire dropped to her knees and O'Rourke unbuckled himself and McGuire pulled down his zipper and his underwear, and then her mouth was on his cock and her hands were under his balls.

"Oh, man," she said, "I missed these."

Soon McGuire was stripped bare and O'Rourke ogled her different naked body. She was bigger and rounder in places and just looking at her made his engorged cock extend well beyond his bellybutton.

"I see you finally got those humongous tits you always wanted."

"There's that word again, Tone, humongous. Your humongous balls and my humongous tits. What a pair of pairs!"

"You're something," was all O'Rourke could muster.

"Man, I just love your cockadoo," said McGuire as she played with O'Rourke's erect penis, pulling it and letting it go as if it was the arm of a slot machine. She giggled at his hardness. "Boy, are you glad to see me!"

"Only you can do this to me."

"I bet you say that to all the girls," replied McGuire.

They went to the bed and O'Rourke's hands were all over her. Before she knew it, she was laid back on the bed and he had buried his head between her legs. All she could see over her bump was the top of O'Rourke's gray head, like he was her gynecologist, but then a shiver ran up her loins.

"My God," she said, "what are you doing down there?"

O'Rourke, from below, replied, stealing a line from Sam Beckett, "I'm between wind and water."

She laughed and grinded her pussy outward to his mouth. "Jesus," she said. "Jesus." O'Rourke finally surfaced and he lay on the bed and she mounted him atop. "Oh, boy. Oh, boy," was all she could muster. Slowly he worked her way into her and she began to ride him.

Then she began to drip milk onto him. "My God," O'Rourke said. "Aren't you a little early with that?"

"Doctor says it can happen to women occasionally. I guess I'm exceptional."

Before she knew it O'Rourke's mouth was on her teat and she came. They found their rhythm instantly. It was as if nothing had changed.

"Stop," O'Rourke suddenly said.

"What?"

"We won't hurt the baby, will we?"

"Tone," she replied, "you're hardly hurting me!"

"Oh, then," he said, "I must have it in the wrong hole!"

She once again hit him on his Vietnam arm, drawing a wince, but she didn't care. "You have, without a doubt, the filthiest mind I've ever encountered!"

"Lucky you," he said and she came down and kissed him and they made love until exhaustion led them into a deep sleep.

55.

McGuire heard O'Rourke working in the living room of their suite at the Shelbourne. She could tell he was talking some of his cousins and Dublin friends on the phone. The dawn in summer came very early to Dublin because of its northern latitude. It was breaking, but Sam ignored it and wrapped her arms around her belly, which seemed to have a mind of its own as a little kicking exercise had begun. This was the first time she would wake up in Ireland and she found it a strange experience.

"Rise and shine," said O'Rourke, sitting on the bed. "Got to get moving. Big day ahead. Limo is picking us up at 8 a.m."

"What's the rush?" yawned McGuire.

"We have appointments. Let's go!" Sam looked at Tone and saw he was wearing a blue suit and tie. She wondered what he was up to. "And wear a dress. We have to look respectable for the people we're meeting."

McGuire got up and slowly made her way to the bathroom where she showered. O'Rourke stuck his head in. "We're running late. I'm going to the limo downstairs. I'll wait for you there. Hurry up."

"Yeah," she thought to herself as she soaped her belly, "don't hold your breath." She really wanted to get back into the bed.

She finally made her way downstairs at 8:15, and O'Rourke looked like he was going to have a stroke. He hopped out of the limo and held the door for McGuire. "Let's go," he said to the driver.

"Where are we going?" asked McGuire.

"To the rest of our lives," he said as he kissed her on her cheek. McGuire wondered why he beamed like he did.

The limo pulled away from the Shelbourne and took a left on Merrion Street, sped past Merrion Square and finally came to a halt in front of St. Andrew's on Westland Row. O'Rourke helped McGuire out of the limo and they headed for the rectory. They were shown in and waited in the hallway. Neither O'Rourke nor McGuire spoke. "Mr. O'Rourke?" asked the priest.

"Yes," he said, "and this is my fiancée"—it was the first time he had used the word and it elicited a smile from McGuire—"Simone McGuire. I hear you spoke to Monsignor Burke in New York and everything is in order."

"Yes," he said, "I'm Father Conway"—O'Rourke shook his head in quiet disbelief—"and after we fill out a few papers we can get onto it."

"Get onto what?" wondered McGuire.

Father Conway pulled out the blank certificates of marriage and McGuire's knees went weak. She took O'Rourke's left arm—his Vietnam arm—in both of her hands and held on for dear life. "Just a few questions," said the priest. "Your full name?"

"Jude Wolfe Tone O'Rourke," he said and McGuire knew his Christian name for the first time.

"Have you ever been married?"

"No."

"So you are a bachelor."

"Yes, I am. Or was," said O'Rourke, with just a tiny bit of doubt in his mind.

"Your name, missus?"

"Simone Elizabeth McGuire."

"Have you ever been married?"

"No."

"Then you're a spinster," said the priest as he filled in the marriage certificate.

"Spinster!" protested McGuire with some fire in her eyes.

"Ah," said the priest, "it's just a term we Irish use for the ould ones without a man."

"Spinster," said McGuire again and the priest gave O'Rourke the eye, knowing full well how sharp his needle was.

"There, there," said O'Rourke trying to hide a smile. "There, there."

"There, there, yourself," replied McGuire.

* * * * *

O'Rourke often thought of himself as the "spinster's son." His mother had not married until she was forty-two and, in reality, should never have married at all. It was funny. He had been all over the world, yet he was almost back to where he began.

His first encounter with the fairer sex was violent. It had been just around the corner at Hollis Street Hospital in 1946 when after two days of excruciating labor they finally yanked him out by the head, clamps scraping, from between his mother's legs. In Dublin you apparently got natural childbirth whether you wanted it or not. Mary Kavanagh was forty-three and this was her first child and, by God, she was terrified.

Her life had been hard after her father had succumbed to Black and Tan thuggery. Out of the orphanage in Sandymount and into her first job in a tobacconist shop in Bray by the sea. His mother was a woman of few vices, but it was here that she acquired her most virulent one. On the counter they sold "Lucys"—single, loose cigarettes. A Woodbine for a ha'penny. If you worked in a sweets shop, you might pop a chocolate. In a tobacconist shop, it was a Lucy. She lit up for the first time at eighteen, and it was three packs a day until she drew her final breath at eighty-two. Her right hand looked like it belonged to a Negro, it was so brown from the nicotine. But she loved her smokes from the first light-up in the morning to the last snuff-out at night.

After the tobacconist there were jobs as scullery maids and housekeepers in all the fine Protestant houses in the wealthy, manicured suburbs of South Dublin. Her life was literally just like *Upstairs, Downstairs*, which became her favorite TV show. She was unlucky in love—as her son would be—but she filled her time away from work with a deep devotion to the church—and a penchant for the movies. When she worked for the Anglo-Irish—O'Rourke couldn't utter the hyphenated words without thinking of Brendan Behan's bulls-eye definition: "A Protestant on a horse"—she found herself with a half day on Thursdays and Sunday evenings off. Thursday afternoons were reserved for the cinema and she took the tram to O'Connell Street for some Hollywood escape at the Carleton, the Metropole, or the Savoy. She confessed years later that Tyrone Power "did it for her" and O'Rourke first realized that she was as interested in sex as everyone else was. Her Sunday nights were different as she would often find herself in the City Centre, on Dame Street, when the loud, solitary bells of Christ Church Cathedral would strike the Angelous at six o'clock. "Oh," she said to her son years later as they walked together on the same Dame Street as the bells sounded again. "I remember them as a young girl and they were so, so lonely." O'Rourke looked across the deserted street—long before Temple Bar became the place to be—and understood completely, for loneliness was another trait he shared with his mother. It was as if loneliness stalked the Kavanaghs, for just down the street was Temple Lane, the girlhood home of her mother, Rosanna.

Her life changed when she went to work during the "Emergency"— as World War II was known in the Irish Free State—for Mrs. Darley out in Foxrock. O'Rourke's mother was a fantastic chef and a superb baker. Her gift was her simplicity. She could take a piece of fish and fry it—*sauté* was not yet in the Irish vocabulary—to a golden, delicious perfection. Mrs. Darley was suspicious of this O'Rourke fellow—a land steward from Donabate—his mother was seeing and demanded that he come to the fancy house in Foxrock for an interview. It did not go well and Mrs. Darley advised against marriage, but Mary Kavanagh was adamant. She was married in July 1945 at Our Lady of Perpetual Sorrow.

O'Rourke, years later, had asked his mother if she loved his father when she married him. "I liked him enough," she replied, which was the wrong answer, for O'Rourke at least. And now he remembered his mother's marriage certificate and the marriage certificate of Rosanna Conway. Spinsters. Spinsters to the core. Now he was about to marry another spinster, one Simone McGuire.

* * * * *

"The maid of honor and the best man?" asked Father Conway.

"They'll be here any minute. Driving down from Phibsborough."

"Fine," said the priest, "I'll meet you in the church momentarily."

O'Rourke took McGuire by the elbow and began walking her toward the church. "So this is it?"

"You sound like a prisoner walking the last mile," laughed O'Rourke.

"Well," replied McGuire, "maybe I am."

O'Rourke tapped her gently on the behind. "I don't think so."

"You can't keep your hands off my ass even in church!"

"And you love it."

"I do love it, and I love you."

O'Rourke and McGuire were joined by O'Rourke's cousins Jerry and Maura Bartley, who would be their witnesses.

The church was empty and the mass was quick. Immediately following the mass, the marriage ceremony took place. It was all over in half an hour. Father Conway pronounced them man and wife, and O'Rourke kissed his bride. The four of them headed for O'Rourke's limo to go back to the Shelbourne for breakfast.

As O'Rourke helped McGuire into the limo, she said, "I guess I'm not a spinster anymore."

O'Rourke smiled, then gave her a peck on the cheek, thinking of two other spinsters. "I guess not."

56.

The fire had gone out of O'Rourke's political belly. After nearly two months in Europe, he had returned to New York in early October with serious doubts about running for Congress. His political drive had taken a backseat to Sam and the baby. He would have pulled out in a second, but he felt an obligation to the party. His poll numbers had been steady while he was away, and he had felt no urgency to return. He and Sam had actually looked at houses in Wexford and West Cork, but he knew that was just fantasy. He belonged in New York. Or did he? Now he couldn't decide.

"Nice of you guys to finally show up," said Clarence Black as they settled in for their first campaign meeting of the fall.

"Did everyone have a pleasant summer?" asked O'Rourke sweetly.

"Yes!" said McGuire, and everyone laughed. She was getting really big now and it took some effort for her to move around. "How are those polls coming, Nuncio?" she asked. Baroody pulled out copies and passed them around.

"Fifty-nine percent overall," said O'Rourke, shaking his head. "That's okay."

"It should be higher," said McGuire and O'Rourke nodded. "Let's look at the breakdown," she said.

"We're doing really well with the gays," said Nuncio. "You're nearly 92 percent. I don't know what the hell the other 8 percent is thinking."

"Ah," said Black with amusement, "the Log Cabin Republicans have spoken!"

"Fuck them," said O'Rourke. "How about the Limousine Liberals on the Upper West Side?"

"Could be better," said McGuire. "You're at 55 percent."

"That sucks," said O'Rourke.

"It does," confirmed McGuire.

"I should be killing Swift up there." There was quiet in the room. "Okay, guys, tomorrow we start hitting the subway stations morning and night. We're going to the Upper West Side first. Seventy-second Street. I hope no one bleeds on me this time."

"Why start uptown?" asked McGuire.

"Because those people would rather vote than fuck and if they don't vote for me I'm fucked. Got it?" Everyone nodded as O'Rourke's phone rang. McGuire came out of her chair to pick it up and O'Rourke waved her off. "My God, Sam, calm down," he admonished. He picked up his own phone.

"Tone, it's Kevin Griffin."

"Bubba," he said delighted, signaling to everyone to stay, "how's it hanging?"

"I hear you got married and didn't invite anyone," said Griffin.

"I got married in Dublin," said O'Rourke in explanation.

"I see," replied the taciturn Griffin.

"Fuck you," said O'Rourke and Griffin laughed. "What do you want?" he asked.

"I got a call last night from someone in Congresswoman Fopiano's office."

"Hold on, Kev. I want to put this on speaker phone." He hit the button and made the necessary introductions. "Kevin and I were in the same outfit in Vietnam. He also took me into custody," he said laughing, remembering that it was to Griffin he surrendered to in 1972 at the American Embassy in Dublin. "So what did Congresswoman's Fopiano's office want from you?"

"They wanted to know if you really earned your medals in Vietnam?"

"What did you tell them."

"I told them you were a big fucking hero."

O'Rourke and the others laughed. O'Rourke turned serious quickly. "What else did they want?"

"They wanted to know about you and me in Dublin in '72."

"Yeah?"

"I told them it was none of their fucking business."

"Thank you, Bubba." Griffin was Bronx Irish tough.

"What are they up to?" asked Griffin.

"I have a pretty good idea," replied O'Rourke. "And it ain't good." O'Rourke looked around the room, and the three faces were dead serious. "Thanks, Bubba. If they call you back again, get in touch immediately."

"Will do," said Griffin.

"*Siemper Fi*," said O'Rourke.

"*Siemper Fi*," responded Griffin, and he hung up the phone.

There was silence all around for a good minute. "What do you make of it?" asked McGuire.

"They're about to try and fuck us. So get ready."

"Get ready?" repeated McGuire.

"Yes," said O'Rourke, "have the ad agency ready to respond within twenty-four hours to any major attack by Swift. Also, start polling the district every Monday and Thursday from now on." O'Rourke looked at his team. "Okay, everybody," he said, "Tip O'Neill 101 . . ."

"Money is the mother's milk of politics," they said in cultlike fashion, and they all laughed.

"As far as we know," said McGuire, "they're hurting for money since Costello was deported."

"Correct," said O'Rourke, "but we must be vigilant. Got that, Clarence?" Black nodded. "Keep a close eye on their bank statements." O'Rourke got out of his chair and stretched. "*Bó airgead*," he said in Irish and laughed. "Cash cow," he repeated in English. "Let's keep a sharp lookout for that GOP cash cow."

57.

Julie-Annie was giving Brogan a headache. She was wailing away as her mother tried to calm her by gently rocking her in her arms. Brogan saw the child as a living insult to her own relationship with

Swift. She wondered, if she had a child with Jackie, would it look like the unfortunately named Julie-Annie?

This was the big meeting Vito had been trying to arrange for weeks. The whole gang, including Georgie Drumgoole, was here. There was only one person missing.

"And how is the scion of Rancho Mirage?" asked Vito.

"He's coming along," said Madonna-Sue. "Rancho Mirage is lovely this time of the year." Rancho Mirage, California, was the home of the Betty Ford Center.

"If he gets his ticket punched one more time, his next stay is free," said Vito, laughing at his own joke. "Maybe he should get a time-share."

It was in the week after the Republican National Convention that Jackie Swift had been packed away to sunny California. Brogan had been awoken by moisture. At first she thought there was a pipe leaking. She had almost been right. There was a leak, but it was Jackie leaking into the bed. He was so coked up on one of Fischbein's Fish-Packs that he had peed on Brogan without even waking up. That was it. Brogan called Vito and Jackie found himself on the first plane out to Los Angeles that morning. This stay was going to take longer, they said at Betty Ford. He might be there for up to twelve weeks, which would get him back into the campaign near the end of October.

"Well," said Vito, "Jackie may as well enjoy his stay out there because we're broke."

"Broke?" repeated Madonna-Sue.

"Bankrupt," said Vito. "Zilch."

"Where's Costello's money?" asked Brogan. "What did Mandelstam do with it?" It was an accusation, not a question.

"We had to get rid of it," said Vito. "Couldn't keep it around."

"Where is it?" the persistent Brogan demanded.

"RNC got it." That was the Republican National Committee.

"Why can't we get it back from them?" asked Brogan. "The laundry should be clean by now." Laundry. That word. Brogan thought that the money had been cleaned by now. This was the kind of talk that got people indicted.

"They won't give it back," replied Vito softly. "They think this campaign is going nowhere. Let's admit it, it's really a Democratic district and O'Rourke has plenty of his own money to spend."

That was part of it. Vito couldn't get it back because he had no clout anymore. D'Amato as a senator was history. Giuliani had dropped out of the senatorial race with Hillary Clinton because of cancer. ("He's out walking his pet prostate," Vito had been heard telling colleagues.) And pretty soon, it looked like his son-in-law would be out of a job, further reducing his influence within the party. It came down to no juice, no clout, no money. The RNC had spoken.

"Well," said Madonna-Sue, "we better do something."

"How did your little fishing expedition go?" asked Brogan of Madonna-Sue. They seldom asked face-to-face questions of each other, but this was business, desperate business.

"Kevin Griffin," said Madonna-Sue, lighting up a Camel, "O'Rourke's buddy from Vietnam, told my guy to go fuck himself."

Brogan gave a cynical laugh. She knew the fucking Irish. "What did you expect?" Madonna-Sue shrugged.

"You know you shouldn't smoke in front of the baby," said Vito. "It's not healthy for her."

"Neither is politics," shot back the congresswoman.

"I guess O'Rourke really is the real thing," offered Vito, quickly changing the subject. They sounded stumped, then Drumgoole piped in. "How about O'Rourke's trouble with the IRA?"

"What about it?"

"I heard he was really connected back in the '70s."

"Can you document it?" asked Madonna-Sue.

"Maybe," said Drumgoole, lowering his head. "If we get something on O'Rourke maybe I can get Wellington Mulvaney to run it in his column in the *Post*," he added, his second idea of the day wearing him out.

"Well," said Vito, "we better get lucky and we better get lucky fast or we're going to be out of one fat salary come election day. One-hundred-sixty-grand down the toilet."

"So much for idealism," thought Brogan to herself as she looked at a bunch of people who saw Jackie Swift as nothing more than a meal ticket for their own greedy aspirations.

58.

New York Post, October 29, 2000

The Terrorist Candidate

By Wellington Mulvaney

It has come to my knowledge that one Wolfe Tone O'Rourke, the Democratic nominee in the 7th Congressional District, has terrorist ties to the IRA.

Between August 1971, the beginning of internment without trial in Northern Ireland, and the spring of 1972, he was responsible for getting dozens of IRA men "on the run" into the United States of America on "lost" American passports.

America is the target of terrorists worldwide. Do we need one representing us in the U.S. Congress?

59.

New York Daily News, October 31, 2000

Eye on New York
by Cyclops Reilly

SMEARING TONE O'ROURKE

If there's one thing you can count on in this town, it is that Wellington Mulvaney will type whatever the right-wing tells him to. I am referring to his column of a couple of days ago called "The Terrorist Candidate." (By the way, Boots, I like it when you have trouble breaking 100 words.) This column was directed at Wolfe Tone O'Rourke who is running against Wellington's boy, Jackie Swift, in the 7th Congressional District.

O'Rourke was a corpsman in Vietnam. I freely admit that he saved my life when I was hit by Viet Cong fire. When the Republicans can't beat you fair and square, they take your strength and try to turn it into a weakness. You can expect another 100-word column from Mulvaney any day now, followed by one after that. These columns will drip pieces of information. O'Rourke called me yesterday and he told me the whole story.

The story is simple. After coming home wounded from Vietnam in 1971 the Navy found out they were running out of corpsmen—that's a "medic" in the movies—for the Marine Corp. O'Rourke's tour was about over. The Navy put a stop-loss on corpsmen to keep them in an extra year and ordered O'Rourke back to Vietnam for another tour. O'Rourke had done his duty. The Navy didn't care. O'Rourke told them what they could do with their extra tour of duty in Vietnam.

O'Rourke left for Dublin just as internment without trial was being introduced in Northern Ireland. Some people think that Britain is a democracy. It isn't. Democracies don't lock their people up without trials. But they do this a lot in Britain, and Belfast, because their injustices drive the poor to rebellion. To make a long story short O'Rourke—proudly—admits to getting IRA men out of the country. He won't say how he did it, but he did it. And he said he would do it all over again.

O'Rourke finally returned to New York and spent some time in the brig at the Brooklyn Navy Yard until everything was straightened out. He was reprimanded for not following an order—going back to be killed in Vietnam for the vainglorious politicians—censured, and given an honorable discharge in 1972.

He went to serve his country when others were running away to Canada.

Where, exactly, was Jackie Swift in 1970, and why wasn't he in Vietnam?

Come to think of it, our glorious Australian ally was also in Vietnam in 1970. Why weren't you there, Wellington? I'm just saying, if the Boots fit, wear 'em.

60.

"Well," said Vito, "that was a fucking disaster. Any other great ideas?"

Madonna-Sue spoke up. "Mulvaney's column was a disaster," she said, "but the premise behind it was solid. Let's face it, Mulvaney doesn't carry much of a punch anymore."

"That's an understatement," agreed Brogan.

"But that terrorist story can still work," insisted Madonna-Sue.

"How?" asked Vito.

"In commercial form," said Madonna-Sue. "A few pictures of Saddam Hussein and Yasser Arafat next to O'Rourke, and we're on our way."

"There's only one problem," injected Brogan, "money."

"Yes, that is a problem," said Madonna-Sue, "but I think we know where we can get some."

"The RNC won't budge," said Vito. "We're on their shit list. If Giuliani was running, it might be different." At the sound of her name, Julie-Annie started to howl.

"Hush, hush," said Madonna-Sue, rising from the chair to walk the infant around the room. The child calmed. Madonna-Sue looked over the baby's shoulder and spoke to her father. "It's about time you called in some chits, Daddy."

"Like who? I told you the RNC won't go for it."

"Fuck the RNC," said Madonna-Sue. "Let's go to all the friends you've been doing business with over the years. The developers, the drug companies, the whole lot of them. You were their boy, now get something for it!"

"Okay," said Vito, "I'll make some calls."

"Just don't make calls, get some money," demanded his daughter. "Let's get enough money to get a commercial together. I'll call the stations and the cable company myself and see if they'll wait a week or so until we can pay for the blitz after Election Day."

"Well," said Vito, "that's fine, but where are we supposed to get the money to pay for the commercial itself?"

"That's where Manny comes in," said Madonna-Sue. "Manny, how about calling Father Costello?"

"Are you crazy?" replied Manny Mandelstam, who was sorry he was mixed up in this whole sordid business. He had been keeping a low profile. His instincts told him that the Fopianos were nothing but a disaster waiting to happen. The less contact, the better.

"Let's make a call," said Madonna-Sue.

"One call, Manny," added Brogan.

"I have a secured cell phone here," said Vito, "from the RNC."

"What do I ask him?"

"Money!" they all said together.

"Call him," said Vito, holding out the phone. Mandelstam took it and dialed.

"Hello," said the voice at the other end.

"Reverend Dr. Costello?"

"Yes, this is he."

"Reverend, it's Rabbi Mandelstam."

"Rabbi, how are you?"

"I have a problem, Reverend."

"What's your problem?"

"Jackie Swift's campaign is broke. Could you help us out?" There was silence at the end of the phone. "Perhaps I could travel to Canada to meet with you?"

"No, rabbi," said Costello, "our last meeting did not go well." Then a pique of paranoia hit Costello. "Is this phone secure?"

"Yes, it is. From the committee."

"Yes," said Costello, "the committee." There was a pause. "No, I will not meet with you, but I will meet with Congressman Swift."

"Ah," said Mandelstam, "the congressman is presently indisposed. Perhaps you could meet with Mrs. Swift." Madonna-Sue shook her head at the mention of the married name she never used. ". . . Or Congressman Fopiano?"

"No," said Costello, "it's Jackie, or nothing."

"Would an electronic transfer be possible?" Manny inquired. Manny could see himself in Leavenworth right now, dressed to the nines in jailhouse pinstripes.

"I do not think so. Your FBI and the RCMP are keeping a very close eye on me. How much will you need?"

"How much?" repeated Manny. Vito help up the five fingers on one hand and one digit on the other hand. "Six figures," said Manny into the phone.

"That is quite a lot," said Costello, "but I might be able to pull it off."

"Should we send Jackie up to Canada to meet you?"

"No," replied Costello, "I'll reenter the country at Windsor, Ontario, across from Detroit. One of the border guards there belongs to the organization and can get me in."

Vito was rolling his hand to tell Mandelstam to hurry up. "When do you want to meet Congressman Swift?"

"How about this coming weekend?"

"In New York?"

"Yes," said Costello, "New York. Maybe I can combine a little business with pleasure. I'll call Congressman Swift on the weekend, if that's convenient."

"Yes, Reverend Doctor," replied Manny. "That would be very convenient," and the phone went dead.

"What now?" asked Vito.

"We gotta spring Jackie from Betty Ford," said Mandelstam, "and fast."

61.

The commercial appeared just before the 11 p.m. Eyewitness News broadcast.

"In this time of international terrorism," the actor's voice said as a film showed a bus exploding on the streets of Jerusalem, "we must be on guard against terrorist threats." There was a film of Jackie Swift shaking hands with Ariel Sharon. The voiceover continued: "We need a representative in Congress who knows the threat and is part of the solution—not the problem." At this point there was a picture of Wolfe Tone O'Rourke laughing with Gerry Adams at a White House reception. "We know the threat to our country," said the voice as pictures of Arafat, Adams, Hussein, and O'Rourke flashed quickly on the screen, "and Jackie Swift is part of the solution. On election day, vote to keep America safe. Vote for Congressman Jack Swift." The commercial ended with Swift saying, "I'm Congressman Jackie Swift and I endorse this message."

It took all of thirty seconds.

62.

"The fucking has begun," said O'Rourke, and Black cursed.

"Nothing," said Black, "nothing, no indication of any money."

"Cash and carry," said McGuire.

"What does Monday's internal poll say?"

"We're dropping fast on the Upper West Side," replied Baroody. "We were 55 percent two weeks ago; now we're at 46 percent. That commercial hurt."

"Yeah," said O'Rourke, "let's get moving. Simone, is the agency ready?"

"Waiting for you."

O'Rourke pulled pictures of George Washington, Nelson Mandela, Martin Luther King, Jr., Michael Collins, Eamon DeValera, David Ben-Gurion, and Menachem Begin out of an envelope and threw them on the desk. "Okay, we're ready. Let's go to the agency and see if we can get this on the air on the 11 o'clock news tonight."

"Tonight?" asked McGuire with alarm.

"Tonight," repeated O'Rourke and he scooped up the photos and headed for the door.

63.

The film was of the president's inauguration on March 4, 1933: "We have nothing to fear," said Franklin Delano Roosevelt, "but fear itself." The voiceover minced no words. "They are trying to scare you, pure and simple. When there are no ideas, they get desperate, and the desperate love fear. They say that Tone O'Rourke is a terrorist." The pictures begin to roll: "Was George Washington a terrorist, or was he a freedom fighter, driving the unwanted British from these shores? Was Martin Luther King, Jr., a terrorist when he broke the law in the South trying to overturn the American apartheid? Was Nelson Mandela a terrorist when he spent thirty years of his life in jail so his country could emerge from a history of bigotry? Were Michael Collins and Eamon DeValera terrorists when they told the British it was time to leave Ireland after seven hundred years? Were David Ben-Gurion and Menachem Begin terrorists when they helped birth the nation of Israel?

"Remember: You have nothing to fear but fear itself. Vote out the fear mongers on Election Day." A picture of O'Rourke, Gerry Adams, Teddy Kennedy, and Bill Clinton taken in Belfast after the

Good Friday Agreement was signed filled the screen. O'Rourke read his own tagline: "I'm Tone O'Rourke, and I approved this campaign commercial."

64.

"How are the daily internal polls?" asked O'Rourke at the morning meeting.

"Better," McGuire and Baroody both replied. "You're back over 50 percent on the Upper West Side," Sam continued. "Overall, you're still at a solid 54 percent throughout the 7th CD."

"Did Swift go on the air last night?"

"No," said Black, "he didn't. Maybe they're saving their money."

"We have to know," said O'Rourke. "The only way they can beat us is with money. You can't find anything?"

"Not a thing in any of their accounts," said Black. "And the RNC has shut them down."

"It's got to be that fucking Costello," O'Rourke said finally.

"He's not allowed in the country," reminded McGuire.

"Allow and enter are two different words, sweetheart. Clarence, can you get someone to check on Costello up in Canada?"

"Will do."

"You know who we haven't seen lately?" said Sam.

"Who?"

"Jackie Swift."

"You get one guess," said O'Rourke.

"Betty Ford," said Black.

"Let's see if he shows up this week," said O'Rourke.

"For a fundraiser?" said McGuire.

"You have a devious mind," laughed O'Rourke.

"So do you," said Sam, rubbing her basketball-sized tummy.

65.

The dirty deed was left up to Brogan, and she felt guilty about it. She had flown out to California to fetch Swift from Betty Ford so they could get the dough from Costello. Jackie's doctor told her that she was interfering with the treatment, and there would be no cure for Jackie without his doing the full program without interruption.

Jackie was glad to see her. But she did not beat around the bush. She read him his poll numbers and told him the only way to win was to hit the airwaves—and they couldn't do that without money. The Reverend Dr. Costello was willing to come up with one hundred big ones, but only if Jackie accepted it in person. Jackie listened patiently to what Brogan had to say, but she could see he was itching for the powder. She thought they would have to lock him up for a good six months for the cure to take.

They caught the first flight back to New York, and she insisted they fly first class. It was bad enough having to fetch him, but she didn't want to be disturbed by little old ladies in tennis shoes who wanted to see the Blessed Virgin's favorite congressman. The sight of Jackie Swift brought them out of the woodwork.

As they boarded they were offered a drink, and Brogan saw that Jackie had that look in his eye. "You might as well have one, Jackie, because Vito and Madonna-Sue will cut you off as soon as you hit Manhattan." He got a double vodka on the rocks with a slice of lime and savored the entire thing before takeoff. Once the plane was airborne, he switched to double vodka gimlets.

Brogan sipped a chilled white wine and wondered how Jackie had gotten from Paul O'Dwyer to Vito Fopiano. He certainly didn't believe all the crap about family values and abortion that Vito spit out like gospel truth. Jackie was a go-along to get-along kind of guy. He couldn't care less what you did in your bedroom. But power had a way of changing people. Sure, it was nice being a congressman and being fussed over and making 160 grand a year for doing basically nothing except appearing on the Sunday morning talk shows. But there had to be more to life than that. Then Brogan thought of Madonna-Sue again. She had kept her legs shut and *still* came up with the baby. Then they compounded the felony by naming it Julie-Annie. Brogan had had enough.

She put her wine down in the little compartment for drinks between their seats. "That's it, Jackie."

"That's what?" he asked. He had a nice glow, and he hoped they were not going to discuss the terrible campaign again.

"We're through."

"We're what?"

"Through. As of Election Day, November 7, I resign. But you're leaving the apartment tonight."

Jackie was in shock. "But that's my apartment!"

"That *was* your apartment. You're getting out. You're going to live with Madonna-Sue from now on. You are going to be a father to Vitoessa and Julie-Annie. You, for once in your life, are going to do the right thing. Do you understand me?" Jackie could see that Brogan was getting red in the face. "You are going to do the right thing—win or lose! Is that understood?"

Jackie hesitated for a second. "Could we talk this over? I really need that apartment."

"No, we are not going to talk this over. It's over. O-V-E-R. Let's get on with both of our lives. There has to be more to life than this lie of ours."

"But the apartment."

"If you get the apartment," said Brogan, "you also get the front page of the *New York Post*."

"What?"

"How does FIRST PIX OF CONGRESSMAN'S LOVE NEST grab you?" She had Swift between a rock and Madonna-Sue and Jackie knew it.

The flight continued in silence. "We'll be on the ground at Newark's International Airport within ten minutes," the pilot said over the intercom.

"On the ground," Swift said aloud, "without an apartment." Then he began laughing, knowing full well that the party was almost over.

66.

O'Rourke loved red-sauce joints.

They were the old-fashioned Italian restaurants that were quickly becoming extinct around the Village. They came by their name honestly—they covered everything with lots and lots of red sauce. They were usually run by families and you could always expect a stiff drink and a red-checkered tablecloth along with your veal parmigiana. Gene's, which had been on 11th Street since 1919, was one of his favorite places, and home to the blue-hair set. It wasn't unusual to see eighty-five-year-old women in long elbow-length white gloves banging down Manhattan after Manhattan at its small bar. The food was delicious, plentiful, and inexpensive. It felt like you were being served in your own living room by your own personal chef.

On the Saturday night before Election Day O'Rourke had invited Monsignor Séan Pius Burke to join him and McGuire for dinner. The place—as usual—was a mad house, but O'Rourke had managed to secure a table for the three of them. The Monsignor showed up with his collar on.

"You trying to frighten people with that outfit, Johnny Pie?"

"Hey," said Burke, "when I'm in civilian clothes, you tell me I look like a cop. If I wear my collar, I'm scaring people. I can't win with you." Burke seated himself between McGuire and O'Rourke and ordered a martini from the waiter.

"I'm glad you could come, Father," said Sam. "We needed a night off from the campaign and couldn't think of better company."

"Thanks, Sam," replied Burke. "How are you feeling?"

"Pretty good. I get tired, and the campaign takes a lot of work, but I'm holding up."

"Tough week, Tone—with that commercial blitz by Swift."

"I'd just like to forget the whole thing," said O'Rourke. "It was a fucking nightmare."

"Tone," said Sam, pointing at the monsignor, "your language!"

O'Rourke smiled. "I'm an old dog—"

"—with no new tricks," finished Burke. The three of them laughed.

"We wanted to ask a favor of you, Father," said Sam. Burke nodded. "Will you baptize our baby when she arrives?"

"I'd be honored," replied Burke, touched. "I'll look forward to that." The waiter took their order, and they toasted each other. "To the conclusion of a successful campaign," said the monsignor.

"And the birth of a beautiful baby girl," added the proud father. Glasses clicked again.

"The Cardinal sends his regards."

"You're kidding," said O'Rourke.

"Not at all. He's been following the campaign closely. He was," Burke stopped to find the correct word, "*piqued* by Jackie Swift's commercials on you."

"Next you'll be telling me he's changing sides."

"I think he changed sides a long time ago." McGuire and O'Rourke looked at each other. "After you got rid of Costello and had that meeting with the Cardinal at the chancellery I think the old man started rooting for you." McGuire, who knew nothing of the meeting, looked at O'Rourke. He obviously didn't tell her everything. "And that six-figure donation didn't hurt either," laughed Burke.

"What six-figure donation?" said McGuire in a louder than normal voice.

"Nothing, dear," said O'Rourke. "Just a small contribution to the archdiocese." O'Rourke gave Burke a look that said *shut the fuck up!* "I hope the Cardinal has some connections upstairs," added O'Rourke, "because I'm going to need them."

"Does it look bad?" asked Burke, concerned.

"It doesn't look good," said Sam, still eyeing O'Rouke. "Swift is marginally ahead of Tone for the first time. Those commercials are having an effect."

"He's killing me on the Upper West Side with the terrorist ties," said O'Rourke. "It's heavily Jewish up there and they think I was a bomb thrower in Belfast thirty years ago. The only reason I'm still in it is because I have the west side sewn up from Battery City up through the Village, Chelsea, and Hell's Kitchen. You're old neighborhood loves me almost as much as the gays do."

Burke laughed, then said: "For a guy who may be going down in three days, you don't seem that annoyed."

"Marriage has changed me."

"Yeah, sure," said McGuire.

"No," continued O'Rourke, "it has. Now I have a wife, and a child on the way. They are my two most important things in my life. Johnny Pie, I've been on one long campaign since Bobby back in 1968. I've gotten some good guys elected. I've gotten some bad guys elected. I fought in two wars for my two countries, and I have the scars to prove it. Enough is enough. I have more than enough money, and I want to make sure this child grows into a positive human being who cares about people. Maybe my wars are over. Maybe it's time for some reflection. I still expect to win, but there are other more important things in life." O'Rourke took his left hand and placed it on Simone's big belly. "You know what I mean, Monsignor?"

Séan Pius Burke nodded. "Yes, Tone. Yes I do."

* * * * *

Zeus, the Moat's three-hundred-pound bartender was keeping an eye on Jackie Swift. He hadn't seen Swift in the Moat in years and wondered why he would show up three days before the election. Swift stood off to the side, Irish whiskey neat, and kept a close eye on the door. Every time the door opened Swift's eyes shot to it. He was obviously waiting for someone. Jackie looked wired, thought Zeus. He kept rocking back and forth on his heels, nervous about something.

The door opened and in stepped a man in a black overcoat and hat, carrying a briefcase. Swift's empty hand shot up into the air and he called out "Doctor, doctor, over here." The man went to Swift and shook his hand. He whispered a few words into Jackie's ear, then handed him the briefcase. There was some banter back and forth between them with Swift gesticulating, as if giving directions. Maybe the man was lost in the maze of Village streets. They shook hands again and the man quickly exited the bar.

Jackie came up to the bar, drink in one hand, the briefcase in the other. "Zeus," he said, "another Jameson neat." Zeus made the drink and handed it to Swift.

"What brings you around?"

"Needed some fresh air," replied Swift. "Tough campaign, you know."

"Yeah," said Zeus, "I've been watching your commercials."

Jackie looked at Zeus and knew it was not the right time to ask him if he liked them or not. He knew Zeus and O'Rourke went back a long way. The whiskey calmed Jackie. He had made his contact, now he could relax. "Any sign of Fischbein?"

Zeus looked at Swift, suddenly knowing his game. "He's expected. Soon."

Swift wanted to say "Thank God," but only uttered, "Good."

Zeus walked to the end of the bar and pulled his cell phone out, then dialed the number.

"Hello," said Sam McGuire as she put her after-dinner coffee down. "Yes, Zeus, he's right here." She handed O'Rourke the phone. "Zeus from the Moat."

"Yes, Zeus," said O'Rourke.

"Tone, Swift is here, and he's waiting for Fischbein. Maybe you should pay a visit. Can't talk. He's at the other end of the bar."

"Thanks, Zeus. I'll be right there."

"Let's go, guys. Jackie Swift is trying to buy dope from Fischbein at the Moat." O'Rourke signed the check, and the three of them were out the door. O'Rourke and Burke would have walked, but Simone was lagging behind. "We better take a cab." O'Rourke hailed a cab and it sped across West 11th Street, then made a left on Seventh Avenue, pulling up at Christopher Street in front of the Duplex.

The three of them headed straight for Hogan's Moat. As O'Rourke descended the steps into the Moat he could see a kerfuffle at the end of the bar. There were several men on the floor, and Barney was yapping at them. O'Rourke rushed in and Zeus joined the fray. O'Rourke saw Jackie Swift on the floor in the fetal position, covering a briefcase with his body. Barney was barking and growling and nipping at his shoulders. Fischbein was trying to inch away, and Zeus pulled him back by the cuffs of his trousers. All the while, Hogan tried to control his dog, who was in an absolute frenzy, white powder covering his nose.

"Must be some good shit here," said O'Rourke, knowing that Barney was a connoisseur of blow.

Monsignor Burke tucked Sam into the far corner and went to investigate. Zeus was beginning to straighten out the bodies. As Hogan held Barney back, Jackie Swift slowly got up off the floor, the briefcase firmly in hand. The floor was covered with white powder, and Hogan had to hold Barney by the collar to keep him from going totally berserk. Then Burke saw it on the flap of the briefcase:

I.

H.

S.

"Where'd you get this, Jackie?" asked the priest.

"None of your business," said Swift, clutching the briefcase to his chest.

"This is Costello's briefcase!"

"You cocksucker," said O'Rourke, "that's the money to pay for those commercials!"

"Where is he?" demanded Burke.

Zeus pushed Jackie Swift against the wall. Burke went face to face with him. "Where the fuck is Costello?" he demanded.

O'Rourke looked for Sam. He found her in the corner with her cell phone pressed to her ear.

"This is 911. What is your emergency?"

"I'd like to report a drug bust at Hogan's Moat Saloon, 59 Christopher Street," said McGuire. "Please send the police, there's a terrible altercation going on here. Someone might get hurt."

The person who might get hurt was Jackie Swift. Zeus was worried that Séan Pius Burke might put him through the wall into the kitchen. "One last time, Jackie, where the fuck is Costello?" Burke grabbed Swift by the necktie and twisted it and Jackie's face looked like it had been painted red. Burke torqued the tie one more time and asked again, "Where is he?"

"He's gone to the Romper Room on Little West 12th Street."

"How do you know?"

"I just gave him directions."

"You should be ashamed of yourself," said the priest.

The squad car from the 6th Precinct was pulling up as Monsignor Burke let the tie loose and Swift slumped to the floor. His beautiful suit was covered in white powder, the result of a broken Fish-Pack.

"I should have known," said Burke to O'Rourke. Burke's black clerical stock was also covered with cocaine.

"Known what?"

"That fucking Costello was a pedophile." Then Burke thought back to young Felipe sitting on Costello's knee at breakfast. "Short and sweet" popped into his head and he felt an awful pain in his gut. "Costello's at the Romper Room," said Burke to O'Rourke. "It's a bar for pedophile priests. I thought the cops shut it down years ago when I was cleaning these bums out of the archdiocese. They must have reopened. Swift says it's on Little West 12th Street. Let's go."

O'Rourke put his hand on Burke's shoulder. "No, Monsignor. We'll let the cops handle this one. It's over."

And it was over, but Séan Pius Burke felt responsible for the child that was probably sitting on the Reverend Doctor Costello's lap right now, probably holding his silver and gold crucifix. He should have known. In fact, he did know.

67.

New York Daily News, November 6, 2000

Eye on New York
By Cyclops Reilly

HOW DO YOU SPELL *SCHADENFREUDE*?

I told you about these bums, didn't I?

Well, this morning I feel like an obese Cheshire cat who's had his fill and is now getting his belly rubbed for eternity.

I believe this is what those guys with high IQs and precise pronunciation call "schadenfreude." It's one those great German words, like wiener schnitzel or sauerbraten. You know, the kind of words you use to rouse up the masses before you take the backdoor into France and invade Belgium again. "We will have wiener schnitzel for our people, or there will be sauerbraten to pay!"

I was informed by *Webster's College Dictionary* that it is the combination of two German words, *schaden*, the word for harm, and *Freude*, for joy. That's how we get the wonderful word "harmjoy." Well, not exactly. Schadenfreude is defined as "pleasure felt at someone else's misfortune."

Well, that's right on the money. Because you cannot imagine the pleasure I find in the misfortune of Congressman Jackie Swift and the Reverend Dr. John Costello. Saturday night, Swift was found at Hogan's Moat Saloon on Christopher Street with a snootful of cocaine and a suitcase full of one-hundred-dollar bills, $100,000 in all. Dr. Costello, the papal nuncio's bagman in this country, was found bouncing a naked 6-year-old boy on his knee at the Romper Room, the underground playpen for pedophile priests in the Meatpacking District. Presently, both are occupying cells at the 6th Precinct on West 10th Street in Greenwich Village. Enjoy the comfort, boys, before you go off on your island vacation—Riker's Island, that is.

It should not be overlooked how pivotal Aloysius Hogan, the proprietor of Hogan's Moat, and his cocaine-hunting dog, Barney, were in the apprehension of Swift and Costello. If it wasn't for the total surveillance that Hogan keeps at the Moat in trying to deter the scourge of cocaine, Swift might have never been apprehended. And without Swift's apprehension and his subsequent cooperation in pointing to the whereabouts of Costello, we would not know how deep the pedophile scandal runs in Holy Mother Church. Few saloon owners would go to the trouble of adopting a former DEA cocaine-detection dog in order to keep our saloons safe from the terrible addiction of cocaine. Hogan and Barney, you are our heroes.

Now there is only one more thing to do. Tomorrow is Election Day, and every New Yorker in the 7th CD should go out and vote with all your heart and soul for Wolfe Tone O'Rourke. O'Rourke may be a lot of things, but he is one of us. He eats, sleeps, and especially drinks in this grand city of ours. He's not in it for the money, the glory, or to compete with Senator Schumer on the Sunday morning talk shows. He's in it for us, to see that those thieves in Washington ante up what belongs to New York. If you think he's a lot of trouble around here, just imagine what he'll do to those pompous asses in Washington.

And while I'm at it, I want to throw a bouquet to Declan Cardinal Sweeney for the wonderful homily he gave at St. Patrick's during yesterday's mass. He admitted he was wrong about Jackie Swift and the Fopiano Gang, and while he didn't endorse Tone O'Rourke, he did say that Tone is "a decent and genuine man and a much better Catholic than many of us are." That's high praise coming from a man like his Eminence.

As for the rest of you, you have your marching orders for Election Day: Vote for Tone—like the Fenians say, early and often.

68.

The election was as anticlimactic as the primary had been. O'Rourke rented the Queer Independent Democrats headquarters on Sheridan Square and the party began early. By 6:30, O'Rourke knew from exit polls that he had won. CNN called his number at 9:35 p.m.

The party already had started at Hogan's Moat. It seemed so much different than only three nights before when Barney had apprehended Jackie Swift with his dope and his bag full of money. Sam looked tired and she sat in O'Rourke's seat at the end of the bar and held onto his arm.

"You okay?" he asked.

"I'm fine. Just very tired. Let's get over to the QID and get this over with. Campaigning is hard enough. Campaigning with a seven-pound belly is even harder." O'Rourke kissed Sam on the forehead and announced they were going across the street for the victory celebration.

The QID was unbelievably hot with all the television lights. CNN, NY1, ABC, CBS, and NBC were all there. Even Fox had shown up, probably hoping for a clip of some O'Rourke outrage they could show over and over again for the next forty-eight hours.

With a great effort, O'Rourke helped McGuire up on the stage where the podium was situated. He looked for Thom Lamè and Lizzie Townsend, but could not see them. "Bad losers," he thought to himself. There were cheers and whistles from the crowd, and O'Rourke actually felt embarrassed. He really didn't like the attention. He held Sam's hand tight and said, "This will be over in the minute."

"Thank God," she said, looking a little wobbly.

O'Rourke held his hand up for quiet, and the room settled down. "My name is Wolfe Tone O'Rourke," he began, "and I believe I'm the Congressman-Elect from New York's 7th Congressional District." Cheers went up, and O'Rourke smiled broadly. McGuire pressed a smile onto her own lips. "I want to thank all of you who worked so hard to make this night possible. I want to thank especially Clarence Black, your own Nuncio Baroody, and most of all, my campaign manager and my wife, Simone McGuire O'Rourke." There were loud cheers. O'Rourke wanted to thank—but knew he couldn't—two other people, Cyclops Reilly and Declan Cardinal Sweeney, who had helped the campaign in more ways then they even realized.

"It's getting late," said O'Rourke, "and it looks like we're going to have a long night waiting for the results of the presidential election. Let's hope for the best with Al Gore, for God help this country if George W. Bush becomes president of the United States of America. That man is dumb with a capital D." There were no cheers for the red meat O'Rourke had just thrown out. It was as if the notion of a second President Bush had sucked the energy out of the room. "The booze and the food is on me. Thank you again. Good night and God bless." With a triumphant wave to the TV camera, O'Rourke realized that his campaign for Congress was over.

* * * * *

It took O'Rourke and McGuire a good ten minutes to work their way through the crowd of well-wishers. Both of them knew everyone loved a winner, especially in America. If they had been losers, the joint would be empty.

Going down the stairs, Sam felt as though she had to take a desperate pee. "Oh my God, Tone, I don't think I can hold it."

"What?"

"Oh, God," she said. She felt wet. "I can't believe I peed on myself." She gripped the banister, as if for dear life. Then it hit her. "Oh my God, Tone. I think my water just broke."

"What?"

"My water broke!"

O'Rourke had heard the line a thousand times in movies and, like most men, he knew absolutely nothing about a woman's plumbing. Especially a pregnant woman's plumbing.

"But the baby isn't due for another six weeks," he said, as if that had something to do with it.

"Baby ain't gonna wait," said McGuire, looking terrified.

"Jesus H. Christ," said O'Rourke looking around for Clarence Black. He saw him at the top of the stairs talking to one of the guys from the Moat. "Clarence, come here," he said, and when Black didn't immediately break away, added "right now!"

"What's up, Tone."

"Sam's water just broke. Let's get to St. Vincent's. Go get a cab." Black went down the stairs in front of them and hailed a cab on Seventh Avenue and brought it around to West 4th Street. Black got in first, then gingerly helped Sam into the middle of the back seat, then O'Rourke piled in.

"St. Vincent's Hospital," O'Rourke said to the Arab cabdriver.

"I don't know . . ." the driver said.

O'Rourke lined the Village streets up in his mind and wanted a direct route. "Drive," he said, "to West 12th Street and make a right." The cabbie put the car in gear and did what he was told. After the right turn O'Rourke told him to go to Seventh Avenue and make another right. Within five minutes, they were in front of St. Vincent's ER. O'Rourke turned Sam over to a nurse and got Black to call Dr. Moe Luigi.

"Yes," snapped Luigi. He was already asleep at 11 p.m. "Moe, it's Tone. I'm at St. Vincent's."

Luigi was instantly awake. "What's wrong?"

"Nothing's wrong, Moe. Simone's having the baby."

"Jesus Christ," said Luigi, rising from the bed.

"Can you get over here?"

"I'll be there in ten minutes."

Sam was taken to the maternity ward. O'Rourke and Black waited for Luigi in the lobby. "You don't look to good," said Black.

"I don't feel too good, either," replied O'Rourke.

Luigi arrived within minutes. "I'll take over from here, Clarence," he said, and Black wished O'Rourke luck.

"Every time it gets exciting," said Clarence, "you send me home!"

"Yeah," said O'Rourke, "exciting."

Luigi brought O'Rourke up to the maternity ward where they were informed that McGuire was in labor. "Why don't you gown up and join her?" Luigi helped O'Rourke into a hospital gown. He could see that he was literally in shock from what was happening.

Hesitantly, he followed Luigi into the birthing room. "How's it going, Sam?" asked Luigi.

"It's tough, doc. It's tough." She saw O'Rourke, almost hiding behind Luigi, and said, "Here's another fine mess you've gotten me into." Even O'Rourke was forced to smile with her Oliver Hardy quote.

God, did O'Rourke hate hospitals. There were probably only two good reasons to be in one and they were to get born or to die. At least this would be a positive experience—he hoped. They were working between Sam's legs and O'Rourke, for once, couldn't look.

"I think this one is going to come quickly," said the birthing nurse.

Soon Simone was pushing and groaning and there was sweat on her forehead. O'Rourke was up top holding her hand and she was in intense pain.

"Come on, honey, push it," said the nurse. "Push it out." With a shriek, Simone pushed, literally, for dear life and O'Rourke heard his child's voice as it cried for the first time.

The baby was squeegeed, scooped, and dried and wrapped in a little pink blanket. O'Rourke wondered how the nurse did it, it was such a little squiggly thing. She had, strangely thought O'Rourke, better hands than a Gold Glove shortstop.

The package was delivered to Sam and the smile told it all. "She's perfect," said the nurse. O'Rourke suddenly felt like the odd man out with his wife and daughter, like a third wheel on a blind date.

"Let's prepare for the birth of the placenta," said the nurse and O'Rourke knew he had to get the hell out of there. That was too much blood, even for him. "Here," said the nurse, "hold your daughter."

"No," said O'Rourke, "I couldn't."

"Won't break. Get used to it," she said, dropping the bundle into O'Rourke's shaking arms.

He took the little brown child into his arms and she looked him intently in the eye, suspiciously, as only an infant can. Then it hit him, like a lovely shock. She had his eyes. Which meant she had the eyes of his mother, Mary Kavanagh, and his grandmother, Rosanna Conway. And the great mystery immediately became clear. He knew who Our Lady of Greenwich Village was. It was his daughter, Rosanna Mary Brigid Kavanagh O'Rourke.

NOW

69.

He couldn't get her out of his mind. Her name was Kathleen Fahey, but everyone called her Kat. She had the most wonderful red hair and a big smile. Only twenty-nine, she was all Irish and a terrible flirt. After a few drinks, she might take you into the bathroom, undo her belt buckle, and drop her jeans just low enough so you could see the discreet green shamrock she had tattooed high on her right buttock. You'd like to touch it, but she'd pull her pants back up and tell you that was enough for now and that you owed her a drink. Oh, what a bargain. That beautiful pink bottom and the solid green of St. Patrick's Holy Trinity. She was O'Rourke's constituent and he thought about her almost everyday. It was a strange one-sided love affair because they had never met. He called Kat his "WTC girl" because that was where she died on September 11, 2001. He had met her over at St. Vincent's Wall of Hope and Remembrance on West 11th Street. Her "wanted poster" was up there on the wall with the others who had perished, now preserved forever under Plexiglas. He felt for all the victims. They were up there, representing every conceivable color, age, and religion. They were there laughing at college graduations, weddings, christenings, all so alive and vibrant. But Kat was the one who became a symbol to Congressman Wolfe Tone O'Rourke. From her picture, O'Rourke could see that she enjoyed a joke and a drink. In fact, she was just the kind of girl O'Rourke could fall in love with.

O'Rourke felt that he had let the WTC dead down. They were working stiffs just like the rest of New Yorkers. They weren't all rich, they weren't all powerful, mostly they were only average people trying to get by. He wondered about all of the Cantor Fitzgerald people and all the people up there at Windows on the World. That was the wonderful mosaic of New York. Guys having their power breakfast who made a six-figure salary and the Hispanic kid in the kitchen who washed their dirty plates and made the minimum wage. Now they were united. The plane had hit under them, destroying their escape. Now all they could do was wait and feel the dread. Did anyone go behind the bar and take a good, stiff drink? Did the executive lend his cell phone to the young Hispanic so he could call his mother in Mexico? What do you think about when you know you're going to die within the next hour? The governor is not going to call with a reprieve. In fact, you'll be lucky if they find a body part. Vaporized is the sanitary word of choice. What people forget about September 11, 2001, is that it was the most beautiful day of the year. Not a cloud in sight, dry and the temperature in the low 80s. O'Rourke often wondered if it had been a cloudy, rainy, mucky day if the attacks would have succeeded. Maybe, maybe not.

Washington was in full cover-your-ass mode. No one was to blame. And the Republicans started lying by noon of 9/11. They lied about the air quality, they lied about their Saudi friends, and O'Rourke could not get a straight answer out of any of them. "Those were my fucking constituents," he had told the Speaker of the House. "I worked for those people so don't patronize me or them with this God Bless America shit." He had upset the Republicans mightily. He had fought against the Patriot Act, reminding people on *Sunday Press Box* that "when Washington puts a label like 'Patriot' on any kind of a missile or a bill you can be sure that the taxpayer is getting fucked." Danny Dorsey had gotten all upset because O'Rourke had used the F-word. "Grow up," he had snapped at Dorsey.

His constituents backed him when he voted against the Iraqi war, but he had been declared "dangerous" by Condoleezza Rice, President Bush's National Security Advisor, on Fox News. The next morning the media caught up with McGuire and O'Rourke as they worked the West 72nd Street station on the IRT line. "What do you think, Congressman, about Dr. Rice's comments?"

As O'Rourke was about to answer, McGuire, who knew how much he despised Rice, stepped forward before he could say something that might come back to haunt him. "I'd like to answer that for my husband," said Sam and O'Rourke realized he had been saved. "Let me say this to Dr. Rice," continued Sam, "from one black woman to another. At least my husband didn't sell out his race, like you did, to work for this bunch of bigots." First there was silence, then deafening applause from the commuters.

"Anything to add, Congressman?"

"Yeah," said O'Rourke with a twinkle in his eye, "I guess we're having Rice-a-Roni tonight!" McGuire turned and kissed him full on the lips and his overnight poll numbers soared.

The Republicans were relentless and mounted a vicious campaign during the 2002 congressional elections. They had spent $15 million and had even talked Vito Fopiano into running against O'Rourke, although he didn't even live in the district. They told every lie they could think of, but O'Rourke was up to the task. He reminded everyone of Vito's connection with the Reverend Dr. Costello, who was doing time in Sing-Sing for child molestation; Menachem Mandelstam, who was hiding out from federal subpoenas in Israel; Vito's son-in-law Jackie Swift, who had finally beaten his cocaine addiction while serving time for money laundering at the Clinton Correctional Facility in Dannemora, New York; and their friend, the devout Robert Hanssen, who was convicted of spying for Russia in 2001. O'Rourke beat them with 67 percent of the vote. "Shout '67 and the Bachelor's Walk," sang O'Rourke.

The day before the election, Sam had told him that she was pregnant with their second child. That was the clincher. "We're outta here," he told her. The next night at his election headquarters, he had stunned the victory celebration by telling the crowd that he was resigning from Congress, effective immediately. He never went back to Washington, and he was amused as Thom Lamè and Lizzie Townsend got ready to fight it out for his vacant seat. He had all the money he would ever need and he had taken Sam and young Rosanna back to Ireland to start a new life and wait for the new baby.

He returned to New York infrequently, the last time for the funeral of Declan Cardinal Sweeney in 2003. The Cardinal had been exhausted by the 9/11 tragedy and had worked himself to death going to funeral after funeral. They had wheeled his fine mahogany casket down the center aisle of St. Patrick's and all the politicians had shown up for one last time. Clinton was there, right next to Senator Hillary. President Bush and his wife were sandwiched between the two Republican Catholics, Pataki, the governor, and Giuliani, the national icon. Giuliani, involved in an ugly public divorce, had actually gone up to the altar rail for Holy Communion, which brought a smile to O'Rourke. Newly minted auxiliary bishop Seán Pius Burke, host in hand, had laughed. "Get moving," he had said to Giuliani and had watched as the comb-over meekly went back, host-less, to his pew next to the President. Bush's expression never changed. It was obvious that he was uncomfortable in a Catholic Church. Johnny Pie stared down the president, who averted his eyes from the *sagart* from Hell's Kitchen. "Fuck Bob Jones University," O'Rourke thought he had read off the lips of Bishop Seán Pius Burke.

A few tourists came into the Moat for the last day and recognized O'Rourke. "Congressman O'Rourke," they said, happy to see what to them was a celebrity. "Could we take our picture with you?"

Shipman started to say something, but O'Rourke raised his hand. "That's okay, Saul," he said. "I'd be delighted to have my photo taken with these nice people." Everyone smiled and said "cheese" and were captured for posterity with the infamous O'Rourke.

He liked the anonymity of Ireland. In Wexford, no one cared about his politics. Their biggest curiosity was why this middle-aged white guy was with the young, beautiful black wife and the gorgeous bronzed children. He thought of Sam, Rosanna, and his baby son Declan, who he had named after the Cardinal. He wanted to go home to Ireland. Right now. He didn't want to wait around and see the old faces again. The Moat was done. It was time to get out before the wake began. He took out his cell phone, which Sam insisted he carry at all times, and called Aer Lingus. There was one seat left on the flight back to Dublin tonight. "Saul, I gotta go. I'm going back to Dublin tonight."

"You're not staying around?"

"Saul," said O'Rourke sadly, "there's nothing to stay around for." He didn't want to see Cyclops, Moe Luigi, Fergus T., or any of the others at what was sure to be a depressing wake. The next time he saw them he wanted it to be on his own turf, in Ireland. Shipman nodded his head, comprehending what O'Rourke meant. "You come visit me and Sam and my little brown babies in Wexford. Promise?"

"I will, pal," said Shipman, his morose eyes black with sadness. "So this is it?"

O'Rourke smiled. "Yes, this is it," he said, now not wanting to leave.

"I hope," said Shipman, "you won't be bored in Ireland."

"I don't think so," said O'Rourke. "*Sinn Fein* is looking for a candidate for the *Dáil* from South Wexford in the next general election."

Shipman raised his eyebrows in shock. "You wouldn't," he said.

"I haven't decided yet," said O'Rourke, a small smile brightening his face, "but as the Bible says, "As a dog returneth to his vomit . . ."

". . . So a fool returneth to his folly," finished Shipman.

"Proverbs 26:11," said O'Rourke.

"I know."

O'Rourke stepped back from the bar and looked at the joint and thought of Joe Flaherty and Nick Pinto and all the laughter and tears he had experienced here over the last forty years. He almost expected Hogan and Barney to come walking out of the back room, but they didn't. Maybe the ghost of Bobby Kennedy was still back there, stuck in a 1968 brood.

He got off his bar stool and smiled at Shipman. "*Slán agat*," he said as he went through the door of Hogan's Moat for the last time.

Acknowledgments

I want to thank some of the people whose kindness and opinions helped shape *Our Lady of Greenwich Village*.

Joanie Leinwoll, who was always willing to read; Tania Grossinger, who kept cheering me on; Michael Coffey, for his wise counsel; Ann Hostetler, who was crucial in reshaping this book; Heather King, a new friend, who shares a keen interest in Holy Mother Church; and Diane Raver for holding my hand during the publishing process.

I'd like to thank my Dublin first cousins for their help in finding missing pieces of the Dublin of one hundred years ago: Monsignor Vince Bartley; Maura and Jerry Bartley; Declan and Adrian Bartley; Mary and Terry O'Neill; Brendan and Geraldine Bartley; Father Kevin Bartley; and Ann Bartley Kelleher, who started the Lombard Street research.

I'd also like to thank four close friends, all Vietnam veterans, for helping me shape the Vietnam career of Tone O'Rourke: John Hamill (USA), Neil Granger (USMC), Kenny Moran (USA), and Kevin Griffin (USMC). I'd particularly like to thank John Hamill, former army medic, for his advice on how a Vietnam corpsman might do his job.

I want to thank Frank McCourt and Rosemary Mahoney for their help and support. Not only are they two of my favorite people, but they are also two of America's greatest writers.

And lastly, I want to thank all the people at Skyhorse Publishing: Tony Lyons, my publisher now on two novels; Bill Wolfsthal, who continues to have an answer to all questions; and Erin Kelley, my editor extraordinaire. I'd also like to thank Tom McCarthy, who first published me at the Lyons Press, for his input on this book.